Media Justice

A Marc Kadella legal mystery

Dennis L. Carstens

Additional Marc Kadella Legal Mysteries

The Key to Justice

Desperate Justice

Certain Justice

Personal Justice

Delayed Justice

Political Justice

Insider Justice

Exquisite Justice

Email me at: dcarstens514@gmail.com

Author's Note

As a lawyer I am asked, as I am sure are almost all lawyers and judges by friends and acquaintances to give my opinion about highly publicized trials. I always tell the person asking that I do not follow trials in the media. Forming an opinion based on what you have received through the media is third or fourth-hand knowledge filtered through any number of people involved in giving you the story.

First there is a reporter or reporters watching the trial, probably part time, who may or may not know what they are watching. Then they write the story for the print media or television which will likely, unwittingly or not, contain their bias. Next it goes to at least one and probably two or more editors who check the story and make corrections, deletions and edits that may or may not be tainted by their biases. Finally, it is printed in the paper or read over the TV news to consumers who also have their opinions and biases. By the time all of this filtering is done, the story may not look at all like what is really going on in the courtroom.

To truly form a reasonably accurate opinion, you have to sit in the courtroom all day every day, listen to the testimony, evaluate the credibility of witnesses and follow the judge's rulings. How many members of the media that report this to you actually do this? I tell people to wait for the jury to decide since their opinion is the only one that matters anyway. When you finish this novel, it is my hope you will appreciate the difference between what is reported and what really happens.

Finally, I must make a minor confession. The courts of Minnesota, much to their everlasting credit, do not allow television cameras in the courtrooms. I may be a bit old-fashioned about this and if so, so be it. In this age of reality TV, this is one place that should not be televised for the amusement of the public. Trials are serious events and should not be shown for voyeuristic entertainment. I allowed a camera in the court for my trial simply for literary license purposes and today's realism.

Dennis Carstens

A very special thanks to my good friend Kathy K. for all of her assistance, suggestions and help. I really appreciate it. Thanks again.

"The fault, dear Brutus, lies not in our stars but in ourselves."

Julius Caesar Act I Scene 2

ONE

October

Eric Carson's eyes snapped open when his internal clock awakened him before the alarm went off. He lay quietly in the dark staring up at the interior ceiling of the topper over the bed of his Toyota Tundra. Eric looked to his left and read the time on the dimly illuminated, portable alarm clock barely ten inches from his face. The alarm was set to go off in ten minutes, at four A.M. He reached over, switched off the alarm, rolled over to his right, and leaned on his elbow to look at his ten-year-old son. Jackson was still asleep, breathing peacefully, his back to his dad, one bare leg outside of his sleeping bag. Eric leaned over, lightly kissed the boy on the back of his head, then quietly gathered his clothes and still in his underwear, slipped out of the back of the truck bed.

Eric quickly dressed, retrieved the thermos of coffee from the front seat of the truck, poured a cup, and then opened the door of the kennel for his black Lab, Blue. Excited to see his master, the dog jumped up and down several times while Eric scratched him behind his ears. Then Blue ran off toward some weeds to do his morning business.

Eric noticed some of the other members of his hunting party stirring in their trucks and tents. He leaned against the side of his pick-up and looked up at the cloudless sky. Away from the lights of the Twin Cities of Minneapolis and St. Paul, the sight of billions of stars never failed to awe him and to make him realize how small and insignificant he was. Once again, he realized this was why God gave us children; to give us a purpose in life.

The dog came back at the same time he felt his son stirring in the back of the truck. He scooped food into Blue's dish and as he was pouring water into the dog's bowl, he heard Jackson jump down off of the vehicle's open tailgate.

"Hey, Dad," he heard Jackson say.

"Morning, bud. Did you sleep okay?"

"Yeah," the boy said while yawning and stretching.

"Get your coat on," Eric told him. "It's chilly out here."

"I'm okay," Jackson insisted, noting his dad wasn't wearing one.

"I didn't ask. Now, get a coat on."

Jackson grumbled as he climbed back into the truck to get his coat. Eric just shook his head and smiled at the knowledge he had been the same way at his son's age.

"It is a little chilly out here," a voice came from behind Eric. He turned to face Chris Givens, his main hunting partner.

3

Chris blew out a long stream of air that was clearly visible and said, "When you can see your breath that much, you know winter isn't too far off. A few more weeks and it'll be starting. Coffee?" he asked Eric as he held out his thermos toward him.

"Sure," Eric replied as Chris filled his cup. "Gonna be a nice day today, though. Too nice. We could use some clouds and rain to keep the ducks flying lower."

"It's been what, a couple months since it rained?"

"Yeah," Eric answered. "The river is pretty much back down to normal."

Jackson re-emerged and the three stood by the truck chatting about the upcoming day while waiting for the other four members of their party to join them. They were more or less camped in a parking area on a public hunting zone. The parking/camping lot was about two hundred yards from the Mississippi River, south of Hastings in Dakota County, Minnesota. It was their favorite spot and normally not too crowded.

Dakota County is located south of the Twin Cities metro area. It is mostly rural farming with the population centers along the Northern border abutting the Minnesota and Mississippi rivers. It is a fairly affluent, second tier suburb of St Paul with great access to both St. Paul and Minneapolis and plenty of parks and recreation areas. It also borders Wisconsin along the Mississippi where our story begins in an open hunting zone along the river that divides the nation.

There was a nice sized backwater of the river here, roughly ten to twelve acres with a little bit of a current but shallow enough for decoys. They hunted on a small peninsula that jutted out about a hundred feet into the water which allowed the six men to cover the entire area. There was also excellent natural cover which they could use for blinds. A thick growth of five to six-foot tall cattails had expanded out approximately ten feet into the river covering the entire shoreline of the backwater.

The other four men joined them, and they carried the three small boats down to the shore where they had cleared a small launch area through the cattails. They quietly loaded the boats with decoys and while Jackson waited on the shore with Blue and Louie, a golden Lab owned by one of the older hunters, the men quietly paddled out into the calm water. As they did so, they could hear the unmistakable sound of ducks flapping their wings and lightly splashing the water as they took off in the dark to flee from the intruders.

Even with two men per boat, it took six of them an hour to set all of the decoys in the water in a pattern to attract their game. Shortly after 5:30 they got back on shore, pulled the boats out of the water and hid them in the weeds.

4

Satisfied the decoys were set and the boats sufficiently hidden, they all hurried back to the parking area to retrieve their shotguns, ammo and other equipment. They carried these things and small portable chairs out to the duck blinds. Still too early to shoot, the group hunkered down in the weeds underneath several small trees on the peninsula to await the sunrise.

This was Jackson's first time out with his dad and he was determined to make him proud. Eric, Jackson and Chris covered the left side of the backwater. The other four men, including Chris's dad, Don, were to their right. They all had lightweight portable stools to sit on. The ground they were on was dry and firm. There were several small trees scattered about. Between the trees, the normal growth, the cattails and their camo clothing, the men were almost invisible.

Jackson sat quietly, content, and happy to be hunting with his dad and Chris even though he wouldn't touch a gun. He had his earmuff style noise suppressors draped around his neck while he quietly ate a power bar and sipped water from a canteen. Blue, a superbly disciplined dog, sat on his haunches, absolutely still, between Jackson's legs. The dog had been hunting many times and was probably the most excited one in the party; anxious for the sun to come up to get the action started.

There was a slight breeze coming across the river out of the east where the sun would rise shortly after 7:00. They could legally start shooting a half-hour before the official sunrise but waiting in the blinds, with the sky full of stars and an almost full moon, it was already light enough to shoot.

Every few minutes they would see a dark shadow flit across the sky. A moment later they would hear wings flap and a quiet splash as the ducks began to drop into their decoys. Blue could also hear them, and he lifted his nose into the wind, his eagerness apparent.

Gradually, the horizon directly across the river began to turn light gray. Eric held up his left wrist into the moonlight to check the time. By prearrangement, the men had decided to stand and shoot at precisely 6:45, exactly a half hour before the scheduled sunrise. He flashed the five fingers on his left hand twice at Chris to indicate ten more minutes. Eric scratched Blue behind the ears, gave Jackson a brief hug then shifted slightly to make standing quicker and easier. Listening to the birds come in, he had mentally calculated there must be close to two dozen on each side of their small peninsula.

By 6:40, the red of the sun was clearly starting to show to their front. At 6:45 all of the hunters looked over their shoulders, nodded at each other and quickly stood up as did young Jackson with his ear protectors firmly in place, his hand on Blue's collar.

The water exploded as the startled ducks jumped into the air, desperately trying to flee from the sudden appearance of the men with guns. In less than thirty seconds, all six guns were empty with decidedly mixed results. Eric and Chris each scored two birds and a fifth one that they weren't sure which one of them had hit. The other four men, all older than Eric and Chris had knocked down only three between them. They were already in a heated argument over who shot what.

Jackson released Blue. The dog was off in a flash through the cattails and into the river. He spent the next fifteen minutes swimming in and out of the decoys retrieving the downed birds. Louie did the same on the other side of the peninsula.

For the next two hours they sat in their blinds patiently waiting for their quarry to come to them. One of the older men was fairly good with a duck call and every few minutes two or three birds would be drawn in. Eric and Chris each bagged two more, a pair of drake Mallards, a male Wood Duck and a Green-winged Teal. Whenever a bird or two showed any interest in the decoys in front of the other four men, all four of them would completely unload their guns at the curious fowl, making the small cove sound like a combat zone. More often than not, the bird would turn tail and speedily fly off, frightened but otherwise unscathed, much to the amusement of Eric, Chris and Jackson.

By nine o'clock the sun was heating up the air, the birds were flying higher over the river and the action had slowed considerably. Jackson, a little bored, though determined not to admit it, had yawned a few times and almost nodded off.

"Hey, bud," Eric said to his son. "Take the keys, go on back to the truck and lie down for a while."

"No, Dad. I'm okay."

"Go ahead," Eric quietly encouraged him. "It's okay. You're doing great. Besides, we'll be taking a break in about an hour to eat. Go lie down and get a nap in."

Secretly happy to get the offer, Jackson took the keys and started back toward where the vehicles were parked. He had to pee and at his age, he was a little too self-conscious to do it in front of the others. When he reached the open space between the river and the parking area, he turned to his right and ran along the edge of the cattails until he found a good spot to relieve himself.

There was a slight indentation in the ground about a hundred feet from the path to the duck blinds. It was an open spot of bare earth, about three feet high at the top edge, sloping down about ten feet into the cattails. The indentation was a semi-circle about fifteen feet across where the river had washed away the foliage and the water had receded leaving the dry ground.

Jackson dropped down into it and walked up to the edge of the cattails. He quickly finished and as he was zipping up his pants, he noticed something in the water. It was about five feet out and looked like it might be a rag or maybe a doll stuck in the weeds. Jackson was wearing waterproof boots that went up to mid-thigh, so he cautiously waded into the water and began to make his way toward the object. When he reached it, he pushed aside several of the tall cattails and bent over to get a better look.

There were some cloth remnants of what could be a small child's pink, flannel pajamas, what was left of a cotton blanket and a smooth, white ball with what looked like several strands of dirty blonde hair attached. He reached down, gently rolled the ball over and instantly recognized it as a mud splattered, human skull.

TWO

July, Two Months Earlier

Brittany Riley stood in the kitchen doorway of her parents' home in Apple Valley, Minnesota. It was 8:15 on a Friday morning of what was predicted to be the first really nice weekend of the summer. Between the cold, snowy winter, the wet spring and summer, pleasant weekends had become a bit of a rarity.

Brittany watched her two and a half-year-old daughter, Becky, sitting on the couch with Becky's grandfather, Floyd Riley, eating her favorite breakfast; a bowl of Honey Nut Cheerios and a sippy cup full of chocolate milk. Becky was the joy of the world. She was a beautiful, little blonde haired, blue-eyed bundle of smiles, hugs and happiness. Becky melted the heart of anyone who came in contact with her. Even her cold-hearted great-grandmother, who disliked just about everyone, lit up like a Christmas tree at the sight of her.

Brittany became pregnant at nineteen by her twenty-one-year old boyfriend, Greg Mead. Greg was a full-time mechanic at a local Goodyear store while attending night school at Dakota County Vo-Tech in their Heavy-Duty Truck Technology program. He was the first boyfriend Brittany had who was employed with a decent paying job, was in school to secure a good career for himself and was more interested in Brittany than video games.

Despite a fairly strict upbringing, or more likely because of it, Brittany had been quite sexually active through most of her high school years. She was a very attractive, blue-eyed blonde, just like her mother Barbara and her daughter Becky. Even so, she was very insecure, sexually naïve and was quite willing to give the boys what they wanted, believing it would make her popular.

Greg knew of her reputation and knew there was a chance that he was not Becky's father, but he didn't care because he was totally in love with Brittany. The thought of becoming a father, something Greg barely had while growing up, brought him a joy he could not possibly have imagined. When Brittany was still nineteen and six months pregnant, much to the disapproval of Brittany's mother, they were married. It was quite possibly the first time Brittany had so blatantly defied Barbara. Even so, the expectant newlyweds, at Barbara's insistence, moved into the Riley home.

She would never openly admit it, but in Barbara's eyes, a mechanic was beneath even consideration as a husband for her daughter. A doctor or a successful lawyer at least, but certainly not someone who worked with his hands for a living. The irony of the fact that Barbara was married to a postal employee shift-worker apparently never occurred to her.

The house was pleasant enough. It was a two-story, three-bedroom located at 2155 MacArthur Street in Apple Valley. It wasn't the best arrangement for the newlyweds, especially for Greg, but as busy as he was, he made the best of it and even started saving some money for a home of their own.

A month after Brittany's twentieth birthday, Becky was born, and the Riley household had a new star to revolve around. Even Brittany's older brother, Tim, who was living back home after another stint in drug rehab, was absolutely smitten by the tiny little girl. Barbara, who had insisted on being in the delivery room practically elbowing Greg out of the way, seemed to soften toward the baby's father. Perhaps it was because Barbara had been the first to hold the child when she took it away from the nurse in the delivery room. Unknown to Greg, Barbara had insisted to Brittany that the child be named Becky, after Barbara's maternal grandmother. The fact that the three females of this family were named Barbara Ann, Brittany Ann and Becky Ann was no coincidence.

Two months after the baby was born, shortly before 10:00 P.M. on a cold wintry night, they received a knock on the door. Floyd answered it and two Dakota County Sheriff's deputies brought them the news that Greg was dead. He had been driving home through Rosemount after classes at the Vo-Tech when a drunk in a pickup barreled through a stop sign, T-boning Greg's car on the driver's side. Medics were there within minutes, but he was already gone. The driver of the pickup was barely hurt. He had a broken nose and two black eyes from the truck's airbag but was otherwise uninjured.

Six months later, the young widow received her lawsuit settlement. After fees and costs, the life of her husband brought her one hundred and forty thousand dollars, all of the insurance money from the driver of the pickup and Greg's policy that was available to pay for the accident. The negligent driver of the pickup would do thirty months in prison and that would be the end of it.

Before Becky's first birthday, Barbara would be seated in a county courtroom while Brittany finished the formality of changing her name and Becky's. With Greg gone, Barbara saw no reason why her daughter and granddaughter should not become Rileys.

While Becky ate her Cheerios and watched a cartoon show on one of the kid's channels, Brittany explained her weekend itinerary to her mother who was already at work. She would be meeting some friends for dinner after her job at Macy's. Saturday, a bunch of them were going to Wisconsin to tube down the Apple River and a campground party would follow tomorrow night. Of course, she would never admit this to her mother, but a girlfriend had provided her with three new condoms that Brittany was desperately hoping would be needed.

"I can't bring my phone with me on the river, Mother. I'll call you before and after."

"Don't worry about it," Barbara pleasantly replied. "You have a good time but be careful," she continued hoping Brittany knew what condoms were for and had enough sense to get some. "Our baby girl will have a wonderful weekend with us."

"Thanks, Mom. I have to get going. I'll call you later."

Brittany placed her phone in her purse then knelt down in front of Becky. "Give Momma a hug, baby," she said as Becky jumped into her arms. She held the little girl for a few seconds then set her down on the couch. "Bye, sweetie, I have to go. Take care of Papa."

"Bye Mommy," Becky said as she wiggled her tiny fingers at her mother.

Brittany blew Becky a kiss and as she opened the front door said, "Bye Dad. I'll call later."

"Okay, hon," Floyd replied. "We'll be fine, and grandma is coming home early."

Brittany worked at the Macy's department store at the Mall of America in Bloomington. She was a sales associate in the men's clothing department and was fast becoming their best salesperson. With her girl-next-door looks and friendly smile, she was overcoming her inner insecurity and discovering a sense of confidence she hadn't known was there. Of course, men of all ages were attracted to her and like the superficial adolescents they naturally were, almost always bought something from the pretty, charming young clerk.

Brittany left work around 6:00 P.M. and drove home to her two-bedroom apartment a half-mile from her parent's house. A quick shower, a change of clothes to something more suited for a night out and she was able to meet her friends by seven at Rick's Café in Apple Valley.

Rick's was a local meat market that had a dining room in one section and a bar with live music in an adjacent room. Brittany and her friends, Kathy, Annie and Julia had dinner in the restaurant. Then, just before 8:30, they moved to the bar to get a table before the music started. The girls found a table with a good view of the bandstand but far enough away, so they could still hear each other while the music played.

The waitress brought their drinks, four small, strawberry margaritas. As she walked away, Brittany, in a gesture of a toast, raised her glass and said, "Here's to getting laid tonight." She had intentionally said this loud enough for the dozen or so people, mostly single guys at the tables around them to hear. The four of them laughed, clinked their glasses together and took a drink.

After they settled down, Annie asked Brittany, "So, how's our little angel doing?"

"She's good," Brittany nodded. "No, in fact, she's perfect."

"Sweetest little baby, ever," Kathy chimed in.

"Yeah, she is but…" Brittany quietly replied.

"But what?" Julia asked.

"I don't know. It's just…"

"You're feeling a little tied down, again?" Kathy asked. "We need to get you out more."

"Yeah, sometimes I just feel like, you know, maybe I'm a little too young or not mature enough for the responsibility. I just can't help but feel, sometimes, if she was gone … but then I see those beautiful little eyes, her smile and I just…"

"Melt," Julia finished the thought.

"Yeah, I do. Maybe I just get a little lonely sometimes."

"Lonely? You've had four boyfriends in the last six months," Annie said.

Brittany waved her hand as if chasing a fly away and said, "All they wanted was to get me in bed. I'd really like to meet someone who, you know, was looking for something more serious than a quick lay then back to the video games."

"When do they start to grow up and become men?" Julia asked.

"Never!" the three other girls answered her in unison.

The music started up, a local rock band made of guys in their late forties called the Heart Breakers. The band was actually quite good, made up of members were musicians who had been together for years and not some kids practicing in someone's garage. Within minutes, all four girls were on the dance floor with guys who had been eyeing them up since they sat down. The music, mostly contemporary and classic rock, was very good and the band normally drew a good crowd and tonight was no exception.

Over the next three hours, almost by silent mutual consent, the guys and girls paired off. The young man who was able to attach himself to Brittany was a twenty-something by the name of Jeff Stevens. Jeff was a student at UW-Madison, Wisconsin and had no intention of getting seriously involved with a girl who had a young kid. To Jeff, Brittany was a 'hottie' and looked to be an easy score which was all either of them seemed to be interested in.

Around midnight, while the band was on a break, having been sufficiently plied with alcohol, Brittany suggested they slip out to her

11

apartment. When she awoke in the morning, Jeff was gone leaving only a thank you note and a hungover Brittany with a slight headache.

THREE

Brittany crawled out of bed and went into the apartment's tiny kitchen. She started the coffee maker and as the machine started brewing the coffee, she found and swallowed several ibuprofen from her medicine cabinet. As she poured her first cup, the ringtone on her phone started up, which did nothing for her headache. She looked at the caller ID, frowned, sighed and rolled her eyes at the name she saw, pressed the answer button and as pleasantly as she could, said, "Hi, Mom."

"Are you up?" Barbara asked.

"Yes, Mom, I've been up for over an hour."

"Tell me your schedule for today, again."

"Mom," Brittany patiently said, "I told you yesterday..."

"Tell me again," Barbara insisted.

"Okay," Brittany said with a sigh. "I'm going to work until around noon," she lied. "Then I'll meet my friends, you know them..."

"Their names?"

"Kathy, Annie and Julia."

"Go on," Barbara said.

"We're supposed to meet at Kathy's around 1:00 and then go to Somerset, Wisconsin. We'll meet up there with a bunch of people and then tube down the river. Afterward, there's a party at one of the campgrounds. Some of the people are spending the night camping."

"Who are these people? Do you know them?"

"I know a couple of them from high school. Most of them are friends of Kathy's."

"Yes, your friend, the party girl," Barbara said with obvious distaste.

"She's not a party girl, Mom."

"Be sure you call me before and after you go down the river. I want to make sure you don't drown."

"Mom, there's a million people tubing on the river in the summer. You know that. It would be impossible to drown."

"Never mind. Just call me."

"Yes, Mom. Can I talk to Becky?"

Barbara had been standing in the kitchen entryway while talking to her daughter. She was watching Becky and Floyd play with some of her granddaughter's dolls. When Brittany asked to talk to Becky, Barbara turned and went into the kitchen before answering.

"I'm sorry, dear. Becky is in the backyard with Floyd. She's playing on the swing set. I don't want to disturb her, okay?"

"Okay, Mom," Brittany answered, obviously disappointed. "I'll call you this afternoon. Probably around 2:00 or 2:30."

Barbara set the phone back in its charger and went into the living room. She sat down on the couch, handed Floyd a piece of paper and as she pulled Becky onto her lap, said, "Come here, sweetheart. Grandpa has his list of things to get at the grocery store and while he's gone, Grandma is going to take you to get your hair done. Won't that be fun? And if you're a good girl, we'll go to the Mall of America for lunch and rides at Nick Universe."

Even though she was barely two and a half, Becky knew what Nick Universe was; an amusement park with rides inside the Mall. When Barbara told her this, Becky's eyes lit up, she let out a delighted squeal, jumped up and wrapped her arms around Barbara's neck.

Floyd stood up with the grocery list in hand. As he headed toward the kitchen to go into the garage, Barbara sharply said, "Make sure the fruit isn't too ripe this time."

"Yes, Barbara. I'll be careful."

"We'll meet you back here in an hour. Don't forget anything on the list either," Floyd heard her admonishment as he went through the door leading to the garage.

Later, around noon, the three of them were finishing their lunch at the Rainforest Café. Floyd was feeding Becky one of his French fries and said to his granddaughter, "Do you like your hair now that it looks just like Grandma's?" Becky shook her head and grabbed two more fries from Floyd's plate and stuffed them both in her mouth.

"Brittany isn't going to like what you did to her hair," Floyd said.

"She'll get over it," Barbara said with a dismissive wave of a hand. "It's summer. She needs it shorter. It's easier to take care of. Sweetheart," she continued. "Papa is going to take you on some rides. Grandma will be back in a little while, okay?

"I have to do something. Take her on a few rides and I'll find you down there," she said to Floyd. With that she stood, bent down to kiss Becky on the forehead and abruptly left.

Barbara quickly walked through the crowd in the mall and a few minutes later hurriedly walked into Macy's. She went right to the men's department which was fairly crowded with shoppers and patiently waited for one of the sales associates to become available. She noticed a young man finish with another customer and lightly waved to get his attention. He hurried over to her and asked if he could be of assistance.

"I was wondering," she politely began with a friendly smile, "if Brittany was in today?"

"No, ma'am, haven't seen her."

"Was she in earlier? I thought she worked Saturdays. She is still in this department, isn't she?"

"Yes, ma'am, she's still in men's clothing but she hasn't been in today. I've been here since 8:00 A.M. and I haven't seen her. Is there something I can help you with?"

"No, no," Barbara said as if it was nothing. "She was such a dear when I was in before and I wanted to thank her. Some other time," she said as she abruptly turned and walked away.

Kathy parked her mid-sized Subaru SUV in the parking lot of the River's Edge Apple River Tubing Company. The girls were a little late and were supposed to meet up with a group that would total almost twenty people.

As they were parking, Annie opened her window to yell a greeting at a young man she knew as he was walking toward the building. He yelled back telling her to hurry, everyone else was already there and anxious to get going.

After the four girls exited the car, Kathy and Julia grabbed the beer cooler from the back. As they started walking toward the tube rental office, Brittany told them she needed to make a quick call to check on Becky. Annie offered to rent an inner tube for her and Brittany handed her the money for it while pressing a button to dial her mother's home.

She spent ten minutes on the call to Barbara then hurriedly ditched her phone in the car and ran to catch up with her friends. They all got onto their tubes, tied the entire group of twenty together with rope along with several coolers of beer and floated out into the lazy current. One of the guys had rigged a small boom box with a waterproof battery from a portable electric drill. He put it on one of the coolers and after two or three beers each, the entire party was floating, singing and bouncing along to the music.

The four girls were all similarly dressed in shorts or cut-off jeans and skimpy bikini tops. Brittany looked especially good in her bikini top. Her breasts had filled out quite nicely while pregnant and did not shrink much afterward. And she certainly wasn't above showing them off to attract the guys.

There wasn't a cloud to be seen and all of the girls in the party were continuously rubbing on generous amounts of sunscreen, the guys, of course, kindly offering their assistance. The temperature was in the mid-eighties, the water was comfortably warm, and the day could not have been more pleasant. It was, in fact, almost perfect.

The river was quite crowded and a couple of times they got caught up in log jams that were created by raucous groups of mostly young men ahead of them on the river. Several groups would band together and block the river. It would cause a pileup of as many as two or three hundred tubers before it became too difficult to hold them all back. No one seemed to mind. Because of the beautiful day and everyone, including older adults and families with children, were having an extremely pleasant afternoon, the log-jams only added to the fun.

About halfway through the four-hour trip, on the bank of the river, there is a snack stand set up. By this time everyone could use a bite to eat and a break from the water, so they all piled off of their tubes for a brief respite. All of the party members ordered up a burger, brat or hot dog, a soda or a beer and many made quick trips to the restrooms.

Around 5:30, just before the end of the ride, the river narrows and forms an easily traversed, white water rapids to bring the trip to a fun conclusion. Plus, by this time, everyone had one or two beers more than they should which made the quick shot down the rapids a little more interesting.

At the end of the trip, the group was shuttled back to the campgrounds at their starting point where the cars were parked. They got together at the campground and set up tents for the night. Annie's parents were campers, so she brought along a tent easily large enough for all of them and their camping gear as well.

The girls fooled around for ten minutes playing the part of helpless females, easily getting some of the guys to put up their tent. While their tent was being erected, the four of them watched and drank more beer, giggling amongst themselves at how easy it had been to get someone else to set up their camp.

The entire group pooled their food, bought more beer and had a great time partying. Around nine, a band began to play on the outdoor stage about a hundred yards from them. There was more drinking, more music and more dancing.

By ten o'clock, Brittany had settled on the guy she wanted. An empty-headed pretty boy who had spent most of the evening bragging about his glory days playing high school football. Around ten-thirty she allowed him to lead her off to his tent. Fifteen minutes later she was back looking annoyed.

"What happened?" Kathy asked her.

"The idiot sat down on his sleeping bag and the next thing I knew he was snoring."

The other three girls all laughed, and Brittany couldn't help joining in.

After a couple of minutes, Brittany popped another brew, looked around and said, "Well, there are other candidates."

"Hey," Julia said. "I thought you told your mother you weren't spending the night. Getting a little brave lying to mommy?" she teased.

"What she doesn't know won't hurt her," Brittany answered setting her sights on one of the guys not yet attached.

Brittany woke up around 3:00 A.M. looked at the bareback of the young man she knew as Ron and felt a pang of guilt. As quietly as she could, she put on her panties, shorts and bikini top, then slipped out of his tent and hurried back to where her friends were sleeping.

FOUR

Bob Olson checked his face in the rearview mirror of his car to give it one last look. His dirty blonde hair was fine but his stylish, black-framed glasses felt and appeared slightly askew. He removed them, gave one of the bows a minor tweak, put them back on and they felt much better. Satisfied, he ran his fingers over his mustache and goatee to smooth them over and checked himself out in the mirror again. Quite pleased with the look, he got out of his car, closed the door and locked it as he started walking toward his goal. He was in a ramp at the Mall of America and was going to Macy's to hopefully meet a girl.

Bob had first seen her a few days ago tubing down the Apple River. She had been in a different group than him, but they had started out about the same time and he saw a lot of her as they made the journey. Later that night, he and the few friends who were with him were camped nearby and he kept a curious eye on her.

Shortly before the music started, he noticed one of the guys sitting with her get up and head toward the restrooms. Bob quickly stood up and followed the young man and was able to stand next to him at the row of urinals. He struck up a casual conversation with him and found out some basic information about the girl such as her name, the fact she was widowed and has a young daughter.

"Why are you asking?" the young man asked.

"I think I've seen her before," Bob lied. "She's pretty hot and I'm sure I remember her from somewhere. Where does she work?"

"Macy's at the mall. You want to meet her?"

"You know, I think that's where I've seen her. Meet her tonight? No, I was just curious. I knew I had seen her before and it was bugging me, you know?"

"Sure, dude," the young man said as he zipped up. "And you're right, she is pretty hot."

A couple days later, Bob had scouted out the Macy's and found her in the men's department. He had nonchalantly observed her while he pretended to check out some expensive watches in a glass case in the jewelry department. When he did this a sales associate, a young girl whose name tag identified her as Julie, approached him. He chatted with her for a few minutes then left. On his way out of the store, he reached a decision on how to approach Brittany and quickly walked to his car to go back to work.

Today, determined to go ahead with his plan, he entered Macy's through the second- floor parking ramp entrance and quickly walked to the down escalator. He went straight to the men's department hoping to find her; both worried that she would not be there and a little anxious that she would be.

He saw her helping a customer at the checkout station, took a quick look around and saw no other sales staff in the department. Bob strolled around pretending to look over dress shirts and after a few minutes, he heard a soft, female voice behind him.

"Can I help you find something?"

He turned around and looked down at Brittany's pretty smiling face and shining blue eyes. Throwing caution to the wind he decided to jump right in.

"Um, yeah, ah, you can," he slightly stammered. "Look," he began over. "I'm going to be up front and honest. I'm not here to buy anything. I'm here to meet you."

When he said this, Brittany's back stiffened, the smile vanished, and she took a half step backward.

"Wait, look, um. I'm not weird or a, ah, stalker or anything like that. It's just, well," *go for it*, he thought to himself. "I saw you at the Apple River a few days ago and I thought you were real pretty; someone I'd like to meet. So, um, I asked a guy who was in your party about you so, ah, I guess, here I am."

Visibly relaxing, Brittany looked at the young man who appeared to be quite sincere and more than a little nervous. She had to admit to herself that she was actually very flattered. This guy wasn't super-hot, but he was at least attractive. She was impressed and more than a little pleased that he would go to this much trouble just to meet her.

"I'm sorry," he said when she didn't say anything. "I just thought, you know, we could maybe get together for coffee or a drink. Or I could take you to dinner. If you tell me to get lost, I'll never bother you again, I promise."

"I think I'd like that," she finally said.

"What, for me to get lost?"

"No, silly," she laughed. "Get together. You can buy me dinner."

"Cool," he answered obviously relieved. "When's good for you?"

"How about tomorrow night? I have to check with my mom to watch my daughter. You know I have a kid, don't you?"

"Yeah, I heard. I'm sorry about your husband. Are you doing okay?"

"Yeah, better. It was tough. Come over here and we'll swap info."

They went to the department's service island where they exchanged names, addresses and phone numbers. As she watched him walk away she found herself thinking, *He might be a definite, solid maybe.* Just before he left the men's department he turned, smiled and waved at her, which she returned. At the same time, he was thinking that his plan was starting out quite nicely.

While preparing for their first date, Brittany thought about how glad she was that Bob knew about Becky. She believed at least a couple of guys she had briefly dated had fled upon learning she had a daughter. Brittany understood why and that her child was not their problem. And it was possibly just as well to find out sooner rather than later that they weren't interested in becoming immediate fathers. This guy seemed different. He had known about her little girl and had pursued Brittany anyway. The realization gave her a nice warm glow and she decided, just to be sure, she would let him pursue her some more.

Bob picked her up in a late model dark gray Camry. He was wearing a decent blue sport coat, a white dress shirt, tan wool slacks and polished cordovan loafers. Unlike most of her first dates, he looked like a grown-up and was clearly trying to impress her, a thought which pleasantly surprised her. Instead of the usual sports bar restaurant, he took her to a nice, quiet, semi-expensive place in Eagan with a real menu, a pricey wine list and a jazz combo to provide background music.

For the next three hours they had an excellent meal, two bottles of an absurdly over-priced wine she had never heard of and they basically smiled at each other, laughed and talked a lot. Or, more accurately, Brittany did most of the talking and Bob did most of the listening. Of course, being a good listener made him even more attractive to her.

Toward 11:00 he checked his watch and reminded her it was a work night for them both. When the bill came, he paid in cash which prompted her to ask about his employment.

"I work at a financial investment firm downtown Minneapolis."

"What do you do?" Brittany probed further.

"I work in the bond department analyzing bonds. It's really pretty boring," he said hoping to change the subject. "How about this weekend? Are you busy?"

"I'm seeing some girlfriends tomorrow night but Saturday I'm open," she hurriedly replied.

"Great! How about I call you Saturday and we'll make plans. Maybe grab a bite and catch a movie. Can you find a sitter for Becky?"

"My mom will watch her."

For the next two weeks, they either saw each other or spent time on the phone every day. Gradually she got to know more and more about him. She discovered that he wasn't a big video game player, he would rather actually talk to her on the phone than send text messages and most importantly he had met and seemed genuinely fond of Becky.

Her initial plan to avoid the bedroom for a while lasted only until their third date. It was a weeknight and he couldn't spend the entire night, but the event left her believing there were good things ahead for them. He had been upgraded from a "definite, solid maybe" to an "almost, certain probable".

The only thing that perturbed Brittany was Bob's reluctance to meet her friends. Every time she brought it up he would find some excuse for why he couldn't make it or another time would be better and he would quickly change the subject.

On a rainy Friday evening, a little more than two weeks after they met, Bob picked up both Brittany and Becky to take them to dinner. While driving to the restaurant down County Road 42 in Burnsville, Bob told her he had forgotten his wallet and needed to stop at his apartment to get it. He turned down County 11, went about a mile, and then took a left into the parking lot of a large apartment complex. He parked in a spot away from the door and because of the rain, Brittany and Becky stayed in the car while he ran in. He was back in barely two minutes.

He drove back to County Road 42 to the Olive Garden and the three of them had a great time together. Becky was really taking to Bob as the two of them almost played like kids during the meal. Later, on the ride back to Brittany's apartment with her baby securely strapped into a car seat in back, Brittany reflected on the evening and realized it was the best night they had since Greg had died. For the first time in a long time, she felt like life could actually work out for them.

At 3:00 A.M. Brittany heard a noise and was groggily awakened. She reached behind her to check for Bob and realized he wasn't there. Believing the noise she heard was probably him in the bathroom, she closed her eyes and quickly went back to sleep.

Brittany awoke at 7:15 and looked at the empty side of the bed where she expected to find her lover. She laid there for a minute listening to the quiet apartment then rolled out of bed and went into the bathroom.

After finishing in the bathroom, she went to Becky's bedroom wondering why she was still asleep. Brittany opened the door and found an empty bed and no sign of her little girl. Alarmed, she quickly went through the entire apartment and found no sign of either Becky or Bob. Suppressing her panic and still in her robe she ran outside and saw that Bob's car was gone. She ran back to the apartment, grabbed her phone and despite how badly her hands were shaking, managed to press the button to dial Bob's cell. Forcing herself to remain as calm as she could with her heart in her throat, she put the phone to her ear praying to hear his voice and tell her Becky was with him. The blood drained from her face when she heard the recording; "This number is no longer in service."

21

Totally gripped by fear, her entire body began to shake, and she dropped to her knees. Staring silently at a wall in her living room, Brittany tried desperately to think. Instead, her mind went blank, she pressed her palms to her temples and she stopped breathing for almost a full minute.

"Okay, okay, okay," she finally said aloud to herself. "He's a really good guy. He has her and he's just taking her for breakfast."

She struggled to her feet and went back into her child's bedroom for another look. That is when she noticed it. On the dresser were the clothes Brittany had set out for her the night before and missing were her baby's teddy bear, the one with the tiny gold chain and little plaque engraved with the word *Becky* on it. Also missing were her favorite blanket and the pink pajamas Becky had slept in that night.

"This can't be. This just can't be. How, how, oh my god! How am I ever going to tell my mother?" Brittany said as the tears began to flow.

Unknown to Brittany, and something she would never learn, three days later a dark gray Camry with stolen license plates was found abandoned in a restaurant parking lot in Robbinsdale, a suburb of Minneapolis. The police identified the vehicle owner by the VIN number and the owner of the stolen plates. Since the car was not damaged and there was no insurance claim, a stolen car returned to its owner did not merit much police attention. Had they done a search of the car, which of course they had no reason to do, they might have discovered several medium length blonde hairs and fibers from a child's blanket and pink pajamas among the usual detritus in the trunk of the car.

FIVE

Brittany didn't remember doing it, but she managed to stagger back to the living room where she collapsed onto the couch. Her mind had gone blank again and she lay on her back staring, unblinking at the white, textured ceiling of the apartment. Thirty minutes passed when suddenly she was snapped back to reality by the ringtone on her phone going off.

Praying it was Bob, she quickly snatched up the phone from the coffee table. Brittany looked at the screen, dropped the device back on the table, raised her hands and jumped back as if it was a poisonous snake. It was actually worse than that. The phone's caller ID showed it was her mother calling to check on her. She waited until Barbara finished leaving a message then quickly erased it without listening to it and started to think again. She looked at the clock noting it was almost 10:00.

Brittany tried Bob's number again and heard the same out of service message. Thoroughly convinced Bob had taken Becky, she calmed down by convincing herself that he was a good guy, everything would be all right, and her baby would be home safe and sound. In the meantime, what to tell her mother?

While in the shower, Brittany came up with an idea of what to tell Barbara. She also decided she wasn't going to just sit, waiting for Bob to call. They had been to his apartment building and she believed she could find it again.

"Hi, Mom," Brittany said into her iPhone. "What's up?"

"Nothing, just checking on you. How're you two? Are you coming over today?"

"Ah, I don't think so. We sort of have plans."

"Who's we?" Barbara demanded.

"Me, Becky and Bob, you know, my new boyfriend. I told you about him."

"Oh, yes, the mysterious boyfriend no one's been able to meet. If you're going to allow a strange man to be around Becky, I have a right to know more about him than just a name."

"I have to go, Mom. We're going to Como Zoo and I need to get ready. I'll talk to you later."

Determined to find her daughter, she spent the next couple of hours cruising the parking lots of every restaurant she could find between her apartment and Bob's. She slowly drove through each lot checking for Bob's car but to no avail.

Just before noon, she stopped at a Perkins to get a bite to eat and consider her options. After the waitress took her order, she found a pen and a small notebook in her purse. Brittany sipped her water and tried to think as calmly as she could. She debated on whether or not to call the

23

police but quickly ruled that out. Bringing them in would require telling her mother. They already had too many disagreements on how Becky should be raised. Barbara had even threatened to get custody of her several times. No, calling the police or telling her mother was not even a possibility. Becky would turn up, somehow, someway, somewhere and she would be just fine; or so Brittany convinced herself.

She made a list of places she had been with Bob and local parks where he might have taken Becky. She tried his phone again, hoping beyond hope that the disconnection of it was temporary. It wasn't, and she once again felt a jolt of fear when she heard the tinny sounding recording.

Brittany finished her lunch and left the restaurant to continue her search. She continued to drive around checking the parking lots of a few places they had been together. No luck. Around mid-afternoon, Brittany decided she would try to find his apartment building.

As best as she could remember, having only been there once, it was one of the places along County Road 11. She drove the entire length of the street checking the lots of every apartment building she could find. Without even realizing it for a certainty she had correctly guessed which one they had stopped at the night before but because it had been raining and she had not paid close enough attention, she couldn't be sure of it. Brittany just cruised through the parking lot looking for the Camry once again with no luck.

Still very worried, but somehow calmer than she had been earlier, Brittany decided to head home. On the way, she received two phone calls, both of which made her grab her phone desperately hoping it was Bob.

The first call was from her friend Annie wanting to know if Brittany could meet the girls for a night out. Brittany didn't tell Annie this, but she just wasn't in the mood. Annie told her the time and place and Brittany said she would think about it.

A few minutes later, Brittany's phone rang again. This time, it was her mother. Barbara had called several times during the afternoon and each time Brittany had let it go to voicemail. Realizing she could not put her mother off any longer, she took a deep breath, sat up straight in the car's seat, cleared her throat, smiled into the mirror, and answered the call.

"Hi, Mom, what's up?"

"Why haven't you returned any of my calls? Do you know how rude and inconsiderate that is? Your father and I worry about you."

"Sorry," Brittany said insincerely.

"Is everything all right?"

"Yes, Mom, of course. We've just been having a nice day and I didn't have my phone on."

"Is Becky there? Can I talk to her?"

"I'm, uh, in the car heading home. She's in the back seat. She fell asleep and I don't want to wake her. I have to drive Mom. I'll call you tomorrow."

After disconnecting the call, she gripped the steering wheel hard with both hands and said out loud while staring straight ahead, almost trancelike, "Everything will be all right. Everything, everything, everything. Everything will be all right." She then inhaled deeply and slowly exhaled.

Brittany sat on the couch in her living room, the TV turned on to a local newscast. Her eyes were fixated on the screen, but her conscious mind had no idea what she was looking at. Thinking through her options, she again decided the best course for her would be to continue what she was doing, searching for Becky herself. The thought of her mother finding out and taking Becky away from her was simply too much to bear. In the meantime, she would act and conduct herself as normally as possible. Brittany wanted no one to think there was anything out of the ordinary going on.

She called Annie back, told her she would meet them, and Brittany decided she would act as if there was nothing wrong. An hour later she was at a restaurant with her three friends laughing, gossiping and giving them no hint of the problem she had.

On Sunday morning, after a fitful night's sleep punctuated with bizarre and disturbing dreams, Brittany awoke with two ideas. The first required a phone call to her mother and the second was a place for her to search.

Monday morning was a workday and Barbara was going to expect her granddaughter to be dropped off. Obviously, Brittany was going to need an excuse for why that might not happen. Still convinced she would find her daughter soon and everything would be fine, she just needed to put off her mother for a couple of days. At 9:00 A.M. she called Barbara to tell her why Becky would not be there the next day.

"Hi, Mom," she said when the call was answered. "Um, Mom, look there's something I need to tell you."

"What's that, dear?"

"I've found daycare for Becky. She's starting tomorrow."

"That's probably a good idea," Barbara answered, shocking Brittany. "She's getting to the age where she needs to be around other children."

25

"Wow, thanks, Mom. I was worried you'd be upset."

"Who is this daycare provider?"

"Uh, ah, her name is Rosalie Parker and she was recommended by my friend Kathy's older sister, Mandy. You remember. She has a little boy. He's in school now, but Mandy used Rosalie and really liked her."

"I suppose. But I'll want to meet this person, Rosalie, sometime."

"Oh, sure, ah, of course. But, um, let me get Becky started there first."

"Is Becky there now? Let me say hello."

"No, she's out in the play area with Bob. Probably on the swing set. Look, Mom, I have to go. I'll call you later." She clicked off before her mother could reply.

The previous Sunday, Brittany recalled, Bob, Brittany and Becky had gone on a picnic at a local park, not far from her apartment. A relatively small two hundred acres, it had a nice picnic area alongside a little lake and plenty of trails, bike paths and a huge playground for children. She had decided this would be a good place to look for them. Still in total denial, she truly believed she was going to find them both. Of course, she had tried his phone again, but she was no longer dismayed by the disconnect message she heard.

Brittany spent the entire day roaming through the park. She hiked every path and bike trail in it. She walked completely around the streets bordering the park and examined every child she saw, even older ones, in a vain search. She stayed at it until early evening then went home for supper. Still calm and relaxed, she simply decided to stop worrying and convinced herself that Becky would be found, and no one would be the wiser.

For the next several days her life took on an odd routine. Brittany would get up like normal, make breakfast, go to work and all the while act as if there was nothing out of the ordinary going on. Her mother would call, Brittany would fill her with convenient but believable lies and the charade would continue. A couple of evenings she spent parked in the lot of the apartment building she was now sure was the one that Bob lived in. She even stopped a couple of the residents and asked if they knew him, which they did not.

A huge clue she wanted to pursue was the place he said he worked. The problem was she simply could not remember the name. Brittany did remember it was an investment firm of some kind and he had something to do with bonds but even looking online at a list of all of the investment firms in Minneapolis had not jogged her memory.

Each day passed, but she never lost faith. Somehow Becky would turn up and everything would be back to normal and no one would be any the wiser. At least she convinced herself this was true.

In the middle of the week, Brittany decided she needed a night out. She met her three friends at a bar with live music and a young, fun crowd. As usual, they all asked about Becky and received the normal answer of "she's fine". They also asked about the mysterious phantom boyfriend, Bob, and chided her for not meeting him. She was able to casually brush them off and the four of them had a great time dancing and partying up a storm.

Around 10:00 Brittany was thinking about calling it a night when her three friends talked her into something she would come to regret. The bar was having a wet T-shirt contest which Brittany would likely win. She went into the women's restroom, took off her blouse and bra and slipped into a T-shirt the bar had provided.

Brittany and another six fairly well-endowed young women spent the next half hour dancing on the bar while being sprayed with water. Unknown to Brittany, her three friends all took several excellent pictures of her and all three would "jokingly" post them on their Facebook profiles the next day. To make the whole thing a little worse, Brittany did win the contest and was made to stand on the bar and hold a trophy over her head while still wearing the extremely revealing T-shirt. Her friends each took several photos of this for internet viewing.

By the end of the week, Barbara was growing increasingly impatient. She had never gone more than forty-eight hours before without seeing her granddaughter and for some inexplicable reason, Brittany had not allowed her to even speak to the child for almost a week.

Friday evening, after she got off work, Barbara drove directly to her daughter's apartment building. Using the key she had, Barbara let herself in and found that no one was home. She walked through the entire apartment and finding nothing out of place, turned on the TV to wait for Brittany.

Brittany drove into her building's parking lot less than ten minutes after her mother. While looking for a spot close to the door, she spotted a familiar Chevy Tahoe parked in the front row. A stab of fear shot up to her chest when she saw the stickers in the back window that spelled out *Becky Ann*. There was only one SUV on the planet with that name in the window. Brittany punched the gas pedal and squealed out of the parking lot bouncing over two speed bumps, scraping the rear undercarriage of her car, fleeing as rapidly as she dared.

She drove to County 42 and went as quickly as she could to the big Target store on 42 and Cedar Avenue. Once parked in the crowded lot, she leaned forward, her forehead resting on the steering wheel, her arms dangling as she tried to normalize her breathing.

Over the past week, she had been living in a fantasy world. Brittany had actually begun to believe she could put off the reality of her baby's disappearance indefinitely. The lies came easily, and she was actually on some subconscious level, starting to believe them herself. Seeing Barbara's car at her building and knowing her mother was waiting for her was like a slap across the face, knocking her back to the real world.

Brittany had a serious decision to make that she would do almost anything to avoid. Sooner or later, and probably much sooner, she would have to face up to what happened. Just then, a plan popped into her head that would at least buy her the weekend. She retrieved her phone from her purse and punched the button to dial Barbara.

"Hi, Mom," Brittany said when her mother answered.

"Where are you and where is Becky?" Barbara demanded.

"We're on our way to Chicago for the weekend."

"Chicago? What for? Let me talk to Becky."

"Ah, we, ah, haven't left yet. I'm on my way to pick her up at the daycare. Sorry, I didn't call sooner. It was a last-minute sort of thing."

"What are you up to...?"

"Sorry, Mom. I gotta go. I'll call you tomorrow..."

"Brittany, goddamnit, I want..." but she was talking to dead air.

Later that night, well past sundown, Brittany snuck back to her apartment, packed a bag and left. She would spend the next two days hiding in a motel on the other side of St. Paul, in White Bear Lake. Barbara called more than ten times all of which were ignored by her daughter.

On Saturday, she answered a call from Annie and agreed to meet the girls at Rick's in Apple Valley. A night out away from her worries was what she needed to take her mind off of Becky and it would also allow her to act normal with her friends.

Brittany did her best to have a good time, but it was too difficult and all three of her friends could see something was bothering her. She managed to dance a few times and Julia took a group selfie of the four of them holding up drinks and mugging for the camera, a nice picture of the gang for posting on Julia's Facebook page the next day. By 11:00 Brittany had enough, called it a night and drove back to her motel room.

Monday morning came and Brittany, delighted to have the work week start again, believed she could hide out there as she arrived at 8:00, two hours before the store opened. Starting early, she began an inventory on the sales floor of her department. She was barely half finished when she heard a familiar voice behind her.

"Where have you been, young lady, and where is my granddaughter?"

Brittany whirled around and to her horror, found herself staring into the furious face of her mother. The blood drained from her face, she dropped the paperwork and staggered backward two or three steps before collapsing to her knees.

Unable to look up at Barbara, Brittany's shoulders and chest began to heave as she started sobbing uncontrollably. Barbara knelt down on one knee directly in front of her, grabbed her daughter's shoulders and forced Brittany to look at her.

"Brittany, for God's sake, what have you done?"

Still sobbing, tears streaming down her face, gasping to catch her breath, she quietly said, "She's gone. Bob took her, and I can't find them."

Stunned but still in control of herself, Barbara firmly asked, "What did the police say?"

"I, I haven't, uh, called them. I was too afraid. I didn't want to hurt you or make you angry."

"What have you done? What have you done?" Barbara quietly said while dialing 911 to begin the ordeal.

SIX

Melinda Pace watched the video of the final cut of today's show, *The Court Reporter*, with a slightly displeased look on her face. She was illegally dragging on the second cigarette she smoked while watching it, impatiently tapping her well-manicured nails on the arm of her chair as the preview finished. She stubbed out her cigarette in the ashtray on her desk and picked up her glass of Chardonnay. Turning to the young man patiently waiting on her couch, she said, "It's fine, Robbie. We'll go with it. I like the story about the judge in New Hampshire giving a child molester probation. Those always get the viewers riled up and will bring in the emails and phone calls."

"Yeah, those are always my favorites too, Melinda," Robbie sarcastically answered her.

"Look, we..." she began.

"I know, we just report it, we don't make the news blah, blah, blah," he wearily said as he rose to retrieve the tape. "At least we don't always make the news."

"We need something juicy, something really interesting. We haven't had anything since the Prentiss trial," she said ignoring his comments.

Melinda Pace was the host of a local half-hour TV show seen daily in the Minneapolis-St. Paul metro area. As its name suggested, *The Court Reporter* was a show about interesting stories coming from the judicial system, both locally, nationally and on a rare occasion, internationally.

Melinda had worked hard, received excellent grades, and a journalism degree from the University of Wisconsin. The fact that she was a blonde, blue-eyed beauty who slept with just about every professor she had, including the women, didn't hurt her academic achievements either.

Upon graduation, she spent a little over three years at a local station in Duluth. Through guts, brains and beauty, she worked hard and proved herself to be a natural on-air talent. She sent audition tapes to stations in much larger markets and quickly landed a job in the Twin Cities as their on-scene court reporter.

Three years later she had transformed herself into a huge asset. Because of this, and the fact she threatened to go to a competitor, the station agreed to send her to law school if she agreed to a five-year contract. She earned her J.D. from the University of Minnesota and did the two more years she had agreed to do with the station. Melinda then decided she wanted to give the practice of law a try.

With the connections she had made working the courts for TV, she easily landed a job with a very prestigious firm in downtown Minneapolis. Determined to give it her best, she stayed for almost two years which, by the time it was over, seemed like ten. In her mind, it was the modern equivalent of being a galley slave, rowing the boat for the benefit of the partners. Up to this point, she had only seen the most interesting part of the practice of law. Reporting on trials was fascinating, glamorous and rewarding. Being expected to bill eighty to ninety hours per week to placate greedy partners was not what she had bargained for. Even sleeping with most of them didn't seem to matter and would not move her up the ladder any faster.

Finishing her time as little more than a well-paid slave at this firm, an exhausted and disillusioned Melinda Pace practically begged her old boss to get her old job back. Her boss agreed, and Melinda gratefully threw herself back into her TV work.

A short while later Melinda made another big mistake. Now in her thirties and having never been married, she decided to accept the marriage proposal of the law firm partner she had been sleeping with. Instead of the charming, take charge man she dated, he turned out to be an arrogant, immature ass who could be as pouty and petulant as a teenage girl. Plus, his ex-wife had hired a female shark to eviscerate him in the divorce leaving him just about broke. Six months into the marriage, a quick, somewhat expensive divorce was necessary to resolve this mess.

It was about this time that she came up with the idea for her show. Melinda took it to her boss as a low cost, half-hour show the station could produce and air daily. The station agreed to let her try and Melinda turned it into her baby. The show became an immediate hit. It quickly evolved into a tabloid-style, salacious, voyeuristic crime and court show that the viewers ate up.

Now, several years later Melinda had a second divorce, a mild drinking problem and a reputation that had moved beyond Minnesota. She also had a mid-six figure salary and was well known as a five-star, prima donna bitch.

"I'd like to go back to doing the show live like we did during the Prentiss trial. It was a little hectic but more interesting and fun."

"Yeah, it was," Robbie agreed. "I'll see if I can get the mayor to kill his wife. Would that work?"

"Very funny, smartass."

Melinda normally hired and fired producers almost at a whim. Robbie was different. He was sharp, worked hard, was careful not to let anything get on the air that might embarrass her and he had the balls to stand up to her. Plus, she genuinely liked him.

Robbie Nelson was a graduate of the University of Illinois at Champaign. He had a degree in communication and after graduation had lived in Chicago for three years trying to find a job that would make use of his degree. At the time, he was a reasonably attractive, well-groomed, articulate young man trying to land his first decent job. Fed up with bartending, cab driving and retail sales jobs, he answered an online ad for an entry level position with a TV station in Minneapolis. His initial position was an associate producer for Melinda's show for a salary barely above the poverty line. But it was an interesting job in a field he found he enjoyed, and he stuck with it.

Robbie "earned" a promotion to producer when his predecessor made a serious mistake. She had provided Melinda with a wrong picture of a judge accused of his third DWI. Melinda had to make an on-air apology and due to the embarrassment it caused Melinda, an absolute no-no, that producer was gone, and Robbie took her place. Along with significantly more responsibility came enough of a raise to allow Robbie to pay his bills on time and an occasional night out. Plus, he quickly discovered Melinda's bark was far worse than her bite if you were organized, efficient and willing to stand up to her.

Robbie took the tape to editing to finish putting the final touches to it before their 4:00 P.M. air time. Today's show was fairly good. The show consisted of the usual tabloid nonsense. The first segment was about a celebrity divorce in California, always a surefire winner for the masses. Then Melinda fed them the juice about a murder trial in Texas of a woman who poisoned her philandering husband then put his body in a freezer for three years. "Who hasn't wanted to do that?" was Melinda's on-air quip. The final story of the day was about a judge in Montana who gave a child rapist a meager thirty-day jail sentence which was certain to bring about a torrent of emails, tweets and phone calls. Of course, as usual, the highlight of the show was Melinda's daily 'Dumbest Criminals' segment. Today's episode featured two genius home invaders in Portland, OR. Police were dispatched to a home where these two idiots were still on the scene. The would-be crooks had convinced the homeowners to tie them up so when the cops came, they would also claim to be victims. The real victims naturally accommodated them and according to the police report, these two geniuses were shocked when the homeowners ratted them out to the cops. Robbie believed the viewers loved these stories because no matter how many mistakes they've made themselves, at least they could believe they aren't that stupid.

Robbie watched the show in Melinda's opulent corner office then went back to his cramped, windowless cubby hole to begin working on the next day's show. He was reading over the draft of a story one of the writers had prepared when he heard a soft knock on the door. He swiveled in his chair as it opened and saw Gabriella Shriqui, a reporter with the station standing there.

"Hey," Robbie began. "Thanks for coming," he added as she stepped into his office and plopped down in the armless uncomfortable chair alongside his gray metal desk.

Gabriella was a couple years older than Robbie and was stop traffic gorgeous. The product of Moroccan Christian parents who emigrated to America when her mother was pregnant with her older brother. Gabriella had silky black hair six inches below her shoulders, light caramel colored skin that looked like a perpetual tan and almost black, slightly almond-shaped eyes.

She and Robbie had worked together extensively on a recent, notorious local trial of a judge, Gordon Prentiss, who had been accused of murdering his wife. For the first dozen or so times they were together, Robbie's knees weakened just at the sight of her. He eventually worked up enough nerve to ask her out, but she very kindly shut him down by claiming she didn't date co-workers. Which, of course, is really code for: "not interested". She told him she had dated a coworker once at a station in Detroit and when it ended, she was out of a job. Robbie took it well and they had become pals, even going out for an occasional lunch or beer together.

"Have anything for me?" he asked.

"Stop staring at my legs," she jokingly chided him.

"I like your legs. If you don't want me to look at them, don't wear a dress. Now, do you have anything?"

Gabriella wasn't just a reporter for the station. She was the main on the scene personality for all of the local courts throughout the Metro area. As such, she was a great source of news, gossip and information about anything of interest that might be happening or in the works around any of the county courthouses.

"I got nothing," she replied. "I can't believe how slow it's been. A couple of gang bangers pleading out to a two-year-old drive-by is the news of the week. Other than that, not much. I'm so bored. Want to go for a beer?"

"Oh, you're bored so now I'm looking good to you," he said with feigned anger.

"Yep," she said. "I'm bored so you'll do. What about it?"

"My fragile male ego is crushed. Sorry, can't do it. I'll be here for at least a couple hours."

"I think I need a vacation," Gabriella said. "When was the last time you took a vacation?"

"Just before the Prentiss trial," Robbie answered her after thinking about it for a moment. "I went to St. Louis for a week and saw the Cubs play the Cardinals. I'm going home for Christmas."

"How was it?"

"The trip to St. Louis?"

"Yeah, was it good to get away?"

"Sure, except the Cubs got their ass handed to them all three games."

She stood up, patted him on the shoulder and with mild sarcasm said, "That's a shame. I'm gonna go. I'll see you later," and opened the door to leave.

"Okay, if you come across anything…"

"I'll let you know," she said as she closed his door behind her.

With that, Robbie went back to the story he was reading. It was about the trial of a thirty-eight-year-old mother of three teenage girls who was being tried for using her daughters as prostitutes. It was taking place in Philadelphia and would be tomorrow's lead.

SEVEN

"Judge Harlan accepted the plea of Demetrius Young to first-degree manslaughter and immediately sentenced the seventeen-year-old veteran gangbanger to forty-eight months in an adult prison," Gabriella Shriqui said facing the camera.

She was standing in the front plaza of the Hennepin County Government Center, with the big granite, glass and chrome building in the background. It was a bit of a breezy day and she was having a little trouble keeping her long black hair from blowing in her face. Gabriella and the remote camera crew she worked with were reporting on a gang shooting homicide case. Demetrius Young, the last of the three defendants, had pled to a lesser manslaughter charge in the tragic death of a seven-year-old little girl.

It had started when Demetrius was picked up a few minutes before the shooting by the two co-defendants and was in the backseat of the car when it happened. Demetrius claimed he had no prior knowledge of what his friends and fellow gang bangers were up to. The other two defendants had both testified that before picking Demetrius up, they had been cruising the streets of South Minneapolis looking for an older man who may have insulted the shooter's sister.

Barely two minutes after Demetrius got in the car, they spotted the man, or at least someone they believed to be him, walking along a residential street. DeShawn, the gang member whose sister was supposedly the grievously offended party, opened up at the man from the passenger seat with a semi-automatic 9mm handgun. His target fled unscathed, but one of the bullets went through a window in the house on the street and struck the seven-year-old girl in the forehead, killing her instantly.

"Primarily, because of his extensive juvenile record, despite his age and his alleged lack of any agreed upon participation in the shooting, the judge was not inclined to allow the probation his lawyer requested. With this final plea, a sad and tragic tale that shocked the Twin Cities last January has come to a close. This is Gabriella Shriqui reporting from the Hennepin County Government Center."

"How was that take? Are we good?" she asked the technician and the cameraman.

"Yeah," the technician answered. "It should be fine."

Gabriella looked at her watch and saw it was almost 3:00. The film would be in time for the 5:00 P.M. news report and would likely be used by Melinda Pace on her show. At that moment she felt her phone vibrate in her skirt pocket. She pulled it out and saw that the caller ID read

Dakota County Sheriff. Suspecting it was someone she didn't want to talk to, she frowned but answered it anyway.

"This is Gabriella," she said as pleasantly as she could.

"Hey, sweetheart, it's Stu Doyle. How've you been?"

"Fine, Stu. What's up?" she said as she sat down on the wall surrounding the fountain on the plaza. The caller was indeed the person she feared it was and she needed to sit down because she wasn't sure she wanted to talk to him.

Stu Doyle was an investigator with the Dakota County Sheriff's office. Gabriella had met him a couple of months ago while covering a murder trial in Hastings, the county seat. Stu was a tall, charming, very good-looking man who made it clear he wanted to get in Gabriella's pants in the worst way. Gabriella, being the stunning beauty she was, had plenty of experience with Stu's type. As politely but firmly as she could, she made it clear to him that she was one conquest he wasn't going to get. And on top of it, she found out later he was married.

"I have a 'no bullshit' hot tip for you, but the price is meeting me for a drink in an hour. Say four o'clock."

"Stu," she said with a sigh, "I…"

"Gabriella, listen. This could easily be the hottest story of your career and so far, no one else has it. I am not exaggerating. Meet me at Giorgio's in Rosemount. You won't be sorry."

Gabriella hesitated for a moment thinking, *why do I doubt that*, then said, "Okay. I'll be there by 4:00. Oh, and Stu, how's your wife?"

The last comment stopped him a bit. Even so, he quietly replied, "See you in an hour."

A few minutes before 4:00, Gabriella entered the dimly lit restaurant. Giorgio's is a small family restaurant with excellent Italian food. She stood in the entryway allowing her eyes a moment to adjust from the brilliant afternoon sunlight. At this hour, the place was almost empty except for a few early birds in the bar.

Gabriella looked to her right into the bar and saw Doyle sitting in a booth facing her. He waved at her. She went into the bar and slid into the booth opposite him.

"As gorgeous as ever," he greeted her flashing his practiced smile as she placed her purse on the table between them.

"Thanks, Stu," she replied.

A moment later the bartender stepped up to their booth and said to her, "What can I get you?"

"I'll just have a soda, a Coke?"

"Coke it is," he replied. "What about you, Stu. You good?" he asked looking at Stu's glass of beer.

"For now, Milt."

The two of them idly chatted until the bartender came back with Gabriella's soda. When he left, she said to the investigator, "Okay. What do you have?"

"Well...'" he started off coyly. "I'm serious about what I told you on the phone. This could be a career maker."

"Okay, I'm listening."

"But we need to get your payment straight before I tell you."

Gabriella knew he would pull a stunt like this. She thought it through, decided to remain calm and interested and hear him out.

"And...?" she replied.

"Well," he quietly said as he leaned forward. "I do for you, you do for me. You know, favors."

"Oh, exactly what kind of favors?" she asked seductively narrowing her eyes at him.

"A little, you know, party favors..."

"Sexual favors?"

"Yeah, sure, why not? If you don't want the deal, I know other reporters who will take it," he said as he smugly sat back and straightened his tie.

"Okay, why not? I've heard you're a good guy and to be honest, I don't have much of a social life. So, tell me what you have."

He wasn't at all surprised she would go for it. He leaned forward again and sincerely said, "You won't regret it, Gabriella. Believe me. Plus, I'm telling you, this is a great story.

"You remember a few years ago, that girl in Florida who got away with murdering her daughter? We may have the same deal here."

"Tell me," Gabriella said as she removed a notebook from her purse and began taking notes.

"This is all on background, an anonymous source in the sheriff's office."

"Yeah, yeah, of course."

For the next half hour, he told her everything he knew about the situation. A young mother, widowed, was brought in earlier that day by her mother and reported a missing child. Doyle explained it all to Gabriella, gave her a detailed report of everything he knew from the statements taken from the two women.

"And she didn't report her daughter missing for what, almost ten days?"

"That's right. Says she thought she could find this guy herself and get the kid back. One more thing, a little bonus for you. I have this," he said as he handed her a print of a photo of Brittany and Becky together.

"That's great. You're right. This could be a huge story. Certainly worth our deal," she said with a wink. "Tell you what," she continued as she started to pack. "I gotta get going. Get this on the air before somebody beats me to it. But," she said as she softly placed a hand on his, "I'll meet you back here at, say 7:30?"

The channel 8 six o'clock news broadcast led off with Gabriella's story. While this was on the air, she was in a meeting with the station's General Manager, Madison Eyler; the station's News Director, Hunter Oswood; Melinda Pace and Robbie Nelson.

"You trust this guy?" Oswood asked Gabriella.

"No, he's a total snake but I can control him," she answered.

"You're sure?" Madison interjected.

"Yes, believe me," Gabriella confidently answered her. "He doesn't know it yet, but I've got him by the balls."

"Melinda," Eyler turned and asked, "You want in on this?"

"Absolutely. After tonight, there's going to be a shit storm in the media around here. You see this picture of that beautiful little girl? This is a ratings wet dream."

"Okay," Eyler said once again looking at Gabriella. "Gabriella, you've got point on this. It's your story, at least for now. I guess that's it for now. You're seeing this source again tonight?"

"In about an hour," Gabriella said as they all stood to leave.

As the four of them started making their way out of her office, Madison said, "And Melinda, let's not have another clusterfuck like Cindy Scarpino."

Without a word, they all left and Melinda, obviously annoyed, stomped off down the hall toward her own office. As she did, Gabriella lightly took Robbie's arm and held him back.

After Melinda was out of earshot from them, Gabriella asked, "Who is Cindy Scarpino?"

Robbie bobbed his head back and forth several times considering if he should tell her or not. After thinking about it for a moment he decided she probably needed to know.

"This was a couple years before me, but I heard all about it. Cindy was a young mother whose kid was taken by the father. There was a big stink about it, nationwide. Anyway, Melinda had her on almost every day for two weeks running the story. Then Melinda found out Cindy had been arrested for solicitation in Miami at age 18. Melinda made a huge deal out of this, you know, for ratings. She ripped this poor girl to shreds, making her look like the guilty one for the kid being taken. After a couple of days of this, Cindy takes a bottle of pills and commits suicide."

"Oh, my God!"

"Yeah," Robbie agreed. "Then it turns out, at seventeen, Cindy ran away from home because her stepfather was abusing her…"

"Sexually?"

"Yep. She was pretty much broke, homeless and ended up on the streets. That's when she got picked up for hooking. And on top of it, two days after she kills herself, the cops find the kid in Montana with his dad. The station got sued over it and I heard they settled but…"

"Yeah."

Right on time at 7:30, Gabriella once again slid onto a booth bench across from Stu Doyle. This time they were seated in Giorgio's dining room. The waitress arrived almost immediately to check with Gabriella.

"I'm not having anything," she pleasantly said to the older woman. "I won't be staying long."

"What, you in a hurry to get a little of the Stu wild ride?" he asked with a smirk after the waitress left.

"Not exactly, Stu," Gabriella replied. She reached into her purse and removed a small cassette player. She placed it on the table between them, pressed the play button and they both listened to a recording of Stu's proposal from that afternoon and his monologue concerning Brittany Riley.

When it finished playing, Gabriella removed the mini-cassette and held it up in her hand. An obviously furious Stu Doyle simply glared at her as she did this.

"This one's for you if you want it. I have others, at least one for your wife and one for the sheriff. No, you don't want it?"

"Fuck you, you conniving…"

"Here's our new deal," Gabriella said cutting him off and ignoring him. "You will be my exclusive source for information about this case. You will talk to no one else. If I find out you have, I mail the copies. And the information better be good and timely, or I mail the copies. Do we understand each other?"

Stu sat silently, still glaring at her. What galled him wasn't the arrangement but the fact he had been played by a woman.

"I want to hear you say it, Stu," she said as she replaced the tape player in her purse.

"Fine, I'll do it," he said through his clenched teeth.

"Good. I'll be in touch," she continued as she slid across the bench seat. She stood up, leaned over to put her mouth by his ear and whispered, "You'll never know what you're missing. I've been told I'm even better than I look."

With that, she straightened up, turned and walked out.

EIGHT

The Dakota County Sheriff was a man named Brian Cale who had been in law enforcement for over thirty-five years. First, he was with the Rochester police department for twenty years, retiring as a sergeant and then decided to double dip his public pension by becoming a deputy with the Dakota County Sheriff's Office. The previous sheriff, his predecessor, retired five years ago and Cale took a run at being elected to the job. Considered a long shot, what probably won it for him was his physical appearance. Brian Cale looked like what a sheriff should look like. A no nonsense looking bald man in his early fifties, he kept himself in good shape and when he made a public appearance, he not only looked the part but gave off an aura of confidence. This was well received in this mostly white, middle-class suburban county and he was elected easily.

When the sheriff's investigators finished interviewing Barbara and Brittany Riley, they met with Cale to review the case. A decision was made for the four detectives to begin preliminary arrangements for their investigation. The first step would be to locate the missing Bob Olson and the child. In addition, after considerable discussion, argument and heated debate, it was decided to hold off informing the media until the next day. Three of the detectives argued strenuously to make an announcement immediately. The other detective, Stu Doyle and the sheriff himself, favored waiting until the next day. Doyle wanted to wait so he could take a run at Gabriella by leaking the story. Cale wanted to wait until they were more prepared for the media storm this news would create. What finally decided it was when Cale stated what they all believed; the odds of finding Becky Ann Riley alive were probably zero.

Despite this obvious fact, the sheriff had authorized the issuance of an AMBER Alert for seven o'clock that evening. His hope was that the media would act responsibly for a change and not come pounding on his door. It was, of course, a vain hope at best and he knew it. By the time Gabriella's report finished airing, the phone lines at the sheriff's office were exploding. It seemed every news source in Minnesota had seen the broadcast and were now clamoring for information. Sheriff Cale decided he had little choice but to hold a press conference that evening and issued the AMBER alert immediately.

The Dakota County Sheriff's Department is located in Hastings as part of the Dakota County Government Center. The Adult Detention Center, the latest "PC" term for jail, the main courthouse and county administrative offices are all part of the same complex. It is about twenty-two miles from downtown St. Paul and almost thirty from

40

downtown Minneapolis. This was a trip the media horde would become very familiar with over the next several months.

After the detectives finished their interview of her, Brittany sat down with a police artist. Between them, they came up with a very good drawing of Bob Olson. The problem was that it was both too vague and too specific. Too vague in that, with the glasses and the facial hair, it could be just about any twenty-something white male. Too specific because remove the glasses and facial hair and it could also be used to rule out just about any twenty something white male.

The department's press liaison officer, Patty Dunphy, prepared a press release package to hand out to the media representatives before the press conference. In it, with the sheriff's approval, were recent photos of Becky, a synopsis of the information available and a copy of the drawing of the missing Bob Olson. By the end of the week, the photo of the missing, beautiful, blue-eyed little blonde girl would be tugging at the hearts of people from coast to coast. The media firestorm it would unleash was about to begin.

At precisely eight o'clock, Sheriff Cale stepped up to the podium. Standing behind and flanking him were the four detectives, two men and two women, who would be leading the investigation. It was a very pleasant, warm, summer evening and because of the size of the crowd, the podium had been set up on the steps of the government center with the courthouse for a background.

Cale started off with a monotone recitation of what had been written and handed out in the press release. Before he was halfway through it, the questions were starting to fly. He did his best to ignore them and continue on, but there was one question repeated over and over that he finally could not disregard: "Why did it take the mother ten days to report her missing daughter?"

Setting aside his notes, he removed his reading glasses, placed them on the podium and looked directly at Gabriella Shriqui standing in the front row. A clearly annoyed Cale said, "She told us that she believed her daughter was safe with her boyfriend, Bob Olson. She believed her daughter would be returned by him."

A murmur went through the crowd and more questions were thrown at the sheriff. Knowing this could very easily be the most important case of his law enforcement career, Cale was doing his best to keep calm and patient. Despite the fact that he was an elected official, his patience with the media was not a strong point in his make up. After gritting his teeth and not answering the howling mob for a full minute, he slammed a fist down on the podium and bellowed for order to be restored. The sheriff's momentary loss of control worked. The noise and the chaotic questioning immediately ceased.

With the unruly mob now more or less under control, Cale began calling on reporters and taking questions one at a time. For the next fifteen minutes, a reasonably polite exchange took place between the press and the sheriff. When it was done, he had revealed everything his office knew which was mostly covered in the handout each had received.

"Obviously, our main priority is to return this little girl to her family. In your information packet, you'll find our 800 number. We would appreciate it if you good people would publicize it and let the public know to call us with any information to help us accomplish that."

This last statement caused all four detectives to silently cringe. With a case like this, the four of them could easily spend weeks, maybe months, running down false leads. Every goofball, crackpot and member of the aluminum foil helmet club would be calling. On the other hand, sometimes these notifications led to legitimate information.

"Now," Cale continued, "if there are no other questions..."

A hand went up in the front row, raised by the reporter Cale suspected had broken the story, Gabriella Shriqui. The sheriff would have loved to have known who her source was but knew she would never reveal it.

"Sheriff," Gabriella began, "is the mother, Brittany Riley, a suspect in your investigation?" It was a question everyone at the briefing wanted to know but for some inexplicable reason had not been asked.

Instead of simply answering "no" he added an innocuous "not at this time" onto his answer. With that, another loud buzz went through the crowd and a half dozen hands shot up.

Without understanding the significance of his seemingly innocent statement, Cale said, "That's all I have folks. We'll keep you posted. Thank you." With that, he turned to his deputies and indicated he wanted to see them. As he walked away, a dozen voices could be heard yelling the word "sheriff" in a vain attempt to get his attention.

Cale, the four detectives and Patty Dunphy beat a hasty retreat toward the entry to the sheriff's department. Waiting inside the door was Cale's personal assistant, Louise Shaffer. Shaffer stepped up to Cale and the six-foot four-inch sheriff bent over as she whispered in his ear to let him know he had visitors. The Riley family was waiting for him in his office.

As they walked down the hall toward his office, Cale quietly asked Louise, "What do they want? Did they say?"

"To see you," Shaffer shrugged. "To find out what's next, I guess."

Cale stopped, turned to his deputies and said, "Shannon, you and Patty come with me. You three go into conference room A. We'll meet in there."

A minute later, Cale, Dunphy, Shaffer and Shannon Keenan entered Cale's office. Shannon Keenan was one of the department's senior investigators. She was an average size woman who dressed mostly in jeans, cowboy boots and casual coats and blouses. Her one indulgence to vanity was blonde highlights in her light brown hair. She was exceptionally good at family matters especially those involving children. At the age of forty-four and the mother of three teenage boys, she had plenty of hands-on experience.

Waiting in his office were all four Rileys; Barbara, Floyd, Brittany and her brother Tim. When the greetings, introductions and handshakes were completed, Cale took the chair behind the large oak desk, leaned forward on his forearms and asked, "How are you folks holding up?" He paid close attention to Brittany who was looking past him at the wall behind his desk.

Flanked by the state and U.S. flags, the sheriff's vanity wall was filled with plaques, awards and pictures of the sheriff with various politicians. What Cale found most curious was the blank, almost indifferent look on Brittany's face and her emotionally empty eyes. He expected them to be red and puffy from crying. Instead, they were quite dry and she looked almost uninterested.

"How did the press conference go? Will they publicize Becky's disappearance? Do you think it will help?" Barbara asked.

"The press conference went fine," Cale answered while stealing a quick peek at Dunphy who slightly nodded her head and shrugged her shoulders a bit. "And yes, they'll publicize this. In fact, they'll be all over it. You folks are going to be in for a rough ride from them."

"Why?" Brittany asked.

"Because they're going to want to know your story. They'll probably be camped outside your house wanting pictures, interviews, you name it. I can't tell you what to do but you might want help handling this. It wouldn't be a bad idea to get a lawyer to represent you and help you with this. Once word gets out, you'll have dozens of them wanting to represent you."

"It's all right," Barbara said glaring at Brittany. She turned back to Cale, smiled and said, "Why would we need a lawyer?"

"Just to help you handle everything."

"What about a reward?" Barbara asked. "We could put up fifty thousand   dollars."

Cale paused for a moment before answering and instead,

Shannon Keenan spoke up. "Mrs. Riley, why don't we hold off on that for at least a few days? We've barely begun. Let's see how it goes first."

"Okay," Barbara said a little disappointed while looking at Shannon who was standing in back with Patty Dunphy. "What next?" Barbara asked turning back to Cale.

Again, it was Keenan who answered. "Brittany, tomorrow I want you to come here at 8:00 A.M. You can come with me and we'll start searching for Bob Olson. Is that okay?"

"Sure," Brittany answered, looking at Shannon and showing real interest for the first time.

"We would like to organize a search ourselves," Barbara told Cale. "You know, get some volunteers to look through parks and other places."

"That would be okay," Cale replied nodding his head. "Why don't you meet with Patty tomorrow and she can help you with that. Get some publicity going and things like that. Is that good with you?" Cale asked Dunphy.

"Sure, no problem," she said as she handed a card to Barbara. "Come in tomorrow at 8:00 and we'll start on it."

Cale and Shannon Keenan took their seats at the conference room table. "Tomorrow?" Cale asked everyone seated at the table.

"Stu and I will start running down known pedophiles in the appropriate age and race group; white males in their twenties to mid-thirties," Paul Anderson said.

"And all Bob Olson's in the Metro area. We'll expand outstate later if we need to," Doyle added. "Same age and race."

"You'll get a shitload of them," Cale said to Doyle.

"We have to start somewhere," Doyle shrugged. "We'll have Curt Thomas run DMV on Bob and Robert Olson spelled with an o-n or e-n and pull photos for Brittany to go over."

"Speaking of Brittany," Cale said turning to the two women, Shannon and her partner, Kristin Williams. "We need to discreetly start looking at her."

"She acted about as upset as if we were talking about her neighbor's cat running off," Shannon replied. "We'll see where this search goes, but I'm not too hopeful."

"I'm not the only one who senses she knows more than she's telling us?" Cale asked looking at Shannon.

"No, you sure aren't," she answered.

NINE

The morning after the press conference, a few minutes before 8:00 A.M. Barbara, Floyd and Brittany Riley arrived back at the sheriff's office. Barbara and Floyd went with Patty Dunphy to set up a public search for their granddaughter while Brittany went into a conference room with the two female detectives. The four investigators, with the sheriff's approval, decided to let the two women handle Brittany. Their reasoning was that until she could be ruled out as a suspect, she must be considered to be one. Their job was to handle her carefully and try not to intimidate her and risk losing her cooperation. Specifically, they needed to keep Stu Doyle away from her as long as possible.

The three women each took a chair at the conference room table. The two investigators were on one side facing Brittany who looked to be a little frightened. Kristin Williams, the other female detective whom Brittany had not yet met, introduced herself and said, "You look a little nervous, Brittany. Believe me, we're here to help you," she finished with a reassuring smile.

"I know," Brittany replied, nodding her head.

"Good," Kristin said. Kristin was ten years younger than her partner, Shannon. A little taller, slimmer and also married but no children, she had been a detective for only two years but had learned a lot from the more experienced Shannon.

The three of them spent the next half hour listing all of the places Brittany could remember having been with Olson. Additionally, even though Brittany had done this herself, they went over a list of all of the investment firms in the metro area hoping that if she heard the name, it would jog her memory. Several of them sounded like possibilities to Brittany but she could not be sure.

"Wait here, Brittany," Kristin said as she stood and walked to the conference room door. "I need to get one of our other guys in here."

"Get Paul," Shannon said.

"I will," Kristin answered as she stepped through the doorway into the hall. She walked down the hall and into the room where the detectives' desks were located. To her relief, she saw Paul Anderson at his desk and Stu Doyle nowhere in sight. Kristin motioned for Paul to come to her, which he promptly did while looking around to make sure Doyle didn't see them.

"Where's Doyle?" Kristin asked as they walked toward the conference room.

"Probably in the john admiring himself in the mirror. What's up?"

"C'mon in and talk to her for a minute."

45

"Hello, Brittany. I'm Paul Anderson," he said with a disarming smile after entering the conference room as he shook hands with Brittany. "I'm a detective and I'll be working with Kristin and Shannon to find Becky," he finished as he sat down next to her. Anderson was the oldest member of the sheriff's office, next to the sheriff himself. A receding hairline, a slight paunch and a bit of a rumpled appearance belied a sharp mind and one of the best-case closure rates in the state.

"She can't remember the name of the investment firm where Olson told her he worked," Shannon said as Kristin sat down again.

"Okay," Anderson said. "I guess we'll have to check all of them."

"You're going to need subpoenas," Shannon said.

"I think we can get a blanket one to cover all of them. It would be helpful if you could remember," Anderson said turning back to Brittany. "Did you ever go there with him?"

"No," she answered.

"You're sure it was downtown Minneapolis?"

"Yes," she answered quickly. "That I remember for sure. At least, that's what he told me. And he said he worked in the bond department, whatever that is."

"Okay," Anderson said in his kind, fatherly way as he patted Brittany on the back of her hand. "You keep thinking about it and try to remember, okay?" He looked at the two women across the table and said, "I'll put Doyle on this. He's actually pretty good at it. And Brittany," he said as he turned back to her. "We're getting photos and information on every Bob and Robert Olson in the Cities. In the next day or two, if we haven't found him, we're going to have you go through them. Okay?"

"Yes, of course," she replied. "Will somebody please tell me something," she continued as she made eye contact with each of the detectives. "Am I going to get my baby back?"

It was the fatherly Paul Anderson who answered her. He took her right hand in his left, looked directly into her eyes and softly said, "I can promise you this: we will do everything we possibly can to make that happen."

With Brittany in the back seat of the unmarked, four-door sedan, the three women pulled into the parking lot of the Buck Hill Apartments. This was the third apartment complex on County Road 11 they had been to that morning. Since Brittany could not remember with any certainty which apartment it was, they decided to check them all.

Of the first two, one of them did have a Bob Olson as a tenant. Even though he was a sixty-four-year old retired postal employee, they checked on him anyway. Fortunately, he was home, very pleasant and cooperative. Obviously not the Bob Olson they were looking for.

Though uncertain of it, the complex they were currently at was the same one Olson had taken Brittany to the night before the kidnapping. Like most people when they are passengers in a car and not driving, Brittany had not paid close attention to where they had gone that night. Assuming Olson knew what he was doing, where he was going and having no reason not to trust him, she simply wasn't watching.

There were three large three story brick buildings housing a total of one hundred and twenty apartments. It also had two long buildings that housed sixty single car garages and a large, open parking area. Kristin Williams parked in a visitor's slot in front of the building that housed the management office.

As the three women walked toward the office door, Brittany looked around and said, "I'm pretty sure this is the one. In fact," she continued as she stopped and pointed at the building directly across the parking lot, "I'm almost positive that's the one there."

The two detectives stopped, turned to her and Shannon said, "But you didn't actually see him go in," a statement, not a question.

"No, sorry. We were parked over there I think," she said pointing at a spot in the lot away from the door. "It was raining, starting to get dark, Becky was in the back seat and we were just waiting for him."

"Okay, let's go see the manager," Shannon said.

The office manager was a well-dressed, professional looking young woman in her late twenties. The detectives introduced themselves, showed her their badges and credentials and explained their purpose to her. As they had done with the previous places they had checked, they showed her the drawing of Olson. The manager could not identify him, but after a search on her computer, she did come up with two Robert Olsons as current tenants. She also did a search for former tenants who may have moved in the past year and came up with two more. Of the four of them, only one was in the appropriate age group. He was listed as married with one child and was a current tenant.

"We'd like to check them all out anyway," Shannon told the manager. "We'll need you to print off the information for each of them."

"Um, jeez, ah, I'm not sure if I can do that, even for the police."

"This is a kidnapping investigation," an impatient Kristin Williams said glaring at the woman. "A little girl is missing!"

"Oh, my God! Seriously? Okay. I'll get them for you right away."

Kristin winked at Shannon as the young woman hurried to comply. Barely five minutes later, with the information in hand and the apartment manager in the lead, they entered the building that was home to the married Bob Olson. They found the right apartment and after knocking on the door, a harried looking woman in her mid-twenties opened the door holding a small boy.

They introduced themselves and explained the purpose of their visit to the obviously distraught young mother. She let them in and politely answered their questions, even getting them a picture of her Bob Olson.

Brittany stared at the photo for thirty to forty seconds then said, "With glasses, a mustache and goatee, it could be him. I mean maybe…" she stammered.

The young mother, whose name was Carly, clutched the young child a little too tightly and said, "No, that can't be. He would never… when did this happen?"

Shannon told her the time frame for when Becky went missing. Carly assured them they were out of town visiting her relatives in Bemidji that weekend.

Kristin who had taken the photo from Brittany asked, "How tall is your husband?"

"Six foot three, six-four?" she answered.

"Too tall," Shannon said then apologized for the intrusion. As they were leaving, a visibly relieved Carly put a hand on Brittany's arm and said, "I hope you find your little girl. I can only imagine the hell you must be going through." Later, after everything had settled down, Carly found herself thinking that Brittany didn't look very upset at all.

Before moving on to the next apartments, as they had done with the first two places they visited, they left copies of the drawing of Olson. The apartment managers would post these along with instructions to call if anyone had information about him.

The three women spent the rest of the morning stopping at every apartment complex between County Road 42 and Highway 13. They obtained information on a total of eleven Bob Olsons that were either current or former tenants. Of those, aside from Carly Olson's husband, there were only two others that could be listed as possible, in the right age range and race. One had moved several months before and one was still living in the apartment. They placed a quick call to the employer of the Bob Olson living at the apartment they were checking. It was a small trucking company in Shakopee. The owner told them this Bob Olson was currently out of town in his truck. Shannon left her name and number and told the man to have him call when he returned.

By 2:00 that afternoon, they had finished the apartment search. Their only interview was with Carly Olson, but they had obtained more names to run down. After arriving back at the sheriff's department, they handed Brittany over to Stu Doyle to go over pictures and bios of the Bob Olsons he had collected from the DMV.

TEN

The two women detectives left Brittany with Stu Doyle to begin going through the photos of all the Bob and Robert Olsons the DMV had provided. In the immediate Twin Cities area alone, narrowed down to the appropriate age and race group, there were over three hundred possibilities. Doyle had also asked the DMV to give him a list of all of the Bob Olsons in Minnesota outside the Twin Cities. The DMV came back with an additional eight hundred from outstate; almost two hundred of those were age and race appropriate. He decided to put aside the ones from outside the metro area and just concentrate on those from the Twin Cities.

Of the three hundred they had so far from just the Twin Cities metro area, Doyle had them further broken down by height and weight and was able to eliminate about a hundred. Brittany would have to sit down with him and go through the remaining two hundred.

Shannon softly knocked on the door of Sheriff Cale's office, opened it and stuck her head in. Cale motioned her in while he listened on his phone. Shannon and Kristin each took a chair in front of the big desk while their boss, who was facing the wall behind his desk, finished his call.

"Well, Commissioner, I appreciate the offer and I'll certainly keep it in mind. I'll let you know as soon as I need something. Thanks again," he said as he ended the call.

Cale swiveled his chair around, placed the phone handle in its cradle, leaned back in his chair and said to the two detectives, "This could get out of hand. That was Cameron Philby, the Commissioner of Public Safety and head of the State Bureau of Criminal Apprehension. Seems he had a chat this morning with Ted Dahlstrom, the governor. Dahlstrom is offering to have the BCA help us which, of course, means they take over and I don't really want that. Okay," he sighed, "what have you two got? Tell me something good."

"Wish I could sheriff," Shannon replied. She filled him in on their day and the fruitless search for the missing Bob Olson.

"The 800-number hotline has been busy. We've had over fifty calls from people who claim to have seen him. Fortunately, every police department and sheriff in the metro area is on board to help us run these down," Cale said. "What do you think of Miss Riley? Is she credible?"

Shannon and Kristin looked at each other and shrugged their shoulders. It was Shannon who answered. "I don't know. At times she seems genuine and other times, not so much. It might be too early to tell."

"This business about not calling to report her daughter missing for ten days, that's total bullshit," Kristin interjected.

"I agree," Cale said as he leaned forward and placed both forearms on the desk. "Paul is running down the Robert Olsons who work for investment firms. Stu can work with Brittany on the DMV photos…"

"Did you tell him not to hit on her?" Kristin asked only half joking.

"That's all I need," Cale said shaking his head with a weary look. "Going through the photos will probably take the rest of today. I've got Patty and Louise plus a couple of uniform deputies working with the Rileys on a public plea for help with the search. We brought in a couple of temp kids to answer phones and Patty and I will handle the press. I'm open to suggestions. Anything else you can think of that we need to do?" he asked his two favorite detectives.

"No," the women said in unison. "I can't think of anything off the top of my head. But," Shannon continued, "things will come up."

"And here's one of them," Cale said as he handed Shannon a piece of paper. "This is a list of Brittany's friends, at least those her mother knows about. I want you two to start interviewing them about their relationship with Brittany and her daughter and anything else you can think of, especially this Bob Olson. Something in the back of my mind tells me this whole thing just isn't quite right. Talk to each of them and get more names and…well, you know what to do."

"Will do, boss," Shannon answered reading the list of three names while Kristin looked over her shoulder.

Patty Dunphy was entering Cale's office as Shannon and Kristin were leaving. She held the sheriff's office door for the two investigators and the three women exchanged a sincere, friendly greeting. Dunphy closed the door behind her and said, "We're all set. The Rileys are here and it looks like we've got some national media showing up as well. CNN has a truck out in the circle along with all of the locals."

"Patty, I'm not going be able to do this every day…"

"I know, sheriff," she interrupted. "But at least for the first few days and then, if we have anything significant to report, you should probably do it."

"Ok, you're right," Cale sighed as he stood. He looked at the clock on his wall and noticed the press conference was set to start at three o'clock, ten minutes from now.

"Let's go," he said as he stepped through his door. "I'm not the President. I don't need to keep everyone waiting just to remind them I'm more important than they are."

Instead of holding the press conference outdoors, Cale had decided to make the media cram into a small briefing room. Cale started off making the announcement that there was nothing new to announce, which each of the reporters dutifully recorded or scribbled into notebooks. The sheriff took a few questions, most of which amounted to no new information. He was again asked about Brittany not reporting to the police that her daughter was missing and again dodged it by making a vague statement that she thought the boyfriend would return her.

At that point, the Rileys took over or, more precisely, Barbara Riley took over. She stepped up to the podium in the crowded room and asked the media to make a public plea for information about her missing granddaughter. She explained to them that an 800 number had been set up and they were looking for volunteers to handle calls and begin searching for Becky.

Without waiting to be called on, a local reporter, a man with Channel Nine, interrupted Barbara and asked, "Where is Brittany now? Why isn't she here?"

"I'll answer that," Cale said as he stepped back to the microphone. "She's working with one of my detectives to track down this Bob Olson who we believe took this child."

There was another ten minutes of questions for the sheriff and Barbara Riley, none of which elicited any new information. Cale called a halt to it and everyone slowly made their way out of the room to make their reports.

"That wasn't very enlightening," Gabriella Shriqui said to her cameraman, Kyle Bronson.

"Not surprising," Kyle replied. "We'll know when they have some news and..." he stopped as Gabriella answered her phone.

"Hey, Melinda," Gabriella said as she and Kyle continued to walk toward their van.

"Anything new?" Melinda asked.

"No, nothing at all. And still pretty vague about why the kid's mother didn't report her missing for ten days. Are you thinking about going live today?"

"No," Melinda answered. "Listen, is the family still there?"

"Yeah, I guess."

"Good, get to them. I want them on my show. And the mother, what's-her-name...?"

"Brittany," Gabriella said.

"Her, too. But separately. Not on the same show as her parents. Can you swing it?"

"I'll see if I can find them. I'll get back to you." Gabriella ended the call.

"I'm going to go back inside and see if I can track down the Rileys for Melinda," she said to Kyle. "Wait for me by the van. Set up for a remote back to the station."

"I'll write up a script for you too," he answered her as Gabriella turned to go back into sheriff's office.

Not wanting to go through the main entrance and be stopped by a locked door in the waiting room, Gabriella went to the door the deputies used. When she was ten feet from the entrance, two male deputies came through it.

"Would you hold it for me, please?" Gabriella said as she flashed a brilliant smile at the younger one.

"Um, yeah, sure," he stammered gaping at her with his mouth hanging open.

"Thank you," she politely said as she quickly walked past the two officers and into the building. The two men stared at her as she walked down the hallway into the off-limits part of the offices.

"Was she supposed to…" the older one finally said.

"Oh, shit, probably not."

"Let's get out of here."

Gabriella hurried away from the deputies who she knew were watching her. She turned a corner and found Stu Doyle coming out of a men's room.

"Stu," she quietly called out as she hurried after him. Doyle turned toward the sound of his name and saw her.

"How did you get in here?"

"Never mind that. I need to find the Rileys. Do you know where they are?"

"Jesus Christ, Gabriella, you can't just come wandering back here."

"Yeah, yeah, whatever," she said dismissing him with a wave of her hand. "Is Brittany with you? I need her too."

"For what?"

"Melinda Pace wants to do a live interview with the family. Brittany separately."

Doyle swiveled his head about, checking to see if they were being overheard, thankful there were no security cameras.

"Tell you what," Doyle began, "Let me see if I can set it up for you. But you gotta get out of here and if I do this, we're square."

Gabriella suppressed a laugh and said, "Not even close."

Thinking quickly, she continued, "Here's what I want: I want you to take me to their home later and introduce me. You talk to them now and I'll meet you at the Rileys' around eight tonight."

"I'll see what I can do."

"No! Get it done. You don't need to set up the interview. Just get me inside."

A couple minutes later, having retreated the way she came in, Gabriella was on the phone to Melinda. She explained the situation and her plan then hurried back to the station's van to report on the press conference.

Gabriella turned onto the street the Rileys lived on, found the house and parked her car. Before she got out of her car, Doyle pulled up behind her and the two of them walked across the lawn to the Rileys' front door. When they were about halfway there, Floyd Riley opened the door and stepped onto the front steps to greet them.

Doyle had called ahead, and all four family members were present and waiting for them. Doyle introduced Gabriella who shook hands with each of them and they all found a place to sit, more or less facing each other in a circle in the living room.

"The reason I'm here," Gabriella began believing she would have to sell them on the idea, "is to…"

"We'll do it," Barbara said, cutting her off. "The more publicity, the better. It can't hurt."

Oh, yes it can, Gabriella silently thought before answering. "Okay. Let me call Melinda's producer and set it up and ah, we'll get back to you."

As Gabriella stood to leave, she noticed Doyle sitting next to Brittany, their knees touching. "Is tomorrow too soon?" she asked the group.

"No that should be fine. We'll make ourselves available," Barbara quickly answered. "I don't know about a separate interview with Brittany. We'll see how it goes."

Gabriella and Doyle said goodbye to the Rileys and as they were nearing their cars, Gabriella said to him, "What the hell is the matter with you?"

"What?" Doyle said.

She turned to him, glared at him and said, "You're hitting on Brittany Riley? What kind of a sick twist are you? Get yourself some therapy!" With that, she hurried off leaving the detective standing on the grass with a stupefied look on his face trying to act innocent.

ELEVEN

The four sheriff's investigators waited patiently in Conference Room A for Sheriff Cale to join them. Because of the importance and publicity being generated by this missing little girl, Cale had decided he wanted a briefing every day, at least as often as practicable.

Paul Anderson, who had picked up pastries and coffee was always available. Doyle was on his third chocolate doughnut when the sheriff, followed by Patty Dunphy and Cale's personal assistant, Louise Shaffer, came in and took their seats at the rectangular conference table with Cale seated at the head. The sheriff took a quick peek at the clock on the wall, noted it was 9:15 A.M. and apologized for keeping everyone waiting.

"Okay, Shannon, why don't you start us off?" Cale said as Dunphy and Shaffer began to take notes.

Shannon Keenan spent about fifteen minutes summarizing the previous day by explaining their search of the apartment buildings. When she finished that she checked her notes and talked about the interviews they had done with Brittany's friends.

"We were only able to get together with the two of them," she said. "A Kathy Franz and Annabelle Oslund. The third one we got from Brittany's mother, a Julia Day, we got her on the phone and will see her later today.

"The first one, Kathy Franz," she continued, "is a bright, pleasant, attractive young woman."

"Very cooperative," Kristin Williams interjected.

"As was Oslund," Shannon concurred. "Franz was very concerned about Becky and said she had trouble sleeping because of this."

"Did you ask about Brittany?" Cale wanted to know.

"Casually. In a roundabout way," Kristin answered. "Not directly."

"And?"

"She had nothing but good things to say about her," Shannon said. "Loving mother, always took care of the child. And according to both Franz and Oslund, Becky was a delight. Bright, happy, bundle of joy. Both said they adored her and claimed Brittany did as well.

"As to Brittany's relationship with her mother," Shannon continued, "they are both of the opinion that Barbara is a total control freak. From what they've been told by Brittany, Barbara is absolutely in charge of that family and Brittany is scared shitless of her.

"Also, and this is an interesting part, neither of them or anyone else as far as they know, ever met this mysterious boyfriend, Bob Olson."

"Seriously?" Paul Anderson said. "She dated this guy for what, two to three weeks at least and none of her friends ever met him?"

"Yep. At least that's what these two said and they were as close to her as anybody," Shannon replied.

"Especially Oslund," Kristin added. "They grew up together and went through school together."

Anderson leaned forward with his elbows on the table, swiveled his head to look at Cale, arched his eyebrows and said, "Curiouser and curiouser."

"Isn't it?" Cale said. He turned back to look across the table at Keenan and said, "Anything else?"

"We got a couple of names of ex-boyfriends to check out and we'll go online and look at social media. Facebook, Twitter, stuff like that to see what's out there about her," Shannon answered her boss.

"So, Brittany is an official suspect?" Doyle asked.

"Right now, everyone's a suspect until we can eliminate them. That is not to leave this room," Cale said as his eyes looked directly at each of them.

"Where are you two?" Cale asked Anderson and Doyle.

"Brittany went over a couple hundred photos of the Robert or Bob Olsons that we got from the DMV. We looked at those that fit the profile and are in the Metro area. We haven't gone outstate or any other states yet," Doyle said. "She found fourteen who, with glasses and the right facial hair, could be him."

"We called all of the investment firms in Minneapolis and faxed over a subpoena to get the information they have on employees," Anderson said. "We should be hearing back from them today."

"There's no way we'll be able to keep all of that quiet," Patty Dunphy said. "The press is going to get wind of it."

"That might not be so bad," Paul said. "If our guy is out there, he may do something. He might not show up for work or he might try to take off. If so, we should hear about it. There aren't that many of them that we won't be able to keep track.

"Stu and I will start tracking down our list of Bob Olsons. In the meantime," Paul continued turning his attention to Louise Shaffer, "We're going to need someone to enter the data about these guys into a computer, including the ones we get back from the investment firms. We have to cross check them and start eliminating them."

"And the information we're getting off of the 800-number hotline," Cale added.

"No problem," Shaffer said. "I'll get right on it."

The meeting broke up and the four detectives went into their squad room to get back to their investigation. While Anderson and Doyle conferred about chasing down their lists of Bob Olsons, the two women went to Shannon's desk. The room itself was a basic, standard, lifeless government office with standard, lifeless government issued desks, chairs, file cabinets and the normal office paraphernalia. The one exception being their computers. Those were relatively new desktops and each detective was also issued their own laptop, an advantage of being in the sheriff's department of a fairly affluent, suburban county.

"Let's check some social media and dating sites to see what we can find out about Brittany. Why don't you take the dating sites and I'll do the Facebook and Twitter," Shannon said to her partner.

The two women spent an hour and a half searching online for Brittany and what she had out there. Shannon found her on Facebook on which Brittany was active and current. It was mostly chatting with other women her age about the usual nonsense. Shannon also came across a Myspace page for her that was not very active and a little old. On it, Brittany had posted several pictures of herself in various stages of undress. There was nothing nude except for a shot of her slightly bent over "mooning" whomever it was that took the picture. Neither site had anything seriously offensive or shameful, at least as far as Shannon was concerned. Being a cop, she had certainly seen more than her share of postings far worse.

"What did you find?" Shannon asked Kristin. The two women's desks were back-to-back, so they could face each while working. "She's on three sites, Match, Zoosk and ClickandFlirt, nothing out of the ordinary except one thing."

"Which is?"

"She doesn't admit to having a child on any of them."

Shannon thought about this for a moment then said, "I'm not sure that's a big deal. She's what, twenty-two? At that age would you advertise you had a kid on a first date?"

"Yes, I would," Kristin said. "But I see your point," she agreed.

Shannon stood up, stretched her back which was stiff from sitting still and staring at a computer screen for as long as she had, then said, "Let's go. It's time to meet with that girl, what's-her-name…?"

"Julia Day," Kristin said.

"Yeah, her. Let's hear what she has to say."

TWELVE

The Riley family waited patiently in the TV station's reception area for Melinda Pace to come for them. They were an odd-looking bunch. Brittany looked good. Her hair and makeup were done well, and she was dressed casually but appropriately for a television appearance. Floyd was obviously uncomfortable in dress slacks and a white shirt, no tie but buttoned at the throat. Timmy looked a bit bored and sported a twenty-something disheveled look of Cargo pants, sneakers and a pullover golf shirt. And of course, his hair looked like he had just gotten out of bed. Barbara, however, looked as if she had just left Neiman Marcus with a stylish new hairdo and designer clothes down to her Jimmy Choo pumps.

They had been waiting barely five minutes when the door opened next to the receptionist's desk. All four of the Rileys looked at the door just as a pretty twenty-something, black woman in gray slacks and a navy-blue blouse came through it. She walked up to Barbara, flashed a very charming smile and introduced herself as Cordelia Davis, an associate producer of Melinda's show. After handshakes all around, she led the family through the building and into a conference room. They had barely taken their seats when Melinda came through the door, whirled around the table greeting each one by name, warmly shaking their hand and profusely thanking them for coming. Of, course, this attention by a legitimate TV star had its intended effect. Instead of taking the chair at the head of the table, Melinda took the chair in the middle directly opposite Barbara.

"First of all," Melinda began making eye contact with each of them, "I can't tell you how sorry I am about what's happened. I can only imagine what you must be going through.

"What I would like to do today," she continued, "since we only have about sixteen minutes of air time is to first introduce each of you. Then, I'll ask each some easy 'How do you feel?' questions to give each of you a chance to let the audience know what you are going through. Especially you, Brittany," she finished looking directly at her.

"If we could…" Barbara said.

"What?" Melinda asked.

"Well, we're trying to get volunteers to start searching for Becky. There's a large park in Dakota County, Lebanon Hills. We'd like to do a search of it, but we'll need all of the volunteers we can get."

"Of course," Melinda said. "That's a great idea. We'll see what we can do to help."

While this exchange was taking place, Cordelia was seated next to Melinda taking notes. She managed to maintain a neutral expression at the same time wondering what the normally cynical Melinda was up to.

"Cordelia will take you to get ready. They'll probably want to put a little makeup on you. The lights will give you a shiny face without it. Then we'll bring you onto the set and start filming. Don't worry about making a mistake. We're not going live so we can edit the tape for the show. Okay?"

"Melinda," Cordelia asked when they were done filming the interview. "I don't mean to be disrespectful but what are you doing?"

Melinda, Cordelia and Robbie Nelson were watching the film of the Riley interview. Robbie was making notes about editing it down to sixteen minutes from the thirty-five minutes of filming that had been done. The problem he was having was, with the possible exception of Barbara, this was a pretty boring group of people.

"I'm building rapport with this family," Melinda answered Cordelia. "My instincts tell me there is something wrong here and it has to do with why Brittany didn't report her daughter missing for ten days."

"I can get sixteen minutes of okay stuff, Melinda," Robbie said. "But it'll be twelve minutes of Barbara and four minutes of the rest of them."

"What's up with the father, Floyd? He's like a potted plant," Cordelia said.

"Two things," Melinda began as Robbie stopped the tape and turned to Melinda to hear her answer a question he also had. "First, he's a closet drunk. Trust me, I know the type. He sneaks his booze in small shots throughout the day. Second, and this is why he's a drunk, his wife is a total control freak. And keep this to yourselves," she whispered conspiratorially even though the three of them were alone, "Brittany knows more than she's telling. From what I'm hearing from the sheriff's office, I'm beginning to believe this boyfriend, this Bob Olson character, is a figment of her imagination.

"But to answer your question, Cordelia, we're going to stir this pot and be the driving force behind this investigation. Why are we going to do that?" she asked looking at Robbie.

"To generate ratings," Robbie answered.

"Never, ever forget, Cordelia, that is always the only thing that really matters," Melinda said. "Without them, we don't get paid."

When Melinda got back to her private office, she called Gabriella Shriqui on her cell phone. Melinda asked to meet with her and Gabriella informed her she was in the building and would stop by right away.

"What's up?" Gabriella asked as she sat down on Melinda's couch.

Melinda, seated in a chair opposite Gabriella, told her about the interview with the Rileys, especially Barbara's role. She went on to explain her suspicions about them and doubts about Brittany's innocence.

"Are you seeing your source in the sheriff's office soon?" Melinda asked.

"I don't have anything set up, but I could call him."

"I need to find out where the investigation is at."

"I talked to him yesterday and all he had was that they are in the initial stages of finding this guy, what's-his-name…"

"Bob Olson."

"Right, the boyfriend. Anyway, he really didn't have anything. I've got a trial to cover in Washington County in Stillwater starting tomorrow. I could try to get a hold of my cop this afternoon. Maybe set something up for tonight or tomorrow."

"I need to pry Brittany away from her mother for an individual interview…"

"My guy could probably help with that. I noticed last night they were maybe getting a little close."

"Brittany and your source?" Melinda asked.

"Yeah. In fact, I think he might be trying to get in her pants. He's a total pig."

"That would be perfect for us," Melinda said.

"Melinda! She's a kid," Gabriella came back at her.

"She's obviously old enough to know what she's doing. I suppose you're right, though. He shouldn't be fooling around with a witness let alone a potential suspect. Find out what you can and get back to me."

Over the next several days the Rileys turned themselves into minor, yet sympathetic, celebrities. They were interviewed by every TV station's news department and appeared on every local, daytime talk show. In addition, reporters from every newspaper in the state were clamoring for an in-depth interview.

Initially, Barbara had planned this media campaign to keep interest in the search for Becky on the front pages. Also, they never failed to make a plea for volunteers to help in the search to be done on Saturday. After a couple of days, Barbara realized she enjoyed the attention and took to it like a fish to water. The culmination came when she watched herself and Floyd being interviewed by a well-known, highly respected, TV personality on CNN. The celebrity bug had definitely taken a bite out of Barbara.

THIRTEEN

Iceland Air flight 451 from London through Reykjavik, Iceland was about an hour out of the Minneapolis-St. Paul International airport. Marc Kadella and his love, Margaret Tennant, were returning from a ten-day vacation. The two of them, seated in coach, had an empty seat in their row. This allowed Margaret to curl up and lie down with her head on a pillow in Marc's lap and sleep for most of the flight home. Marc, who found it almost impossible to sleep on an airplane, was left with little to do after being forced to watch a terribly boring kid's movie but contemplate their trip.

Marc was a lawyer in private practice and as a sole-practitioner rented space in a suite of offices shared by other lawyers. His landlord, Connie Mickelson, a crusty, older woman working on her sixth marriage, did mostly family law and personal injury work. Also, there was Barry Cline, a man about Marc's age, who was becoming modestly successful at business litigation. The fourth and final lawyer was Chris Grafton, a small business, corporate lawyer with a thriving practice who was a few years older than Marc and Barry.

Marc was sandy-haired, blue-eyed of Scandinavian and Welsh ancestry. He was a little over six feet tall, in his mid-forties and the recently divorced father of two mostly grown children; his son, Eric, age nineteen and a daughter, Jessica, age eighteen. The vacation with Margaret was his first in years and became affordable when he received a very nice check from Connie Mickelson. Marc had referred a personal injury case to her for a client of his. The case had recently settled, and the check was his portion of the attorney fees. A standard and quite ethical, practice among lawyers.

He had needed the trip, despite the cost which would be over five thousand dollars for each of them. Marc had recently finished a highly publicized, stressful trial in which he had unsuccessfully represented a local judge for murdering his wife, a man whom Marc loathed, and the feeling was reciprocated by his client.

Margaret Tennant was the woman Marc had been exclusively involved with for well over a year. She was a few months younger than him, a very attractive woman of about average height who had done an excellent job of taking care of herself over the years.

Margaret had divorced her first husband a self-absorbed investment banker with a lot of money of which Margaret had taken a healthy proportion. She was also successful on her own. A district court judge in Hennepin County, she had worked hard and had a well-deserved reputation as a fair, efficient and exceptional jurist.

They had flown into Charles de Gaulle outside of Paris to begin their first extensive vacation together. The twelve-hour flight, which included a stop in New York, arrived in France at 7:00 A.M. and had given Marc his first real experience of jet lag by the time they arrived at their hotel, a Westin on the Rue de Rivoli near the Louvre and the Tuileries Garden. The two of them had spent the next three days roaming around Paris, a place Margaret had visited before but was still amazed by the beauty of the city. Even Marc, about as Midwestern American as any man could be, was absolutely astonished by Paris.

On the fourth day, they took a day trip by tourist bus across France to the beaches of Normandy. Margaret especially had wanted to take the trip. She had a great uncle, an older brother of her grandfather, who was buried in the giant American cemetery behind Omaha Beach. They found his grave and while looking down at the white marble cross with the name of a man she had never known etched into it, she realized what he and the almost ten thousand others buried here had done. The emotion brought tears to her eyes and Marc held her as she gently sobbed. Later they would admit the visit to the cemetery was the highlight of the trip.

The next day they took a train from the Gare du Nord in Paris to London. Except for the older, smaller houses of mostly brick construction, the French countryside appeared little different than Wisconsin or Minnesota.

Going through the Chunnel, the tunnel between France and England under the English Channel, had been a disappointment, at least for Marc. There were no lights inside of it and it was just a half hour trip in complete darkness.

Like Paris, this was Marc's first visit to London and it too was not a disappointment. He found London to be not as beautiful as Paris and more crowded and expensive. London, however, is still one of the world's truly great cities with an enormous number of things to see and do.

It was while visiting London that Marc noticed a subtle change between himself and Margaret. It was nothing overt or even all that noticeable. Just a barely perceptible shift in the way they communicated, or more precisely, were not communicating. A couple of days after arriving in Britain, it was Margaret who brought it in the open by admitting they were getting on each other's nerves a bit. They talked it out and realized that they had been together twenty-four hours a day for over a week and grating on each other a bit would be only natural for any couple.

The Boeing 757 hit a patch of turbulence and the plane's sudden jostling bounced Margaret awake. She sat up, yawned, stretched, ran her fingers through her hair to fluff it a bit and rolled her head back and forth to take the kink out of her neck.

"Hey, sleep okay?" Marc asked.

"Um, yeah. I guess. How about you? Get any sleep?" she said as she slipped her shoes on.

"Not much. I've never been able to sleep on planes. Can't get comfortable."

"Where are we?" she asked.

"About another hour," he answered.

"It'll be nice to get home," she said.

Margaret looked him in the eyes without saying anything, then after a half minute or so Marc broke the silence and said, "What?"

"Are we okay?"

"What do you mean?"

"You and me. Do you still love me?" she seriously asked.

"Relax. Of course...pretty much...more or less....ouch! Why'd you kick me? I was kidding."

"Are you all right?" the female flight attendant who was passing by asked him.

"This woman just assaulted me. I want her arrested," Marc said trying to sound serious.

"He had it coming," Margaret told her.

"Don't they all?" the attendant said with a smile. "I'm guessing you'll live," and walked away.

The next day, at 9:00 A.M., Marc trudged up the back stairs of the Reardon Building on Lake Street and Charles. When he reached the second floor, he stood in the empty hall in front of the entry to his office and stared at it for several long seconds. He was trying to decide if he wanted to go in, uncertain what awaited him on the other side and if he wanted to deal with any of it. He took a deep breath, turned the handle, opened the door and stepped into the office's reception area.

The first thing Marc noticed was a middle-aged couple sitting on client chairs obviously awaiting an appointment. He said a pleasant hello and felt a slight twinge in the back of his mind. There was something familiar about the woman, but he couldn't place her as a client.

"Hey, here he is," his landlord, Connie Mickelson, said when she saw him come in. Connie had the corner office directly across from the entryway. With her door open she could see whoever came through the hallway door.

Marc spent the next ten minutes giving his officemates a brief description of the trip. When he was finished, Connie asked, "So, are you and her Honor still good? Those kinds of trips can be relationship killers."

"Yeah," Marc said looking directly at her. "You would certainly know about killing relationships. And yes, we're still good."

The office settled down and Carolyn, one of the secretaries, said, "Marc, this is Charlotte and John Daniels. They've been waiting since 8:00. You don't have any other appointments this morning."

Marc turned away from the Daniels, looked directly at Carolyn and with a serious look including raised eyebrows, sending her the clear silent message, "What were you thinking making this appointment this early my first day back?" He turned back to the patiently waiting couple, stepped over to them, extended his hand as they stood and said, "Hi. I just got here, which is obvious. Give me a few minutes and we'll talk." Of course, they both readily agreed.

Marc headed toward his office and gestured for Carolyn to follow him. When she closed the door he asked, "What's going on with them?"

"Marc, they were here at 8:00. They're walk-ins. Just showed up. Said it was important to see you today."

"Who are they? Did they say why…?"

"No, not really. Sorry," she said.

"No, it's okay. I'll see what's up."

Three minutes later he held the door for them and politely invited them to sit in the client chairs in front of his desk.

When he was seated he looked at the husband and pleasantly asked, "What can I do for you, Mr. Daniels?"

"It's my niece," the wife answered. "She's been arrested."

When Marc turned his head to look at her, the light in his memory clicked on as he recognized her. "I remember you," he said. "You were juror number, let me think…seven," he said as he snapped his fingers. "I thought you looked familiar, but it took me a few minutes."

"You're right," she said clinging to the purse she held in her lap. "I hope this is all right, me being a juror on a case you tried."

Marc sat silently for a few seconds thinking it over then said, "As far as I know, it's okay. The trial's over and I don't represent Prentiss anymore."

"I thought you did a really good job so here we are."

"We both did," John said. "I sat in on the trial a few days and you were really good."

"Well, thank you, I appreciate that. Now, tell me about your niece. What's her name and why was she arrested?"

"Her name is Brittany Riley," Charlotte said then waited for a response from Marc.

He looked at her for a few seconds then said, "Doesn't ring a bell. Should it?"

FOURTEEN

While Marc Kadella and Margaret Tennant were still sightseeing in London, Sheriff Cale, in a freshly laundered uniform complete with a new campaign hat, looked over the crowd of volunteers that were gathering at the entrance of the Lebanon Hills Park. Barely 7:00 A.M. on Saturday morning, he estimated the crowd to be close to three thousand people. While cruising through the main parking lot he had noticed license plates from all of the Upper Midwest states and as far away as Texas and Pennsylvania.

Cale saw Patty Dunphy and Louise Shaffer near the park's visitor center and made his way through the crowd to them. The two women, along with Barbara and Floyd Riley and several volunteers, were setting up behind several tables.

"Quite a turnout," Cale said to Shaffer. "What's the plan?"

"We're going to line them up along Dodd Road," Shaffer said pointing off to the east, shielding her eyes from the morning sun. "We'll get them stretched out all the way south to 120th. Then we'll sweep west until we come out on Pilot Knob."

"How many lakes and ponds are there?" Cale asked as he watched a couple of his deputies directing people to their start-up positions.

"Seven lakes and I don't know how many ponds. It won't be easy. We figure it will take all day. There are restrooms at picnic areas throughout the park that people can use. Plus, we have several places set up in picnic areas to feed people as they make their way through it. We've got burgers, hotdogs, brats and soda."

"Where's Brittany?" Cale quietly asked.

"Not here. I don't know why," Shaffer replied.

"Where'd the money come from for all of this?" Cale asked.

"Barbara has been on every TV show in town and I hear she's going national. She has a website set up and an 800 number. People can donate money through the website."

"How much has she gotten?"

"I don't know. But Barbara told me paying for all of the food wasn't a problem," Shaffer said with raised eyebrows.

"Interesting. Well, I have to take off. Let me know if you find anything."

"Of course. I'll call you later and let you know how it went even if we don't find anything," she answered.

For the next six hours, the massive horde of searchers swept through the large park. The length of their search line ran a little more than a mile. With the number of people in line, they started off almost elbow-to-elbow. The park was over two miles long and because of the terrain and the bodies of water to work around, the going was a little slow. When the search was finished, the park was virtually litter free from the searchers scooping it up and several dozen articles of clothing, including a significant number of the size for small children, were found. Unfortunately, none of them could be connected to Becky Riley. The day wasn't a total loss though because Barbara was able to collect another fifty thousand dollars in donations. Then plans were made to search other parks and open places in Dakota County.

When the Rileys returned to the park's visitor center at the end of the search, there were almost twenty media members waiting for a press conference. Barbara spent an hour in front of the cameras answering the same questions over and over about the search. When she finished, she went inside the building and per prior arrangement, spent another half hour with Melinda Pace doing an exclusive interview. Melinda was the only media person who noticed the absence of Brittany. She asked Barbara about it and received a non-answer excuse claiming Brittany was simply too distraught to attend.

On Monday, Brittany Riley arrived at the Channel 8 TV station promptly at 9:00 A.M. for her second solo interview with Melinda. Brittany had been reluctant to do it but her mother had insisted. The first interview, done the week before, despite Brittany's obvious discomfort, had gone smoothly enough. The young woman had been visibly stiff, uncomfortable and nervous. Melinda had treated her with kid gloves and the interview had gone off without a hitch. Brittany even came across as genuinely stressed, nervous and sympathetic. Unknown to the guest, today's show was going to be quite different than the first.

Robbie Nelson, Melinda's producer, as he had been during the first interview of Brittany, was in the control room handling the technical aspect of the taping. Brittany and Melinda had finished with the makeup and were on the set. Cordelia Davis hooked the mic up to Brittany, did a sound and light check and they were ready to roll.

The two of them were on a casual set. They were each seated in a comfortable cloth-covered, swiveling armchair with a glass-topped coffee table between them. Brittany and Melinda were actually close enough to each other to be able to reach across the table to shake hands.

Melinda looked into camera one. They were using two cameras to tape both women for the entire session then edit the good parts. Melinda read a brief intro to get this show started then looked at Brittany, smiled and said, "How are you feeling today, Brittany? I understand you were too upset to attend the big search that was done on Saturday."

"I'm okay today," Brittany answered.

"Good. You don't seem as nervous as you did the first time I interviewed you. Are you getting a little more comfortable being in the spotlight?"

"No, not really," Brittany replied.

The two of them chatted amiably for the first few minutes about Becky's disappearance and the stress Brittany and her family were going through. Melinda spoke softly, asking her easy questions about the situation, the toll it was taking on her and what they were doing to find the missing little girl.

"You must be having a lot of trouble sleeping?" Melinda asked.

"I've been getting only a couple hours sleep each night," Brittany agreed.

Ignoring her answer, Melinda leaned forward placed her elbows on her knees, looked directly into her eyes and said, "Can you explain why, the very night you claim your daughter went missing," at which point a picture of Becky went up on the screen behind them, "you were out partying at a bar with your friends?"

Brittany's back stiffened and she leaned back in her chair, her eyes wide-open and her jaw hanging loose as if Melinda had just slapped her. "What, um...uh...how, what? I don't know, I mean I don't think..."

"What?" Melinda asked. "Are you denying it?"

"I guess, um, no. I mean how do you know that and what does that have to do with anything?" Brittany said, trying to maintain some semblance of calm.

At that moment the background photo of Becky was replaced by a selfie taken by one of her friends that was date stamped the same day Becky disappeared. It was a photo of Brittany and her three friends taken at a bar.

"This is a picture that was posted on the Facebook page of a Julia Day. She's a friend of yours, isn't she?" Melinda asked while still staring directly at Brittany.

Brittany turned her head to look at the photo and said, "Yes, ah, she's my friend, but um, I don't, um I don't remember when this was taken."

"It's dated," Melinda replied. "Isn't that the same day Becky disappeared. Or so you claim."

"Yes, it is. But I remember now, I, ah, I spent the whole day looking for her and I just wanted to get out. I needed to get out because I was so upset..."

"Yes, you certainly look upset. In fact, you were so upset you went out a few nights later, didn't you?"

The background selfie of the four girls disappeared and was replaced with a new one. This time, it was a photo, again clearly dated, of Brittany standing on a bar with several other attractive young women, all posing, smiling and wearing identical white T-shirts with the name of the bar on the front. As Brittany looked on in horror, a series of five more photos of Brittany on the bar in various poses were shown. The last one, uncensored, showing her standing triumphantly holding a small trophy above her head, the T-shirt now soaked with water, Brittany visibly braless.

"Funny," Melinda deadpanned, "you don't look too upset in these pictures either do you?"

While the photo of Brittany showing off her wet T-shirt contest trophy remained on the screen, Melinda said, "All of these events and pictures were taken during the ten days you couldn't be bothered to call the police and tell them your baby was missing. That beautiful little girl was gone, and you were out partying."

A silent moment passed between them that seemed longer than it was. Brittany remained in her chair but just barely. She was looking at Melinda with a shocked, almost numb expression on her face. Her hands were tightly clutching the arm rests on the chair and pushing her back almost out of the seat.

"How did you get these? What are you trying to do…?"

"That doesn't matter," Melinda said as she sat back in her chair and casually crossed her legs. She held out her right-hand palm up, and her arm extended toward the picture.

"If this isn't enough, two nights ago, Saturday night, the same Saturday you said you were too upset to look for Becky at Lebanon Hills Park, you were out partying again, weren't you?" At that moment another shot of Brittany in a bar went up on the screen, this one taken by the man Melinda had hired to follow her.

"How do you know that?"

"You didn't show up to search for Becky because you knew she wasn't in that park, isn't that true?" Melinda asked as if she were a prosecutor cross-examining a defendant.

"What?" Becky answered Melinda with an incredulous look on her face. "You think I had something to do with Becky being gone? You're insane!" she yelled.

"Am I? Then, explain your behavior, if you can."

Brittany stood up, removed the mic from her blouse, threw it at Melinda and screamed, "Fuck you, you crazy fucking bitch! I had nothing to do with it. I told you, a man named Bob Olson took her!"

Before Melinda could respond, Brittany burst into tears and ran off the set. Melinda looked around at the film crew and said, "Please tell me you got all of that."

FIFTEEN

Patty Dunphy, Sheriff Cale's press officer, her three-inch heels clicking on the tile floor, hurried down the hall toward Cale's office. Cale's assistant, Louise Shaffer, heard her coming and from her desk in front of Cale's office, looked up at Patty as she hurried past toward the sheriff's office door.

"What?" Shaffer asked her friend.

"Is he in?" Dunphy said then knocked on the door and opened it without waiting for a reply.

"Come in," Cale said looking up to see Dunphy come through the door, "What's up?" he asked.

"We just got a call from Channel 8 telling us to watch their four o'clock show, *The Court Reporter.* Do you know the show?"

"No," Cale shrugged. "I don't think so. Why?"

"It doesn't matter," Dunphy said with a slight hand wave as she stood in front of his desk. "We were told Brittany Riley is being interviewed and we should watch it."

Cale looked up at the clock on his wall and saw it was two minutes before four. "Okay," he said. "Let's take a look."

Dunphy retrieved the remote control sitting on the TV in the right-hand corner of Cale's office in front of his desk. At that moment, Paul Anderson and Louise Shaffer came into the office. Cale looked up and gestured for them to take a seat as Dunphy turned on the TV set.

For the next twenty minutes, the four of them sat silently watching the trainwreck that was Brittany's interview with Melinda. When it was over, after Brittany had fled the set and following a commercial break, Melinda took a few minutes to solemnly stare into the camera and review what she assumed was the evidence against Brittany and all but declared her guilty of Becky's disappearance.

When it was over, Cale dismissed the two women after politely admonishing them to keep quiet about this for now. Even though it had been publicly aired he didn't want a lot of office gossip about it. Cale sat back in his big, brown leather desk chair, laced his fingers behind his head, looked up at the ceiling and silently thought for a full minute. Paul Anderson waited patiently for the ass-chewing he was sure was coming.

Cale sat up, placed his forearms on the desk, looked at Anderson and said, "There's not much point in recriminations, but we do need to get this information."

"Agreed. Apparently, we need to start going through social media sites of Brittany's friends. Her behavior is suspicious, to say the least. I'll put Kristin Williams on that. She's very good at it. I know she has been through Brittany's online stuff. Apparently, we need to look at everybody who knows her," Anderson said.

"Where is everybody today?" Cale asked.

"Stu is running down alibis of a few Bob Olsons. So far, no luck…"

"I'm not surprised. I'm beginning to think this whole boyfriend story is bullshit," Cale responded.

"Williams and Keenan are out interviewing ex-boyfriends of Brittany," Anderson continued.

"Get a hold of everyone. I want a meeting at six today to review everything. I'll call LeAnne Miller and see if she can sit in," Cale told him referring to the Dakota County Attorney.

At that moment, Patty Dunphy knocked on Cale's door and stepped back in. "We're getting calls from the media asking about that TV show. What do you want me to tell them?"

Before Cale could answer, Anderson said, "Let's tell them we had all of that information and are reviewing it and all other information related to this case. Other than that, we have no comment."

"And deny that Brittany Riley is a suspect," Cale interjected. "Tell them we are still pursuing the boyfriend, Bob Olson, as the primary suspect."

"When they ask if we have found him?" Dunphy asked.

"Tell them we are pursuing a number of leads and we won't comment about an ongoing investigation," Anderson said.

"That should work," Cale said.

"Not for long it won't. This thing is starting to generate some serious media interest. Good looking young, blonde mother and beautiful blonde baby missing. The public eats this stuff up and the media loves feeding it to them. As disgusting as it may seem, this sleaze sells," Dunphy replied.

The four investigators waited patiently for their boss and the county attorney to arrive for the meeting. They were sitting around the large table in the main conference room discussing the investigation and their findings. Kristin Williams was using a laptop to check out the pictures of Brittany that were used by Melinda to ambush Brittany that afternoon. Shannon Keenan and the two men were sharing the contents of the case file paying particular attention to the photos and reports of the crime scene unit's search of Brittany's apartment.

"Nothing here out of the ordinary. Nothing that you wouldn't expect to find in a young woman's apartment," Anderson said.

"What is this?" Shannon asked while staring intently at a photo.

"What's what?" Anderson asked while he leaned over to take a look. Stu Doyle stood, got behind Shannon's chair, and bent over Shannon's shoulder and also focused on the photo.

"This right here," Shannon said pointing at a barely visible, dark object that appeared to be attached to a door.

"It's a hasp," Doyle answered her. "Looks like what is called a rotating eye hasp. It's used to lock a door from the inside."

"Okay," Anderson said. "But this is a photo of the kid's bedroom. It was taken from the hall looking into the room. That's the bedroom door and…"

"And Brittany had a lock on the outside of the door, so she could lock Becky inside," Shannon quietly finished the thought.

"Looks like it," Doyle said.

Shannon looked at both men with a puzzled expression and said, "Why would anyone…"

"To lock the kid in her bedroom so she could…" Doyle began.

"Do anything she wanted," Anderson finished.

The conference room door opened, and Cale held it while LeAnne Miller entered. The county attorney was a small woman, barely an inch over five feet and a hundred pounds with rocks in her pockets. Pushing fifty and starting to show the years of job stress, she had been a prosecutor with the U.S. Attorney's office until a few years ago. The Democrats found her, convinced her to give politics a try and she was now in her second term as Dakota County Attorney. Everyone, cops, lawyers and judges were all very positive about her job performance.

She went around the table shaking hands and greeting the deputies then took a seat at the head of the table. Cale had taken the chair to her right.

"Okay," she began in a firm voice looking over the detectives to let them know who was running this meeting. "I've been over everything you have with Sheriff Cale. Anything new, anything positive about the boyfriend, this Bob Olson?"

"Nothing so far," Doyle answered her. "We're running down as many Bob or Robert Olson's as we can in the metro area especially the ones that fit the age, weight and height description. Or, at least, those that are possible. So far, they've all alibied out. But there are more to look at."

"We interviewed a couple of Brittany's ex-boyfriends," Shannon began. "One by the name of," she continued as she opened her notebook, "Dustin Barnes. Age 24. He lives in Bloomington and says he met her at a party about nine or ten months ago. He says, they dated for a few weeks and were sexually involved. He believes Brittany wanted a father for

Becky and that's what caused the breakup. He wasn't ready for fatherhood.

"The second one we talked to this afternoon," Shannon continued. "An Alex Walker who lives in Burnsville. He works for Canon Copiers in sales and is out of town a lot which is why we had trouble tracking him down. Anyway, pretty much the same story. Casual dating, casual sex, at least on his part. But," she stopped and made eye contact with Kristin.

"But," Kristin said continuing,

"They both made a similar comment about something Brittany said. They both said, after she had a couple drinks, that sometimes she wished she wasn't stuck with a kid. They both claim those were her words. Stuck with a kid."

"What do you think?" Cale asked Miller.

"I think if I was a twenty-one-year-old widowed, single mother, I'd have times where I felt the same way," Miller said. "By itself it doesn't mean much."

"You don't think we've got enough for an arrest?"

"For what? We could make a case for child neglect, maybe, if you read the statute broadly. An arrest for the kid's abduction? No, not even close," Miller answered.

"The little girl is dead," Shannon Keenan quietly said. "We all know it."

"Yes, you're probably right," Miller replied turning her head toward the investigator.

"And this Bob Olson business is a wild goose chase," Paul Anderson interjected. "She's seen DMV photos of every Bob or Robert Olson in the state of Minnesota. A few maybes are all we have, at best. I think it's bullshit."

Miller leaned forward, placed her left elbow on the table and covered her mouth with her left hand. She stared at the opposite wall thinking over what she had been told, trying to decide what to do. After a full minute, she straightened up, looked over the four detectives and said, "Tell you what. It's now Monday. Keep at it a few more days." She turned to Cale and continued with, "I understand the family is still out searching the county with volunteers."

"Yes, that's correct," Cale nodded. "I've got a couple deputies working with them. Louise and Patty are also. They're actually working pretty hard at it."

"Okay," Miller said. "Keep at it. Continue interviewing friends, family co-workers, anyone who knows her and knows how she treats the child. We're looking for opinions, statements and any evidence she wasn't a happy loving mother. Does she take care of the kid? Is she a good mother? Does she complain about being stuck with a child? Maybe she didn't want the kid around because she was a burden, all those types of things. We'll meet again on Thursday and take another look at it. If nothing turns up by then we can arrest her late Friday, keep her over the weekend and squeeze her. We won't have to arraign her until Monday. Maybe we can get a confession or more information out of her."

Late that night, Bob Olson twisted the cap off of his third bottle of Miller Genuine Draft. He flopped back down on the couch in his two-bedroom apartment in South Minneapolis. He put his feet up on the cheap coffee table in front of the couch and tossed the bottle cap onto it and watched it clatter about among the detritus before it settled down. Olson hit the play button on the DVR recording of Brittany's appearance on *The Court Reporter*. It was the fourth time he would watch it and each viewing brought a large smile and a warm glow of anticipation as he thought about what he had done and how well it was coming together.

SIXTEEN

"The reason Brittany was arrested began last week…" Charlotte Daniels continued the story to bring Marc Kadella up to date.

"On Monday," her husband John interjected. "A week ago, today."

"Yes, that's right. Brittany was being interviewed by that TV person, Melinda Pace, do you know her?"

"I know who she is," Marc answered. "Excuse me a second," he said as he swiveled in his chair and lifted open the window behind his desk. "It's nice this morning and this office could use a little air," he said as he turned back to the couple in front of his desk. "Sorry, go ahead."

"This Melinda Pace," Charlotte continued, "practically accused Brittany of kidnapping her own child right on TV. Then all week long, the interview she did was all over the news. You couldn't turn the TV on without seeing it."

"It went national too," John said. "And it was all over the papers. The media's gone a little nuts with the story."

"There is a lawyer involved, sort of, a guy named Alan Reeder," John said. "Do you know him?"

"No, never heard of him," Marc replied.

"He's a personal injury lawyer who handled the wrongful death case for Barbara when Brittany's husband was killed in a car accident a couple years ago," John told him.

"Okay," Marc nodded. "What's he doing now?"

"He's helping the family with all of this," Charlotte said. "Anyway, he set up an interview for Barbara with a woman from ABC news. It was not a good idea. Barbara got hammered by this woman, I forget her name now, about Brittany, why she didn't report Becky missing for ten days and why Brittany lied to everyone she knew about where Becky was during that time."

"Now the media is camped out on their doorstep," John added. "Wait till you see this. It's like a circus on their street."

"And protestors are starting to show up at their home," Charlotte said. "Then Friday night, a little after midnight, the sheriff's deputies knocked on her door and arrested her."

"And dragged her out in handcuffs, in her pajamas, in front of the TV cameras," John said.

"The press was there?" Marc asked.

"Yes," Charlotte said while John nodded his head. "Obviously tipped off. Why they waited until the middle of the night like that…?"

"Because they can hold her all weekend before they have to bring her to see a judge. Plus, they wanted to embarrass her and cause her as much discomfort as possible," Marc said answering her question. "Has she seen a lawyer? Did she ask for one?"

"Alan Reeder saw her Saturday afternoon. I don't know what he told her," John answered him.

"We talked to Barbara on Sunday. I called her," Charlotte continued. "We wanted to know what was going on and if we could help. We talked about lawyers and I told her about you. She said this Alan Reeder guy wants the case but isn't a criminal defense lawyer. Do you think that would matter?"

"To be honest, yes, she needs a criminal lawyer. But I don't know Reeder. For all I know he may be a great lawyer and can handle her case just fine," Marc said.

"You're trying to be professionally polite and not say anything bad about another lawyer," John perceptively said.

"What is she charged with?" Marc asked.

"Child neglect," John answered.

"Child neglect! All this over a gross misdemeanor child neglect charge? They're trying to squeeze her for a confession. Did Reeder at least tell her to keep her mouth shut?" Marc asked.

"We don't know what he told her," John said.

"We're sorry about just showing up like this but I think Brittany is going to get railroaded. She needs somebody who is really good. I saw you represent that judge and you did really great," Charlotte said.

Marc looked at her and with a conspiratorial tone, raised his eyebrows and quietly said, "I came close to getting him off, didn't I? What got him convicted?"

"Really close. If it wasn't for the picture of him lying on top of her with the knife in his hand well, we just couldn't get past that," Charlotte answered.

Marc smiled slightly, nodded his head a little and said, "Yeah, I thought that was it. That's a tough image to get out of your head."

"I still wake up some nights…" Charlotte said. "Could you at least meet with Brittany and Barbara and talk to them?"

"Give me a minute," Marc said as he rose from his desk chair. He went out into the common area of the office and walked up to Carolyn.

"Hey," he said to her while she looked up at him. "Is there anything on my desk that needs immediate attention?"

Carolyn thought about it for a moment, looked over at the other secretary Sandy who looked back, shrugged and shook her head. Carolyn looked up at Marc and said, "No, nothing I can think of."

At that moment the office paralegal, Jeff Modell, stepped out of the office of Connie Mickelson and quietly closed the door behind him.

Carolyn saw him and said, "Jeff, is there anything on Marc's desk you know of that requires his immediate attention?"

"No, I don't think so," Jeff answered.

Marc was reading the A section of that morning's Star Tribune. On the left side of the front page was a one column story about Brittany. As he skimmed over it, Carolyn said, "So what's this about? Who are they?"

Without answering, Marc flopped the paper in front of Carolyn and pointed at the story he was reading.

Recognizing it immediately, Carolyn said, "Are you serious?" She was talking to Marc's back because he had turned to go back to the office. Upon hearing what Carolyn said, both Sandy and Jeff hurried over to Carolyn's desk to look over her shoulder at the newspaper.

Marc closed the door, sat down in his chair again and said, "Okay, I'll go out to the jail and see her and," he shrugged, "we'll see." He picked up the phone on his desk, punched one of the speed dial buttons and said to the obviously relieved couple, "I need to make a call."

"Do you want us to leave?" John asked as he started to rise.

Marc shook his head and silently mouthed the word "no" and gestured with his hand for John to remain seated. A moment later his phone call was answered.

"Hey, counselor, what's up?" he heard Madeline Rivers say.

"Hi, kid," Marc said. "Are you doing anything right now? Are you busy for the next few hours?"

"No," she said. "I'm good until this evening. Why? What do you need?"

"I'd like you to come with me to meet someone out at the jail in Hastings. It's important. Can you do it? I'll buy lunch."

"You're on," Maddy laughed. "I'll be at your office in ten minutes."

After saying goodbye and hanging up the phone, Marc looked at the Daniels and said, "It sounds like the mother, Barbara, calls the shots. Is that fair to say?"

"Yes," Charlotte nodded. "She likes to be in control of..."

"She's a total control freak," John said.

"She's your sister?" Marc asked Charlotte who nodded in assent. "Okay, I need you to call her and have her meet me at the detention center in Hastings. Make sure she knows where it is."

"You want me to call her now?"

"Yes, tell her I'll be there in about an hour."

Charlotte spoke to Barbara who enthusiastically agreed. When the call was finished, they spent the next fifteen minutes going over the Riley family dynamic and as much of Brittany's life and upbringing as they knew. Charlotte, being Barbara's younger sister, wasn't exactly privy to much of what went on in the Riley home except to know that Barbara

76

was in total charge of everything. About the time they finished, the intercom on Marc's phone buzzed. He answered it and was told Maddy Rivers had arrived. With that, the three of them stood up to leave.

"Would you mind if we went out to the jail also?" Charlotte asked.

"Sure, why not?" Marc replied. "You can introduce me to Barbara. I probably won't let you sit in but it won't hurt to have you there," he continued as he put on his suit coat and opened the door for them.

As the Daniels went into the common area of the office, Marc watched the husband for his reaction. Madeline was standing in between Carolyn's and Sandy's desks with her back to them chatting with the two secretaries. She turned to face Marc when she heard the door open and when she did, John Daniel's eyes noticeably widened, he wiped his palms on his pants and swallowed hard which caused Marc to suppress a laugh.

Madeline Rivers was an ex-cop with the Chicago Police department in her early thirties. In her three-inch heeled suede half-boots she liked to wear she was over six feet tall. She had a full head of thick, dark hair with auburn highlights that fell down over her shoulders, a model gorgeous face and she had a body worthy of Playboy. In fact, foolishly posing for that magazine was what led her to quit the Chicago P.D.

Maddy, as she was called by her friends, had moved to Minneapolis after quitting the Chicago cops following her Playboy pose. At the same time, she went through an ugly breakup when she found out the doctor she had fallen for was married. After arriving in Minnesota, she got a private investigator license. Maddy befriended a retired Minneapolis cop, Tony Carvelli, who was also a P.I. and she was now doing quite well for herself. It was Tony who originally introduced her to Marc to help with a case he was handling where they became good friends and business associates.

The reaction of John Daniels to his first sight of the stunning Ms. Rivers was actually subdued compared to most men. No doubt his wife, sneaking a peek at the same time to catch his reaction, contributed to it.

Marc introduced Maddy to the Daniels and briefly explained where they were going. A few minutes later, with Maddy in the passenger seat, Marc was driving toward Hastings, with the Daniels following.

SEVENTEEN

They were driving east on 494, the southern half of the freeway that encircled the Twin Cities, with the Daniels following behind him in their car. Marc and Maddy were discussing Brittany's arrest and what little they knew about her situation. Maddy was able to confirm what Brittany's aunt told Marc about the media coverage.

"You can't turn on the TV without hearing about it," she said. "They haven't said it, but the impression I got was they believe the kid is probably dead and Brittany did it."

"Where is that coming from?" Marc asked.

"Anonymous sources involved in the investigation is the usual attribution," Maddy answered.

"Dakota County Sheriff's office."

"Sounds like it," Maddy agreed. "So how was the vacation? You and the judge still speaking to each other?"

"The trip was great and why wouldn't we be speaking with each other?" Marc asked glancing over at Maddy who was leaning forward slightly, her head turned toward him, with a tiny smirk and a little twinkle in her eyes.

"Why are you looking at me like that?" Marc asked.

"Gauging to see how much you're lying."

"What? Why would I lie?"

"Because trips like that are relationship killers," she said.

"No, we're okay," he asked. "Or, mostly…I think. We did get on each other's nerves a bit," he admitted.

"I remember one," Maddy said. "This guy I was seeing, I thought he might be the one, you know? Anyway, we went together to Lake Geneva, in Wisconsin. It was a long weekend thing. When we got back, and he took me home, I got my luggage out of the trunk, looked him in the eye and said, 'We're done. Don't call me again.'"

"Why, what happened?" Marc asked laughing at her story.

"It took two days for me to find out he was a totally self-absorbed momma's boy. Literally. During the first two days, he called his mother four times. By the end of the second day, I was checking bus schedules to see if I could get back to Chicago."

"Seriously?" Marc laughed as he turned from the freeway onto Highway 61 southbound, the same Highway 61 Bob Dylan made famous in '65. "Why did you get involved with him in the first place?"

Maddy didn't answer the question but just stared straight ahead through the windshield.

"Well?" Marc asked.

"I don't want to say," she answered.

"Oh, okay. I get it," Marc said smiling. "He was pretty and charming and a male bimbo and…"

"Never mind," Maddy said trying to suppress a laugh. "I was young and stupid."

"Be thankful you got out when you did."

"For sure," she said.

"When we get to the jail and meet with her," Marc said turning serious, "I want you to be the big sister type. Try to be empathetic, is that a word?"

"You see me as the big sister type?" she said smiling.

"Um, actually, ah no. As much of a hard ass as you are…"

"Don't say anything bad about my ass," she admonished waving an index finger at him for emphasis.

"I said hard ass, not fat ass…"

"Ahhhhh!" she said as she leaned toward him straining at the car's shoulder harness. "You think I have a fat ass!" she yelled as she slapped him hard on the shoulder.

Marc took a deep breath, shook his head and wearily said, "No, I do not think you have a fat ass and that's all I'm going to say. Anything else will just get me into more trouble. I just want you to be nice to her, okay?"

"Okay," she said as she folded her arms across her chest and looked straight ahead pretending to pout. After a few seconds, she turned her beautiful head toward him, smiled and said, "I'm just having a little fun with you."

"I know," he answered her.

Twenty minutes later, Marc parked his car in the lot of the Dakota County Government Center. The Daniels parked next to him and the four of them made their way to the detention center facility. As they reached the front entry, Marc could see Maddy sneaking a peek at the reflection of her backside in the door's glass.

"There's nothing wrong with my ass," she whispered to him.

"I can't believe you did that," he whispered back quietly laughing.

"What was that?" John Daniels said to the two of them.

"Nothing," both Marc and Maddy answered in unison.

They entered the reception area where they found Barbara and Floyd Riley seated, patiently waiting for them. Charlotte introduced them to the Rileys. Marc went to the glass-enclosed counter where a deputy sheriff stood behind the glass, waiting for him. Marc had removed his attorney license card from his wallet and slid it through the opening on the counter to the deputy. He told the man why they were here and wanted to see Brittany. The deputy opened the door for them, showed them into a conference room and said Brittany would be down shortly.

There was a cheap, formica-topped table in the middle of the room with about a dozen uncomfortable plastic chairs scattered about. They each grabbed a chair and sat as close as they could to the small table. The table itself could only accommodate four and Barbara, Marc and Maddy took up those places.

The six of them made light conversation for a few minutes then Barbara said, "Charlotte said you did an excellent job on the trial that she was on jury duty for, the one about the judge that murdered his wife."

"I do my best," Marc answered modestly.

"How much do you charge?" Barbara bluntly asked.

"It depends on what is involved," Marc coyly answered. Charlotte had warned him about Barbara's need to control everything, so Marc was ready to politely fend her off. "I'll have to talk to Brittany first and see if she even wants me as her lawyer. That's her decision."

"No, it won't be," Barbara curtly replied. "She's too young and immature for that."

"Well, I tell you what, let's get her down here and see what's what and we'll take it from there. Right now, as I understand it, she's charged with child neglect, is that right?" he pleasantly asked Barbara.

Barbara nodded, and Marc continued. "But I believe there will be more serious charges coming."

"Why?" Floyd Riley asked.

"Because our baby girl is still missing, and the police think Brittany had something to do with it," Barbara quietly answered him.

After that brief exchange, they sat around in awkward silence waiting for Brittany to appear. A half hour passed, and Marc got up and went into the reception area. He looked at the deputy still seated behind the glass partition, paging through a magazine. When the deputy noticed him standing there, Marc raised his hands palms up with a quizzical look on his face.

The deputy spoke into the speaker and said, "She'll be down when we get to her. We have other things to do." At that point, he looked down at his magazine and continued to ignore Marc.

Marc went back into the little room and told the others what happened. He paced around for a few minutes, sat back down and Maddy said, "Want me to try?"

"Sure, go ahead," Marc shrugged.

Less than two minutes later she was back with the news that the deputy at the counter was personally going to get her.

A few minutes after that the deputy came in through the door to the conference room from the interior of the jail and uneasily informed them that someone screwed up and Brittany had been taken before a judge. He told Marc the judge's name as Marc was going out the other door.

Maddy stopped, looked sharply at the deputy as if scolding a small child and said, "I am very disappointed with you."

"Look, I'm sorry, really..." he stammered. "It's not my fault. Let me make it up to you..."

Madeline held up her right-hand palm toward him, lightly flipped the hand at him as if in dismissal and tersely said, "No," as she followed Marc out the door.

When they got outside Marc laughed and asked, "What did you say to him to get him to go get her?"

"Not much. I just asked him to do me a small favor," Maddy replied.

"And he started panting like a puppy," Marc laughed. "But it pisses me off because they're jerking us around."

They hurried into the main building, made it through security and without waiting for the Rileys and Daniels, Marc and Maddy ran toward the courtroom where Brittany had been taken. They walked through the doors just as Brittany, still in handcuffs, wearing a blue jumpsuit and shower clogs, was called to appear. Her hair was unwashed and stringy, she had no makeup on and looked as if she had not slept well for several days.

Marc hurried up the aisle toward the gate in the bar as every head in the gallery, packed with media representatives, turned toward him. As he reached the gate, the judge looked up at him and Marc said, "Marc Kadella, your Honor. If I may approach on the matter before you."

"Certainly," the judge replied as he motioned for Marc to come ahead. There was a young man standing to Brittany's left and another older man, to her right. The one on her left was a Public Defender assigned for today's appearance and the older man was with the County Attorney's office. Marc joined them at the bench while a confused Brittany silently watched.

"I apologize for the intrusion, your Honor. I've been asked by the family to look into possibly representing this defendant," Marc said.

"Where've you been?" the judge quietly asked.

"Cooling my heels at the jail for the past hour waiting for the deputies to get off their ass and bring my client down for a conference," he testily replied looking at the attorney for the county.

"Hey," the man shrugged. "I don't control the jail."

"You want a chance to talk to her?" The judge politely asked Marc while giving the same attorney an admonishing look.

"Yes, your Honor," Marc said.

"Okay. Use the jury room. Take all the time you need. Let me know what's going on when you're ready."

Marc turned to Brittany, looked at the deputy standing a few feet away and said to him, "Take these things off of her," indicating the cuffs.

"Can't," the deputy said. "She's considered a flight risk."

Marc looked around at the other four deputies, all of whom were good sized men. He turned back to the one who had spoken and said, "Seriously? The five of you are worried this one hundred ten-pound young woman is going to get loose? You guys can't handle her without the handcuffs?"

Everyone in the room, including the judge, burst into laughter and the judge said, "Take them off. We'll risk it."

The red-faced deputy stepped up and glared at Marc as he unlocked the cuffs. Marc stepped up to Brittany and whispered to the embarrassed deputy, "You asked for that."

Maddy had been standing by the outer doors and Marc motioned to her to join them. As she walked through the courtroom, a noticeable buzz was heard, and the judge and clerk waited and watched as she, Marc, Brittany and the Public Defender, Tom Goins, went into the jury room. Just as they did, the Rileys and Daniels came through the outer doors and into the courtroom. As the door to the jury room closed, Barbara rushed forward but was stopped by a deputy when she reached the gate.

"Your Honor, judge, sir," she said. "I'm her mother and…"

The judge held up a hand to stop her and asked the prosecutor, "Is she a juvenile?" he nodded toward the jury room door.

"No, your Honor," the man answered.

"Then, ma'am, you'll have to wait until she's done here to talk to her," the judge said to Barbara.

"But I'm her mother," Barbara repeated.

"I understand ma'am. But you have no status in my courtroom. You'll have to take a seat if you can find one or wait in the hall if you cannot. I don't allow people to stand and watch," the judge said politely but with obvious authority.

Barbara, visibly annoyed, turned and looked at Floyd and John and Charlotte Daniels who were still standing just inside the outer doors. Charlotte was looking over the packed gallery for a place to sit. Not finding one, she looked at her sister, shrugged her shoulders and opened the door to leave. Barbara, undaunted, found a row with a small space in it and stepped up to it. She glared down at the man in the aisle seat, gave the other occupants on the long wooden bench a fierce look and they all silently slid down to make room for her.

The judge watched this little drama with a tiny smirk and a suppressed laugh. When Barbara was done disrupting his court, he nodded at his clerk to call the next case.

EIGHTEEN

Introductions were made and Maddy took the disheveled, slightly bewildered Brittany and gently sat her down in one of the juror's chairs. Maddy sat down to her left and the public defender took the chair to her right, next to Marc at the head of the table. The P.D., Goins, who Brittany had already met, briefly told her what was going on to calm her down and let her know she was among friends.

"How are you doing?" Maddy quietly asked the noticeably distraught girl.

"You have to believe me," Brittany blurted out. "I had nothing to do with Becky being gone. They questioned me all weekend about it. I told them it was my boyfriend, Bob Olson, but they don't believe me. I've never been more scared in my life. I've barely slept at all since they arrested me," she replied close to tears. "Who are all those people out there?"

"They're mostly from the media and others who are just curious about your case," Marc told her.

"It's because of all the publicity surrounding your daughter's abduction," Maddy quietly added.

"My folks told me they're camped out across the street from our house. They have the whole street blocked off. Can they do that?" Brittany asked. "Can't someone make them leave us alone?" she added looking at Marc, almost pleading.

"Not really," Marc said. "Maybe if they trespass we might be able to get them to back off. We'll see.

"I need to talk to you about your case…" he continued. Marc took a few minutes to explain to her how he came to be there today. He told her about the Daniels and the discussion he had with her parents. He let her know he was willing to talk to her about taking her case but right now was probably not the best time.

"When we're done here, Tom and I," he continued nodding at the P.D., "will talk to the judge. I think what would be best is to let Tom handle today's hearing. The judge will ask you to enter a plea," he said then looked at Goins and asked, "she's charged with gross misdemeanor child neglect?"

"Yeah, that's it," Goins answered.

"Did he explain this to you?" Marc asked Brittany.

"Yes, he did," Brittany said becoming calmer as Marc spoke. It helped to have Maddy sitting next to her literally holding her hand.

"Good. When we go out there, try not to show any emotion at all. Don't look happy or sad or confused or anything. The judge will tell you your rights and the charges against you. He'll ask you to plead guilty or not guilty. You just say 'not guilty'. Then they'll argue about bail and we'll see if we can get you out of here," Marc said. He looked at Goins and said, "We good?"

"Yeah, that'll be fine," Goins replied.

"Wait a minute," Maddy said. She retrieved a small hairbrush and some makeup from her purse. While Brittany brushed her hair, Maddy lightly applied some makeup just to make her look a little more presentable.

While the women attended to Brittany, Marc said to Goins, "One other thing. Make the demand for a Rule 8 hearing, omnibus hearing and a speedy trial. Let's get the clock ticking."

"Okay, will do. What about assignment of counsel? The judge is going to want to assign someone today."

"You want the case if I'm not retained?" Marc asked.

"Sure, but she'll have to apply for a Public Defender."

"If my aunt Charlotte thinks you're a good lawyer, then that's good enough for me," Brittany told them. "I trust her more than I trust my mom."

At that moment, there was a knock on the door and a deputy looked in. He told them the judge sent him in to find out how they were doing.

Marc looked over everyone and asked, "Everybody ready?" They all nodded affirmatively, and the deputy held the door as they re-entered the courtroom.

Marc whispered to Maddy for her to take a seat in the jury box. He led Brittany back to the spot she was in before, in front of the bench. Marc and Goins, along with the lawyer from the county attorney's office had a quiet conference at the bench. Marc quickly filled in the judge what they were planning to do. The judge had no objection to it nor did the prosecutor. Goins and the prosecutor took their places by Brittany and Marc sat down next to Maddy who had again created a bit of a stir among the male members of the gallery.

The lawyers introduced themselves for the record and the judge quickly went over the charges against Brittany, read her the Miranda rights, asked if she understood everything and asked her to plead. Brittany quickly glanced at Goins who smiled reassuringly and nodded his head. Brittany pled not guilty. Goins requested, for the record, an omnibus hearing and a speedy trial. Then the argument over bail began.

"Our office is requesting that bail be set at five hundred thousand dollars your Honor," the prosecutor said.

"What!" Goins and Marc both said loudly and simultaneously. At the same time, a significant buzz went through the gallery. The judge loudly rapped his gavel a couple of times, sternly looked at Marc, pointed an index finger at him and said, "Either get over here and get in or keep quiet, Mr. Kadella." An admonition to which Marc was apologizing before the judge finished it.

"Mr. Goins?" the judge asked waiting for a rebuttal while Goins solemnly looked at the prosecutor. "Mr. Goins?" the judge politely asked again.

"I'm waiting to see if this is a really late April Fools joke, your Honor. A half a million? That's absurd," Goins replied.

"We are dead serious. We anticipate…"

"Your Honor," Goins interrupted. "She's charged with a gross misdemeanor, not multiple homicides. She has no criminal record and has strong ties to the community. Her family is here to support her. They have presented nothing to indicate she's a danger to the community or a flight risk. The defense believes an NBR, no bail required, release is clearly appropriate."

"As I was saying, your Honor, before Mr. Goins interrupted. There is a small child missing which is involved with this matter. We anticipate more serious charges in the near future."

There it is, Marc thought to himself while silently listening.

"…and we believe she is a flight risk and a danger to the community," he concluded.

"Your Honor," Goins said, "clearly he's grandstanding for the media and…"

"I resent that!" the lawyer said.

"…and," Goins continued ignoring him, "trying to inflame any potential jurors by making baseless claims about possible charges they can't make…"

The judge held up his hand to stop Goins, then said, "Okay, I get it. I'll set bail at three thousand dollars, the maximum amount of the possible fine."

"Your Honor, that's hardly…" the prosecutor sputtered.

"You got more charges to bring, then bring them," the judge almost snarled at the county attorney's rep. "We'll cross that bridge when we get there. We're adjourned."

Barbara Riley posted the bail and what should have taken no more than an hour took over three to get Brittany processed and released. Once she was out, by previous arrangement, Marc and Maddy followed the Rileys back to their home. The Daniels had waited for Brittany's release, then left.

Melinda Pace's show was done live later that same afternoon. She had film of the short hearing and heated argument concerning bail and a shot of Brittany leaving the jail. Unknown to Marc and the Rileys, the reason for the long delay was to give the media time to get their noon reports in and set up cameras for Brittany's release. Melinda also showed film of Marc, Maddy and the Rileys pulling into the driveway of the Rileys' home.

Following a commercial break, Melinda spent two minutes on a live feed with Gabriella Shriqui with the Rileys' home in the background. Melinda tried to make a big deal out of the fact that Brittany showed no emotion. She tried to make it sound as if Brittany didn't care about what had happened to her daughter and was not the least bit concerned. Gabriella neither agreed nor disagreed just evenly and professionally answered Melinda's questions.

They talked a bit more about the scene across the street from the Rileys' house. There was virtually nothing of newsworthy content in this except to show the shot of the five or six media vans lined up on the Rileys' street. Clearly, the circus was getting started.

"Obviously," Melinda began her final remarks looking directly into the camera with a solemn expression, "the police and prosecutors believe this young woman, Brittany Riley, is lying about her daughter's disappearance. And I have to say, I personally find her story not only hard to believe but quite frankly, ridiculous. This is Melinda Pace and be sure to tune in tomorrow to *The Court Reporter*."

The station had promoted Melinda's show with titillating promos that were little better than tabloid journalism. That very night ratings would show a whopping fifty percent jump in her viewership. This caused Melinda and the station execs to meet the next day with everyone who was involved with Melinda's show and brainstorm how best to exploit Brittany's case and give the public more of what they unmistakably wanted. Before the day was done, Melinda would be interviewed by three national TV networks. She would repeat for the nation what was said on her show the previous day.

NINETEEN

Marc stood in the Rileys' living room in front of the picture window looking out over the front yard. The curtains were closed, and he separated them with his left hand just enough to observe the scene in the street.

"Is there anything we can do to make them go away?" Barbara asked.

Marc removed his hand which allowed the heavy drapes to fall back into place. He turned to face the people in the living room. Maddy was on the couch in between Brittany and Floyd. Barbara was seated in one of the two cloth covered matching armchairs. Marc pushed the second one up to the coffee table in front of the couch and sat down on it. He placed his small leather portfolio briefcase he had been holding on the table, looked at Barbara and said, "Not really. If they trespass or become too intrusive, maybe the sheriff will do something but," he shrugged, "right now they are entitled to be on a public street.

"Getting down to business," he continued looking at Brittany, "you need to decide what you want to do. We haven't had much time to talk, to discuss your case or my representation. Did Tom Goins, the guy who was in court with you today, explain things to you? Tell you what was going on and the process and procedures?"

"Yeah, pretty much. Alan, Alan Reeder, did too. He came to see me on Saturday," Brittany said.

"Okay. What did Alan tell you?" Marc asked.

"We talked about the charges against me and I told him the cops wouldn't leave me alone. They questioned me about Becky and where she is. And they kept bringing up stuff about me, about what I did before Mom called them to tell them Becky was missing," Brittany answered.

"What's the deal with Alan Reeder?" Marc asked looking at Barbara.

"He's a lawyer who represented Brittany in a wrongful death suit when her husband was killed in a car accident. He got a settlement for her. Alan would like to get this case, but we told him we wanted a lawyer who does criminal defense. He went to see Brittany as a courtesy."

When Marc heard the word settlement, he immediately realized Brittany probably had some money. Relieved that he was likely going to get paid, he turned back to Brittany and said, "I think we need to talk alone. Is there somewhere we can go?" he asked nodding at both Brittany and Maddy.

"She can sit in," Barbara said a bit testily referring to Maddy, "but we can't."

"Mrs. Riley," Marc politely began. "Madeline is an employee of mine and as such she is also covered by attorney-client privilege. She cannot be forced to testify against Brittany. You and your husband," he continued looking at Floyd who had been sitting quietly, "are not covered and could be forced to testify about anything that you hear or anything Brittany says."

"They can make her mother testify against her? That's ridiculous," Barbara said.

"I'm afraid so. Is there someplace we can talk?" Marc asked Brittany.

"We can use the basement," she replied. "It's finished."

The three of them went down into the finished basement and took seats in the family room.

"First of all, do you want me to take your case?" Marc asked.

"Yes, absolutely," she replied. "I liked the way you took control of things in court. It made me feel better and definitely made me feel more confident."

"Okay, tell me about what's going on here; about your daughter and everything up to today."

For the next half hour, Brittany went over the entire story. She began with first meeting Bob Olson at work, their dates together and with Becky. She talked about the night Becky went missing, the panic she went through and the efforts she made to try to find her that first day and over the next ten days. She skipped over the parts concerning her social life during that time and the stories she made up to keep her mother at bay. She told them about the public pleas for help, the TV appearances and that awful Melinda Pace which seemed to upset her more than discussing Becky's disappearance.

"Ever since then, when she practically accused me of hurting my little girl, the news people have been all over us. They're such assholes!"

"Tell me about the arrest and this weekend," Marc said.

Angry now, Brittany started in on the arrest. "They banged on my door at midnight, almost busted it in. It scared the hell out of me. I was sleeping, and I heard them pounding on the door. I got up, looked through the peephole and the hall was full of cops. I opened the door and they came barging in. They almost knocked me down. One of them pointed a gun at me and another one made me kneel down and put my hands on my head. Three or four others went through my apartment and tore the place up. They made a huge mess. My mom spent the weekend putting my apartment back together."

"Your mom cleaned up?" Maddy asked.

"Yeah," Brittany nodded, smiling slightly, answering her beautiful new friend.

"That's too bad," Maddy said to Marc. "We could've taken some pictures."

Marc nodded to Madeline, turned back to Brittany and said, "Then what happened?"

"The sheriff was there walking around glaring at me trying to intimidate me, which he really did. I was so scared I almost wet myself. Then they put handcuffs on me, behind my back and really tight. One of them got a pair of flip-flops for me for shoes then they took me out to the front."

"Did they read you your rights?" Marc asked.

"Maybe, I don't remember. I was so shocked and scared," Brittany replied.

"Okay, go on," Marc said.

"We went out the front, there were lights all over and people with cameras and microphones yelling questions at me about Becky, did I kill her and things like that," she said as the tears started to flow and she began sobbing. "They put me in a car and made me sit there while they kept taking pictures and filming me. Then the sheriff stood in front of the cameras and talked to them. I couldn't hear what he said but my mom told me she saw it on TV and the sheriff made me sound like a terrorist or something. They asked him if he thought I killed my little girl." She started sobbing then and Marc and Maddy waited for her to calm down to continue.

"How could they think that? How could they believe I could hurt my baby?" she asked after she had calmed down. "Why are they such terrible people?"

"I don't know," Marc shrugged. "I guess they just believe they have a job to do."

They took a brief break, so Brittany could use the bathroom. Maddy went upstairs and came back with a glass of water for her. Brittany drank half of the water, thanked Maddy, and then told them about her weekend in custody.

The cops questioned her almost the entire night. She had been booked into the jail around one o'clock and four of them, all in plain clothes kept after her, off and on, until 6:00 A.M. They went over the same things without let up. Where was Becky? What did she do with Becky? Why did she get rid of Becky? Over and over.

"I got so tired and worn down. I kept telling them it wasn't me; that Bob did it but they didn't believe me. They couldn't find him, and they no longer believed me because they couldn't find anyone who had seen Bob except me. Like I said, I was so tired that I almost said I did it just so they'd leave me alone."

"Did you say that?" Marc asked.

90

"No, I definitely did not," Brittany said, almost defiantly. "Because I didn't do it. I didn't hurt my little girl. Do you believe me? I have to know you both believe me."

"Yes, I do," Marc sincerely answered her pleas.

"Of course," Maddy said as she reached over and took Brittany's hand and gently squeezed it.

"They finally put me in a cell with another girl and I lied down and slept. Then around one o'clock Saturday afternoon, I was taken to see Alan Reeder."

"What did you talk about?" Marc asked.

"Why I was in jail. That stuff. He told me he told the cops they couldn't question me without a lawyer so after that they didn't. Then Monday I was brought to court."

"And you didn't admit to anything?" Marc asked.

"No, absolutely not. I was scared but I was really pissed too. In fact, I told the young cop, Stu, to go screw himself. Of course, that's not the word I used. He had been nice to me before but now he was being an asshole."

"Good for you," Maddy laughed. Marc smiled and said. "Okay. Here's the deal. Right now, you're charged with child neglect. It's punishable by a three-thousand- dollar fine and up to a year in jail, maximum. It's pretty obvious they're after you for your daughter's disappearance," he added being careful to use the word disappearance and not death.

"To take your case I'll need a five-thousand-dollar retainer," he said as he pulled a sheet of paper from his briefcase. He took a few minutes to go over the details to explain it to her. She signed and he was now officially her lawyer.

Before they left, Barbara wrote a check for the retainer which Marc promised to hold for a couple days so she could transfer some money to make the check good. Marc then took a few minutes to politely explain that even though Barbara wrote the check, he represented Brittany and no one else. He could tell Barbara was a bit annoyed with that, but she managed to put on a phony smile and assure him she understood. The entire time Floyd sat on the couch and had not said a word.

Before leaving, Marc went over her current case, the child neglect charge and explained the process to everyone. He made it very clear Brittany was not to speak to anyone, including family members, about anything unless Marc was present. Barbara began to protest this but stopped herself when Marc held up his left hand to her.

"You can be forced to testify," he reminded her.

"I'm sorry, you're right," she sincerely answered him.

"Keep up the search for Becky. Right now, that's the most important thing. Nothing else matters compared to that," Marc told them.

"We've got more searches planned all week," Floyd said speaking up for the first time. "In fact, I've taken a leave of absence from work."

"Great," Marc told him. "And keep up the publicity. You can talk to the press about the search but be very careful what you say about anything else especially Brittany's case.

"We're going to take off now," he said as he stood up. "I'll go out and talk to the media and try to get them to back off. At some point, you might want to get a lawyer for yourselves to help protect you and look out for you."

"Do you really think that's necessary?" Barbara asked as she shook Marc's hand while Maddy walked to the front door with an arm around Brittany's shoulders.

"Yes, I do. If I think of someone, I'll let you know," Marc said as he shook Floyd's hand.

Marc joined Maddy and Brittany at the door. As he began to extend his hand to Brittany, she stepped up to him, wrapped both arms around him and buried her head in his chest. He returned the hug a bit awkwardly as she looked up at him and said, "Thank you, so much. I feel better already."

"Good," he replied as they released each other. "You have my card. Call anytime and leave a message if you have to. Even on my cell. I'll find out what the cops and prosecutors are up to and get back to you."

A minute later, Marc and Maddy walked to the end of the Rileys' driveway to face the mob. The moment they saw the lawyer and his assistant step through the Rileys' front door, they grabbed their video cameras, recorders and microphones and scurried toward the driveway like hyenas after fresh road kill.

"That's first," Marc said pointing at several of them who had intruded onto the Rileys' front yard. "That right there is trespassing and it's a crime which could include jail time." Marc continued to stare at them until they backed off into the street. He turned to face the rest of them and at least two of them shoved microphones toward him and began asking questions.

Marc stood quietly, patiently waiting for the noise to die down. After thirty seconds or so it finally did.

"Let me make a statement then I'll take a couple of questions," Marc said.

Without waiting, one of the male reporters looked at Maddy and asked, "Can I get your name?"

"And phone number?" A second man chimed in.

Maddy looked at Marc who shrugged and said, "Go ahead."

She gave her name and explained who she was and what she did, taking the opportunity to get a little free publicity. Marc intervened and told them she was working with him. He confirmed he had been retained to represent Brittany and the shouting of questions erupted again.

Somehow Gabriella Shirqui had managed to squeeze her way through the crowd and was standing quietly in front of Marc. She was a reporter he knew from a previous case. He could not resist looking into her beautiful dark eyes then said, "Gabriella, do you have a question?" This managed to quiet the rest of them in anticipation and brought a tiny smile to Maddy's lips.

"Do you have any new information about Becky's whereabouts?" Gabriella asked.

"No, I don't," Marc said. "In fact, I've been out of the country for the past couple of weeks so, I probably know less than all of you."

The noise began again but Gabriella beat them to it by asking, "Do you anticipate more serious charges to be brought against Brittany?"

"Same answer," Marc said.

"We've heard rumors that…" Gabriella began.

"No, you've been given leaks out of the sheriff's office or the county attorney's office. That's where you're getting these rumors from," Marc interrupted her, smiling at her. He continued to look at her to see if she would deny it. When she didn't, he looked over the unruly mob.

"Brittany is charged with child neglect. I have been retained to represent her on that charge. That's all there is for now.

"However, it would be nice if the members of the media, that would be all of you, would conduct yourselves as professionals. These people are searching for a missing child. Ms. Riley, Becky's mother, maintains her daughter was taken by a man she was dating. I understand you all have a copy of the drawing of this man. We would appreciate all of the help you can give to find this beautiful little girl. At the very least, respect their privacy and stay off of their property. Really," he continued, "that's all there is for now. Thank you."

With that, Marc and Maddy walked back to his car, got in and slowly drove off.

TWENTY

Gabriella and her cameraman, Kyle Bronson, walked up the street away from the Rileys' house toward the station's van. Marc drove past them and as he did so, Gabriella looked at him and smiled as he gave her a friendly wave. A thought occurred to her and she pulled out her phone, dialed information for the number and had the phone company dial it for her. On the second ring, it was answered by a woman who identified herself as Louise Shaffer whom Gabriella knew was Sheriff Cale's assistant.

Gabriella identified herself and told Louise about Marc's assertion that the sheriff's office was leaking to the media. Even though Gabriella knew perfectly well they were since she was one of the people they were leaking information to, she wanted to get Cale's reaction. By doing that, she believed she might get an interesting squabble going between the cops, the prosecution and the defense. Of course, she didn't tell Louise any of this.

Within a minute of Louise asking her to hold, Cale himself came on the phone. Still standing in the street by the Rileys' house next to the van, Gabriella told him what Marc had said, rattled Cale's cage a bit but managed to get invited by him to an exclusive interview. A few seconds later, Gabriella and Kyle were hurrying out of the suburban, residential area and headed toward the sheriff's office in Hastings. On the way, Gabriella called the station and told them they would have Cale's rebuttal of Marc's allegations concerning leaks, which had already been transmitted back to them.

Gabriella and Kyle, who was holding his video camera, barely had time to sit down in the office's reception area when Shaffer came out to meet them.

Shaffer led them back to Cale's office and on the way, Gabriella saw Stu Doyle who watched her walk by. Shaffer opened the office door, smiled and politely stepped aside as they entered. Seated in a chair to Gabriella's right with her back to the wall facing Cale's desk was Patty Dunphy. She rose from her chair as the two news people entered.

"Hi, Patty," Gabriella said as she shook hands with Dunphy. She turned to Cale who had been sitting behind his power desk. They shook hands, took their seats and Gabriella said, "Thanks for agreeing to this, Sheriff Cale. I wasn't expecting an interview, I thought I'd just get a quote from you over the phone in reaction to the defense lawyer's claim."

"I'm going to try to be calm," Cale said, "but I'm pretty angry over what he said."

Gabriella turned around in her chair and said to Kyle, "How's the lighting? Are we good?"

"Yeah," he answered checking his meter.

"Tell you what, can you back up and get a shot of the sheriff with the flags behind him? I think that would make him look really authoritative," Gabriella said stroking Cale's ego knowing Cale would love that thought.

Kyle backed up and adjusted his lens a bit to get the shot. Kyle told Gabriella he was all set then there was a knock on the door and the county attorney, LeAnne Miller, came in and took a chair next to Dunphy.

"I hope you don't mind," Cale said, "I asked Ms. Miller to sit in. Have you met?"

Cale introduced Miller to Gabriella who leaned forward to exchange a quick handshake and greeting. Gabriella asked her if she wanted to make a statement as well and Miller informed her she probably would which delighted Gabriella with the thought of beating everyone else to this interview.

Kyle and Gabriella did a quick sound check and Kyle got the camera rolling. Gabriella took a couple of minutes to explain to Cale and Miller what Marc Kadella had said at the Rileys'. For the camera, she asked Cale for his reaction then sat back and let him talk.

"This office does not conduct its investigations by leaking information to the media. We stick strictly to the facts, then present them to the county attorney's office for their decision on whether or not charges are warranted.

"The decision to charge Brittany Riley with child neglect was done in strict compliance with the proper policies and procedures established to adhere to the law," he said jabbing an angry finger onto his desk blotter for emphasis. "I am both personally and professionally extremely offended that some lawyer would make such outlandish and insulting allegations. This office has and will continue to conduct itself in a professional manner, at least as long as I am sheriff."

While listening to Cale's attempt at righteous indignation, Gabriella almost had to bite her tongue to stop from asking him whose idea it was to arrest Brittany at midnight, to practically kick in her door while she slept, trash her apartment then haul her out before the media in handcuffs, in her pajamas in the middle of the night. Plus, who had informed the media an arrest was going to be made to make sure they were in attendance? She had gotten to know Marc Kadella well enough to know that sooner or later, and probably sooner, Marc would be in front of a camera asking that question for her.

"Thank you, Sheriff Cale," Gabriella said. She then turned to Kyle and asked, "Did you get that all right?"

"Yeah," he replied. "Really good."

Gabriella turned to Miller and asked if she would like to comment for the record. Miller answered affirmatively, and they took a moment to reposition her chair for a better angle while Miller, with Patty Dunphy's help, checked her hair and make-up.

When they were set and the camera started rolling again, Gabriella introduced Miller then asked her the same question she had asked Cale.

"It's a tired, old story," Miller said attempting to look both weary and annoyed. "It's a constant problem with the defense bar. None of them can resist getting in front of a camera and making outrageous statements they can't back up.

"Sheriff Cale is absolutely right. Brittany Riley has and will be treated no differently than any other citizen accused of a crime. I've known Sheriff Cale for a long time, he is a true professional. And it is the strict, carved-in-stone policy of my office that we will not try cases through the media.

"Defense lawyers love to hold press conferences to talk about their case. We will not do that."

"Can you tell me if Brittany Riley is the subject of an investigation into her daughter's disappearance?" Gabriella asked, turning back to Cale as did Kyle's camera.

"I will not discuss an ongoing investigation," Cale said. This is the answer that the authorities always give when the answer to the question is yes, Gabriella knew. Otherwise, the cops will just say no and move on.

The impromptu interview wrapped up after that. Gabriella thanked them both and Patty Dunphy led them back to the front door and pleasantly said good-bye.

Before Gabriella and Kyle were out of the building. Cale and Miller were having a brief meeting in Cale's office.

"What exactly did your guys get out to them?" Miller asked referring to their media contacts.

"Just what we had, so far," Cale replied. "We don't have much, just enough to let them know we're not buying her story about Bob Olson."

"Okay. Let's start putting out the things we do have. Put special emphasis on her not reporting the kid missing for ten days. This Gabriella chick," Miller said, "is someone talking to her?"

"Yeah, Stu Doyle."

"Good. Make sure he tells her about all of the lying Brittany did. We need to ratchet up the heat on her."

"We're working on it. Don't worry. In a couple weeks no one will buy her story," Cale said.

By the time Gabriella and Kyle were onto Highway 55 for the drive back to the Cities she found Marc's business card and was dialing his cell. He was back at his office going through the pile of mail on his desk when the phone went off. Marc checked the caller ID, saw who it was and politely said hello.

Gabriella told him about her interview with Cale and Miller, what they said and asked if he wanted to respond. Marc thought about it, then simply said, "No comment".

"Off the record?" he asked.

"Sure," Gabriella replied.

"I'll watch the news and think about it. Call me tomorrow."

It was almost midnight when Bob Olson finally turned off his television set. He had set his DVR for Melinda's show and for the five, six and ten o'clock newscasts.

Melinda's indignation and borderline hysteria for the missing kid was the best part. She was practically accusing Brittany of at least being involved with the kid's disappearance and she walked right up to the line of saying Becky was dead and Brittany did it.

He put the empty beer bottle on the coffee table, loudly belched, smiled and headed for the bedroom.

TWENTY-ONE

Marc and Maddy parted company in the small parking lot behind Marc's office. Marc had a pile of work waiting on his desk and Maddy had other clients to check in with. She was developing a steady stream of business doing background checks on individuals for various reasons. Initially, her clients were mostly women checking on potential lovers and future husbands. Lately, with the help of a P.I. friend of hers, an ex-cop named Tony Carvelli and Marc, she was expanding into business and corporate work. It paid the bills but her real love, what really got her juices going, was helping Marc with criminal cases. It was interesting, rewarding and a lot more fun than checking up on boyfriends. And it didn't give her the sleaze factor she got from doing the occasional divorce case.

Marc got off the phone with Gabriella, finished going through the pile of mail on his desk then used the office intercom to ask the office paralegal, Jeff Modell, to come in. Marc gave Jeff instructions to open a case file for Brittany and draft a discovery request, including the video of the interrogation of her while in custody. As Marc was finishing, his landlord and good friend, Connie Mickelson came into his office and took the chair next to Jeff.

"So, you're getting yourself into another one of these high profile clusterfucks," Connie said. "When are you going to learn?"

"Do not light that cigarette in my office," Marc admonished her as she put it in her mouth. Jeff laughed, stood up, asked Marc if he had anything else and left when Marc shook his head.

"You know smoking isn't allowed in Minnesota. Why do you do it?"

"Just to piss off the do-gooders," she replied. "What about your new case?" she seriously asked. "Where's it going?"

"Not sure," Marc said. "Right now, she's charged with child neglect but I'm pretty sure they're going to try to nail her for the kid's death."

"You figure the kid is dead?"

"Don't you? Yeah, unless and until they find her I'm going to start working this as a homicide of some kind. Not sure what yet."

Barry Cline, another lawyer in the office came through the open door and sat next to Connie just as she asked, "If you march her in and plead guilty to the child neglect charge, wouldn't double jeopardy attach?"

"No," Barry answered her. "They can still charge her with the murder. It's a separate act and can be charged separately. What's going

98

on? Are we going to have another extremely unpopular client around here?"

Marc leaned back in his chair, frowned, shrugged his shoulders and said, "We might. I've been retained for the child neglect charge only. If she's charged with more serious stuff, I could get out of..."

"The hell you will!" Connie growled. "You do what you have to."

"Agreed," Barry said. "Even if business gets a little tight, we'll manage."

"Do you believe she's innocent?" Connie asked.

"I don't know yet," Marc said. "My gut tells me, yes, but I've been fooled before," Marc said.

"Carl Fornich!" both Connie and Barry said in unison.

"Thanks for the reminder," Marc said with a smile.

At that moment Carolyn yelled through the open door, "Hey Marc, there's a Robbie Nelson on the phone for you..."

"We have an intercom, or so you keep telling me," Marc yelled back.

"I think I like this one better. The one you normally use. Anyway..."

"Who's Robbie Nelson?" Marc asked.

"He says he's a TV producer for that show, *The Court Reporter*, the one with that person," Carolyn hesitated, "that b-i-t-c-h, Melinda Pace."

"There aren't any kids here and we can all spell, Carolyn," Connie yelled back laughing.

"He wants to talk to you about an interview on the show," Carolyn said ignoring Connie. "What do you want me to tell him?"

"I'll take it," Marc said as he reached for the phone. When he did this Connie and Barry started to rise and Marc said, "No, stay. We'll see what they have to say. Marc Kadella," he said into the phone. Connie gestured to him about closing the door, but Marc just shrugged to indicate his indifference.

"Mr. Kadella, my name is Robbie Nelson and I'm the producer of *The Court Reporter* on Channel 8. Do you remember it?" Marc heard the young man ask.

"Yeah, I'm pretty sure Gabriella Shriqui interviewed me for the show a couple of months ago about a case I handled."

"Yes, in the government center on the walkway bridge," Robbie said. "Gabriella interviewed you for the news broadcast. That was me and a cameraman who filmed you for *The Court Reporter*."

"Oh, okay," Marc said. "I remember that now. That was you who asked to watch?"

"Yes, sir," Robbie replied. "I'm calling, first of all, to find out if you've been retained by Brittany Riley and if so, would you be willing to appear on the show for an interview?"

Marc had placed the call on the phone's speaker, so Connie and Barry could listen in. Connie silently mouthed the words to Marc that he didn't have to answer that.

"I put the call on speaker," Marc said to Robbie. "There are two other people here with me. I hope you don't mind."

"Not at all, sir," Robbie said.

"When does she want me?" Marc asked.

"Whenever it's convenient for you. There's been a lot of news coverage and Ms. Pace thought you might be interested in giving Brittany Riley's side of things."

"Just a second," Marc said as he turned off the speaker and said to Connie and Barry, "What do you think?"

"Might not be a bad idea. The press is already crucifying her. Wouldn't hurt to throw some cold water on that," Connie answered.

"Never a bad idea to get some free publicity," Barry said.

"Never? Remember Carl Fornich?" Connie asked. "This could turn into another one of those. That case damn near bankrupted both of you guys."

"True, but business took a big jump once it was over," Marc reminded her. "Besides, here's a chance to take a shot at the Dakota County Sheriff's office. I know damn well they're leaking things to the media and then acting so pious and indignant about it."

Marc picked up the phone and agreed to do the show the next day. Robbie gladly accepted and told Marc the time for the taping.

"We won't be live for this," Robbie explained. "We always like to tape these things if time and circumstances permit. So if ten o'clock tomorrow morning is okay with you, we'll see you then."

Marc, being a defense lawyer and not a prosecutor, was used to being required to be punctual so it had become habitual. He arrived at the Channel 8 building in Minneapolis fifteen minutes early. Marc checked in with the very professional receptionist, took a seat and picked up the sports section of the morning Star Tribune. Marc had barely started reading about the Twin's latest loss when a familiar looking younger man came out and introduced himself as Robbie Nelson.

Robbie led Marc back to the same set on which Melinda had ambushed and humiliated Brittany a couple of weeks ago. Marc, having been out of town at the time, had not seen that show, but of course, had heard all about it. Robbie introduced Marc to everyone on the set whose names he immediately forgot except for the striking Cordelia Davis whom Robbie introduced as an associate producer.

Marc was directed to a chair off camera and a woman began to prep him with makeup to dull the bright lights. While she did this, Robbie explained to him how the taping would go so he would know what to expect.

"I understand my client was interviewed on this show a couple weeks ago. I didn't get a chance to see it. I'd like to get a copy of it on a DVD format," Marc said to Robbie while the woman worked on his face.

"Um, I'm not sure I can do that," Robbie answered. "I'll have to check with..."

"I can get a subpoena," Marc said with an authoritative look.

"Get him a copy of the show," Marc heard a woman's voice say.

Marc tilted his head to look behind Robbie and saw Melinda Pace walking toward them. Marc had seen her show, or at least parts of it, several times enough to recognize her. She always appeared to be an attractive woman, borderline beautiful even. Seeing her in person, Marc thought the cameras did not do the woman justice.

"Melinda Pace," she said introducing herself as she extended a well-manicured hand toward Marc. They shook hands and Marc was immediately impressed with the firmness of her grip and her obvious take charge attitude.

"A subpoena won't be necessary," she said as their hands separated. "We'll be happy to get it for you, won't we?" she said smiling at Robbie.

"Sure, no problem," Robbie answered. He turned to Cordelia who nodded and walked off.

"Robbie explained everything to you?" Melinda asked Marc.

The make-up woman indicated she was finished, and Marc stood up and said, "Yes, he's been very helpful."

"Good," Melinda said with a dazzling smile as she hooked her left arm through Marc's right arm to guide him to the set. She led him to the same chair Brittany had used and the two of them took their seats. At that point, Marc was glad he had worn his best-looking suit, a light gray Armani pinstripe and Hermes tie Margaret had bought for him in Paris.

The crew completed the sound and light checks then Melinda started the show and introduced Marc. She explained who he was and reminded the audience of two infamous cases he had handled recently.

The two of them amiably chatted for almost ten minutes about those cases. Melinda even gave Marc a little ego boost by complimenting him on the job he had done on both cases.

"It was pretty obvious," Melinda said, "that Judge Prentiss was guilty of murdering his wife..."

"He maintains his innocence and I believe he is innocent," Marc replied.

"Seriously? Even after the guilty verdict. I mean twelve jurors heard and saw all of the evidence and they agreed with me," Melinda said.

"Agreed with you? That's an interesting way of putting it," Marc said with a smile.

"You know what I mean," Melinda lightly said in rejoinder. "Are you handling his appeal?"

"No, I don't do appellate work. He has an excellent lawyer working on his case."

"You made some serious accusations about the Dakota County sheriff and county attorney's offices leaking reports to the media," Melinda said abruptly changing the conversation.

"Yes, I did. And I saw the sheriff and county attorney being interviewed by Gabriella Shriqui. They both did an excellent job of appearing indignant especially when he claimed his office always acts professionally and follows appropriate procedures. I was quite impressed. Of course, if it was me questioning him, I would have asked him if it is proper procedure to show up in the middle of the night like the Gestapo and pound down a young woman's door, then trash her apartment searching for evidence of child neglect, which is what she's charged with and at gunpoint, make her kneel down while they put handcuffs on her, dragging her out in her pajamas in the middle of the night in front of a horde of media who just happened to be there."

Marc turned away from the camera, looked at Melinda and said, "You wouldn't happen to know how all of those news people found out about the arrest of a twenty-two-year-old girl, at midnight, would you?"

"No, I really don't. But even if I did, I couldn't tell you," Melinda answered him.

"That's right. Whoever leaked this to the media gets to hide behind the journalist shield laws. And I'm sure this leak didn't come from Sheriff Cale's office," Marc added with obvious sarcasm.

"Those are all excellent points, Marc. I'm glad you brought them up," Melinda said. She turned and said to the camera, "We'll be back after a short break."

The filming stopped while the makeup woman checked over both of them. As she was doing that, Melinda said, "Marc that was fabulous. The audience will eat it up and you made some great points. Keep it up."

When the filming started again, Melinda turned to Marc and said, "The audience has a right to know: What is Brittany Riley's involvement in the disappearance of her daughter?"

Marc, a little stunned by the question and wondering if she was joking, just stared back at her for a full fifteen seconds. Realizing she was serious, he finally said, "Melinda, I understand you have a law degree and even practiced for a while. Is that true?"

"Yes, it is," she answered him.

"Then you know I can't possibly answer that question."

Getting the answer she knew she would get, the answer she wanted, Melinda quickly moved on before Marc could explain.

She spent a few minutes asking him questions about the Riley family, how they were holding up and the searches being conducted. Melinda asked about a possible reward for finding Becky, a subject Marc knew nothing about. At one point, Marc looked at a clock on the wall and noticed they had gone beyond the amount of time the show would be aired. It was then that Melinda asked, "Isn't it true that many criminal defendants look at their lawyer as a sort of father figure?"

"Sometimes, I guess," Marc answered wondering where this was headed.

"Did Brittany confess to you and tell you where her daughter is?"

An exasperated Marc looked at her and said, "Melinda, stop it. You're not going to get me to talk about something that is covered by attorney-client privilege. You should know better."

"The audience wants to know, and I have an obligation to ask," she said. Melinda then stood up as did Marc and they shook hands again.

Marc said. "Are we done?"

"I'll film an ending but yeah, that's it. You were great and came across really well. I'd love to have you back. In fact, how about dinner sometime soon?" she asked still holding his hand.

"Are you asking me out for a date?" Marc said coyly.

"Sure, why not? You're an attractive, interesting man."

"Um, well, that's flattering," Marc said as they released their hands. "But I'm involved with someone."

At that moment Robbie Nelson joined them on the set, handed Marc a DVD in a plastic case as Melinda said, "Too bad. But if you change your mind, give me a call."

With that, Robbie led Marc back out to the reception area, thanked him and said goodbye. When Robbie got back to the set, Melinda was beginning to film the closing sequence.

"I asked him if Brittany Riley was involved in her daughter's disappearance and if she had told him where her daughter was. Like any good lawyer, he refused to answer either question. But remember something. He didn't say no to either one of them. I'll let you decide for yourselves what, if anything, that tells you.

"This is Melinda Pace and you've just seen *The Court Reporter.*"

The show aired at 4:00 P.M. that same day. By 4:30, Marc's office phone was ringing off the hook with inquiries from reporters and angry viewers who believed he knew where Becky was. Starting the next day, there were a dozen picketers marching up and down the sidewalks alongside his office building, carrying signs demanding to know where Becky Riley was.

TWENTY-TWO

The morning after Melinda's outrageous and borderline libelous statement hinting that Marc had knowledge of Becky's whereabouts, he did the first of many interviews. This time it was a one-on-one with Gabriella Shriqui in the conference room at his office building.

Having been interviewed by her before, he felt comfortable with the belief that Gabriella would play it straight and not sandbag him the way Melinda had. She apologized for Melinda's conduct before they were on camera and assured him she would not pull a similar stunt.

The purpose of the interview for Marc was to give him an opportunity for two things. First, to make it clear that his client maintained her innocence on both the current child neglect charges and Becky's disappearance. Second, to allow Marc to take a shot at Melinda and categorically deny any knowledge of where Becky was. For Gabriella, she had enough professional savvy to know this story was just beginning. It was her opportunity to do a puff piece interview with Marc and get on the good side of Brittany's lawyer. She really didn't have to worry about that. Gabriella's almond-shaped, beautiful dark eyes made Marc's knees buckle a bit every time he saw them.

The actual interview took less than twenty minutes, but Gabriella was very satisfied. Marc assured her he would not give another one to any of her competitors that morning. This would allow Gabriella to get it on the station's midday news show at noon. It would also allow the station time to promote it as an exclusive to attract more viewers. If she was lucky, there would be three minutes of airtime devoted to the story and would lead all of the newscasts for that evening as well.

Marc held the hallway door for Gabriella and her cameraman as they were leaving. When he closed the door, he heard the gruff voice of his landlord, Connie Mickelson say, "Hey, Mr. Showbiz, come in a second."

"Give me a break with the showbiz stuff," he answered as Carolyn handed him a stack of a dozen or so phone messages.

"All media people," Carolyn said.

"Any client cancellations?" Marc asked as he shuffled through the messages.

"Not yet," Carolyn told him as she retreated to her desk.

Marc stepped through the open door of Connie's office at the same time the hallway door opened. Chris Grafton, one of the lawyers in the office, was just arriving and Connie invited him in as well.

"I just saw that smoking hot TV reporter on the back stairs," Chris said as he took the client chair next to Marc. "Was she here to interview you?" he asked looking at Marc. "I need to do something, so she'll interview me," Chris said before Marc could answer him.

"Take up criminal defense work," Marc told him.

"Ah, no, I'm not that desperate. I was thinking more like, maybe kill someone myself. Did you see the idiots out on the sidewalk?" Chris said with a laugh. "Some of their signs are great. 'Baby Killer', 'Defend a Monster', and my favorite one: 'Lawyers Are Gutless Scum.'"

"At least they got that one right," Marc said to which they all laughed.

"Did you watch any news last night?" Connie asked Marc.

"No," Marc said shaking his head. "Once I heard about what Melinda did after I left the station, I avoided it completely."

"Every station in town and most of the ones around the state used it as their lead story and they all used the same lame-ass, gutless, cover-your-ass disclaimer. 'It has been reported that the lawyer for Brittany may have knowledge of…'" Connie said.

"Have you seen this morning's papers?" she continued. "Both the St. Paul and Minneapolis papers have it on page one. The whole world's blowing up and this is what these idiots have on page one; a rumor started by a drunken TV slut."

"What do you want me to do?" Marc asked Connie.

"I want you to defend this girl like it's the last case you'll ever have, of course," Connie said with a puzzled look.

"We'll stand with you on this," Chris added. "We took an oath to represent our clients zealously and we always do. This case is no different."

"Hell, Barry has a serial child molester on his hands," Connie said referring to Barry Cline.

"Alleged child molester," Marc said.

"Nah", Connie said. "Barry's going to plead him out today. That's where he is now. He's going to prison and probably an inpatient sex offender facility after that. He may never get out. Barry did the best he could for the pervert. Once the judge ruled his confession was admissible, his goose was cooked."

"One less child molester on the streets. What a shame," Marc said.

"Why can't these guys keep their mouths shut?" Chris asked.

"Because they want to tell the cops, so the cops will be nice to them. They figure if they explain it the right way, it will all come out as a misunderstanding or some excuse that will make the cops see they're not really to blame," Marc answered.

"What about our girl Brittany?" Connie asked getting back to the subject.

"Where's the kid? You think she's still alive? More charges coming against your client?" Chris asked.

"I don't know," Marc said. "I doubt she's still alive. I think more charges are coming. This Sheriff Cale out in Dakota County, I think he's the one behind the child neglect charges. He's trying to squeeze her. There's not much I can do about it. Wait and see," Marc shrugged.

"Are you going to call all of them back?" Connie asked referring to the messages in his hand. "If you don't they'll just keep calling."

"I know, I promised Gabriella I would wait until after noon."

"Why the hell did you do that?" Connie demanded.

"You explain it to her," Marc said to Chris.

"Because if you look in those eyes, that face and body, well, she'd give Madeline a good run," Chris said.

Connie looked at both of them to see if they were pulling her chain. When she realized they weren't, she shook her head and said, "Men. Jesus Christ give me a break. Get the hell out of here, both of you," but she was smiling when she said it.

Marc gave Carolyn and Sandy instructions to only take messages from clients or potential clients. All calls from the media were to be told Marc would not be in today and no messages would be taken.

"What about the obscene calls from assholes like those dipshits out on the sidewalk?" Sandy asked.

"You decide for yourself what to do with those," Marc replied. "Hang up or record them for listening to on lonely nights, I don't care. Do what you want."

Both women laughed at that, then Marc said, "How bad are they?"

"Not too bad. Nothing we haven't handled before," Carolyn said. "We'll take care of it."

Gabriella and her boss, the station news director Hunter Oswood, reviewed the three minutes of the interview that Oswood had decided to put on the air. Gabriella had also interviewed several of the protestors marching on the sidewalk in front of Marc's office. She asked each of them for a quote about why they were protesting in front of Marc's building and their answers were all about the same in content. "Why are lawyers such scum that they'll defend baby killers?" and "How can this piece of shit (bleeped out but still clear) sleep at night knowing where this little girl is?"

Gabriella tried to inform the irrational nitwits that Marc denied knowing where Becky was. She also tried to point out that no one knew if Becky was dead and in America, everyone is entitled to a lawyer. Oswood decided to include comments from two of the protestors but not Gabriella's reply to them. Oswood was quite pleased with Gabriella for getting the exclusive with the lawyer and because of that, invited her to accompany him to a meeting.

They left the editing room and went upstairs to the office of the station GM, Madison Eyler. Waiting for them was Eyler, Melinda, Robbie Nelson and Cordelia Davis. After greetings, everyone found a seat in the large corner office. Eyler started the meeting by congratulating Gabriella for the interview and her overall performance of reporting the Riley story.

"How pissed was the lawyer this morning about what Melinda said," Eyler asked Gabriella.

"Very," Gabriella replied. "He felt she had sandbagged him by adding that last bit after he left."

"She did sandbag him," Eyler said. "But it was carefully planned, and it worked."

"I cleared it with legal beforehand and stuck strictly to the script. Every word was true, so…" Melinda interjected.

"It was a little sleazy," Oswood said.

"It was very sleazy," Eyler corrected him. "But it worked. We ran it at 5:00 and 6:00 and our overnight ratings for the ten o'clock show were up over ten percent. Plus, we scooped every station in the cities and the newspapers. They all ran it but had to give us attribution. That will do even better things for our ratings. And Robbie," she said turning to Robbie Nelson, "what does that translate into?"

"More money," Robbie answered with a cheery smile.

"Besides, the public eats this stuff up with a spoon. We're just giving them what they want," Melinda chimed in while Gabriella sat taking it in with a queasy stomach.

"I'm not complaining," Oswood said holding his hands up, palms out in protest. "It was very well-done sleaze."

"Are you good with your interview for the noon show? How much do you have?" Eyler asked.

"A little over three minutes. It's an exclusive we can use all day," Oswood answered her. "I have a production meeting right after this. We can start running promos right away."

"Great. Melinda, I want you to use it on your show too," Eyler said.

"Robbie and I will go over the entire interview. We may use more than just the three minutes," Melinda said. "I'll promote it as our sense of journalistic integrity giving him a fair and balanced blah, blah, bullshit…"

"Good work everyone. I think we have a hit on our hands. Keep it up." With that, Eyler ended the meeting.

Marc spent the rest of the morning catching up on his pile of mail, reviewing a draft of a divorce settlement and another criminal matter for which he had a settlement conference to attend later in the week.

At eleven o'clock he called his lady friend, Margaret Tennant, and asked if she was free for lunch. Instead, Margaret asked him, "Is this true?"

"Is what true?"

"That you know where that little girl is? That Brittany Riley told you what she did?"

"First of all," an irritated Marc began to reply, "You're a judge, you should know better."

"I'm also human," she snapped back at him.

"And second," he continued ignoring her. "No, I don't know where she is! My client maintains her innocence. Look, I'll call later. I've got to go," and he hung up without waiting for a response.

Marc leaned back in his chair, folded his arms across his chest and stared at the wall for a full minute. He needed to talk to someone who could give him some advice. Someone who would give him sound, common sense, normal people counsel.

He reached for his phone, found the number he wanted in his phone log and pushed the speed dial button. After two rings he heard the rough, reassuring voice of a good friend.

"Hey counselor, how was Paris?" he heard Tony Carvelli ask.

"How about I take you to lunch and tell you all about it?" Marc answered.

"Usual place?"

"Usual place."

"You're buying?"

"I'm buying," Marc answered with a laugh.

"See you at noon," the retired Minneapolis cop turned private investigator replied.

TWENTY-THREE

Marc was at the restaurant before Tony and went ahead and got a booth for them. He was seated facing the door to watch for his friend and saw the P.I. come in a few minutes after the waitress brought Marc a soda. He waved at Tony who immediately saw him, and Marc watched as the man walked toward him.

Tony Carvelli was in his early fifties and due to his years on the streets of Minneapolis, looked it but could still make most women look him over. He had a touch of the bad boy image they couldn't resist plus a flat stomach and full head of thick black hair, touched with gray highlights; a genetic bequest from his Italian father.

Carvelli was an ex-Minneapolis detective and had the reputation of being a street predator which was well deserved. He looked and acted the part as well. Dressed in a tan suede jacket, black silk shirt, light gray slacks and Italian loafers, he could easily pass for a Mafia wiseguy. Growing up in Chicago, he knew a few of them and could have become one himself and very likely, a successful one. Instead, after his family moved to Minnesota, he became a cop.

"Hey, counselor," Tony said as he slid onto the bench seat opposite Marc and extended his hand for a shake. "How was Paris? Weren't you going to go to London too?"

"Yeah, we did. It was nice. Two great cities. Have you ever been?"

"No, neither one. I went to Italy with my parents when I was a kid. Rome was amazing. So what's up?"

"What can you tell me about the Dakota County Sheriff, Cale?"

At that moment, the waitress arrived. The two men gave her their orders and since they had eaten there many times neither of them bothered to look at the menu.

"I know of him a little," Tony said when the waitress left. "I met him once or twice. Why, what do you want to know?"

"You know about the missing kid? The little girl, Becky Riley?"

"Sure, I saw on TV last night you're representing the mother."

"Right now, she's only charged with child neglect, but the sheriff's office is looking at her as suspect number one for the disappearance," Marc said.

"You think the kid's still alive?"

"I don't know. Probably not," Marc said a bit sadly. "What I want to know is: how far will Cale go to get a conviction? I know the County Attorney, LeAnne Miller. She's always seemed pretty straight, but Cale, I don't know."

"Will he manufacture evidence? I doubt it," Tony said. "But I don't know him that well. I've never heard of anything like that about him.

Most cops will stretch the truth a bit to convict someone they know is guilty. If you're wondering if he would do something like Jake Waschke, I doubt it but I couldn't say for sure. I wouldn't have thought that of Jake either."

"What about using the media?" Marc asked.

Their lunches arrived before Tony could answer. He waited for the server to set their meals in place then said, "Every police department in America will use the media. You leak information to them that you want publicized. Some true, some not so true. It's done all the time. We, I mean cops, all have media sources. Some of the guys even pick up a few bucks tipping off reporters."

"You?"

"Sure. I had a couple guys would flip me fifty or a hundred for a juicy tidbit. Why not?"

"Because it's morally, ethically and probably legally wrong. Or at least questionable," Marc replied.

"Give me a break. You're a big boy. You've had cases that got a lot of publicity. You know the deal," Tony said.

"Yeah, but this is different. She's being tried and convicted before being charged. I know damn well it's coming from Cale and probably the county attorney's office. I just wanted your take on it. You know anybody I can talk to about Cale?"

"As I recall, he's not from the Cities. He's from Duluth or Rochester. I can't remember which. I'll check around and see what I can find out and let you know."

The two men spent the rest of their lunchtime chatting about another case Marc had tried. Tony was still a bit involved with the extremely wealthy matriarch of a well-known local family. He had met her doing some investigation for her that became connected to Marc's trial. A romantic spark ignited between them and Tony was still seeing her. After the small talk petered out, Marc picked up the check and they parted in the parking lot.

Marc arrived back at his office and decided to set up a press conference for that afternoon to tell his and Brittany's side of the story. There is a local community center about a mile from his office. Marc knew the director; an ex-con Marc had represented whom Marc called. He gladly allowed Marc the use of the gymnasium for his event. Marc then called Brittany to explain to her what he was up to and as the client, get her permission. She offered to attend but Marc emphatically told her not to and again warned her not to talk to anyone. It was at that point Barbara took the phone from her daughter and listened while Marc told her what he was up to.

111

"Do you want me there?" Barbara asked. "I'd like to be," she quickly added.

Marc thought it over for a few seconds then said, "Okay. I guess it might not be a bad idea for someone to be there from the family. I'll schedule it for three o'clock." He told her where it was and gave her directions to the community center then said, "Be a little early."

He disconnected with Barbara and called back all of the media people who had called for him that day. He explained to them his plan for a news conference and gave them the information.

At 2:45, while the small crowd of journalists began setting up in the gym, Marc met with Barbara Riley. They discussed what they were going to say and agreed Marc would take most of the questions. The two of them were using the center's director's office and Marc was a little fidgety.

"Are you okay?" Barbara asked.

"I'm a little nervous," Marc admitted. "Don't ever believe these people are your friends, they're not. They'd like nothing better than to have one of us say something that they could use to sensationalize the story. Blow up what you said and take it out of context. Being a little nervous is a good thing. It will keep me on edge."

Marc started the press conference right on time by making a statement he had prepared ahead of time. He denied any knowledge of Becky Riley's whereabouts, re-stated Brittany's innocence and slammed Melinda Pace for waiting until he left the building to tape the ending to her interview of him. When he did this, Robbie Nelson, who had entered the room shortly after the event began, had to suppress a smile. He had taken a seat close to Gabriella and the station's cameraman who were here to cover it for the news department. Robbie prayed the other stations would use the remarks about Melinda's ethical shortcomings as a lead for their story. That kind of publicity would cause another jump in viewers to Melinda's show and make her very happy indeed.

Barbara took a turn at the podium and did an excellent job. She made it clear that the family was one hundred percent behind Brittany and their efforts to locate her missing granddaughter would continue. Barbara listed several more searches that were planned over the next few weeks and made a plea for more volunteers. At the end, she announced that a reward of fifty thousand dollars for information that led to Becky's discovery had been established.

The reporters took turns asking questions, mostly of Marc. None of them elicited any new information and by 3:45 the press conference was over. Marc was at least hopeful that he had set the record straight regarding his knowledge of Becky's whereabouts. All he could do was get in front of the cameras and say it. He couldn't make them use it in their news shows.

The evening news for all channels that night had a brief story about the press conference. They did report Marc's denial but most of the emphasis was on the reward being offered. In the next day's morning papers, unlike the original story which was on the front page, the denial was on page three of the Metro section.

When Marc returned to his office after the press conference, he was feeling a little guilty about his phone call to Margaret. He dialed the private line to her chambers and she answered after the fifth ring. He apologized to her for hanging up on her, but she sounded a little distant. When he asked to see her for dinner she hesitated before responding.

"Marc, um, look. I've been thinking these past couple of days and I think we need to take a break. I just think we could both use a little time out to think about where we are, what we want and where we're going."

"Oh, um, sure," a stunned Marc stammered. "I see that, so okay. I'll talk to you later," and he hung up the phone without waiting for a reply.

TWENTY-FOUR

"Your Honor," Marc began with more than a touch of annoyance in his voice, "I've been trying to get the prosecution to send my discovery request for three weeks. She just handed it to me today when I got here."

Marc was in the judge's chambers with the prosecutor who had been assigned Brittany's child neglect case. Along with the lawyers, Brittany and the judge, was a court reporter to make a record of the hearing. They were conducting the required omnibus hearing and since there were no witnesses giving testimony, the judge, James Connors, decided to do it informally in chambers. The hearing itself amounted to little more than the judge making a record of the charges and having Brittany enter a plea again.

"What about that?" the judge asked the prosecutor, Marcia Lindquist.

"I was assigned the case yesterday, your Honor," she said. "It was with Bob Swanson but he's out sick so..."

"How convenient," Marc said.

"What does that mean?" Lindquist asked indignantly.

"It means, your Honor," Marc said to the judge, "she's now the fourth lawyer in that office to have a hand in this case. Obviously, they're passing it around to avoid responding to my discovery requests! Plus, I've been seeing things on the news, such as witness statements being reported that I have not received. Things are being leaked to the media before they're given to me."

"What about that, Ms. Lindquist?" Connors asked the prosecutor.

"I have no knowledge of that and resent the implication!" she angrily replied.

"Okay, put a stop to it, both of you," the judge said. "Are you satisfied you have everything?" he asked Marc.

"No, I'm not. The night my client was arrested she was interrogated for five hours, from 1:00 A.M, until 6:00. I want a copy of the video of that interrogation."

"The sheriff's office denies that, your Honor..." Lindquist started to say.

"That's a lie!" Brittany said almost jumping out of her chair next to Marc. "I was there..."

The judge held up a hand to her to get her to stop and Marc gently placed a hand on her shoulder.

"Let your lawyer speak for you," Judge Connors politely admonished. "Remember, if you blurt out something you shouldn't," he continued, "It could be used against you."

114

"Yes, sir, sorry," Brittany meekly replied. She looked at Marc who gave her a reassuring smile.

"As I was saying," Lindquist continued. "The sheriff's investigators read Miranda to her and she signed the form agreeing they read her rights to her. Then they questioned her for, according to them, maybe half an hour."

"Where's the video?" Marc asked.

"They didn't make one," Lindquist replied. "This wasn't a drunk driving case. They saw no reason to make a video."

The judge stared directly at her for almost fifteen seconds to show his displeasure, and then said, "I'm ready to rule. I find there is sufficient probable cause, on the face of the complaint to deny your motion to dismiss, Mr. Kadella. I will reserve ruling on evidentiary admissibility until the defense has had sufficient time to investigate the discovery material he was just given. As to any statements the defendant may have made during the night of her arrest, I am ruling them inadmissible. Now, a trial date," he said.

"My client refuses to waive her right to a speedy trial," Marc said. "Plus, at the initial appearance, we requested a trial date which, by rule, must be set within sixty days of that date."

"Unless the court finds good cause for a later date," the judge said.

"Yes, your Honor. I'll settle for sixty days from today. There's no reason to drag this out longer than that," Marc replied.

"Your Honor. There's still a missing little girl out there and we anticipate more charges," Lindquist said.

"We'll cross that bridge when we come to it," The judge replied. "Okay, it's now September twenty-third." He looked at the calendar on his desk then said, "How's November tenth sound?"

The two lawyers checked their pocket calendars, and both indicated this date would do.

"How long?" he asked them.

"I'll want at least two days for rebuttal witnesses to testify that she is not a neglectful mother," Marc said.

"Marcia?" the judge asked.

"This case speaks for itself, your Honor. We'll only need a couple days," she replied.

"Okay, we'll pencil it in for the entire week." He then looked at the stenographer and told her he wanted to go off the record.

"Marcia, what about a deal? I don't see me giving her any more jail time based on what I've seen so far."

"I'll check with my boss," she said.

That evening on the newscast of one of the local stations, the afternoon's hearing was reported. Even though it was not held out in the courtroom, the reporter had a fairly accurate description of what occurred. It was the only station to mention it and the reporter claimed Brittany was said to have been bored with the whole thing. The anchor stated Brittany acted as if she didn't have a care in the world and even seemed to be a little annoyed to be there. Marc didn't see the newscast himself but was told about it the next day by Sandy, one of the office assistants. Knowing he didn't talk to a reporter and it was safe to assume the judge and court reporter didn't, the list of suspects who leaked this information was quite small.

TWENTY-FIVE

Sheriff Cale, in civilian clothes, along with Paul Anderson, Stu Doyle and two uniformed deputies, stood just outside the yellow crime tape. The five of them were patiently watching three members of the county crime scene unit go over every square inch of grounds where the small skeleton was found. The three of them, two men and a woman were carefully looking for any possible piece of evidence. One of the men moved slowly behind the other two people and videotaped their search.

Cale turned away from the scene and walked back toward the parking lot. There was a crowd of gawkers gathering and several members of the press were present and filming. Cale ignored them and sought out Shannon Keenan. Shannon was seated on the tailgate of a pickup truck next to the young boy who had discovered the remains.

"How's he doing?" Cale softly asked looking first at Shannon and then the boy's dad. Jackson was seated between them solemnly looking down at the gravel-covered parking area. Shannon wiggled her hand back and forth several times to indicate he was so-so. To that, Cale indicated with his eyes he wanted a private word with Shannon.

"Seriously, how's the kid?" Cale asked as they stepped away from the truck and out of earshot.

"He'll need some counseling," she said. "That's not a pleasant thing for anyone to find, let alone a ten-year-old."

"Did you and Kristin get statements from everyone?" Cale asked.

"Yeah, but we didn't get much. Not much to get. They were out on the peninsula," she said pointing to where they were hunting. "The kid went to pee and saw something in the water. He waded out and found her. At least, we think it's her. He ran back scared to death and got his dad. The father went into the weeds, saw the remains and they called it in. Can we let them go?"

"Yeah, do that. But I want a word with the father first."

Cale went back to the truck and took Eric Carson aside. They stepped away from the truck and Cale asked, "How's he doing?"

"He was pretty scared. Upset. But he's a tough kid," Eric replied.

"How about you?" Cale asked.

"I don't know. I'm okay, I guess. Though I didn't need to see that," Eric said. "It's awful."

"Some counseling will help, especially for Jackson. Probably wouldn't hurt you either. Listen," he continued. "This may not be appropriate, but I'll tell you anyway. If that is who we think it is…"

"That missing little girl, Becky?" Eric said.

"Yeah. If it is, there's a reward for it…"

"I don't know. I doubt we'll want a reward. That's a little too…"

117

"If it is, use the money. It's fifty grand. Pay for his counseling, college, whatever."

"We'll see," Eric said.

"You don't have to decide anything right this minute. Go on home, we'll be in touch," Cale said extending his hand.

Cale turned back toward the crime scene area and rejoined his deputies. The crime scene people had finished and a couple of people from the medical examiner's office were in the water. They drove a six-foot metal pole into the river bottom to mark the location of where the body was found. The tiny skeleton had a piece of clothesline attached to the left ankle. One of the men carefully held the remains while the other one cut the clothesline a couple of inches from the little ankle bone. The two of them placed the skeleton in a small body bag, closed it and the man who had been holding the skeleton brought it out and placed the bag on a gurney.

While he was doing this, his partner was lifting a cinder block out of the water to which the clothesline had been attached. All of this had been filmed by the crime scene crew and by several media cameras. The media camera operators were standing on the roofs of their vans using long-range lenses to get very clear images of the tiny body being removed from the river.

While the gurney with the small black body bag was being wheeled toward the parking lot, Cale walked over to where the media was waiting. Before he could get within fifteen feet of them, the questions were already being shouted at him. Cale stopped at the rope line and held up both hands indicating a request for quiet. When the reporters settled down, Cale cleared his throat and began.

"I have a brief statement to make and then I'll take a few questions. A young boy who was with his dad and several other men duck hunting on the river discovered the skeletal remains of what we believe is a very young girl. She was attached by a rope to a cinder block and left in the water. By the shape of the skeleton, we're certain it was a girl. At this time, that's about all we know for sure."

Immediately several voices practically shouted out the question they all wanted answered: "Is it Becky Riley?"

Cale hesitated for a moment, not sure if he should answer at all and said, "I can only speculate but I do believe it is most likely her. We'll know for sure in a few days."

He felt his phone vibrate in the back pocket of his jeans and while other questions were being hurled at him, he looked to see who it was. When he saw the caller I.D. displayed, he held up his left hand and said, "That's all I have. Now you'll have to excuse me. I need to take this call." With that, he turned and walked away.

"I just got your message," Cale heard LeAnne Miller say. "What do you have?"

Cale quickly told her the details of the finding and the condition of the body.

"Do you think it's her? Becky Riley?" Miller said.

"I can't say positively but according to the M.E.'s guys, the size of the skeleton is right and there were a few strands of blonde hair attached to the skull."

"How horrible. That poor little girl. It breaks my heart," she said with a heavy sigh. "Okay, now what?"

"We need a search warrant. Make it cover Brittany's apartment, car, her parent's house and their cars," Cale said. "Do we have enough to get one?"

"We may have to wait until we get a positive ID on the remains," Miller said.

"That's going to take some time to do a DNA comparison. We need to move now," Cale replied.

"I'll go into the office now and draft it myself. I'll call Judge Stinson and see if she'll sign it for us," Miller told him.

"Good, let me know right away. I'd like to execute it today. They're going to find out about this and we want to do the search before they can remove anything they haven't already."

"You keep saying 'they'. Do you think the parents are in on this?"

Cale thought about that for a few seconds, then said, "No, probably not. But who knows at this point?"

"I'll call when I have the warrant. Where will you be?" Miller asked.

"I'll be back at my office organizing the search warrant search teams. We're pretty much done here."

Cale disconnected the call and took a few minutes to talk to the crime scene investigators. Except for the remains and a few scraps of cloth, there wasn't much left. He then decided some more positive news coverage would not be a bad thing so, he let the press roam around the crime scene filming and destroying any evidence that might be still there.

Miller called Cale a couple of hours later with the news that the warrant would have to wait until they were certain the remains were Becky Riley. Cale assured her he would get right on it and asked her to use her political connections, if need be, to make the DNA results a top priority from the state's crime lab.

While Cale and Miller were discussing obtaining a search warrant, the Rileys, with Brittany in the back seat, were driving down the street where their house was located. The three of them stared through the windows, surprised at how much the crowd had grown. They were getting used to seeing four or five TV vans lined up on the street but not this many people. There were at least another fifty, none of whom appeared to be with the reporters. Many of them were carrying signs and marching up and down in front of the Rileys' house.

Just before Floyd turned into the driveway, ten or twelve news people, reporters and cameramen, rushed in front of their car and blocked it off. Floyd quickly opened his window and angrily yelled at them to get out of the way. Instead, one of the women reporters from a local station stuck her head in Floyd's window and shoved her microphone at Brittany who was seated directly behind her dad.

While her cameraman filmed through Brittany's closed window, the female reporter said, "How do you feel about the news that the police have found your daughter's body?"

Of course, Brittany had not heard a word about this and she was stunned, her mind could not even compute what she had just heard. Instead of responding, she simply stared forward at the back of her father's head.

Seeing the Rileys' car, several of the protestors broke ranks and began running toward it. Barbara, realizing what was taking place, pushed the button for the garage door opener and yelled at Floyd to get going. Floyd hit the gas and the people in front of the car scattered as Floyd blew by them and into the garage. He slammed on the brakes, jumped from the car and grabbed an aluminum softball bat leaning against the wall. While Barbara and Brittany scrambled into the house, Floyd ran down the driveway waving the bat, shouting obscenities and chased the crowd back into the street.

Every local TV station in the state and virtually all of the national television newscasts led their evening news with the story of Becky Riley's remains being found. Not a single one of the reports even mentioned that a positive identification had not been made. They all simply stated that "it had been reported that the remains of the missing girl, Becky Riley, have been found." The envy of all of them was the woman who "scooped" them by getting a mic inside the Rileys' car while Brittany was being filmed. The reporter, a very attractive, fair-skinned Latina woman named Candida Morales, appeared live, on camera with the station's blonde-haired, blue-eyed anchorwoman. The two of them made a stunning pair.

"What was your impression of how Brittany took the news?" the anchor asked Candida.

"Oh, obviously she couldn't have cared less. Just look at the film. She barely even blinks or reacts in any way."

"Did she ask anything, such as where was her daughter found or who or how, anything at all?"

"No, nothing. In fact, the way she looked makes me think that she knew where the body was," Candida said.

"That's quite an allegation," the anchor said in mock surprise even though the two of them had rehearsed this.

"Well, just look at her reaction. She could not be more uninterested."

At seven o'clock, Bob Olson shut off his television set. He had been captivated by it since 5:00 when he watched the late afternoon local newscasts. The story had jumped off the screen and slapped him in the face when he saw the images of the body being removed from the water. A momentary feeling of fear gripped him at the thought they somehow knew and were coming for him. He quickly calmed down with the realization that if that was true, he'd be in custody by now.

Olson had been glued to the screen for two hours, first switching back and forth watching the five o'clock local reporters. Then he did the same thing at 5:30 to check out the broadcast networks evening news, all of which had film of the tiny body being recovered. At 6:00 he went back to the local news and then, until 7:00, the main cable networks. All of them gave the story significant airtime which left Bob with a fuzzy feeling, a glow that he couldn't define.

At 7:00, it was time to get ready for his date. It was with a pretty girl but no child. *Too bad*, he thought. Then again, he couldn't do another one for a while. Not until Brittany was locked up and even then, possibly not another one locally.

121

TWENTY-SIX

"Hello, Mrs. Riley," Shannon Keenan said when Barbara opened their front door. "May we come in for a minute, please?"

"Why?" Barbara asked. "Did you hear what those despicable people did?" she said indicating the press and protestors.

"Yes, we did, and I am truly sorry that Brittany and the rest of you found out what was discovered today in this way. That's why Sheriff Cale sent the two deputies here, to keep the crowd under control and off your property. But we need to see Brittany. We need to get a DNA sample."

"If I say no?" Barbara replied.

"Who is it, Mom?" Shannon heard Brittany say.

"We'll get a court order," Shannon politely replied. "Please don't make us do that."

"Let them in, Mom. I'll call Mr. Kadella and see what he says," Brittany said.

While Shannon and the woman who was with her took their seats in the living room, Brittany could be heard on her phone in the kitchen. Barbara apologized for being rude, which Shannon brushed off while they waited. A couple of minutes went by in awkward silence between the three women in the living room.

"He wants to talk to you," Brittany said to Shannon as she handed her phone to the detective.

Shannon said hello and Marc introduced himself, then said, "You're there to get a DNA swab?"

"That's correct," Shannon answered.

"Okay," Marc said. "I'm okay with that since I know you can get it. But absolutely no questions or conversations with Brittany or anyone else that are not directly related to the DNA swab and only for identification purposes or to help identify the remains."

"Understood," Shannon said. "That's why we're here."

Shannon introduced the woman who came with her to Brittany. Her name was Courtney and she was with the crime scene unit.

"I just need a small sample of saliva," Courtney told Brittany as she held up what looked like a long Q-tip. She swabbed the inside of Brittany's cheek with two of the swab devices, placed them in sealed containers and the women left.

The samples taken from Brittany and samples from the remains found in the river were rushed to the Bureau of Criminal Apprehension, the State of Minnesota's crime investigation agency. Sheriff Cale had no problem getting their lab to make the testing a priority. Three days later, the results were in. It was a ninety-nine-point eight percent match that the skeleton was Becky Ann Riley. The results were emailed, faxed and sent by messenger to Sheriff Cale's office early Tuesday morning. By ten o'clock, Channel 8 was airing an on-site report by Gabriella Shriqui from the Dakota County Government Center. By 10:15 A.M, every TV and radio station in the Upper Midwest was reporting the results. Because he was working in his office with no television or radio on, Marc Kadella didn't find out the results until several hours later. As the lawyer for the mother, Brittany, he should have been the first one called. The sheriff's office was a little busy and Cale had consciously decided not to call the defense lawyer.

Cale entered the crowded conference room down the hall from his office. As soon as he did, people waiting for him quickly quieted down. Cale stood behind the chair at the head of the table and looked over the twelve deputies and investigators seated or standing along the back wall.

"All right, people. Does everybody know their assignment? Any questions?" he asked as he looked them over. "Is everything set?" he continued looking first at Paul Anderson and then Shannon Keenan who both nodded their heads to answer affirmatively. Anderson and Doyle would be doing the search at the Rileys' home and Keenan and Kristin Williams with two deputies would do Brittany's apartment even though it had been done twice already; once with Brittany's permission and once without at the time of her arrest.

"Okay, let's go," Cale said.

Twenty minutes later, Paul Anderson parked his unmarked sedan in the Rileys' driveway. Stu Doyle was in the passenger seat and as the two detectives got out of the car, a sheriff's squad car parked behind him. In it were four more deputies. Two of them went with Anderson and Doyle up to the front door. The other two walked across the front yard to join the two men Cale had already assigned for crowd control.

Cale pulled up and parked his personal squad car on the street blocking the Rileys' driveway. Before he could exit the car, the TV reporters and their camera operators began to scurry over to him. The four deputies immediately jogged into place to block them from their boss, but Cale waved them away. He had deliberately worn his best, freshly laundered and pressed uniform and hat to make a good impression for film. Before they could get within ten feet of him, the questions had already started to fly.

Cale held up his hands to quiet them and said, "As you probably know, Becky Riley's remains have been positively identified. We are here to execute a search warrant to look for evidence to help us in our investigation. At this point, that's all I have to say. Thank you."

While the sheriff was making his statement to the media, Paul Anderson, Doyle and the two deputies had muscled their way past Barbara. As they entered the Riley house, Anderson handed a copy of the warrant to a steaming mad Barbara. Brittany and Floyd entered the living room as the other three scattered to begin the search. Anderson politely explained to them to please not interfere. An obviously stunned and shaken Brittany asked if she could call her lawyer, which she did. Marc took her call and told her he would be there as soon as he could.

A few minutes after the search began, a car pulled up and a pair of crime scene technicians got out to search the Rileys' cars. While they were doing that, the four-man team went through the house and garage. Paul Anderson was in the den going through papers when one of the deputies came in and said, "There's something in the garage you need to see."

Instead of replying, Anderson ignored the man for a moment and continued to read the document he was holding. "Jesus Christ," Anderson softly said. He folded the papers, placed them in a plastic evidence bag and then followed the deputy through the kitchen into the garage.

"Check this out," the deputy said. He leaned down to look under a shelf that had been built along the back of the garage on which was the usual garage detritus. Under the shelf were six cinder blocks, all of which appeared to be the same size as the one pulled from the river; the one Becky had been tied to.

"And," he continued, "check this out," he said pointing at an item on the shelf above the bricks.

Anderson leaned over to look at the item in the back of the shelf at which the deputy was pointing. Neatly coiled was a length of clothesline rope that, on first inspection, looked like the same rope used to tie Becky to the cinder block.

"Okay, let's get some pictures," Anderson said. He caught the attention of the tech who was working on Floyd's car. The woman took a dozen photos of the cinder blocks and rope. When she finished, the rope was tagged and bagged and the deputy began loading the blocks in the back of his car.

Cale entered the garage and Anderson told him about the bricks and rope. He also held up the bag with the document in it and quietly said, "This may be the smoking gun. It's an insurance policy on Becky Riley in the amount of a half a million bucks."

"And Brittany's the beneficiary," Cale said.

"You got it."

Cale turned his head when he heard the voice of the second CSU Tech speak his name. The man walked up holding another evidence bag and said, "We found several blonde hairs in Brittany's trunk."

"Could they be Brittany's?" Anderson asked.

"Can't tell for sure till we can do a lab check, but I don't think so. These are too blonde and too short," the tech said.

"Sheriff Cale?" a man's voice asked.

"That's me," Cale answered as the three of them turned to look at the man in a suit enter the garage.

The man walked up to Cale, extending his right hand and said, "I'm Marc Kadella, Brittany's lawyer."

Cale shook his hand and introduced the two men with him.

"Could I get a copy of the search warrant?" Marc asked.

"We gave one to your client, actually her mother, and the homeowner. Sorry, but we didn't bring one for you. We'll get you one though," Anderson responded.

"Okay," Marc said. "Now, I'll try to be polite about this, but you knew she was represented. I should have been called."

"We're under no legal obligation..." Cale started to say.

"I know," Marc stopped him. "No one talks to my client without me being present and..."

"I'm glad you're here," Cale said. "We were just about to arrest your client on suspicion of murdering her daughter. You can witness us reading her Miranda rights. Go get her," Cale said to Anderson.

Marc did his best to shield her from the cameras and the crowd as she was being led to one of the squad cars. It didn't help much. The film of the pretty, blue-eyed, blonde, All-American girl, her hands cuffed behind her back would be shown nationwide on every national newscast that day. But not before Melinda Pace got a crack at her on her show that same afternoon.

125

TWENTY-SEVEN

Robbie Nelson filled Melinda's wine glass half-full, set the bottle on the table and chastised her for her drinking. Despite feeling a little guilty because she knew he was right, she still brushed him off with a casual hand wave.

"Why do we need to edit any of it?" Robbie asked. "It's not that long and it's great stuff. The audience will eat it up."

The two of them, along with Cordelia Davis were watching the film of the events at the Riley residence. Robbie looked at the clock, saw that it was almost 2:00 and realized if they were going to tape the show, they had to get started soon.

"I agree," Cordelia said. "Are we going live today just in case we get some last-minute information?"

"I was just thinking," Melinda said, "I want a lawyer on screen, a talking head to give an opinion. Who do we have?" she asked looking at Robbie.

"I can probably get someone," Robbie answered. "We'll have to offer more money than usual. Can I go up to a thousand dollars?"

"Sure," Melinda answered. "Get a prominent defense lawyer. Too bad Bruce Dolan's dead. He was always great. Good looking and smart."

"And corrupt as hell," Robbie reminded her.

"So what? Anyway, find someone good."

"I'll get on it. What about the film?" Robbie asked.

"We'll use all of it. First, we'll show the sheriff's statement to the media when he got there. I'll talk about how I predicted she was a suspect. Get something typed up Cordelia," Melinda said.

"No problem," Cordelia replied.

"Then we'll use the arrest film, which is just great stuff. Then I'll talk some more about that and drop the bomb on them about the life insurance policy. I want to end that with 'she killed her baby for money'. Cordelia, type it up. Let me see it and then we'll get it on the prompter. After that, we'll go to commercial and come back with the lawyer, he or she. In fact, a woman might be good," Melinda said going off track a bit. "That one we had during Prentiss' trial would be good. What's her name?"

"Andrea Briscomb," Robbie said, knowing the main reason Melinda wanted her was because she was fairly good looking but not better than Melinda in makeup, so she wouldn't show up Melinda.

"That's right," Melinda said, snapping her fingers in recognition. "Anyway, after the first break, we'll just have a conversation with her about the case. No big deal. Then we'll go to break and wrap with our dumbest criminals."

126

"So, we're going live?" Robbie asked.

"Unless you can get the lawyer here by three," Melinda said. "Don't worry, it'll be fine."

Robbie stood up, picked up the bottle of wine, replaced the cork and said, "In that case no more of this."

The four o'clock show went so well that the station decided to preempt the show that normally aired right after the six o'clock news to rerun Melinda's show.

As she had outlined it at the meeting, they started off with Sheriff Cale's statement in front of the Rileys' house. The station cameraman had positioned himself to have both Cale in the foreground and the deputies at the door. It was obvious even from a distance that Barbara Riley was vigorously arguing with the men trying to get in.

When the film of Cale's statement finished running, Melinda solemnly looked into the camera and all but claimed credit for making Brittany the prime suspect.

"I suppose they had to wait to see if a body turned up," Melinda said as the background screen on the set behind her changed to an adorable picture of Becky Riley. Melinda turned her head to look at the little girl, looked back at the camera, stifled a sob and said, "She killed her beautiful little girl for money. I'm, ah, really sorry, but I need a break. We'll be right back," she said as she dabbed her eyes with a Kleenex.

"How was that?" she asked with a smile as the entire crew broke into applause.

Cordelia led the lawyer, Andrea Briscomb, onto the set. She shook hands with Melinda and took the empty chair. They were using the set with the anchor desk and not the more casual setting with two chairs and a table. Melinda preferred the anchor desk. It made her look more dignified and she believed gave the show a more professional appearance.

The set director cued Melinda when they came back from their commercial break. Melinda, with a weak, sad, smile, looked at the camera and said, "I'm sorry about getting emotional. I take pride in my professionalism but sometimes these things just get to you a little bit."

She introduced her guest and the two of them had an exchange about the evidence against Brittany.

"A good strong circumstantial case can be more difficult to defend than eyewitness cases," Briscomb said.

"Why is that?" Melinda asked.

"Eyewitness testimony can be very unreliable. If five people witness the same event, you can very easily get five accounts that differ enough to create reasonable doubt. But evidence such as her not

127

notifying the police that her child was missing is going to be difficult to explain," Briscomb said.

"And the same kind of rope that was used to tie Becky to the cinder block and the same type of cinder blocks were found in her parent's garage won't help her case either," Melinda added.

"Exactly, that type of circumstantial evidence can be very persuasive," Briscomb agreed. "Then there's the life insurance policy. Five hundred thousand dollars can be a huge motive."

The two women spent a few more minutes discussing the court process and procedures. When they finished, there was another two-minute commercial.

"Hey," Melinda said to her guest after the break began. "You did really well. I'll want to use you some more on this thing. You interested?"

"Absolutely," Briscomb replied as the two women shook hands. "Try to give me a little more notice but I'll do what I can to keep myself available."

After Briscomb was escorted out, Melinda wrapped up the day's telecast with her dumbest criminals segment. It was about a Florida man named Dan Springer who pleaded guilty to breaking and entering. In an attempt to burglarize a home, he entered through the roof but became trapped, upside down, in the bathroom. The would-be burglar tried to retrieve his phone from his pocket to call for help but it slipped out of his hand and landed in the toilet. Unable to extricate himself, he remained hanging upside down for an hour until the homeowner found him and called the police.

"I always like to add a little humor to the show, folks," Melinda said. "Thank you and tune in tomorrow."

Marc Kadella had spent several hours at the Dakota County jail, court and sheriff's office, basically accomplishing nothing. Brittany would be brought to court the next day at 1:00 P.M. for her first appearance. He hoped some kind of reasonable bail would be set and had discussed this with Barbara and Floyd. As he was leaving the government center to go back to his office, Marc had to wade through a small herd of media types, a couple of them even followed him to his car.

Arriving back at his office, he turned left off Lake Street onto Charles to put his car in the lot behind his building. As he did this, the first thing he saw were the twenty or so protestors, back again marching up and down along the sidewalk next to his building. Marc parked and before the protestors saw him, he ran through the back door and up the stairs taking them two at a time to the second floor. When he reached the top of the stairs, he had to stop and lean over at the waist, huffing and puffing to catch his breath. "I have to get back in better shape," he said aloud to himself. "When this is over I have got to get back into the gym."

When he entered the office, he found everyone staring at the television. They were all watching Melinda Pace's show. "Don't any of those people out there have jobs?" Marc said referring to the protestors down on the street.

"We were going to get a bucket and dump water on them," Sandy answered without taking her eyes off of the TV screen.

"Mother Nature's going to do it for us," Connie Mickelson said. "There's a big storm coming through."

"What are you watching?" Marc asked as he set his briefcase on the floor and dropped his suit coat over it. No one bothered to answer him as Barry Cline and Carolyn stepped aside so he could see it.

"I thought so," Marc said.

"You looked good trying to shield Brittany from the cameras," Carolyn said.

"They showed that? Was I able to shield her?"

"Yes and no," Carolyn answered. "Yes, they showed it and no you didn't shield her."

At that moment, Melinda looked at the camera and delivered the news about the life insurance policy.

"Is that true?" Connie asked Marc.

"Damned if I know," Marc said. "Probably. She seems to be better informed than I am, which is really starting to piss me off."

The small group watched the interview with the woman lawyer and by the time it was over, Marc was steaming mad.

"I'm going to call LeAnne Miller and find out what the hell's going on here," he said as he angrily retrieved his coat and briefcase and stomped off toward his office.

While everyone else stood passively watching him, knowing he had every right to be outraged, Connie went after him. She closed the door of Marc's office as he was picking up the phone to make the call to the county attorney's office.

"Don't do it," Connie said as she gently closed the door behind her. "I know you're pissed but calm down before you make the call. You won't do your client any good by getting into a screaming match with the county attorney. They hold too many cards. They have much more clout than you do. It's better for Brittany to keep things as calm as possible, at least for now."

Marc stared silently at her as he stood behind his desk. Connie sat down in one of the client chairs and waited for him. After a moment, he heavily sighed and replaced the phone.

"I'm already sick to death of finding these things out on TV," Marc said as he sat down in his chair. "It's bullshit. I'm learning about things on TV that I should be given before the media."

"I know," Connie replied. "And you have every right to be mad. I would be too. But…"

"You know what's really frying my ass? This is just the beginning. They'll be at this for months. And on top of it, the media has already convicted her," Marc said.

TWENTY-EIGHT

Gabriella Shriqui woke up at precisely 6:00 A.M, wide awake, flat on her back staring at the ceiling. Brittany Riley had been arrested the day before and it was Gabriella, through Stu Doyle, who obtained the information about the evidence found at the Rileys' home that was used in the station's news broadcasts. Gabriella had appeared live on the 5:00, 6:00 and ten o'clock reports and when she left the station she was almost floating. Not only had she scooped every local station and newspaper in the Upper Midwest, but the story had gone national. Gabriella was scheduled to give a live report for the network noon news show today. She was looking forward to it and an appearance like that wouldn't hurt her career.

She thought about how well everything was going, how well she was handling the story and how effusive just about everyone had been in their praise. Then why, she wondered, was she lying in bed at 6:00 A.M, staring at the ceiling? Something was nagging at her and even though she knew what it was, she tried her best to suppress it.

Gabriella lay like this for fifteen minutes trying to go back to sleep. Unable to do so, she glanced at the clock, threw the covers off, got up and went into the kitchen. She started the coffeemaker and by the time she was done in the bathroom, the coffee was just about ready.

She carried her coffee into the living room turned on the television then spent the next hour bouncing from one morning news show to another. First, she checked out the local shows, then the networks and finally the cable shows. Every one of them had at least a brief spot about the arrest. Although none of the people on any of the shows were as blatantly biased as Melinda Pace, virtually all of them walked right up to the line. It was obvious they believed Brittany was guilty.

Gabriella watched with a mixture of pride and uneasiness. The professional in her was warmly pleased because they all used a version, almost word for word, of the statement, "It has been reported that…" in reference to what they had to say. Gabriella knew that who and what they were referring to was her and the information she had obtained. The uneasiness came from the realization that this was common in the industry. If one reporter used something, reported some tidbit as fact whether it was or not, then it became fair game for others to report and no fact checking need be done. Little better than rumor reported and repeated as news.

"We just report the news," Gabriella said out loud as she pressed the button on the remote to shut off the TV. "It's up to the viewers to decide for themselves what to make of it."

A phone message marked 'urgent' was waiting for her when she arrived at the station. It was from the network news associate producer who had set up the report she was to give. Before she even sat down at her desk, Gabriella dialed the woman's number and plopped into her chair when it started to ring. She was worried she had been canceled and wanted to find out right away. "Hi, Patty," Gabriella said and then told the woman who was calling.

"I'm glad you called. Look, Hamas started shooting rockets into Israel again so, that's the main story right now."

"There wasn't anything about it in any of the morning shows," Gabriella said, worried she was being cut out completely.

"It just started up about a half hour ago. Anyway, we're going to tape you instead of doing it live. I'll still get you on, there's a lot of interest in your story. But we may need to edit it down a bit. Can you be ready in thirty minutes?"

"Sure, I wrote it up last night. I'm ready whenever you are," Gabriella said, obviously relieved.

"Great. I'll get back to you."

Gabriella had worn casual business clothes to work and carried her best dress in a garment bag. She went to makeup and in twenty minutes her hair was done, she was dressed, ready to go and looked fabulous. The taping took less than twenty minutes and Gabriella hoped they would use two minutes of it on their newscasts throughout the day. When she finished the taping and had changed out of the dress, she hurried to the office of her boss, Hunter Oswood. His door was open, and he waved her in as soon as she appeared in his doorway. She closed the door and took one of the chairs in front of his desk.

"What's up?" Oswood asked as he stopped what he was doing, leaned back in his chair and put his feet up on the open desk drawer he used for that purpose. Oswood truly liked Gabriella and not just for her physical attributes. He was just as warm-blooded as any man when it came to beautiful women, but he had grown to admire Gabriella for her commitment and professionalism. Plus, she was still young enough to not be reeking of cynicism.

"I was thinking I would like to be a little fairer to Brittany Riley. Melinda has pretty much found her guilty and what if she isn't? What if she didn't do this?"

"It's not our job to make that decision," Oswood said. "But go ahead. What did you have in mind?"

"I know her lawyer a little. I could do more to get him to talk to me," she replied.

"Go ahead," Osgood said with a shrug. "You don't need my permission. The arraignment is at one, I hear."

132

"I'm planning on going. Is anyone else?"

"Yeah, we'll send Harvey with a camera crew. You go too and see if you can get an interview with her lawyer, what's-his-name?"

"Kadella, Marc Kadella," she answered.

TWENTY-NINE

Marc leaned forward with his forearms resting on the windowsill behind his desk and slowly poked his head through the open window. A huge storm with window shaking thunder, crackling lightning and roaring winds rumbled through the city the day before dumping over an inch of rain on most of the metro area. It was the first rain the Cities received in more than a month and it cleaned the air, the streets and scattered the protesters alongside his building. It was now after 10:00 the next morning. The sun was shining, the air smelled fresh, the streets were not yet dry and fewer than half of the protestors were back on the sidewalk. While Marc watched them trudge up and down, he noticed their enthusiasm, as well as their numbers, was significantly reduced. The traffic going past was fairly busy for that time of day. Most of the drivers ignored them but a few honked and several others flipped off the protesters which brought Marc a flicker of a smile.

The intercom on his phone sounded and he swiveled around back to his desk to answer. It was Carolyn informing him that Madeline Rivers was returning his call.

After greetings, Madeline said, "I figured you'd be calling. I saw the arrest on TV. How is it the media just happens to be there every time something happens?" She asked.

"They're camped out at the Riley's, so they are always there. Are you busy today?"

"I can make time. Why?"

"Brittany's first appearance is at 1:00. I'd like you to come along and be there. Plus, it looks like we're going to have to find this Bob Olson guy. I think the cops are done looking for him," Marc said.

"What time?" Maddy asked.

"Is 11:30 okay? I'll buy you lunch and then we'll drive out together."

"Deal. See you then," she replied.

At 12:45, Marc held open the courtroom door allowing Maddy to enter ahead of him. There was barely an empty seat in the place, including the jury box which was filled with lawyers, most of whom did not have a case before the bench and were there out of curiosity. The only open place to sit was the table for the prosecutors and a couple of chairs along the rail.

Not everyone was in attendance to see the now notorious Brittany Riley. There were several other felony first appearances to be dealt with and several lawyers were there for those. Also, among the crowded gallery were friends and relatives of the various defendants, including

134

Barbara, Floyd and Tim Riley who had managed to get seats in the very front row.

As the two of them walked up toward the gate, a noticeable buzz swept through the crowd. Marc suppressed a smile while wondering if it was for the two of them or just Madeline. She always had that effect.

When they entered the courtroom, Gabriella Shriqui, who made sure she obtained an aisle seat, turned her head and saw them. She was seated on the left side of the courtroom in the second row and she waited until the stunning woman walked by then stood to intercept and talk to Marc.

"Hi, Marc," she said. "Can I talk to you for a minute?"

"Should I be mad at you?" Marc said. "That station you work for isn't doing me any favors."

"That's what I want to talk to you about."

Marc leaned forward and whispered in her ear. "I'll see you when we're done here." As he did so, he lingered a moment to take in the scent of her perfume. Madeline, who turned to watch, noticed it and was giving him an arched eyebrow look when he caught up with her.

"So, how'd she smell?" Maddy whispered to him.

"I don't know what you mean," Marc said with a smirk to which Madeline lightly laughed.

The court clerk was in her chair next to the bench and she gestured for Marc to approach her. When he did, Maddy stood behind looking over the crowd while Marc conversed with the clerk.

The woman leaned forward and quietly began by saying, "Judge Connors told me to keep one of the conference rooms available for you. Your client may even be in the hallway in back waiting by now. Why don't you and your assistant go in the first one," she said nodding toward a door along the wall by her chair. "I'll go see if she's back there and have her brought in."

"Okay, thanks," Marc quietly replied.

Marc and Madeline waited in the conference room for a deputy to bring in Brittany. They were seated in two of the four uncomfortable plastic chairs surrounding a small, round wooden table. Maddy sat patiently, her hands folded together in her lap. In contrast, Marc fidgeted like a kid waiting to see the principal. He smoothed his tie several times, swiveled his head looking over the small room and when he began drumming the fingers of his right hand on the table. The irritating finger drumming caused Maddy to reach over and take his hand in hers to stop it.

"Are you nervous?" she asked when he jerked his head toward her. She let go of his hand and he smiled.

"Yeah, I am. I always am before one of these things. I don't know why. It's not like I haven't done this before. I've just learned to accept it and go with it. Once things get started, I'll be fine. It's the waiting."

They turned their attention to the door when they heard a fairly loud knocking on it. Without waiting for a response, it opened, and a male deputy was standing there with Brittany. He followed her in and Marc gestured to the man to close the door behind him.

Brittany was dressed in an orange jumpsuit. There was a chain around her waist and her hands were shackled to it. Her ankles were locked together with a restraining chain that was barely twelve inches long which caused her to shuffle like an old man. Her hair was uncombed, she looked as if she had not slept well for several days and in general, she was basically a mess.

"You walked her through that courtroom looking like this?" Marc snarled at the deputy as he stood to pull out a chair for Brittany to sit down. She looked extremely relieved to see them.

"Hey, I just…" the deputy started to protest.

"Do you know there's a TV camera in the courtroom? Do you know how much media is sitting out there?" Marc said cutting him off.

"That's not my problem," the man answered.

"There's a door right there," Marc said pointing at the door to the hallway that he could have used to bring her in. "Take these things off of her, right now."

"I don't take orders from you," the deputy said uneasily.

Marc looked the man right in the eye and said, "I remember you. We went through this once before. Do we have to talk to the judge again?"

"Look," the deputy said holding up his hands, palms out with a worried expression on his face. "I got my orders direct from Sheriff Cale. He told me how to handle this. He said that she had to be shackled."

"Cale told you to do this?" Marc asked. "Cale himself specifically told you to do this? He said to shackle her and march her through that courtroom in front of the media?"

The deputy, realizing he was about to step in it no matter how he answered, nervously shifted his eyes around the room then quietly, almost in a whisper, said, "Yes."

Marc looked at Maddy and Brittany who had silently observed the exchange and said to them, "Wait here, I'll be right back. Let's go," he said to the guard as he pointed at the door.

The two men went into the courtroom and Marc was relieved to see that the judge was not on the bench yet. The prosecutor, the same one who had handled the child neglect hearing, had arrived. Marc walked over to her and whispered, "We need to see the judge."

136

"What about?" she asked.

"Give me a minute and I'll tell you." With that, he stepped to the rail and leaned over to speak to Barbara Riley.

Before he could say anything, Barbara said, "Why isn't she wearing the clothes I brought her last night?"

"You did bring her a change of clothes?" Marc asked.

"Yes."

"Okay, that's what I wanted to find out."

By now there was a discernable murmur rippling through the crowd as the reporters began to wonder what the problem was. Marc ignored them, spoke quickly to the prosecutor to tell her why he wanted to see the judge and the two of them, with the nervous deputy in tow, went back to Judge Connors' chambers.

Marc explained the situation to the judge and requested that the judge order the removal of the chains from Brittany. The judge promptly and with clear annoyance did so. The chastened deputy beat a hasty retreat back into the courtroom to wait for Marc.

"I can't tell Sheriff Cale how to run his jail," Connors said. "But I will make it clear that as long as she is in custody she is not to be shackled like that coming into court. I watch the news too, Ms. Lindquist," he said to the prosecutor, "and I am none too pleased with what I am seeing."

"Your Honor, we have no control over…"

"Yeah, yeah," Connors said holding up a hand to stop her. "You want a gag order?" he asked Marc.

"No, your Honor. That will only pertain to me. They'll ignore it and still leak whatever they want through the cops…" Marc replied.

"I resent that!" Lindquist exclaimed.

"I'm getting a little tired of getting my discovery requests while watching TV," Marc said.

"Your Honor, our office will comply in strict accordance with the rules of discovery and any court orders," Lindquist stiffly replied.

"That's big of you, Marcia," Connors said with mild sarcasm. "Okay, no gag order for now. I'll be out in a few minutes. Get your client ready, Marc. I'd like to take care of her case first. We're arguing bail today, right?"

"Yes, your Honor," the two lawyers replied.

"Is LeAnne taking this to a grand jury?" Connors asked Lindquist referring to the county attorney.

"Yes, your Honor. We'll be getting an indictment for first-degree murder," she answered.

Marc, standing between Brittany on his left and the prosecutor on his right, stood before the bench. Maddy had applied a little makeup to

137

Brittany to give her some color. Her hair was brushed out and the chains removed. Fortunately, the courtroom camera was not turned on until the judge came out of chambers. They waited silently while the judge went through the legal formalities. He read off the charges, repeated Brittany's rights to her and asked her to plead. When this was done, he allowed the lawyers some time to argue bail.

Lindquist argued for a total remand to custody without allowance for any bail. She tried to claim that the nature of the crime itself was sufficient to warrant this but it was a losing effort. Connors is well known as a pretty fair and impartial jurist and made the point of reminding her that bail is to be set unless the defendant is a flight risk or a danger to the community. Lindquist tried to argue that Brittany fit both conditions, but it was a weak argument and she knew it.

On the other hand, Marc tried to argue for a minimum bail. Marc's statements about the weakness of the prosecution's case; the nonexistent danger to the community if Brittany was released and a flight risk sounded much more realistic. "Where could she go?" he asked. "Her picture has been shown all across the nation."

Connors patiently waited for the lawyers to finish then abruptly set bail at two million dollars. It was obvious Connors had decided on the amount before he came out on the bench. He let the lawyers argue just so they could get their arguments on the record in case of an appeal.

THIRTY

"Two million?" Barbara despondently asked Marc, more a statement than a question. "We can't possibly come up with that."

After Brittany was ushered out of the courtroom, Marc, Madeline and the Rileys quickly exited to the hall. Before they could say a word, a stream of reporters came through the doors. Some were on their phones to call in the story and several others tried thrusting their microphones into Marc's face for a comment. Marc saw Gabriella Shriqui and remembered he had promised to talk to her. He was surrounded by other reporters and could only shrug his shoulders and indicate he would call her later. Maddy and the Rileys stood behind him as he calmly answered a couple of questions. One of the idiots actually asked if his client was ready to take a plea. Marc ignored the man and they all managed to leave and were now in a conference room at the jail waiting for Brittany to be brought down.

"Could they get a bond?" Madeline asked Marc.

"For that amount? Two million? I doubt it. It would cost at least two hundred thousand and a bail bondsman would want every bit of it collateralized," Marc replied.

"Would we get the two hundred thousand back? We could come up with that much," Barbara said.

"No," Marc answered. "That would be the fee for the bond."

They heard someone rap on the glass of the door. Marc looked up and saw that it was the sheriff himself. The sheriff opened the door and stepped inside to allow Brittany to enter the room. She was once again shackled at the waist and ankles and could only shuffle along while trying to walk. Cale asked Marc if he could talk to him for a minute. While her parents and brother greeted Brittany with teary-eyed hugs Marc followed Cale into the jail.

The two men went into another, smaller conference room where attorneys meet with their clients. Inside, standing around the table were three deputies. All of them were staring at Marc with blank but serious expressions on their faces and beefy arms folded across their chests.

Cale closed the door behind Marc, pulled a chair out from the table and sternly said, "Have a seat. We need to talk."

The instant Marc stepped inside and saw the deputies, he knew what was coming. Suppressing a smile, in fact almost laughing, he took the proffered chair and innocently looked at the sheriff.

Instead of sitting down himself, Cale placed both hands on the table, leaned down and glared at Marc for a long ten seconds. While he did this Marc continued to look back at him with a calm, innocent expression as if he did not have the slightest idea what was going on.

"I understand you have a problem with how I run my jail?" Cale calmly said while continuing to glare at Marc. "If I give one of my deputy's instructions on how to handle an inmate, you don't go running to a judge to complain about it. You come to me. Understood?" Cale continued to glare at Marc while Marc simply stared back at him without changing his expression or responding to his question.

"When I give one of my deputies an order, there is a reason for it and I don't need you or some judge to second-guess me," Cale continued his attempt to intimidate Marc.

With that Cale straightened up and began to reach for the door handle.

"Are you done?" Marc quietly asked.

"What?" Cale said.

"Are you done?" Marc repeated more slowly as if speaking to a child. "Can I say something now?"

"Sure, why not?" Cale said with a chuckle as the three deputies all broke into sneers.

"Have a seat," Marc said motioning at the chair across the small table. "First of all," he began as Cale sat down, "except as it relates to my client, I don't give a damn how you run your jail. Second, if I have a problem with how my client is being treated, I'll go to anyone I damn well please about it."

At this point, the smiles had vanished on the faces of the guards who all fidgeted slightly. Cale looked as if smoke was going to come out of his ears.

"Third," Marc continued holding up three fingers, "the next time you try to intimidate me, you better bring more than the three stooges with you. In fact, if you try it again, I'll have your ass before a judge so fast your feet won't touch the ground. And my client had better be treated with kid gloves while she's in here. From now on, she gets treated no differently than anyone else. When I come to see her, there had better not be any delays and she better not be shackled the way she is now. You get someone in there to take those things off. I know for a fact that prisoners are not shackled when they visit with their lawyers.

"Finally," Marc said leaning forward and staring directly at the sheriff, "as an experienced trial lawyer, something you should keep in mind. I know more ways, legally, to make your life a living hell than you can possibly imagine. Don't you ever pull a stunt like this again!"

With that, he stood up and knocked his chair over. Marc grabbed the door handle and flung it open so hard it banged against the wall and walked back steaming to where Brittany and the others were.

As Marc stomped off, Cale sat at the table strumming the fingers of his left hand almost boiling over at what had just happened. He looked

140

at the three deputies and calmly said, "Go back to your duties. And one of you go unlock prisoner Riley." The three of them quickly went around the opposite side of the table, the first one picked up Marc's chair, and they hurriedly left the room. Cale continued to sit in the room thinking about what happened and steaming over the impertinence of the lawyer.

When Marc returned to the client conference room, Maddy, seeing he was not happy asked, "What was that all about?"

Marc took a deep breath, sighed and said to her, "I'll tell you later. We need to talk about money," he said looking at Brittany. "This is going to get expensive."

At that moment one of the deputies came in and unlocked the restraints on Brittany.

"How much?" Barbara asked after the man left.

"How much do you think you can come up with?"

"I still have a little over a hundred thousand in an investment account from Greg's accident," Brittany said. "I haven't spent much of it. I bought my car and put thirty thousand in the insurance policy for Becky."

"We can come up with another two hundred," Floyd said. "It could take a few days."

"Why do these things cost so much?" Barbara asked.

"I'm going to have to hire several experts," Marc said. "First, a criminalist to go over everything, especially the crime scene. We'll probably need our own pathologist and a psychiatrist to testify. Plus, I'll need to pay her," he said nodding at Madeline, "and maybe another investigator to do a lot of legwork. A lot of witnesses to interview and she'll start looking for Bob Olson. You have to understand in a case like this, the prosecution will spend whatever they need to and we have to be ready."

Marc removed a sheet of paper from the folder he had placed on the table. He began filling in some blanks on the document and said, "Here's what I'll do, I'll take a fifty-thousand-dollar retainer to get started. I'll bill against that at two-fifty an hour and pay costs as we go along. You put the other two-hundred-fifty into a bank account, set it aside to be used as needed and we'll go from there. It can be an interest-bearing investment account, but it needs to be a cash account, so we can get at it in a short period of time. Do you know someone to help you with that?" Barbara said she did as Marc slid the document to Brittany and showed her where to sign.

Marc removed another sheet of paper from the file, handed it to Barbara and said, "I'm going to need another contract from you guaranteeing the costs and fees, whatever they turn out to be."

141

Barbara read the one-page contract, looked at her frightened daughter, smiled at her, brushed Brittany's face with the back of her hand and said, "Of course, whatever we have to do." Marc handed her the pen and she and Floyd both signed it.

The Rileys left shortly afterward so Marc could converse with Brittany. Madeline stayed since the attorney-client privilege extended to her and the three of them went over potential witnesses. Plus, Madeline wanted every detail Brittany could give her about Bob Olson, how they met and every place they had gone including dates and times. Their best chance to end this case favorably would obviously be for Madeline to track him down.

On the way back into the Cities to his office, Marc told Maddy about his confrontation with Sheriff Cale.

"What an asshole," Madeline said. "You just couldn't keep your mouth shut though could you?"

"You had to be there. And if you were, you would've handled it worse than I did."

"Probably true," she agreed. "Not the best idea to make an enemy of the sheriff."

"He already was," Marc said. "I just got it confirmed today."

THIRTY-ONE

Sheriff Cale and the four investigators waited somewhat impatiently in a conference room at the county attorney's office. LeAnne Miller summoned them to this meeting but had not bothered to explain why. Cale sat at one end of the table while the four detectives were seated to his right, along the wall, opposite the room's entryway door. The sheriff was a bit peeved to be summoned at all since he didn't work for the county attorney. To make it a bit worse, it wasn't even Miller herself who called him but an assistant of some kind. On top of that, he was still stewing from the arrogance of the lawyer talking to him the way he did.

The door opened as Miller and her chief deputy, Judy Kennely came in with Kennely carrying a case file with her. Miller sincerely apologized for the short notice and making them wait. The two lawyers took seats in the middle of the table opposite the detectives. Kennely placed the file on the table and flipped it open.

"I wanted to get together and go over the Riley case. Her bail was set at two million, which means she's not going anywhere. We've done some research on her lawyer, Kadella, and we've found he's quite good. He's very competent, knows his business and will give us a fight.

"We have a solid, circumstantial case with Brittany's failure to report her daughter missing, her behavior during that time, this nonsense about a mysterious boyfriend, her many lies to friends and relatives about where the kid was, all casting serious doubt on her credibility. But each one separately can be explained away by a good lawyer. I doubt those things, by themselves, would get a conviction," Miller explained.

"Finding the life insurance policy on Becky is a godsend," Kennely interjected. "It is certainly strong motive. We'll see about the other evidence gathered at the search when the test results come in."

"I see a problem though," Miller said picking up after Kennely finished. "So far, we have no evidence that Brittany was anything but a caring, loving mother. If I was defending her, I would hammer away at that. He'll want to try to create reasonable doubt and we have to anticipate that one of the things he'll try is that. He'll tell the jury it defies common sense to believe this loving, young mother got up one day and decided to kill her beautiful baby girl for money. Will that work? I don't know. What we need is testimony to refute the loving, caring mother image."

"So, what we want from you," Kennely continued looking at each of the four investigators, "is to go back and tear her life apart. We need to know everything about her. Especially people who knew her and the kid. Find someone to refute her loving mother image."

"We interviewed a couple of ex-boyfriends who told us she sometimes wished she didn't have the kid," Kristin Williams said.

"We know," Miller said. "It's a start and we'll use them but it's a little thin. Go out looking, specifically for something more substantial. Interview the ex-boyfriends again."

"Help them along to make their story a little stronger," Cale said. "Don't put words in their mouths, but you know what to do."

"Absolutely," Paul Anderson said while thinking putting words in their mouths is exactly what you want.

"Apparently we're all done considering that Brittany may be telling the truth." Shannon Keenan said, a statement, not a question, "We decided Bob Olson doesn't exist and this is all on Brittany."

LeAnn Miller looked at Shannon and amiably said, "Do you have any reason to believe otherwise?"

"No," Shannon sighed. "Not really. It's just that we, Kris and me, believed her."

"She seemed totally sincere," Kristin added.

"If you two have doubts, say so now," Kennely said. "We need to know if we can count on you. If you get on a witness stand and start expressing doubts, it could sink us."

The two women detectives look at each other then turned to Kennely. "I'm good," Kristin said. "I'll go with the evidence. In fact, I feel a little foolish that the psycho bitch jerked us around the way she did."

"I'm a professional," Shannon answered Kennely's query. "The evidence is what it is and I'll go with it."

"It's a little disheartening," Miller quietly added, "to think that a mother could murder such a beautiful little girl."

With that, the meeting ended, and they all got up to leave. As they were filing out the door, Cale told Shannon and Stu Doyle to wait a moment.

Cale sat on the edge of the table which brought the tall man down to eye level with Detective Keenan. "Are you on board one hundred percent?"

"Yes, sir. I'm good. I think what LeAnne said about it being so sad to think of a mother doing that kind of thing hit home. I might've been feeling that a bit. But I'm fine," she finished with a sad smile.

"Good, Shannon. I'm glad to hear that. I need to talk to Stu so please excuse us," Cale said.

After Keenan had left and closed the door, Cale said to Stu Doyle, "That line about it being disheartening about the mom and kid thing..."

"Yeah?" Doyle said.

144

"Get that out to your media source. We're all sad and sickened about it and blah, blah, blah. The public will eat it up."

"You got, it boss," Doyle said.

Barely two hours after the bail hearing had concluded, *The Court Reporter* went live. Robbie Nelson, Melinda's producer, had expected the show to air live today and restricted Melinda's wine intake to a single glass at lunch.

The show began with a live report from Gabriella Shriqui standing outside the Dakota County Government Center. By this time, knowing Brittany was back in her cell, and her lawyer had left, the crowd of protesters and most of the media had dispersed. Gabriella was reporting the hearing with no embellishment.

Melinda did her best to get Gabriella to make a disparaging comment or two about Brittany but failed. Gabriella did use the leak from Stu Doyle to tell the audience that morale at the sheriff's office was down and that almost everyone there was having a difficult time with what Brittany allegedly had done. "A source close to the investigation," she said, "was shocked that something like this could happen in such a nice community."

Melinda finally gave up on it, politely ended the interview and went to a commercial break.

"Sometimes she's a little too professional," Melinda complained to Robbie while lighting a cigarette. The makeup woman was checking her over as Melinda took several long drags on the cigarette.

"I tell her to be like that," Robbie said as he took the cigarette away from her and chuckled when Melinda childishly stuck out her tongue at him.

Robbie held up a finger to her to stop her from speaking while he listened into his headset. "Good, thanks, Cordelia," he said into his mouthpiece, "We're all set with the video from the courtroom when we come back," he told Melinda, then turned and went back to his seat.

After the break, Melinda read the intro of the court video into the camera. Melinda stayed silent while the courtroom scene was shown. They edited it down to just the bail argument and when it was finished, Melinda was back on screen. She took about two minutes to explain to the audience what had taken place before the bail argument especially the not guilty plea which Melinda commented on with a weary expression and a sad shake of her head.

"I must say," Melinda continued, "the judge was very kind and generous to Ms. Riley. I find it hard to believe he allowed bail at all, even two million. Hopefully, she'll be kept locked up because she won't be able to come up with it."

145

Following another commercial break, Melinda wrapped up the show with another dumbest criminals' story. This one about a bank robber who tried to cash a check at a small bank in Georgia. Because he did not have an account there, the teller, following bank policy, refused to cash the check. At that point, the twenty-two-year-old pulled out a gun and made the terrified teller fill a bag with cash. The young man ran out of the bank and forgot that he had given his driver's license to the teller when he tried to cash the check. According to the police, he was shocked to find them waiting for him when he arrived back at his apartment.

Melinda's show was rerun at 6:30 following the six o'clock news. The viewing public was anticipating this, and the overnight ratings showed a thirty percent increase for the time slot. Of course, there were smiles all around at the jump in numbers and the additional revenue this would bring in along with bonuses to be paid out.

THIRTY-TWO

Marc and Madeline departed in the parking lot when they arrived back at his office. Maddy was going to start interviewing Brittany's friends and ex-boyfriends first, then try to track down Bob Olson.

Marc opened the office's exterior door and immediately saw a small, mostly bald, older man with an obvious uninterested look on his face leafing through an issue of *People* magazine. As the door automatically closed behind him, Carolyn told Marc the man's name as their visitor arose from his chair. The two men shook hands and Marc invited the man to join him in his office.

His name was Jason Briggs and he was a criminalist Marc had been in touch with regarding Brittany's case. A criminalist is basically an independent CSI type investigator. Briggs was in his early fifties, though he looked older because of his bald head and diminutive frame. He had earned a bachelor's degree in forensic science from Northwestern and a Masters from Boston University. Briggs had spent ten years with the Chicago police department and six more in the Chicago office of the FBI. He had watched many people of lesser ability making a lot more money as independent agents and decided to go that route himself over ten years ago. Because of his reputation from the CPD and FBI, he immediately tripled his income and worked less doing it.

Marc, having never met the man before, looked him over and saw a fairly small man dressed casually in brown loafers, tan Dockers and a light blue polo shirt. Briggs sat down in one of the client chairs while Marc hung up his suit coat.

"I'm not what you imagined," Briggs said smiling.

"Actually, you're exactly what I expected." Marc smiled. "Maybe missing a bow tie." Both laughed at the image then Marc asked, "Can I call you Jason?"

"Of course."

"How was the drive up from Madison?" Marc asked.

"Uneventful," he shrugged. "Would it be possible to go out and look at the scene where the body was found? The sooner the better."

"Did you get a chance to watch the DVD I sent that was taken by the cops?"

"Yes," Briggs shrugged as he reached in his leather satchel, retrieved the disk and placed it on Marc's desk. "I hope you don't mind, I had a copy made."

"Sorry," Marc said as he picked it up. "I should've told you. The one I sent you was a copy for you."

"Not much on it," Briggs said. "I really need to get out there before the area becomes any more degraded."

147

Marc looked at his watch and did a quick mental calculation of the time and how much daylight was left. "How much time will you need?"

"A couple of hours should be enough for now," Briggs answered. "I can go back tomorrow if I need to."

"Let's go," Marc said as he removed his tie. "Do I need to bring anything?"

"No, we'll take my van. I have my cameras and equipment in it."

As they were walking through the office, Carolyn handed Marc a message from Gabriella Shriqui. He folded it in half and put it in his shirt pocket and the two men left. On the drive to the crime scene, Marc returned Gabriella's call and they set up a date and time to meet for another interview. Marc told her he had serious misgivings, but she assured him she would be fair, objective and professional. Having dealt with her before, Marc figured it was probably worth a try to counter at least some of the reports that were so grossly biased against Brittany. And if nothing else, she was nice to look at and pleasant to be around.

Next, he placed a call to Marcia Lindquist to let her know they were going to the crime scene. Marcia answered on the second ring and after Marc told her why he was calling, she said, "Go ahead. I don't know what you'll find that wasn't on the video. Plus, Cale let the media go over it after the crime scene people were done."

"He did what?" Marc practically shouted into the phone.

Lindquist repeated what she told him about the media being allowed onto the grounds. "What's the big deal?" Lindquist asked. "Everything you need is on the disk. There had already been hunters and who knows how many others through the place anyway."

"You allowed the media to trample over a crime scene, Marcia," Marc said as patiently as he could. This statement caused Briggs to jerk his head toward Marc and stare at him with his mouth hanging open.

"They did what?" Briggs said before turning back to his driving.

"Goodbye Marcia," Marc said and cut off the call without waiting for a reply.

"Did I hear you right?" Briggs asked. "They didn't cordon off the grounds and keep people out? They let the media trample all over the place?"

"Yep," Marc quietly said.

After a minute of silence between them, Briggs finally said, "What kind of Mickey Mouse outfit is this?"

"Don't kid yourself," Marc said. "They knew exactly what they were doing. They didn't want us to find anything that they didn't find."

"Well, we'll go out there anyway but I'm not optimistic," Briggs replied.

Some of the yellow crime scene tape was still up but most of it had blown away. The two men walked slowly and carefully over the entire area, including the parking lot and the small peninsula that jutted out into the river. They spent over an hour doing this with the criminalist leading the way while Marc carefully followed behind. Occasionally, Briggs would stop, stoop down to examine something and usually take several pictures when he did and then make a notation in his notebook about the picture to remind himself later what it was.

They methodically worked their way over to the spot where the body had been found. Briggs had put on waterproof rubber hip boots when they first arrived. While Marc waited, he jumped down into the washed-out spot that led to the river bank. The long metal pole the CSU people had placed in the water where Becky's remains were found was still there. Briggs slowly, very carefully began wading out toward the pole. As he did so, he moved his camera back and forth over the entire area taking still photos of all of it.

Briggs worked his way out to the pole and even went out several feet more beyond that spot. When the water reached the top of his boots, he stood up straight, looked around and satisfied he had covered it all, cautiously made his way back to shore.

Marc held out a hand and helped the smaller man climb out of the washed out spot up onto the grass. Briggs stood there, the river water dripping from his boots and casually looking over the crime scene. Facing the parking lot while looking to his left, he noticed a brown spot in the grass a short distance past the peninsula about three hundred feet away "What's that?" he asked rhetorically as he started walking toward the object, Marc trailing behind.

Before the two of them reached the spot Briggs was looking at, they could see what it was. It was a patch of dried grass, leaves, sticks and twigs about a foot long and six inches wide. It was a small spot of river detritus that had been left over when the river had swollen from the spring and summer rains then receded back to normal.

"Hold this," Briggs told Marc as he handed him a tape measure. "I want to measure the distance to the shoreline."

Marc knelt down and held the end of the tape on the patch of washed up grass while Briggs walked down to the river's edge. The spot measured almost exactly fifteen feet. The two men then went back to the place where the body had been found. Marc held the tape at the spot where the washed-out indentation was farthest from the river's edge. Briggs walked it down to the shoreline and measured it. The distance was exactly the same as the place where the detritus they had just checked was from the high-water mark just past the peninsula.

For the next half hour, Briggs, with Marc's help, took multiple pictures of both spots. He retrieved two metal poles from his van, four-foot sections of half-inch rebar, and used them as stakes. Briggs pounded one into the ground where the river wash remained and at the place where the body had been found. He then strung a highly visible yellow rope between them and took several shots of the marker from both places.

Briggs then took the yellow rope and walked it out to the metal pole in the water and took a few pictures of this as well. By this point, the sun was starting to set and the two of them decided to knock off for the day.

"So, what significance do you think the high-water mark means?" Marc asked as Briggs rolled up the yellow rope.

"I don't know," Briggs answered. "At this point, maybe nothing. Pull up the stake, will you please?" he asked Marc. "We need to find out when the river was this high. And then when it started to recede in relation to when the body was placed in the water."

"We had a pretty wet spring and early summer," Marc said. "Not much flooding but every lake, river and stream was full. We can find out but as I recall, it was rainy up until about mid-July."

"About the time the child went missing," Briggs said.

"That would be about right," Marc agreed. "This is an open hunting and fishing area. Being this close to the Cities, the state DNR probably patrols it regularly. We can find out from them which of their deputies has this on his route. He would know when the river was at its peak. Again, though, I'm not sure why that matters."

"Let's find out then we'll see how, if at all, it fits in with the other physical evidence," Briggs said.

THIRTY-THREE

Marc arrived at the Channel 8 building intentionally fifteen minutes late. He realized this was an almost childishly petty thing to do, but he really didn't care. The station was located in the western part of Minneapolis not too far from downtown. If need be, he could always claim there were traffic problems. He parked in a visitor's slot next to the handicap parking and sat in his car for a couple of minutes before going in. Marc stared at the array of satellite dishes behind the building. They were situated in a large lot surrounded by an eight-foot, chain-linked cyclone fence topped by two feet of razor wire. Marc thought the setting gave the place an almost eerie, government-like, Big Brother appearance.

Gabriella came through the security door behind the receptionist less than a minute after Marc checked in. She greeted him warmly, almost too effusively and ignored his tardiness. As she was leading him back toward the soundstage where the interview was to be filmed, Melinda Pace saw them and immediately made a dash to catch up with them. Marc sensed someone approaching from behind and turned his head to see who it was.

"Hello, Marc," Melinda chirped as if they were the best of friends.

Deciding to play her game a little bit, Marc stopped, turned around and said with a smile, "Why hello, Melinda. You're looking lovely today. How've you been since you backstabbed me?"

"You're not still angry about that, are you?" Melinda sweetly asked. "That's just showbiz."

"And that's probably the number one problem with the news media these days. It's all just show biz," Marc said mimicking her.

"We don't make the news, we just give them what they want," Melinda countered still smiling.

By this point, Gabriella was standing next to Marc with a tiny smirk on her face. She was thoroughly enjoying watching Melinda squirm.

"How about you come on my show again? I swear you'll be glad you did."

"Well, maybe if you stop proclaiming my client guilty, I'll consider it," Marc replied. "Bye, Melinda." At that Gabriella lightly took his arm and they continued on their way.

The makeup woman finished applying just enough makeup to Marc's forehead, cheeks and chin to reduce the shine. The camera crew did their sound, light and video checks and the interview began.

Gabriella and Marc were seated opposite each other at a small, round, wooden table in two comfortable chairs. They both had a camera pointed at them to simultaneously record the questions and answers that would be edited afterward and shown as one continuous conversation.

Gabriella started out by tossing a few easy questions at him likely to be left on the cutting room floor, just to get the ball rolling. They almost casually conversed about the case, the presumption of innocence and burden of proof. She let him take a shot at the police and prosecutors whom Marc believed were using the media by leaking damaging information. While he was making this point, the station's news director, Hunter Oswood, quietly slipped in and settled into a chair to watch.

"You believe that the police and prosecutors are leaking details about the case?" Gabriella asked.

"I don't know for sure exactly who it is, but I am seeing things on TV that should have been sent to me first. Things that could only have come from them."

"Can you give me an example?"

"The DNA results of the remains that positively identified Becky Riley," Marc replied. "Worse was when Brittany was arrested the first time. The cops show up just past midnight on a Friday night to arrest her for child neglect. You were there," Marc continued. "How did you just happen to be there with a cameraman? And was it really necessary to kick her door down at midnight and then parade her out in the middle of the night in her pajamas in front of the cameras? Of course not. The cops should be embarrassed about pulling a stunt like that."

"You've insisted from the beginning," Gabriella said changing subjects, "that Brittany is innocent and had nothing to do with the death of her daughter."

"That's right," Marc agreed.

"Why not have her take a lie detector test and prove it?"

"Take a what?" Marc asked with a puzzled look on his face.

"A lie detector test. Would you be willing to let Brittany take a lie detector test?" Gabriella repeated, uncertain why Marc appeared not to understand her.

"There's a test people can take that can tell when someone's lying?" Marc asked keeping a straight face. "When did this happen?"

Gabriella's brow furrowed, a look of confusion on her face not quite comprehending why Marc appeared not to know what she was talking about. "Well, um, yeah," Gabriella responded. "In fact, it's been around for a long time."

"Oh!" Marc exclaimed with an acknowledging expression. "I know what you mean. You're talking about a polygraph machine."

"Yes, that's right, a polygraph lie detector," a relieved Gabriella said.

Marc leaned forward a little, looked at the beautiful reporter and with a sly smile said, "Gabriella, there's no such thing as a lie detector. At best, that's an urban legend," he finished as he sat back.

"Would she be willing to take the test?"

"Gabriella," Marc politely continued, "polygraphs cannot detect when someone is lying. They detect certain bodily functions. Skin temperature, pulse rate, breathing and those kinds of things. Some people believe this allows them to tell when someone is lying. It's nonsense. There's a good reason the results are not allowed in court. They're not reliable."

"Still, if the police believe them, wouldn't that help your client if she passed?"

After a moment of silence went by as if Marc were thinking it over, he said, "No, it wouldn't. Think about it. Let's say she took the test and passed. The cops believe they have enough evidence to prove her guilty. If she passed the poly, do you think the cops would say: 'Well, she must be innocent' and the prosecution would drop the case? Of course not. They would believe she figured out how to beat the machine."

"Probably true," Gabriella conceded.

"Now say she took it and failed. What good would that do her?"

"As you say, it's not admissible in court."

"Yeah, but if she took it and failed, I guarantee you the media would know about it and report it before Brittany and I left the building."

"That's probably true too," Gabriella agreed with a big dazzling smile and mischievous look in her eyes. "But if she passed it, you'd be sure to leak that to the reporters yourself."

"You're right, I would," Marc said nodding his head. "But I can see it now. Melinda Pace would have an expert," — Marc made air quotes with his hands at this point — "to convince her audience that beating the machine was simple. And she wouldn't be the only one.

"There's nothing good that can help my client by agreeing to a polygraph. So, to answer your question, I would not allow her to take the test. In fact, I can't think of a single reason to ever allow anyone to submit to a polygraph."

Having received a huge piece of news, Gabriella decided the best thing to do was wrap up the interview. She genuinely thanked Marc for coming and cut it off at that point.

Hunter Oswood stood up, pleased with what he had witnessed and motioned for one of the assistant directors. Oswood quietly told the woman to have Gabriella come to his office when she was finished and left as quietly as he entered.

"What did you want to see me about?" Gabriella asked after knocking on Oswood's door and entering his office.

"Have a seat," he gestured. "I watched your interview with the lawyer."

"You did? I didn't see you because of the lights," Gabriella said a little nervous at being summoned so abruptly.

"It was terrific," Oswood said to which Gabriella visibly relaxed. "That stuff about the polygraph was great. Do you think you can get twenty-two minutes of it after editing?"

"Easily," Gabriella answered.

"Good. Here's what I want to do. First, on her show this afternoon, we'll have Melinda break it that the lawyer, Kadella, won't let Brittany take a lie detector," he said, then quickly held up his left-hand palm out when Gabriella started to speak. "Let me finish. We'll go with that angle for today for all of the newscasts. We'll have you do a little Q & A with Melinda on her show, so you can say you interviewed him, asked him about the lie detector and he said he would not let her take one.

"Then, tomorrow evening, we'll preempt the 6:30 show and run your complete interview. We'll promo it after the 6:00 and during the ten o'clock newscasts. The competition and the newspapers will pick it up. It will go national as well. Hell, it will create a shit storm. Then we run the full interview, you'll end up looking great and so will we."

"I thought he made me look like an idiot," Gabriella said.

"No, not at all," Oswood chuckled. "He just took a little shot at everyone who believed in the bullshit about lie detectors. Don't worry about it."

While Gabriella walked back to her cubicle after leaving Oswood's office, her phone went off. She checked the ID, frowned but answered it anyway. Stu Doyle got right to the point. The lab tests of the rope and cinder blocks found in the Rileys' garage matched the ones discovered at the crime scene. Gabriella thanked him then returned to Oswood's office to tell him what she had just learned.

That afternoon, Melinda once again did her show live and had Gabriella on as a guest. It went exactly the way Oswood predicted. Gabriella explained about Marc stopping in for the interview and adamantly declining to allow his client to take a lie detector test. Gabriella was a little uncomfortable calling it a lie detector, but Melinda insisted. Between Marc's refusal to allow the lie detector to be administered and the news about the cinder block and rope to which Becky had been tied, Melinda had one of her best shows ever. It was again replayed at 6:30 and the public couldn't get enough of it. The overnight ratings for the metro area of the 6:30 showing came in with an almost unheard-of sixty percent of all homes with TVs on tuned to her show. Even Melinda was staggered by the number.

Oswood was right about the reaction. Every television news report in the Upper Midwest led with the lie detector refusal. It also was prominent on every cable news channel that evening and the next day. In the morning, almost every paper in America ran it somewhere on their front page and all of the national morning news shows devoted time to it. Every one of them used the same basic disclaimer. "It has been reported that the lawyer for Brittany Riley will not allow her to take a lie detector test." Then, of course, the reporter would follow with the obvious question: "I wonder what she has to hide?"

THIRTY-FOUR

Vivian Donahue, seated on the loveseat in her home office, was watching the replay of the interview Gabriella had done with Marc Kadella. She was born Vivian Corwin, the only daughter of Robert Corwin, Jr. the great-grandson of Edward Corwin. Edward had moved to the Minnesota prairie in the 1840's and began farming. Having a natural head for business and a serious ruthless streak, Edward had founded Corwin Agricultural. Forbes listed the Corwin family eighteenth on its list of richest Americans. Vivian, as the undisputed head of the family, was one of the wealthiest women in the country. When she spoke, people listened. In her mid-sixties, she was still a very attractive woman and she could proudly boast, with the exception of her hair color, it was all natural.

Vivian was dressed casually in tan Armani slacks and a robin's egg blue silk Hermes blouse. Her legs were crossed, and her right arm rested comfortably on the armrest of the small sofa. The door to her office opened, her favorite granddaughter, Adrienne came in and plopped down on the small sofa next to her. At nineteen, she was also Vivian's oldest grandchild and practically lived with her in the family mansion.

"You really need to learn to knock, dear," Vivian said as Adrienne affectionately looped her right arm through her grandmother's left.

"What are you watching, Gram?" Adrienne asked.

"Ssssh. An interview," Vivian answered patting Adrienne's knee.

The two women sat quietly while Gabriella asked a question. "I'd kill to have her eyes," Adrienne observed. "Hey, that's Marc Kadella," Adrienne exclaimed when the picture shifted to Gabriella's interviewee. "Tony's lawyer friend. He's kind of hot, in a lawyerly sort of way," she added knowing the statement would mildly needle her grandmother.

"Ssssh," Vivian admonished her again.

For the next several minutes the two of them quietly watched and listened. Marc was patiently explaining to Gabriella the pitfalls of allowing Brittany to take a polygraph test. When the interview ended, Vivian leaned forward, picked up the TVs remote and turned off the power.

"Was that about the girl who murdered her baby?" Adrienne asked.

"Accused of," Vivian corrected her.

"I hope she rots in hell," Adrienne said. "How could she..."

"I don't believe she did," Vivian said.

"Grandma! It's all over the news. It's obvious she's guilty."

"Why, because the media says so?" Vivian asked her granddaughter. "They're never wrong? They never have their own agenda? You should know better."

After a long ten seconds, Adrienne meekly said, "Yeah, okay, point taken. But if not her, then who, this mystery boyfriend that no one has ever seen?" she said as Vivian stood up, walked to her desk and picked up her private cell phone. She punched a speed dial button and put the phone to her ear while Adrienne watched with a puzzled expression.

"Hello, Anthony," Vivian said. "I was wondering if you could find time to stop by this evening."

"I can be there in about twenty minutes," the private investigator said.

Tony Carvelli, an ex-cop turned private investigator, had both a professional and personal relationship with Vivian Donahue. Tony had investigated the murder of Vivian's nephew and while doing so, the two of them had become good friends and even part-time lovers. It was through Tony that Vivian had come to meet Marc Kadella. Despite the fact Marc had represented one of the men involved in her nephew's murder, Vivian had grown to respect the lawyer.

Adrienne answered the door when Tony arrived and gave him a huge, affectionate hug when he came into the foyer. She led him into the office where Tony and Vivian exchanged a kiss and a hug. When all three were seated, Tony in a chair, the two women on the small sofa, Vivian began the discussion.

"What can you tell me about this case your friend is handling?" Vivian asked.

"You mean the murdered little girl," Tony said.

"Yes."

"Not much," Tony shrugged. "I had lunch with him the other day. We talked about it a little. Some things I don't want to get into."

"Is his client really innocent?" Vivian asked. "I haven't watched all of it but you can't pick up a newspaper or turn the television on without being hit over the head with it. And they certainly imply she's guilty."

"Why do you want to know? This isn't something you should get involved with. It's not something you should have your name attached to," Tony said.

"Anthony, stop it. I quit worrying about my name and reputation years ago. You don't get to our level of prominence without stepping on some toes."

"Or doing a little bootlegging," Adrienne said lightly poking Vivian with her elbow, referring to rumors about activities Vivian's grandfather may have done.

"Shush. Let's not air the family's dirty linen in front of our guest," Vivian said with a smile.

"I was thinking if she is really innocent she shouldn't be in jail."

157

"You want to post her bail?" Tony asked incredulously. "I heard it's two million bucks. Are you sure…"?

"I could do that. Besides, I will get it back when the case is over. Will you call Marc and ask him if he will meet with me? I want to get his opinion."

Tony stared at her for a few seconds then looked at Adrienne who shrugged her shoulders and raised both hands, palms up. Tony took out his phone, made the call and after Tony convinced him it was important, Marc agreed to come to the Corwin mansion at nine the next morning.

The Minnesota Attorney General, Anne Peterson, was relaxing in her husband's multi-million-dollar home in North Oaks. Peterson had graduated from the University of Minnesota law school twelve years before. Her husband, Arthur Peterson, was a very successful investment banker almost twenty years older than Anne. Using her husband's political connections, she had obtained a job in the former attorney general's office. Six years later, the AG ran for the US Senate and lost. But his misfortune opened the door for Peterson. She obtained the nomination for the state attorney general's job and despite not having been in a courtroom since moot court in law school, won the election.

Peterson shut off the TV and called her chief deputy, H. Lowell Vanderbeck. She had been watching Gabriella's interview of Marc and decided it was time to act.

"Did you watch the interview of Brittany Riley's lawyer on Channel 8?" she asked.

"No, I didn't, why?" Vanderbeck answered.

"It's time we took over the prosecution. The publicity for this is too much to pass up," Peterson said after sipping her twenty-year-old single malt.

"Are you sure LeAnne Miller won't kick up a fuss?"

"Sure she will," Peterson replied. "I'll smooth that out. I'll hint around that when I run for governor, I'll recommend her for the AG's job."

"Where does that leave me?" an anxious Vanderbeck asked. "That was supposed to be my…"

"Relax Lowell. I said I would hint around about it. I didn't say she would get it. I'll call her tomorrow and let her know we're taking over. I think you should handle the case personally with Danica Hart."

"What if we lose," a nervous Vanderbeck asked. He was always one to look at the downside of everything.

"Don't. I'll talk to you tomorrow," Peterson said, then abruptly ended the call.

158

THIRTY-FIVE

Marc arrived at the Corwin Estate on Lake Minnetonka ten minutes early. As he was walking toward the granite stairway that led to the front door, he saw Carvelli's Camaro come roaring up the driveway. He waited for his friend and as the two men walked up the stairs, Marc tried to find out why Vivian wanted to see him. Tony, having been asked by Vivian not to reveal the purpose, would only say Marc would find out soon enough.

The housekeeper let them in and as they were being led across the large, marble-floored foyer, the two men saw a bikini-clad Adrienne going out the back door to the pool. Both men watched her go through the door and both felt a little guilty staring at the backside of the young girl. Marc had been in the house before, but even so, he was still a bit awed by it. The housekeeper opened the library door and stepped aside so the two men could enter.

Vivian came toward them, offered a cheek for Tony to kiss then warmly and graciously greeted Marc. She followed them to the two matching couches. They were facing each other with a beautiful mahogany topped coffee table between them, all positioned in front of a large exquisite, gas fireplace.

Vivian poured the two men coffee from a sterling silver pot on the table. While Marc sipped from his cup, which he really didn't want, Vivian said, "Marc, I want to talk to you about your client, Brittany Riley, if you don't mind. If I ask anything out of bounds, please just say so."

"Sure," Marc said as he set the cup on the table.

"This is a bit awkward," she began.

"Brittany Riley is innocent," Marc abruptly said. "If that's what you're wondering."

Visibly relieved Vivian replied. "That was the question I had, and I wasn't sure how or even if I should ask it."

"Why do you want to know?" an obviously puzzled Marc asked her.

"Because I am sick to death of turning on the television or picking up a newspaper and having her guilt shoved in my face."

"You think you are?" Marc laughed. "Try it while wearing my shoes."

"How is she holding up?" Vivian sincerely asked.

"Not well," Marc admitted. "Brittany and her family are pretty stressed, and I'm worried about Brittany's health. She's quite depressed. It would help if they could make bail but…"

"That's why I wanted to see you. As I understand it, bail is used to make sure she shows up in court. Correct?"

"Yes, essentially," Marc agreed.

"How much is it?"

"Two million dollars," Marc said.

"If someone were to put up the money do they get it back if she shows up for her trial?"

"Yes," Marc said, a little too eagerly. "Are you thinking about...?"

"I'll put up the money, but I would like it to be anonymous," Vivian said.

"That's going to be difficult," Marc said. "We can use a cashier's check, but the reality is, if the media wants to track it back to its source, I'm sure they could do it."

"What about cash?" Tony asked.

"You want to deliver two million dollars in cash?" Marc asked. "And even then, despite whoever brings it, they'll still figure out that it came from Vivian," Marc said turning back to her. "Where is this money coming from?"

"That's not really your concern," she politely replied.

He held up a hand to her and said, "I realize that. I'm thinking as a lawyer. Are you going to have family members or investors or anyone like that making a stink about...?"

"No," Vivian smiled. "I'll deal with that. So, what do we do? Cash or check?"

"A cashier's check would be best. Vivian, I can't tell you how grateful I am."

"Stop," she said. "I'll have the check tomorrow. It will be delivered here. I'll let Anthony know when for sure. Then the two of you can go get her out."

They all stood up and as they were leaving, Marc turned to Vivian and said, "I want to tell her the news. Are you sure about this?"

"Yes, of course. By all means, go tell her in person right away. It will cheer her up."

When the two men got outside, they stood by their cars for a couple of minutes discussing how best to handle this.

"What about security?" Tony asked. "If word gets out, and it probably will, every goofball in town is going to show up at the jail. Protesters, media, you name it."

"The sheriff can provide security," Marc said.

"You trust him to do it? No, we'll need our own. You want me to make a couple calls?"

"Wait," Marc said snapping his fingers. "I know just the guy. And he owes me a favor. Besides, who are you going to call, cop friends?"

160

"Yeah," Tony answered.

"Do you think they are going to want to get involved with this?"

"Maybe, maybe not," Tony agreed.

"I'll check with my guy and let you know if I need you to get some help. Talk to you later," Marc said.

Marc left the Corwin Estate and drove directly to the jail in Hastings. The forty-mile drive took almost an hour. As a criminal defense lawyer, it was not often he was able to bring good news to a client. Knowing how much it would boost Brittany's morale was a tonic to his disposition and put him in a very good mood.

He stepped up to the glass partition and slid his attorney license card through the opening on the counter. The deputy recognized Marc and told him he would have his client brought down right away.

While waiting for Brittany, Marc paced around the conference room, too wound up with the good news to sit down. He barely had to wait five minutes before the door opened. A different deputy stepped aside for her and Marc immediately noticed she was not shackled or handcuffed at all. The deputy stepped into the small room, closed the door behind himself and quietly said, "I just want you to know, most of the deputies heard about what you did to Cale the other day and we're all pretty pleased with it. Take all the time you need. Let us know when you're done."

"Thanks," Marc said with a large grin as he and Brittany sat down while the deputy closed the door and left.

Marc reached across the table and took both of Brittany's hands in his. He quickly told her why he came, and she immediately burst into tears, sobbing almost uncontrollably. He let go of her hands, so she could use them to cover her face. Marc removed a handkerchief from his back pocket and handed it to her. It took more than a minute, but she finally got herself under control.

"Why is she doing this?" Brittany asked.

"I know her a little bit. A good friend of mine and Maddy knows her a lot better. She's a terrific lady. She thinks the media is screwing you over and is willing to help."

"Please, tell her, I'm so grateful. I don't know what to say."

"I have, and you'll probably get the chance to tell yourself," Marc said. "We'll do this tomorrow as soon as we can. In the meantime, you keep this to yourself. We're going to try to get you out of here without making a big circus out of it, okay?"

"Sure. Yes, I will."

"I'll go see your parents yet today. In fact, I'm going to go now. Maybe you'll be able to sleep tonight."

161

While they waited by the door for the guard, Brittany weakly smiled up at Marc then threw her arms around his neck. "Thank you," she said as she kissed his cheek and Marc hugged her back.

The sheriff's deputy, standing in front of the Rileys' house, recognized Marc when the deputy stopped him before the Rileys' driveway. With a pleasant grin and a tip of his cap, the deputy waved Marc forward to allow him to park his car. Marc got out of his car and started up the walkway toward the house. Halfway to the front door he stopped and looked across the street at the people and TV vans.

Recognizing him, the protestors began booing, yelling obscenities and several of them slowly walked toward him. Marc saw a few of the media cameras pointed at him then he turned back toward the protestors in time to see the two deputies intercept those coming at him. Marc impassively stared at the scene, wondering at the ignorance of these misguided fools. Did they really not understand how the justice system worked? That the accused is only that, accused? Could they not grasp how easily any one of them might find themselves wrongly accused of a crime and be in Brittany's place? What is wrong with people in this country?

He saw one of the men who walked across the street pick up a rock and hurl it toward Marc. He watched the rock's flight and it landed harmlessly in the front yard several feet from him. At the same time, one of the deputies hit the man with a Taser and dropped him onto the asphalt. The sight of this idiot flopping around on the ground with the wires protruding from his chest made Marc laugh and stunned the crowd into silence which made them all back up. While one of the deputies stared down the crowd, the one with the Taser cuffed the rock thrower and put him in the backseat of the deputy's car.

With that, Marc hurried up the sidewalk and into the house where Floyd was holding the door for him. Once inside he greeted an angry Floyd and frightened Barbara.

"Sorry," Marc said as they all took seats in the living room. "I didn't mean to get them riled up."

"Are you all right?" Barbara asked.

"Yeah, I'm fine. They'll have something to show on the news tonight," he added indicating the events outside. "I can just hear them now," he continued mocking the voice of an anchor. "We, of course, the members of the media, strongly condemn this type of behavior even though we do everything we can to help create it and film it so we can bring it to you for higher ratings to make more money."

His mocking of the phony piety of reporters brought a hearty laugh to both Barbara and Floyd.

"The reason I stopped by is, I have great news," Marc said turning serious. "We are going to get Brittany out on bail."

"Oh, my God, how? I mean that's wonderful!" Barbara exclaimed.

"When?" Floyd asked.

"Tomorrow," Marc replied. "We're getting the money together."

"Where is the money coming from? Who is doing this?" Barbara asked.

"For now, this person wants to remain anonymous." His phone buzzed, and he looked at the screen. Seeing who it was, he figured it was important. "I need to take this," he told the Rileys.

He listened to the caller for almost a minute then quietly said, "Thanks, Carolyn. I'll be back in a while." He ended the call and said to the Rileys, "Turn the TV on. That was my office. The news is reporting that the grand jury has returned an indictment."

Barbara picked up a remote and turned on the flat screen in the corner of the room. She found a local channel with the news being reported. An attractive middle-aged man with a perfectly styled full head of blow-dried hair and brilliantly white, capped teeth was solemnly reading the news.

"Again, we have been informed that Brittany Riley, the young mother who allegedly murdered her daughter," — a picture of Becky came on the split screen — "has been indicted with several counts of first and second-degree murder. We'll pass along more information as it becomes available."

While Marc was driving back to his office in Minneapolis, he became curious about something. He took out his phone, found the number he wanted in his cell log and dialed it. Before the second ring had finished, it was answered.

"Hi, Marc," Gabriella answered. "What can I do for you?"

"I saw the midday news show and your anchor reported the indictment of Brittany. I was wondering, did the station receive a copy of it or were you just tipped by a leak?"

"Ah, I'm not sure…"

"I'm not asking for your source, Gabriella. I just want to know if you got a physical copy of the indictment itself."

Gabriella, sitting at her desk in her cubicle, looked around to make sure no one was listening. Satisfied and realizing what the lawyer was asking for was harmless, she said, in a whisper, "We got a copy of it by fax. I think it came in around 11:00. Why?"

"I thought so," Marc said, the annoyance obvious in his voice. "I still don't have it. I first heard about it from one of the women in my office who saw it on TV. Then I saw it on TV. So, once again, the media gets important information about my client's case before I do."

"Sorry, Marc," Gabriella said.

"Don't be. It's not your fault. Listen, thanks. I have to go."

"You owe me one," Gabriella said.

"No, I don't," Marc laughed. "Bye, Gabriella."

"This just came by messenger," Sandy said as she handed Marc a large manila envelope when he returned to his office.

Sandy had already sliced open the envelope and as Marc pulled the document out of it, he looked around the office and said, "Where is everybody?"

"Chris is at a real estate closing. Barry and Connie are in court, Carolyn is in the ladies' room and Jeff is off this afternoon," Sandy answered.

"Oh, okay," Marc muttered while he paged through the indictment.

"And here's a message for you. It says it's urgent and to call him right away. It's from a Lowell Vanderbeck of the Minnesota Attorney General's office."

Marc took the message slip from Sandy and with a puzzled look, asked, "What did he want?"

"He didn't say."

Marc went into his office, closed the door behind him and called the lawyer back.

Vanderbeck's secretary put him on hold which lasted over a very long minute while he waited listening to ear aching bad music. Finally, he heard a nasally voice that came across as a bit annoying.

"Thank you for calling," Vanderbeck said. "I just wanted to let you know the attorney general's office has taken over the prosecution of your client, Brittany Riley."

"Really?" a surprised Marc responded. "How come?"

"Well, ah, that's not something I care to go into," Vanderbeck said. "Your client is set to be arraigned tomorrow at 1:00 on the full indictment. Are you aware of that?"

"Yes, I got the arraignment notice delivered with the indictment just now."

"We can postpone if you need to. I realize it's pretty short notice," Vanderbeck said.

"No, let's not. 1:00 tomorrow is fine. Are we still in front of Judge Connors?"

"Yes, as far as I know, he is still assigned to the case. Personally, I don't know anything about him."

"He hates prosecutors and thinks all cops are lying assholes," Marc said looking for a reaction. After twenty seconds of total silence between them, Marc said, "Are you still there?"

"Um, yes, I am," Vanderbeck meekly replied.

"I'm kidding. I don't know much about him either except so far on this case he's been pretty straight."

"Oh, good. Well, um, I guess I'll see you tomorrow then."

"One other thing," Marc said. "Are the leaks of evidence and discovery material to the media going to continue?"

"I resent that," Vanderbeck said. "We do not try our cases in the media!"

"I'm glad to hear that. Is that a yes or a no?" Marc asked.

"I will see you tomorrow," Vanderbeck icily answered and hung up.

Marc replaced the phone and chuckled at how easily he had jerked the man's chain.

Marc leaned back in his chair, slipped his shoes off, placed his stocking feet on his desktop and began reading through the indictment.

There were five charges in total. The big ones were two first-degree murder charges, a single second-degree and a third-degree murder charge. Also, the original charge of child neglect was included as well.

The indictment was basically a list of each charge and a statement of the facts of the case the prosecution believed supported a finding of guilt on each one. The document itself was barely ten pages which was an indication, Marc believed, of how thin their case was and what little evidence they had. The most significant fact that was missing was the cause of death. The reality was they had no idea how this child died.

"Hey," he heard a voice say and he looked up to find his friend and officemate, Barry Cline, standing in his doorway.

"You know a guy in the AG's office named...," Marc paused to read the name from Sandy's message slip, "Lowell Vanderbeck?"

"Nope," Barry said. "Sounds like an East Coast, old-money name."

At that moment, Connie Mickelson crowded in and Marc asked her the same question to which she also replied negatively.

"Why would the AG's office take over the prosecution?" Marc asked them both.

"Publicity," Connie replied. "A high-profile case like this will get Peterson's picture in the paper a lot. Don't ever get between that woman and a camera. The word is she's going to run for governor next time around."

Marc dropped his feet off of the desk, stood and held the indictment out for Barry. "Read this and let me know what you think."

"Make a copy for me too," Connie said.

Ten minutes later, having read the document through, they both took seats in Marc's office.

"It's probably a decent circumstantial case except for..." Barry began.

"No cause of death," Connie finished.

"Thanks," Marc said. "That's what I thought too."

"Juries have convicted on less," Barry reminded him.

"I know," Marc sighed. "Hell, she's already been convicted."

Connie and Barry left and a few minutes later Marc opened his computer file of clients to find a phone number. The number he was looking for was for a client by the name of Butch Koll. Butch had been involved with a gangster named Leo Balkus. While doing a little collection work for Leo, he had been at the scene when his fellow thug, Ike Pitts, had inadvertently killed a man. In fact, the man Pitts had accidentally killed on behalf of his gangster boss was the nephew of Vivian Donahue. Marc had represented Butch and had done a good job for him despite the crooked judge and Butch would be forever grateful.

Marc found it, dialed and Butch answered with a cheerful, "Hey counselor, how've you been?"

"Good, Butch, listen," Marc continued, "I need a favor from you."

"Name it, Marc. You got it. I've been seeing you on the news lately, helping that young girl."

"That's what I'm calling about. I need some security for her. Tomorrow."

"When and where?" Butch asked. "Whatever you need."

"Here's the deal," Marc said. "I need a couple of big guys to run interference for her. We're getting her bailed out of jail tomorrow. Keep that to yourself. I'm expecting a big crowd so I'm guessing I'll need some help just getting her to a car to get her home. I'll even toss you a couple hundred bucks cash for the afternoon. It shouldn't be that big a deal. I just don't think the cops will be much help. Do you know somebody who can lend a hand?"

"Yeah, I know a guy. Maybe a little bigger than me. He'd do it. Can I tell him two hundred cash?"

"Sure. Is he reliable? Will he keep cool if he's hassled?"

"Yeah, he's good. I've worked a couple of concerts with him. Nothing fazes this guy."

"Perfect. You know where the Dakota County Government Center is in Hastings?"

"No, now that you mention it, I don't. I've been through Hastings a few times but never been to court out there. What's the address? I'll look it up and find it."

166

Marc gave him the address and told him to be there by 1:00. Butch gave Marc the second man's name, Andy Whitman, then ended the call.

When Vanderbeck hung up the phone after talking to the defense lawyer he opened the door of his private bathroom and went inside. He checked himself in the mirror and unnecessarily tightened the knot of his four-hundred-dollar tie. While leaving his corner office, he slipped into his Brooks Brothers suit coat and headed toward the press briefing room.

Barry Cline had been absolutely correct. Vanderbeck was from East Coast old money. At least his lineage was East Coast money. A long succession of inept Vanderbeck men, including, if not especially, his father and grandfather, had squandered the money part of the East Coast old money heritage.

Lowell, as he preferred, had moved to Minnesota after graduation from Dartmouth for the sensible reason that his wife's wealthy family was here. Tall and good-looking, charming when necessary, he had landed Victoria his senior year and upon graduation, they married after Lowell found out about her very substantial trust fund.

Nearing forty and with the obligatory two children produced, he saw his job as Chief Deputy in the Attorney General's office as a potential escape route. He secretly loathed Minnesota as a backwater, provincial hell and would use politics to force his wife out of here. She loved the place, especially the winters and since it was her money, a divorce was not an option.

Vanderbeck joined Anne Peterson, the Attorney General, on the dais for the press conference. First off, Peterson made a brief statement about the AG taking over the Riley case. The reason she gave was the significance of the case and the resources of her office would make certain that justice would be done. While she said these things, LeAnne Miller, the Dakota County Attorney looked on and did her best to act as if she agreed, even making a statement of her own supporting the decision. Vanderbeck and Danica Hart were both introduced as the lawyers who would try the case. Then Peterson spent twenty minutes in front of the cameras taking questions and acting as if this was all being done for the people of Minnesota.

Marc Kadella would later, somewhat cynically, remember how phony he believed the whole thing was.

THIRTY-SIX

Madeline Rivers, dressed for court, walked a couple of steps ahead of Marc as the two of them made their way toward the courtroom door. There were at least a hundred people milling about in the hallway, disappointed and grumbling about being refused admission. How these people always managed to find out about these hearings was a mystery to Marc. Maddy, sporting a grim look of determination, marched straight toward the double doors where the two deputies stood guard. Marc, along with Butch Koll and his friend Andy Whitman, followed right behind her. Butch was a six-foot-four-inch two hundred forty-pound weightlifter and he looked small next to Andy. Butch had suggested that he and Andy lead the way through the crowd but Maddy assured them that wouldn't be necessary. Not with these people at least. Marc followed right behind her. He had his briefcase in hand wearing his best suit, the charcoal gray Armani with light blue pinstripes and acting as if this was all routine business. Suppressing a laugh, he watched as the mob silently parted to allow the dazzling Ms. Rivers to march past them. Without a word and without breaking stride, Maddy smiled at one of the deputies who opened the door for her as she marched into the courtroom with Marc on her heels.

"That's too much fun to watch you do that," Marc whispered to her.

The two of them went through the gate and took the table on the right-hand side of the courtroom. The first row of the gallery on that side of the room had been reserved for the defense, mostly for family of the defendant. Butch and Andy slid into it next to the Rileys who looked at the two large men with trepidation in their eyes. Marc turned around in his chair and leaned over the rail to talk to Barbara, Floyd and Tim, who was far more interested in Maddy than what Marc had to say about his sister. He introduced Butch and Andy and briefly explained again, what would happen today.

Marc took a moment to look over the crowd. Seated behind the Rileys were the fortunate few court junkies who had managed to get seats. On the other side of the aisle were the media members. He looked up at the camera on the back wall and noticed the little red light was not on. Whoever was remotely operating it was apparently waiting for the judge to come out.

Marc turned back around and pushed his chair up to the defense table. As he did so the door behind the judge's bench opened and two people, a man and a woman came into the courtroom.

They were both very well dressed, carrying briefcases and obviously lawyers. The man was about six feet, around forty years old, a full head of hair and could pass for a TV news anchor. The woman was a little older, had short brown hair and dressed conservatively in a navy-blue matching blazer and skirt. They both put their briefcases on the other table and walked toward Marc.

Marc stood and the three of them introduced themselves. They were the lawyers from the attorney general's office who had taken over the case. The man explained to Marc that they had been in chambers with Judge Connors to let him know what was going on with the prosecution and the AG's office was handling it. Clearly, Lowell Vanderbeck was quite impressed with himself.

"That's interesting. I'll tell you what, Lowell," Marc said with a sarcastic smile. "I don't care who you are or who you work for. If you ever talk to the judge again without me being there, I'll have your ass up on charges before the Office of Professional Responsibility faster than you can say 'bad publicity'."

"Well, ah, I didn't think…"

"That's obvious," Marc said. "Don't do it again."

The woman with him, Danica Hart, was trying hard not to smile while this exchange took place and Marc noticed it. Annoyed, Vanderbeck turned and went back to his table. As he did this, Hart stepped up to Marc and whispered, "I warned him." She then turned and joined the chastened Vanderbeck at their table.

A minute later, Brittany Riley was led into the courtroom. She was wearing the slacks, shoes and blouse Barbara had brought for her. Her hair was brushed out and she had enough makeup to look healthy and fresh. Brittany and Maddy exchanged a warm hug and she took the chair between Maddy and Marc.

Marc looked up at the clock and noted it was already 1:15 and still no judge and no Tony Carvelli with Brittany's bail check. Simultaneously, the door to the judge's chambers and the door to the hallway both opened. Judge Connors came out, the bailiff said, "All rise" and Vivian Donahue with Tony Carvelli at her side strolled up the aisle as the audience stood. A surprised Marc looked at Vivian and Tony as the two of them reached the front row and waited for Butch, Andy and the Rileys to make room for them. Marc turned to them and with his eyes indicated it was okay for the newcomers to sit with them.

The media knew who Vivian was and a noticeable buzz was going through their side of the gallery over her presence. Judge Connors also knew her and although a little puzzled himself, rapped his gavel and called for quiet. Vivian, ignoring it all, simply adjusted her skirt after she sat down, smiled and nodded at Marc and Maddy and quietly waited for court to begin.

The judge called the lawyers forward along with Brittany and the four of them stood before the bench. Connors looked at Maddy and gestured Marc to come to him. Hart went up front also while Vanderbeck stayed back.

"Is she a lawyer?" Connors quietly asked indicating Madeline.

"No, your Honor. She's an associate working with me. I hope it's okay for her to sit at the table," Marc replied.

"She can sit wherever she wants," Connors said.

"Am I detecting a little bias?" Hart playfully asked.

"Step back," Connors said trying not to smile.

The judge went through the preliminaries of reading the case and having the lawyers identify themselves for the record. He asked Marc if he had received a copy of the indictment and would he waive reading it for the record to which Marc answered in the affirmative.

Connors again read Brittany her rights and made her verbally answer for the record that he had done so, and she understood them. He then listed the charges against her which were two counts of first-degree murder, one count of second-degree, one of third-degree and the child neglect charge and asked her to enter a plea.

The judge then ordered that the two million in bail be continued and asked Marc if bail would be posted. He turned and looked at Tony who nodded his head.

"Yes, your Honor. We will be posting bail right away," Marc said which sent a current of electricity through the crowd.

"You will, huh?" a surprised Connors said. "Okay, then..."

"Your Honor," Vanderbeck interrupted. "Clearly bail is not warranted in this case."

"She's hardly a flight risk. Where is she going to go where she won't be recognized, and she is certainly no threat to the community?" Marc replied.

"I've already ruled, Mr. Vanderbeck. But I'll tell you what," he continued turning back to Marc. "Does your client have a passport?"

Marc looked at Brittany who shook her head to indicate she did not.

"No, your Honor."

"I'm going to put her on home monitoring. She can wear an ankle bracelet monitoring device. Have probation services set it up," he said to his clerk. "Anything else? Good. We're adjourned."

With that, there was a mad rush for the doors.

The deputy who had brought Brittany into court came over to collect her and told Marc that he would take her to probation to set up the monitoring. The deputy and Brittany left, and Marc introduced Vivian and Tony to the Rileys. Butch and Andy led them all through the mob of reporters, but Vivian stopped to address several of them.

"I'm here," she began answering the obvious question they were all wondering, "because I think this young woman deserves to be treated

170

like anyone else. The media, that's you people," she said with a disdainful glare while looking over the crowd standing in front of her with lights blazing, cameras whirring and microphones in her face, "have already convicted her. And that's something you should all be ashamed of. It would be refreshing if just once you showed a glimmer of professionalism. Finally, you will probably find out anyway, so I may as well tell you. I was the one who put up her bail. I believe in the presumption of innocence and her lawyer, whom I know, assures me that she is in fact innocent. Because of that and the way she has been hounded by you and the public, I decided this young woman deserves to at least get out of jail. That's all I have." With that, she turned and followed Butch and Andy through the building and out to her car with the chauffeur waiting illegally parked in the fire lane in front of the building.

Within an hour there was a crowd of at least three hundred people in front of the government center. Marc, Maddy, Butch and Andy were in the jail's entryway looking over the sea of angry faces trying to figure out how to get Brittany to a car. Having assured the Rileys that they could get their daughter home, Marc had them leave right after court.

"Look at that man!" Maddy said pointing to a man holding up what looked to be a two-year-old boy. The child had a sign hanging around his neck which read, "Would you kill me too?"

"And that one," Butch said pointing to a woman holding a young girl about Becky's age with a sign that read "Please don't kill me". There were dozens of signs of a similar nature throughout the crowd.

"You'd think she was Charles Manson," Maddy added.

"I don't think Manson is hated as much as she is. You should read some of the death threat letters she gets and some of the stuff I get," Marc quietly said.

"I can imagine," she answered him. "What do you do with it?"

"Turn it over to the cops. There isn't much they can do except make a file and monitor it. Most of it is from the aluminum foil helmet crowd and probably harmless."

"Probably?" Maddy asked.

"Hopefully," Marc smiled.

The interior door behind them opened and Sheriff Cale appeared. He had two good sized male deputies with him, both wearing vests.

"Your client's on her way," Cale brusquely said.

"We can't take her out this way," Marc told Cale. "We need to go out the back."

"No way," Cale said. "These guys will run interference. They can keep the crowd back. She's not getting any special treatment. Your car is right there," he continued, indicating Andy's large Suburban parked about a hundred yards from the door.

At that moment, one of the three news helicopters that were circling overhead went roaring by barely twenty feet above the building. The noise was so loud, Marc had to pause.

"If anything happens out there, it's on you," Marc snarled.

"Fuck off, lawyer," Cale whispered so only Marc could hear him. The sheriff turned and abruptly walked back into the jail area.

Another guard brought Brittany to them and Marc was somewhat relieved to see Brittany and the deputy both wore vests.

"Are they all here because of me?" the terrified young woman asked.

Maddy put an arm around her shoulders and assured her she would be all right. Marc, Butch and Andy huddled with the three guards whose names were Tom, Dick and Harry.

"Seriously?" Marc smiled when they told him their names.

It was decided that Andy and Butch would go first, and Marc and the deputies would be on the sides surrounding Brittany and Madeline in the middle. All three deputies offered Maddy their vests which she politely declined.

"I think they are more noise makers than anything else," she said.

When they were ready, Butch pushed the doors open and out they went. As soon as the crowd saw them, pandemonium ensued. The mass of people, most of whom were yelling obscenities, began to push their way toward the phalanx surrounding Brittany.

With Butch and his large friend easily knocking people aside, the group was actually making pretty good progress. Most of the protestors were to their left and Andy's SUV was over to the right. They kept pushing and even knocked a few of the protestors down as they gradually made their way to the big SUV.

The man sitting in the back of the pickup truck with the matching topper was no more than a hundred yards from the crowd. The back window of the topper was open, the truck parked, engine running, pointed away from the building with his wife behind the wheel.

He had watched the small group surrounding Brittany as they made their way toward the big SUV. As they broke into the clear, the circle of the 8-power scope framed her face and the crosshairs were dead center on Brittany's nose. *Pretty girl*, he thought as he waited for the right moment. He had seen the vest she was wearing so he moved the scope for a head shot. At this range, with his expertise, he couldn't miss.

The deputy named Dick was on Brittany's left so close that her head brushed his shoulder three or four times. Marc was moving with her on

Brittany's right. A member of the crowd, a man about Marc's size squeezed past Butch and Marc stepped forward to stop him from grabbing Brittany. As he did this, a large woman on Marc's right reached behind Marc and tried to grab Brittany. Seeing this, Dick stepped in front of Brittany and reached over with his left hand to stop the woman. At that exact moment, a loud *CRRRAAACK!* echoed between the buildings.

At first, everyone in the crowd and those surrounding Brittany went absolutely still and silent. No one was quite sure what that was except it was loud, out of place and somehow familiar. Before anyone knew what happened, Dick collapsed on top of Brittany taking them both to the ground.

Blood began to spurt out from Dick's underarm, a spot not protected by the vest. Madeline, who had been behind Brittany calmly but loudly yelled, "He's been shot! Everybody down!"

In a wild panic, three hundred people began to scatter. Maddy and Marc went for Brittany and pulled her out from under the wounded deputy. She was covered with the man's blood and seriously shaken but they believed she had not been hit and the two of them with Butch leading the way, hustled her to the SUV. The unhurt deputies went into action to save their friend. Tom put pressure on the wound while Harry called for a car to get him to a hospital.

It was Andy who had seen the pickup. He heard the shot and looked right at it as it took off to get out of the parking area. Andy ran to an open space, looked up and began waving at one of the helicopters. The pilot noticed him, waved back and when Andy pointed at the pickup, the pilot gave Andy a thumbs up and took off after the fleeing suspects.

A couple of minutes later, a calm Bob Olson stood on the sidewalk of the government center and watched the SUV taking Brittany away. He was wearing a wig with brown hair down over his ears, a black baseball cap, aviator sunglasses and the mustache and goatee were gone. Had Brittany looked right at him from ten feet away, she would not have recognized him. There were a couple of dozen other protestors who had not panicked still milling about so he didn't stand out in the crowd. Some of them were helping the thirty or forty people who had been trampled and injured during the mad scramble after the shooting. The rest, like Bob, seemed to be enjoying the show. And of course, there was still several cameras filming the aftermath of the melee.

When he could no longer see the truck, he turned to watch the deputies who were working on the wounded man. Gauging from the amount of blood and how pale the man's face was, Bob believed the deputy's chances were not good. Hearing sirens close by, he turned his attention toward the sound and saw four sheriff's cars screaming away

173

from the government center. He shrugged his shoulders, carefully stepped around several of the injured protestors and headed toward his car. "That was pretty exciting. Glad they missed her. Would have ended the fun," he quietly said to himself.

THIRTY-SEVEN

October in Minnesota, in fact, the entire Upper Midwest, like New England can be and normally is, a month that makes life worth living. Comfortable, sunny, pleasant days and cool nights perfect for sleeping are the norm. The only drawback that the natives never completely forget is what lies ahead. Summer is over and Old Man Winter is not far off.

East Coast winter is a source of amusement for the people in "flyover" country. If New York gets eight inches of snow and the temperature drops below thirty, the national TV networks act as if Armageddon is descending upon them. Minnesota, the Dakotas and Wisconsin get Real Winter. What the Easterners call "brutally cold" temps, Midwesterners call "get out and enjoy", which is why October and normally November are months to appreciate.

The October of our story was, if anything, even better than normal. Dry and as pleasant as any month in memory during most of the month and the meteorologists were predicting it to continue and even be a mild winter. A forecast everyone wanted to believe but no one really did. On Halloween, of course, the last day of the month, the kids had mid-fifties temps, dry and calm. It would be the last such day for months.

In the early morning hours of November 1st, a cold front was moving down from Canada into and across the Dakotas. At the same time, warmer, extremely wet air dropping rains across Kansas, Missouri and Nebraska moved north into South Dakota. The TV weather forecasts, usually bordering on hysteria over something like this, were predicting as much as a foot of snow for South Dakota, North Dakota and Minnesota. Later, after the storm passed, they tried to claim they downplayed the actual amount of snow so as not to upset people.

The storm roared across South Dakota, through Western Minnesota during that first day of November, which was, fortunately, a Saturday. After dumping as much as thirty inches in some places, the storm then moved into the Twin Cities mid-afternoon and early evening on Saturday leaving twenty-two inches of wet, heavy snow before moving on into Wisconsin on Sunday. Normally, a storm this early would melt off within a few days. Unfortunately, the upper atmospheric jet stream had shifted southward bringing arctic air and biting winds with it. Winter had abruptly dropped out of the sky and would stay until April.

By the Monday morning, after the storm went through, the streets were plowed and the morning rush hour, while moving a little slower than normal, was barely affected. The freeways were clear, businesses and schools were open and except for the enormous mounds of snow piled up, the Cities were pretty much back to normal.

Marc Kadella, having been stuck at home most of the weekend watching football, set his briefcase on his desk. He slipped out of his overcoat and suit coat, hung both on the coat tree in the corner of his office and sat down in his desk chair. He swiveled around to look out the window at the bundled-up people scurrying along the sidewalks fighting the northwest wind that whipped between the buildings. He was happy to see that the weather had chased off the protestors that had been making fools of themselves along the side of his building. While watching the traffic below, his mind wandered back to the events of the shooting.

The people responsible for the death of the sheriff's deputy, Richard 'Dick' Leakey, a twelve-year veteran who left a widow and two young children behind, were Lester and Clara Young. They were a childless couple, in their mid-thirties from Albert Lea, a small city in southern Minnesota. Neighbors would describe them as a bit of an odd pair. Pleasant enough to say hello to, but they were hard-core, anti-abortion, right-to-life advocates. They erected a large sign in their yard that they fought the city over because of its size and gruesome pictures of aborted fetuses on it. Clara's sister would tell investigators that she believed it was because Clara was unable to conceive.

The attempted murder of Brittany Riley by these two surprised no one that knew them. Clara, and to a lesser degree Lester, had both made comments to friends, relatives and co-workers that Brittany should rot in hell for killing her baby.

The police surmised that they had seen the news reports about Brittany's court appearance. They then drove to Hastings to watch it and were unable to get a seat in the courtroom. After finding out Brittany had made bail, the pair apparently became so incensed they decided to take the law into their own hands.

With a TV helicopter, the sheriff's departments of several counties and half of the state highway patrol chasing them, the couple headed south attempting to flee. With Clara driving, they led their pursuers across two large counties on county highways, small-town streets and even dirt roads for over fifty miles. Unable to shake the helicopter, they finally came to a halt on a dirt road in a Goodhue county farm area with a police roadblock dead ahead. Instead of surrendering and with several firearms in the back of the pickup truck, Clara drove them through a ditch, across an open field to an old, abandon farmhouse a couple hundred yards off of the road.

For the next two hours, law enforcement from all across southern Minnesota poured into the scene. At first, nothing much happened. The back of the dilapidated weather-beaten structure was barely fifty feet from a large cornfield that bordered the empty field where the house stood. A dozen officers in camo gear had slipped into the cornfield behind the house and were watching from the rear.

One of the deputies could see their truck and read off the license plate number from which the suspect's name, address and cell phone numbers were obtained. A captain with the highway patrol, Don Bellows, the senior on-scene officer tried calling the cell phones but received no response. Next, he tried a bullhorn and again no response. By now, there were a total of four news choppers circling overhead, filming the entire episode.

Bellows, the Goodhue County Sheriff and Sheriff Cale discussed their options which were obviously limited. They all agreed that when night came, the fugitives could easily slip out of the house and if they got into the cornfield, it would be hell finding them in the dark. Bellows volunteered to try to walk up to the house to see if he could talk them out. To make everyone just a little edgier, they had all received the news that Deputy Leakey had been DOA at the hospital in Hastings.

Bellows, hands raised, Kevlar helmet and vest on and bullhorn in hand began to slowly walk through the ditch and across the field. He stopped about a hundred yards from the house and used the bullhorn to announce himself and his intentions. As an answer, Lester who had spent four years in the Army and was an excellent rifleman, fired at the captain probably intentionally missing. The bullet struck the ground between Bellow's feet who immediately dove to the ground and began to roll backwards to make himself harder to hit.

Sheriff Cale, boiling mad at the death of his deputy, was closely watching while Bellows made his way toward the house. He had his radio mic in his handset to give the order in case anything happened. The instant he heard the shot and saw Bellows go down, he pressed the send button and barked, "Fire! All units fire! Now!"

Two hundred cops opened up with everything they had. Within a minute, the fragile, crumbling old structure was literally blown apart. Amazingly with the place encircled and bullets coming in from every direction, none of the law officers hit each other. The autopsies of Clara and Lester would find more than twenty bullet holes in each.

For the next several days the massacre, as it came to be called, dominated both the local and national news. With the film provided by the helicopters, the cops shooting, and the house being blown apart, the public couldn't get enough. This was Reality TV at its best, or worst depending on your point of view.

It also engendered pious editorials on TV, in newspapers and magazines from coast-to-coast. Ninety-eight percent of the news stories and editorials were clearly negative toward the police in general and the on-scene officers in particular. Not surprisingly, they managed to overlook their own role in this sordid affair by stirring up the public in general and Clara and Lester Young in particular.

The media opprobrium was not limited to the police. Judge Connors was also in their crosshairs for allowing bail in the first place. Strangely, despite the fact that Marc had made a point of telling several reporters that it was Cale's idea to send Brittany into the middle of the mob, there was very little airtime or newsprint given to this fact. Cale had leaked to his media sources the story that there was no way he could anticipate a lunatic couple in the parking lot shooting at Brittany. Oddly, he came across as almost heroic for his role at the farmhouse. Cale had it reported that he was certain Captain Bellows had been shot and Cale was trying to protect him. After all, the story went, Cale was the one voice of reason who wanted to wait out the suspects and take them into custody to answer for what they did.

Fortunately for all concerned, the attention span of the public and the media isn't much longer than your average six-year-old. A few days after the shooting a married Republican congressman got caught in the backseat of his car, literally with his pants down, receiving oral sex from a prostitute. Much to the relief of the Republican Party hierarchy, the hooker was an adult female. However, she was African-American and the race hustler industry of America, having had a slow summer, decided to use this as an opportunity to further their personal political and financial agenda. The controversy over the exploitation of poor black women raged for a few days. Then, of course, the knucklehead congressman made the obligatory mea culpa apology with his poor, humiliated wife being forced to stand up on the stage with him.

Luckily for him, the next day something truly significant to feed the public's appetite for news occurred. A rumor came out of Southern California that one of the Kardashian sisters was having marital problems. The story turned out to be untrue or at least denied, but no matter. A Kardashian marital rumor normally garnered the same level of media attention as the return of Halley's Comet. And much to the media's delight, a Kardashian family catastrophe occurred almost weekly rather than every seventy-five years.

Marc pushed open the window behind his desk and was shocked by the blast of arctic wind that hit him in the face. Using his bare hand, he brushed off the eight inches of snow that had accumulated on the window's ledge then quickly slid the window back down.

"Hey, sunshine," he heard Carolyn say as he tried to dry his half-frozen right hand.

He spun his chair around and saw her holding a cup of hot coffee for him. "Thanks," he said as he held the cup in his cold hand. "That feels good."

"How was traffic?" Carolyn asked as she sipped at her own cup.

"Not too bad. What a pain in the ass this is. Two days ago, it was beautiful and now this," he answered.

"And according to the weather geeks, it's here to stay," Carolyn said. As she turned to leave she asked, "Open or closed?" referring to his door.

"Leave it open," Marc said.

Despite the early hour, Marc dialed Madeline's cell. She usually slept late because of the hours she routinely kept, but Marc wanted to talk to her, so he tried her believing her phone would be off if she didn't want to be disturbed.

"Hey, Marc," she said before the first ring was completed. "What's up?"

"You're up early."

"I wasn't out much this weekend. Have you looked outside?"

"Good point. Where are we with witnesses?"

"I didn't get a chance to get in touch with the new list you got for me. I'll start working on them this week. How about you?"

"I'm working on my motion to suppress the evidence found at the Rileys during the search. They didn't have any real grounds to search her parents' home. At least I don't think so."

"What happens if you win? Will they throw the case out?"

"I doubt it, although it would exclude some evidence, maybe."

"Why only maybe?"

"It would exclude the life insurance policy, but they could reasonably argue inevitable discovery anyway. That they would have found it with a routine review of Brittany's finances, which is probably true.

"Then there's the cinder block and rope. They could argue that they would have noticed the cinder block around the patio and the Rileys' expectation of privacy in the backyard is thin. I haven't researched it yet. There's also the problem that the patio wall in the backyard is in plain sight and the cops could have easily seen it. If so, is that sufficient probable cause to obtain a search warrant for a sample of the cinder blocks? I'm just not sure."

"When's your hearing?"

"About two weeks. The judge wants to hear all motions, set discovery timetables and a trial date."

"Why are you pushing for an early trial?" Maddy asked.

"I don't want to give them any more time than I have to for them to come up with more evidence. There will be more witnesses for you to interview. The prosecution is doing everything it can to find someone to testify that Brittany was a bad mother and wanted to be rid of the kid. Be ready. Any luck on the Bob Olson search?"

"I'm pretty much going over the same ground the cops did. So far, nothing even close."

"You know, I had a thought…"

"You did? You had a thought?" she teased.

"Yeah, about once a month or so I get one, smartass. Anyway, I was thinking: Did you and the cops check other people, other employees at Macy's? Brittany says that's where she met him. He had scouted her out and approached her at work. He must've been hanging around for a while checking her out. Maybe someone saw him."

"Yes, I have a list of all the mall employees, not just the ones at Macy's, but every one of them that the cops interviewed. I have talked to each of them either in person or on the phone. We talked about this," she reminded him.

"I know, but did they get all of them? Everyone who worked at Macy's around that time? You could use your obvious charms to get a list from someone in their human resources and check. Maybe someone who isn't working there anymore."

"Hmmm. Not bad," Maddy admitted. "Let me see what I can do. It's a long shot but worth a try."

Carolyn walked in and silently handed Marc a note. He read it and said, "I got another call I have to take. I'll talk to you later," and ended the call.

He immediately punched the button for the caller waiting for him. Without even saying hello, Marc blurted out, "I forgot. You were supposed to meet with the DNR agent this week to go back out to the crime scene. Now what?" he asked referring to the snow that had obliterated whatever might have been found there.

"We're okay. I got together with her and we got out there again on Halloween day and went over everything. We also did the measurements and got all of the pictures to show what the actual water level was in July. Plus, she has a record and dated pictures of the water level during that time," Jason Briggs, Marc's criminalist said.

"She did? That's great," a relieved Marc said. "But why would she…"

"She's a bit of a camera buff. Has tons of wildlife pictures and even has a website and sells them. Says she takes pictures of everything.

"She said she took pictures of a lot of the high water along the river and at lakes she has in her zone. They like to keep track. She even has some using a measuring device like a long yardstick. She didn't mention it before and I didn't think to ask. She was going to email them to me, but I talked to her yesterday and she has been really busy since the storm hit digging out campers and other idiots who didn't get their asses home when they should have. She'll send them to me the first chance she gets. Probably in the next day or two. I'll let you know what I find."

"Okay. Good." Marc said. "Anything else?"

"I'm still waiting for the results on the rope and cinder block. Don't hold your breath. What about an autopsy?"

"I don't see where it can help us. They can't find a cause of death, why should we help them?"

"Agreed. I'll call you later this week."

THIRTY-EIGHT

Melinda Pace yawned and rubbed both eyes with her knuckles. She had just finished watching the final edit of the show that would be aired later today. Melinda and her producer, Robbie Nelson, were in her office reviewing the taping. They were reporting on the trial of a suburban man who shot and killed a neighbor over a dispute about feeding local deer. The accused had been feuding about this with the victim and several of his neighbors for years.

The accused and his live-in girlfriend, both in their fifties, had been feeding the deer since moving into the neighborhood. Just about all of the people living within a half a mile had been trying to get them to stop. The accused had a double sized lot and on any given day, as many as forty or fifty deer would wander onto the property for food.

Deer may be beautiful and nice to look at but they are also dangerous, a health hazard due to Lyme disease and very destructive of lawns and gardens. Deer do not clean up after themselves either and everyone had to deal with the excrement they left behind.

A couple of months ago an argument between the deer-lover and the man who lived directly across the street became a bit heated. While the girlfriend stood on the front lawn screaming at the neighbor across the street, the accused went inside and grabbed a shotgun. He came out and stormed across the yard toward the victim who watched in apparent stunned disbelief. Witness' stories varied about the number of shots but the best guess was somewhere between four and six. Whatever the number, the poor man was lying dead in the street in a massive pool of his own blood and internal organs when the police and paramedics arrived.

The victim's wife accused the girlfriend of encouraging the shooting by screaming over and over for him to keep shooting. The girlfriend was subsequently acquitted of aiding and abetting a homicide. The deer lover was now being tried for murder claiming self-defense and temporary insanity.

Melinda wrapped up that day's show by sarcastically explaining this somewhat novel concept. "What he is claiming to the jury is that: One, I acted in self-defense, in fear of my life. Or two, if you don't believe I acted in self-defense, then I was temporarily crazy. I'm a little skeptical that he'll be able to pull that one off. I'm not sure he'll be able to get away with saying 'I acted in self-defense and was crazy at the same time.'"

"Not bad," Melinda said, yawning again.
"Are we boring you?" Robbie asked.

"Oh, shut up," she mildly rebuked him. "We need something else. Something more about Brittany Riley. This trial of the deer feeder is pretty good, but it just doesn't grab people the way Brittany does. Let's face it; the deer feeder is just a crazy old goofball. What's Gabriella been up to? Does she have anything going on with Brittany?"

"Gabriella's been covering the deer feeder trial," Robbie answered her. "I'll talk to her. Maybe she can find some time to get together with her source in the sheriff's office. That's the way these things go. You know that," Robbie continued. "There are periods where there isn't much going on. There is some kind of court hearing scheduled I think. If I remember correctly, it's in a few days. We'll have the live feed come into the station and record it. If there's anything worthwhile, we'll use it."

"See if Gabriella can find out what the hearing is about and if anything, interesting is going to come out of it."

"Will do," Robbie said as he left Melinda's office.

Gabriella hung up her winter coat and slid into the booth opposite Stu Doyle. She set her purse on the bench seat next to her, stretched her back and turned her head from side to side as if getting out a kink in her neck. Just before she arrived at the restaurant, she reminded herself to eat something and limit herself, at most, to two glasses of wine. The last time she met Doyle like this, having not eaten anything since breakfast, after four glasses of wine, Doyle was starting to look pretty good to her. Fortunately, her rational brain was still working, and she managed to get out of there and home unsullied.

"Hey, Gabriella," Stu said while giving her what he believed was a seductive look. "You're looking particularly delicious this evening."

"Don't bother, Stu. Ain't gonna happen," she abruptly answered him.

"No harm in trying," the married detective said with a slight grin and a shrug. "Aren't you at least a little flattered?"

"Terribly," she answered with a bored inflection. "Wait, I'm sorry. That was mean and unnecessary. Look, Stu, you're not unattractive but you're married, and I don't approve of married people, men or women, cheating. So, give it a rest.

"I'm hungry," she said when the waitress arrived. "You want to split a pizza? I'll buy and expense it."

"Sure, why not," Doyle agreed.

"What's going on with the Riley case?" Gabriella quietly asked after the waitress had taken their order and left.

Doyle shifted his eyes back and forth as if making sure they were not observed before saying, "We've dug up more dirt on her. More stuff on the internet. Plus, we've found old high school friends and acquaintances who tell us she was quite the little party girl."

"Exactly what?" Gabriella asked.

"You know, the school bicycle. Everybody rode her."

"That is really disgusting, Stu," Gabriella said with a look of distaste. "Plus, is that fact or rumor?"

"It's probably a little of both. Even these days it doesn't take much for a girl to get a reputation. Give it to Melinda Pace, she'll use it."

"Is there anything else going on?"

"Yeah, there is. The sheriff knows about our little arrangement, he doesn't know why I talk to you, specifically. He probably thinks we're sleeping together," Doyle said holding up a hand to Gabriella as she started to protest. "I didn't tell him that. Anyway, he told me to ask you, as a payback favor, to cover a bust we're gonna do in the early morning, day after tomorrow. There's a pretty good size meth lab on a farm about ten miles southeast of Farmington. We've been watching it for a while. After the shit hit the fan when Brittany made bail and we had the shootout a couple weeks ago, Cale figures, politically, he could use some good press. What do you think?"

The pizza arrived before Gabriella could answer and as hungry as she was, she wolfed down two large slices. She drank most of her glass of Miller Lite, mulled it over for a bit then agreed to cover it. A little quid pro quo for the information she was being fed never hurt and besides, a meth lab bust could get interesting. Some of these biker types were not shy about a gunfight with cops.

The raid was timed for dawn and Gabriella, along with a cameraman named Ramone who also drove the van, followed the caravan of cops south to the farm. Robbie Nelson had talked Gabriella into letting him ride along. All three wore Kevlar vests and were given Kevlar helmets as well.

Fortunately, or unfortunately, depending on your point of view, the raid went off without a hitch. The northwest wind that had blown across the state for the past several days was gone. It was an unseasonably cold twenty degrees this morning and the farm and surrounding countryside was blanketed by almost two feet of snow.

The twenty sheriff's deputies and state troopers had stealthily surrounded the property just before dawn. There was a total of four buildings, a rundown old farmhouse and barn, a newer shed for farm implements and equipment and a shiny new pole barn sitting off by itself. The raid was over in less than ten minutes and for the next hour, Gabriella and Ramone filmed just about everything that happened. The best shot, the one Cale pressed her to use was when she was interviewing him, had been set up so the eight scraggly looking prisoners, including three women, hard, foul-mouthed biker chicks, were used as a backdrop. The eight of them were sitting in the snow, cursing and cold on the ground with their wrists flex cuffed behind themselves. All of this was filmed in front of the new pole barn meth lab while deputies were carrying out the evidence.

It turned out to be one of the largest meth lab busts in the state for the past several years. The state BCA and Federal DEA office made sure they got in on it as well by running out to Hastings to get filmed with Cale. Every newscast the station aired that day ran between five and seven minutes of the raid along with Cale being interviewed. Sheriff Cale could not have been more pleased.

THIRTY-NINE

Marc drove his new Buick Encore north on Third Avenue in downtown Minneapolis. The small SUV was a bit of an indulgence he gave himself after being fully paid for the Prentiss trial. Mother Nature dumped another three inches of snow on the city the night before. He was again being taught that four-wheel drive isn't a big advantage in slick, wet snow. Marc was running a little late for a settlement conference of a DUI client and it annoyed him. Marc wasn't what anyone would call punctual obsessive, but he did like to be on time for court appearances. As he approached the big granite, glass and chrome building, he cursed a little when he saw the "Full" sign turned on for the building's underground parking ramp. Just before he reached the corner of Third and Fifth Street, a man in a Ford F-150, going much too fast, cut in front of him, slid into the curb and spun the pickup completely around before it stopped on the light rail tracks on Fifth. Marc was lucky to have seen him coming and was able to stop in time. The driver of the pickup was even luckier. The truck came to a stop in the middle of the intersection astride the train rails. Fortunately, there was no train in sight. Even luckier for the knucklehead behind the wheel was the fact that there weren't any cops around even though this happened in front of the Old City Hall building which also houses the police department.

Traffic on Third Avenue and Fifth Street came to a complete halt, including pedestrians. Everyone watched in stunned silence. The intersection remained still for what seemed like five minutes but was, in reality, only a few seconds. The pickup driver put the truck in reverse, backed off of the rails, swung the vehicle to head it north along Third again and then hit the gas. He took off just as fast and recklessly as he had been driving when he caused all of the commotion. Marc just watched the idiot go, shook his head, and then took a right on Fifth to go to a parking ramp.

Marc hurried down the hallway to the courtroom 1520 and went inside. The courtroom was almost empty. The prosecutor from the city attorney's office, a young man named Mike Upham was talking to a defense lawyer, a young woman Marc did not know. Marc greeted his client, Scott Tanner and then took a seat at the defense table.

When he finished with the other lawyer, Upham looked at Marc and said, "Do you need some time, or should we go back and get it done?"

"We're all set, aren't we? Nothing else?" Marc answered. The case had been settled quickly over the phone and this court appearance was to take the plea and finish it.

"Nope," Upham said as he stood up. "Let's do it."

After finishing the plea, Marc had reduced the charge to careless driving which had pleased his client, he took the elevator up two floors to seventeen. He went into 1745 through the hallway doors to find court was in session and Margaret Tennant on the bench. She was listening to one of the lawyers drone on about some obscure, probably outdated point of civil law. When Marc came in, she looked at him and involuntarily smiled and her eyes noticeably lit up. She almost waved but stopped herself and put her hand back on the desktop. Marc quietly took a seat in the empty gallery and patiently waited for her to take a break.

Margaret immediately stopped the verbose insurance defense lawyer by asking, without apologizing for the interruption, "Do you have anything new to tell me that isn't contained in your one hundred thirty-eight-page brief?"

"Well, um, no, your Honor," the man said after looking at his two associates, both of whom shook their heads.

"How about you, Mr. Markham?" she asked the lone plaintiff's attorney.

"No, your Honor," the man said while rising from his chair.

"Good. I'm ready to rule. Defendant's motion for summary judgment is denied. Mr. Benson," she said looking at the lead defense counsel. "There are a number of issues of fact for a jury. This motion was a waste of time and should not have been brought." She continued as she held up his large "brief". "I'm fining you, personally, one thousand dollars, your firm five thousand and ordering you to pay plaintiff's lawyer a thousand dollars in attorney fees."

"Your Honor," the red-faced Benson said as he stood to protest.

"Not a word!" Margaret said as she glared at the man. "You want to appeal, go ahead. Be thankful I'm not bringing a bar complaint against you. You'll have my order for mediation within thirty days. We're adjourned." Margaret stood to leave, looked at Marc and indicated with her eyes and head he should follow her.

Marc quietly closed the door to her chambers and watched her remove her robe to hang it on a coat rack. She turned back to him, looked him over with a sad smile and said, "Hi. How are you?"

"Missing you," he said as he took a couple of hesitant steps toward her, uncertain of how she would respond.

"Really? Me too," she said as they rushed to each other. She jumped in his arms and kissed him on the mouth and face many times while muttering, "I'm sorry," over and over. After a minute of this, they parted, stepped back and looked each other over.

"That went pretty well," Marc said, and Margaret laughed. With a sly look, he turned his head to her couch, raised his eyebrows and said, "Hmmmm?"

Margaret laughed again then said, "Not a bad idea, but I have another hearing in about five minutes."

"That might actually be enough."

"You're probably right," she agreed.

"How about lunch?" he asked.

"Oh damn, your timing isn't the best. I have a full schedule. I was going to grab a bite at my desk and look over some case files. Come by tonight and I'll make you dinner and well, you know...."

"About six?"

"Perfect," Margaret said as she stepped into him again. "How's your case? I'm sorry I maybe prejudged her."

"She's innocent. The case itself is moving along slowly. We have a lot of witnesses to interview. In fact, there's an omnibus hearing today at 1:00," he concluded while looking at her wall clock.

"A spring trial date?" she asked.

"No," Marc replied. "Probably right after New Year's. Maybe mid-January. I don't want to give them any more time than I have to.

"See you later. I'm really happy you stopped."

"Ah, well I guess I should tell you the main reason I stopped was to find out how Bubba's doing?" Marc said referring to Margaret's Himalayan Siamese.

"He's fine, smart ass. Now beat it. I have work to do."

Marc laughed and feeling better than he had for weeks, with a noticeable spring in his step, walked out of her chambers.

The media and court junkies were in full attendance for the omnibus hearing which began promptly at 1:00. An omnibus hearing is essentially a time for the judge to decide issues before trial. Marc argued that there was no probable cause for the search of the Rileys' residence and any evidence obtained should be excluded. Also, the search warrant was too vague and even if the search was allowed, the life insurance policy should be excluded.

Marc got his first look at Lowell Vanderbeck in action and he came away impressed. The man thought highly of himself, but that didn't preclude him from handling himself in court with poise, skill and confidence. He deftly countered every argument Marc made, exactly as Marc had anticipated.

No witnesses were called which made the hearing go faster and shortly after two o'clock, Connors stopped the lawyers to rule on what had been argued so far.

"Your Honor," Marc said. "I haven't had a chance to talk about venue."

"I know, Mr. Kadella," the judge politely said. "We'll get to it in a few minutes." Connors then went on to make his ruling. Even though he took the time to make a couple of points seemingly in Marc's favor, he came down on the prosecution's side right down the line.

"As to a change of venue," Connors continued. "If it's all right with you," he said looking at the lawyers, Brittany was not in attendance, "I want to discuss that issue in chambers. We'll take a fifteen-minute break then reconvene in chambers."

When the lawyers had taken the chairs in front of the judge's desk Connors asked the court reporter if she was ready. She answered affirmatively, and he turned to the lawyers.

"I thought we could do this informally and I think it's best to keep the media in the dark for now. There is an obvious problem with publicity in this case," he said to Vanderbeck and Hart who both agreed.

"However, Mr. Kadella, I'm not sure what we can do about it," he said to Marc. "Where can we go in Minnesota where publicity isn't a problem?"

"Plus, the defense has not demonstrated his client cannot get a fair trial because of it," Hart interjected.

"She has a point," Connors said. "I have an idea. This case is going to require a sequestered jury, no matter where we go. How about this; instead of moving the trial to a different county, how about we go somewhere else, pick the jury, move them back here and put them up in a hotel? That way, all the rest of us can stay home. It's no hardship on the jury. They're going to be sequestered in any event. There would be no need for the rest of us to live out of a suitcase and pay the extra expenses of hotel living."

"Good idea," Marc agreed and Vanderbeck and Hart both concurred. "Let me make a suggestion, your Honor."

"Sure," Connors said.

"You alone decide where we're going to go. You set it up and you keep it to yourself until the very last minute. The minute it becomes public, the media will be all over it. And if you tell anyone else at all, the news people will find out about it."

"Mr. Vanderbeck, any suggestions or objections?" Connors asked.

"The obvious one, your Honor. How will we prepare our voir dire of the jury pool if we are not told who they are ahead of time?" Vanderbeck replied.

"I won't know either so neither side has an advantage," Marc said.

"He's right," Connors said to Vanderbeck. "No side will have an unfair advantage or disadvantage. I like the idea. I'm going to order it."

FORTY

Marc hung up the phone on his desk, slapped his hands together, pumped his fist and said, out loud, "Yes! Finally, I get some good news."

The call he just finished was from his criminalist, Jason Briggs. Briggs had completed his analysis of the contents of Brittany's car trunk. The CSU team had vacuumed the trunk and sent the contents to Briggs after they had gone through it. What Briggs found was a lot of blanket and other fibers that are normally found on children's toys, such as stuffed animals. He had compared those to items found in Becky's bedroom and could testify that there was an absolute match. Briggs could also conclude that the hairs found in the trunk, positively identified as Becky's, could have easily been transferred from a blanket or toy into the trunk.

Because the defense need only show reasonable doubt, Marc could use these findings to argue Becky was never in the trunk. Her blanket and stuffed animals were placed in there and that's how the hairs got in there. The prosecution could not even speculate with any degree of certainty when the hairs got in there, so Marc had some good news about some of the evidence.

Marc asked Briggs about the evidence of the cinder block found in the trunk.

"There was a lot of it," Briggs answered. "Much more than there would have been from just one brick. It's certainly more consistent with what Floyd told us, that Brittany's car was also used to haul the cinder blocks from the store back to the Rileys'."

"Was it spread out throughout the trunk as if several blocks were in there?"

"I don't know," Briggs said. "They vacuumed everything up and their report doesn't have anything in it about that. I just know there was too much for just one brick unless it fell apart."

"Which didn't happen, the one pulled out of the river was intact," Marc said.

"Right, you want a written report?"

"No. I would have to turn that over to the prosecution. If they want to interview you, cooperate and be honest. No written report." With that, he ended the call.

A short while later, Marc heard loud laughter coming from the receptionist's area of the offices. He opened his office door to find Madeline chatting with the staff and Connie.

"Oh, shoot," he said. "I forgot we're meeting now."

Maddy gave him a dirty look, turned to Connie and said, "I should be offended. He forgot about me!"

191

"He's a man." Connie sighed. "You learn to live with their many shortcomings."

"Ha, ha. Too funny," Marc said. "Come in here," he said feigning annoyance at Maddy.

He stepped aside holding the door for her as she walked past and playfully gave him a light punch on the shoulder.

Marc told her the news he just received about the contents of Becky's trunk. When he finished he asked, "Where are we with the witnesses?"

Maddy, reciting from memory, said, "I've interviewed twenty-seven people, everyone on the list they gave us. Of the twenty-seven, most are acquaintances or people she worked with who don't know her very well. None of those have anything bad to say about her relationship with Becky. In fact, the ones who did have knowledge of her relationship with Becky all told the cops she always talked about how much she loved her little girl. How Becky was the best thing in her life.

"The list also includes a few relatives; John and Charlotte Daniels who you met and an older brother of Floyd, Martin Riley. He doesn't see him much. He says it's because Barbara doesn't like him, and the feeling is mutual.

"There are the three close girlfriends Brittany goes out with that we've talked about that want to testify for her. That leaves three ex-boyfriends who may be a problem. All three of them told the investigator and me that Brittany, after a few drinks, made comments about not wanting Becky. That maybe Becky was kind of a drag on her life. None of them could remember her specific words, just…"

"A twenty-two-year-old widow with a young child on her hands to raise," Marc said.

"That's what it sounded like to me. The prosecution will use them for motive, that and the life insurance. Do you want to meet with them? They're decent guys and all of them said they'd be willing to talk to you," Maddy said.

"Yeah, I do. Set it up, please. What about the mysterious Bob Olson, any luck?"

"I've been over the same ground as the cops. I don't think they missed anything. I did, finally with your subpoena, get a list of all the employees that worked at Macy's last summer. There's about a dozen I need to contact, people who worked there that the cops didn't interview. When's the trial set for?"

"I have a scheduling conference set for tomorrow. We'll set it then. I want to go as soon as possible. We'll see," Marc shrugged.

"Um, Marc, about my bill…"

"Oh, yeah, sorry," he said as he pulled a checkbook from his desk.

"It's just that Christmas is only a week away and if I want to get you a gift…"

"Don't do that," Marc said as he finished writing the check and smiled as he handed it to her.

"Thanks. I said 'if' I want to get you a gift," she laughed. "Seriously though, how's the money situation for the case?"

"Okay for now," he answered her.

"How's business for everyone in the office? Is this case causing problems?"

"Hard to tell," Marc answered. "December is always slow around here. The Holidays are always bad for business. We'll see once the trial starts. At least with the cold, snowy weather, the idiots aren't marching up and down the street outside."

Maddy stood up to go then said, "I'll set up those interviews and let you know. Most of the people I talk to say she was a great mother, at least the ones who know."

"We'll get subpoenas for them when we have some dates set. In the meantime, keep digging for Bob Olson."

Marc parked his car in the Dakota County Government Center lot in the closest spot he could find. The complex was out on the fringe of the small city adjacent to mostly open fields. Overnight the sky had cleared leaving a bright sunshine day, but the temperature was barely ten above zero, cold for December. To make it a little worse, the wind whipped across the open, snow-covered fields bringing the wind chill well below zero. Along with several other people scurrying to get inside, Marc almost ran the last fifty feet to the door.

Marc seated himself at one of the tables in Connors' empty courtroom. A few minutes later the court clerk came out, cheerily said hello and noted his appearance on the record. The conference was scheduled for 10:00 and at 10:15, Vanderbeck and Hart showed up. The clerk immediately took them back and the judge rose to greet them as they entered his chambers. Hart apologized for their tardiness while Vanderbeck said nothing about it.

"Okay, let's get started," Connors said. "Any motions today?"

"Yes, your Honor," Marc answered as he handed copies of a document to all three of them. "I realize you have already ruled on the admissibility of evidence gathered at the Rileys' home. I would like to revisit the hairs found in Brittany's trunk. They are highly prejudicial and offer nothing in the way of proof of the crimes charged. They can't tell you how the hairs got in the trunk, when they got in there or anything whatsoever…"

"Points I am sure you'll be able to make to the jury. I'm letting them in Marc," Connors said cutting off Hart who had started to refute Marc's contention. "Do you want me to bring in a court reporter and put it on the record?"

"No, your Honor," Marc answered. "If you'll note in the court's file that I requested it again and you turned me down."

"I'll put it in my order that I will issue from today's conference," Connors said.

"Judge, if I may?" Vanderbeck asked.

"Sure, what is it?"

"I would like to make a plea offer and get some input from you." Vanderbeck turned to look at Marc who was now looking at him.

"We're willing to let her plead to the second-degree murder count and drop everything else. We would recommend twenty years in prison, she would do less than fifteen. She's a young woman. She would still have a long life ahead of her when she got out. Would you agree to the twenty-year recommendation, judge?" Vanderbeck asked Connors.

"Yeah, I could probably go along with that," Connors said. "What do you think, Marc?"

"I'd recommend no. My client maintains her innocence," Marc said. "I'll put it to her, but when she asks for my opinion and she will, I'll tell her no."

"Okay." Connors shrugged. "Let us know if she agrees. What about scheduling?"

The four of them spent the next half hour discussing deadlines for discovery, witness lists and any more motions to be brought. Vanderbeck and Hart argued vociferously for a trial date to be scheduled in June at the earliest. Marc would have none of it. He was adamant that his client would not waive her right to a speedy trial. Pushing as he was for an early trial date was quite risky. It shortened the time the police and prosecution had to find evidence and prepare witnesses. It had the same effect on the defense, but Marc was willing to risk it.

"A trial date?" Connors asked rhetorically. "How long will we need?"

"Six to eight weeks," Vanderbeck replied.

"Not a chance," Connors said to him. "Four at most. Get your act together. Marc?"

"I'm thinking three to four," he quickly agreed just to stay on the judge's good side.

"Okay, we'll schedule it for four and be prepared to take testimony evenings and weekends if necessary. I'm not going to keep the jury sequestered any longer than necessary." Connors looked at the calendar on his desk then said, "Monday, January twenty-sixth."

"I'm okay with that," Marc said.

"I have a conflict," Vanderbeck said. "I was planning a vacation then."

"Where are you going?" Connors affably asked.

"Florida to visit friends," Vanderbeck lied.

"Have a good time. I'm sure Ms. Hart can handle things until you get back. Get your discovery done. I don't want to hear any excuses. All motions to be completed by the twenty-fourth."

"Have you decided where we're going to pick the jury?" Danica Hart asked.

"Yes, and it's in the process of being arranged. How much notice will you need?"

"We'll be starting jury selection on January twenty-sixth?"

"Yes," the judge answered.

"When can we get a list of the jury pool?" Vanderbeck asked.

"The twenty-fourth. In fact, let's schedule another conference for that day for any last-minute problems, motions or whatever needs to be done."

"That's not enough time with the jury pool," Vanderbeck objected.

"How about we just take the first twelve people through the door?" Marc challenged.

"Seriously?" Hart asked. "I'm tempted." She said with a twinkle in her eye and a mischievous smile.

"Don't be silly," Vanderbeck practically barked.

"Anything else?" Connors asked. "No? Good. I'll have an order out in the next couple of days. If I don't see you before then, have a Merry Christmas."

The three lawyers went into the courtroom to leave and found it almost full of media people. The horde rose as one when the attorneys passed by and exited through the hallway doors. When they got out into the hallway, several of them went after the state's attorneys while others stayed with Marc. Vanderbeck was only a few feet away and Marc could hear him piously informing them that they would have no comment since their policy is and always will be to not try cases through the media.

Gabriela Shriqui had squeezed through the crowd to stand directly in front of Marc. Smiling directly at her he told them the hearing was no big deal. It was just a conference to discuss and resolve some routine issues. Gabriella was the first to ask specifics. Despite the fact that Marc suspected she was the main recipient of leaks from the sheriff, he couldn't help liking her. She was just doing her job.

"Nice try, Gabriella," Marc said as he turned and walked away.

When Vanderbeck and Hart reached the exterior doors leading out to the parking lot, Vanderbeck said to her, "Get the car and pull it up in the circle. I have a call to make."

Hart gave him a nasty look and said, "You're quite the gentleman, Lowell."

Ignoring her and stepping away, he placed the phone to his ear. A moment later, Sheriff Cale answered. The two of them had a brief exchange then Vanderbeck turned to wait for Hart and at the same time, Cale called Stu Doyle into his office.

FORTY-ONE

When Marc left the courthouse, he drove straight to the Rileys' house to give them an update. Although she was not strictly confined to the house by the terms of her bail release, Brittany Riley did not like to go out in public. The few times she did, people immediately recognized her. A couple of times someone would make a nasty comment but mostly they would stare then move away as if she might be contagious. Brittany tried her best not to show the hurt those actions caused. Bad enough she had lost her baby so cruelly but to be tried, convicted and treated like a leper by the public was immensely painful.

Marc had not bothered to call ahead. They knew about the conference he was coming from and would be waiting for him. Although Floyd was back to work, Barbara had been granted a leave of absence and could take as long as she wanted. Even so, rather than hang around the house, she went into work two or three times a week anyway. The tension, stress and depression, with which everyone in the family had to deal, needed to be relieved. Barbara, Floyd and Tim could at least go to work where there were friendly, supportive people. Brittany was stuck.

Marc turned the corner to drive down the street to the Rileys'. He had not been here for almost a week and what he saw shocked him. There was only one TV van parked across the street looking cold and forlorn. And there wasn't a single protestor marching up and down. Apparently, Old Man Winter had tested their commitment and resolve and found them wanting.

He parked in their empty driveway and as he strolled up the walkway to the front door, he couldn't resist waving at whoever was in the van, probably filming him. Floyd opened the door before he could knock, and they greeted each other as Marc stepped into the house.

The four took seats in the living room and Marc explained what happened in court. Brittany was not looking well at all. The bags under her eyes, the disheveled, apathetic look of a very pretty young woman were certain indications of the stress she was under. When Marc told her about the trial date, she became visibly more alert. The news that the case had a finite time limit had a very positive effect.

"I need to talk to Brittany alone about something," Marc said to her parents. Barbara had heard this so many times by now it no longer annoyed her, especially since she knew she could get out of Brittany what they talked about once Marc left.

"Let's go in the dining room," Brittany said.

They looked at each other across the dining room table. Marc reached forward, took her hand and said, "You're not looking well.

You're not eating, sleeping or taking care of yourself. You're depressed, and you need to be in therapy."

"I know," Brittany said with a weak smile as she squeezed his hand.

Marc released her hand and sat back in his chair while saying, "I have a psychiatrist I want you to see. We need to have a plausible explanation for the jury of why you took so long to call the cops and report Becky missing."

"You know why." Brittany bitterly replied as she turned to look at the living room where her mother waited.

"I need to have you see a professional, an expert we can call at trial. Plus, the prosecution will want to have an expert to talk to you if we do. It's very important."

"Okay, if you think it will help. Whatever you say, Marc," Brittany agreed. "When?"

"Tomorrow. She has set aside two hours tomorrow afternoon. Two o'clock." Marc handed her a business card with the doctor's name and address on it.

"She's in Eagan?" Brittany asked rhetorically after reading the card. "My mother will want to sit in."

"I've already warned Lorraine about that. She'll let Barbara sit in for a while but then ask her to leave. She's an M.D. which means she can write prescriptions. Ask her for something to help you sleep."

Marc took a few minutes to tell her about the plea offer from Vanderbeck. He barely got the words out before Brittany was emphatically telling him no. She would never say she hurt Becky, even if she went to prison for the rest of her life.

Marc turned his head toward the back of the house. He looked past the drawn curtains, through the patio doors and out at the snow-covered patio. With a curious expression, he stood and walked to the patio doors and looked over the backyard.

"What is it? What's wrong?" Brittany asked as she came up behind him.

"Get your dad for me please."

While Brittany went to retrieve Floyd, Marc continued to look at the patio area, especially the wall around it.

"What's up?" Floyd asked when he arrived at the window with Brittany and Barbara trailing.

"How many bricks did it take to build that wall?" Marc asked.

"Oh, geez, I don't remember. It's been what," he turned to look at Barbara, "three years ago last summer when we built it?"

"Yes, it was," Barbara agreed.

"And you had a few of the cinder blocks left over when you finished?"

"That's right," Floyd agreed. "I don't remember how many. Maybe five or six. I shoved them under the shelves in the garage and haven't looked at them since. Not till the cops were here."

"We need to figure it out. We need to know if one of them is missing. Did you give any of them to anyone…?"

"No, uh uh," Floyd said with certainty.

"…for any reason? Where did you get them?"

"Menards."

"Did you pay cash or use a card?"

"I have a Menards card that I use there," Floyd answered.

"Would you still have the receipt?" Marc asked Barbara.

"I doubt it," she answered shaking her head. "I'll look but I don't usually keep them that long."

Marc sat down in the same chair at the dining room table. He placed his left elbow on the table and his hand cupped over his mouth while he stared at the opposite wall. After a minute or so he removed his hand and looked at the three Rileys.

He turned to look at Barbara and said, "Okay, Barbara, try to find the receipt or at least figure out when they were bought. If you can't find the receipt we'll subpoena Menards and see if they can pull it out of their computer. Let's hope so."

Robbie Nelson was on vacation. He was taking a few days off to visit his mother's home in Rockford, Illinois for Christmas. This was a bit of a problem because that meant there was no one at the station to babysit Melinda. When he was absent, Melinda's wine consumption during the day had a tendency to start earlier and last longer.

It was barely two o'clock and Melinda was about to finish what had been a full liter of Chardonnay. She and Cordelia Davis were reviewing all of the film for today's show to make editing decisions. They were in one of the station's edit rooms when they heard a light knock on the door. Cordelia opened it to find Gabriella Shriqui standing in the hall.

"Hey!" Cordelia said. "What's up?"

"Is Robbie in there?" Gabriella asked as she peeked around Cordelia to look in the room.

"He's on vacation for Christmas," Cordelia said. "Come in," she added as she stood back to allow Gabriella to enter.

Melinda turned to look at Gabriella standing in the doorway. "What do you have? Anything I can use?"

"Maybe," Gabriella answered trying not to commit.

"What? Tell me."

Gabriella stood silent for a few seconds deciding how much to tell her. "I got some information from a source about Brittany Riley. I have a meeting with Hunter now and I wanted Robbie to sit in."

"What do you have? Can I use it?"

"That's what I'm seeing Hunter about," Gabriella answered. "Maybe Cordelia could…"

"No," Melinda said as she stood and walked toward the door. "She can stay here and start editing. I'll go with you."

"That's not necessary…"

"Yes, it is! Let's go."

The two women took chairs in front of the news director, Gabriella's boss, Hunter Oswood.

"What do you need?" Oswood asked.

"I got a tip from a source over lunch," Gabriella began. "There was a scheduling conference with the judge and lawyers this morning on the Riley case."

"They set a trial date?" Oswood asked.

"January twenty-sixth."

"That's pretty quick," Oswood said.

"Yeah, it is. That's not what I wanted to talk to you about. My source claims Brittany's lawyer, Marc Kadella, offered a plea deal. She would plead to second-degree murder if the judge would agree to a maximum sentence of twenty years."

"That is huge! I want it for today's show," Melinda said practically jumping out of her chair.

"There's more." Gabriella turned away from Melinda and looked back at Oswood. "There's a big deal going on about jury selection. They're selecting the jury in a different venue. Kadella's worried about all of the publicity. He believes his client has already been tried and convicted by the media," she continued turning to look at Melinda who ignored the comment.

"One of the prosecutors suggested they simply take the first twelve people through the door to use as a jury. Kadella about had a fit that anyone would even suggest that. Finally, Kadella tried to get some evidence excluded but the judge turned him down."

"I want it! I want to use all of it," Melinda repeated.

Oswood held up a hand to quiet Melinda, then said to Gabriella, "You don't seem quite as enthused about this as Melinda. Why not?"

Gabriella hesitated for a couple of seconds then said, "It doesn't sound right to me. I know Marc Kadella a little bit and I'm just not sure I buy this. I've talked to him several times and he is adamant that Brittany is innocent. This sounds like bullshit coming from the prosecutors to taint the jury pool."

"Oh, nonsense…" Melinda started to say but Oswood cut her off.

"Is there any way you can verify this?" Oswood asked.

"I could call Kadella," Gabriella said.

"He'll just deny it," Melinda protested.

"She's right. Anyone else?"

"I've tried talking to the prosecutors on other things. They just say 'no comment' then leak what they want through the sheriff," Gabriella said.

Oswood picked up his desk phone and dialed an extension. "I have Melinda and Gabriella in here. Could you come in and join us? I'd like your input."

After replacing the phone, in less than a minute the station G.M., Madison Eyler came through the door. Instead of sitting down, she leaned against the window frame next to Oswood's desk.

"Tell her," Oswood said to Gabriella.

After repeating the story for Eyler, including her misgivings about the story's veracity, Gabriella sat back and waited for a decision.

"I'm not real crazy about it," Eyler said to Oswood. "It would be nice if we had another source for verification. Have you used this source before?" she asked Gabriella.

"Yes," Gabriella nodded her head.

"And?"

"The information has always been good before," Gabriella answered.

Eyler turned back to Oswood and said, "This is going to make her look really guilty."

"I know," Oswood agreed.

Eyler said to Melinda, "You want to run with this?"

"Hell yes. She is guilty for Christ's sake. What's the problem?"

"We're going to have to put you on the air, Gabriella," Eyler said.

"I know, how about if I say we have not been able to confirm this from any other source?" Gabriella answered.

"Good idea," Eyler said.

"Bullshit!" Melinda yelled. "It's still my show and…"

"You still work for this station. Have her say the disclaimer. Relax Melinda. The audience won't even hear it. Do you have time to film the show again?"

"No, but we can do it live. I'll lead with this and the rest of it I can do from the teleprompter."

"Okay, we'll go live on your show. Use a tape for the newscasts then promo your show to repeat at 6:30," Eyler decreed.

Melinda's show went on live at 4:00 and led with Melinda interviewing Gabriella reporting the leak. Gabriella was her normal, professional self and truthfully reported what she had been told and gave the ass-covering disclaimer.

Unfortunately, since Robbie was not around to monitor and curtail Melinda's drinking problem, the effects of the three additional glasses of wine she drank after leaving the meeting in Oswood's office were kicking in about this time. Melinda completed the interview of Gabriella and after Gabriella left, she got through the scripted part of the remainder of the show just fine. Melinda decided to wrap up the show by proclaiming that Brittany must be guilty, otherwise, why offer to plead? Also, her lawyer is using every trick in the book to prevent the jury from seeing damning evidence.

"I hope you have a very Merry Christmas, Brittany. I hope the death of your beautiful little baby girl doesn't prevent you from a joyous Christmas and a very Happy New Year. And folks, if you're out and about on Christmas Eve or Christmas Day, be sure to stop by the Rileys' and wish Brittany a very Merry Christmas."

As bad as that was, her alcohol-addled mind decided it would be a good idea to read the Rileys' address to the audience, which she proceeded to do three times.

Oswood and Eyler argued for a half hour about a rerun of the show at 6:30. Eyler, being Oswood's boss, had the final say and the show was put on as scheduled. She did agree to cut out the part where Melinda gave the Rileys' address. Too little, too late. The damage had been done.

Melinda was forced to take a vacation through New Year's, a suspension that was rescinded the very next day when the overnight ratings came in. The four o'clock show was up almost fifteen percent and the 6:30 was up almost forty percent over the time slot's normal audience. The viewing public had spoken loud and clear. Their voyeuristic appetite for the Brittany Riley reality show could not be sated.

Gabriella Shriqui called in sick the day after the broadcast and did not return to work until December twenty-ninth.

FORTY-TWO

Christmas Eve day was a balmy, sunny, wind-free thirty degrees. The winter had been prematurely harsh, and the Cities had already received almost three feet of snow. This day was fairly mild and actually quite pleasant to be out, in fact, too much so.

They had started showing up on the Rileys' street the day after Melinda's grossly negligent broadcast. That day there had been almost two thousand of them lined up and down opposite their house. Many carried homemade signs of varying degrees of quality, none that were favorable on behalf of Brittany and many over the line and quite obscene.

As a condition of being reinstated, Melinda had promised no more drinking during the day, a promise she had no intention of keeping and station management was under no illusions that she would. She did cut it back to, at most, one or two glasses of wine and was always sober in front of a camera. The result was that she did scale back her accusations of Brittany Riley. Not that Melinda suddenly became ethical. The real reason for it was because her little on-air stunt when she gave out the Rileys' home address had gone national. Most, not all, of the reports deleted that part, but Melinda herself had become the story and not in a positive way. A lot of sanctimonious editorializing and criticism hit her, and station ownership was not pleased with the publicity.

Marc Kadella spent the better part of the next two days after the broadcast answering reporter's calls and denying Melinda's claims. Reporters bombarded him with requests for comment which he did his best to patiently accommodate. The damage had been done. The various media outlets dutifully reported Marc's denials with little effect. A couple of TV stations even aired film and comments from other lawyers smiling while claiming that, of course, he's going to deny it.

Marc turned the corner on the Rileys' street with Maddy in the passenger seat and slowly drove past the crowd toward the Rileys' house. The street was already quite narrow as a result of the snow piled up along both sides by the plows. Without the crowd, there was barely enough room for two cars to get past each other. With the Christmas Eve crowd lined up along the street, the people had to move aside to let one car pass.

"It's Christmas," he quietly said to Madeline. "Don't these people have better things to do?"

"How many do you think there are?" Maddy asked him.

"I don't know," Marc replied. "There has to be two, three thousand. Maybe more."

"They seem pretty well behaved at least."

"The neighbors must be really tired of this," Marc commented.

"God yes," Maddy replied. "What a pain in the ass for them to deal with. We need the temperature to drop below zero with a good wind. That would send them packing."

"You'd think Christmas would send them home!" Marc exclaimed as he pulled into the Rileys' driveway.

The two of them stood in the driveway looking over the crowd. Despite the fact they both wore sunglasses, they still shielded their eyes from the glare of the sun coming off the pristine snow. Several of the protesters recognized Marc and started yelling obscenities and booing the two of them.

Marc looked at Maddy and said, "Can't be me, it's gotta be you they're pissed at."

Maddy flashed a smile and said, "Yeah, I'm sure that's it."

Sheriff Cale came storming up the driveway to them. "It's bad enough I have to keep a dozen deputies out here on Christmas Eve. What I don't need is you standing here inciting them and getting them all worked up." By now the booing and yelling was so loud Cale could barely be heard.

Marc just shrugged, took off his glasses so the sheriff could see his eyes, then said, "I didn't cause this. Some asshole leaked some lies to the media. That's what caused this." He leaned his head a little closer to the taller man and severely said, "You wouldn't happen to know who that was, would you Sheriff?"

"C'mon," Maddy said as she took Marc's arm and began to pull him away. Instead, Marc continued with an impassive expression to watch the sheriff's face for a reaction.

"Please, just go inside," Cale said much more calmly.

Floyd closed the door behind them and Maddy asked Marc, "What was that about?"

"I just wanted to see his reaction. He did it. He leaked that stuff about the plea offer. Someone in the AG's office called him and had him or a deputy leak it. I could see it in his eyes," Marc said.

Floyd led them down to the basement where Barbara and Brittany were waiting. Brittany and Maddy exchanged a warm hug and the five of them each took a seat in the large family room. There was a beautiful, nicely decorated tree in one corner next to a gas fireplace that warmed up the room. A few presents had been placed under the tree. The absence of Becky hung over the room and a Merry Christmas in the Riley house was not going to happen this year or maybe never again.

Marc and Maddy had been invited to dinner but had respectfully declined. Both had plans and if they could be totally honest, spending Christmas Eve in this depressing environment was not what either would have preferred. It is always best for a lawyer to keep his or her emotional

204

distance from a client. It's important to be a professional and maintain your objectivity to give the client the best representation you can. Despite what is generally believed, lawyers are flesh and blood humans too and maintaining that professional detachment is not always easy. Marc and Maddy both genuinely liked Brittany and felt horrible about what was happening to her. But as for her family, they didn't know her brother, Tim, considered Floyd a eunuch and flat out did not like Barbara at all. Socializing with these people was not high on the "to do" list for either Marc or Maddy.

Over the next couple of hours, the five of them had an amiable, if somewhat strained, conversation. They talked about anything, but the case and it seemed to help Brittany's disposition. The stress was quite obvious. As they were seated together on the couch, she practically held onto Maddy as if she didn't want her to ever leave.

As they were preparing to leave, Marc took a moment and pulled Brittany aside. He asked her about her session with the psychiatrist.

"I like her," Brittany said referring to the doctor. "She's really nice and easy to talk to. I think she'll help. I'm going to see her twice a week for a while."

"Good. Did she prescribe anything for you?"

"Yeah, um, Citalopram for depression and sleeping pills to help me sleep better."

"Did you get them filled?"

"Yeah and I'm taking them. She said the Citalopram will take a while to really work, but you know, we'll see."

Marc slipped on his overcoat while Maddy gave Brittany a big hug and wished her a Merry Christmas. It sounded a little hollow with the specter of the missing Becky so obviously in the house. Even so, Brittany smiled and threw her arms around Marc. Marc returned the embrace, gave her a quick peck on the cheek and wished her and all of them a Merry Christmas.

Once outside they hurried to Marc's car. It was almost 5:00, the sun was gone, and the temperature had already dropped ten degrees. The crowd had dwindled to a few hundred die-hards and only two deputies were still present. Both of them waved at Marc or, since they were both men, likely the wave was meant for Maddy.

"That was pleasant," Maddy sarcastically said as Marc drove away. "It's hard not to feel terrible for those people with their baby being murdered and now it's Christmas. How do you do it?"

"You don't, really. You just have to learn to bury it and move on. There's nothing I can do to alleviate their pain. That's not my job and I don't know how. Do my job. That's the best I can do."

205

Marc's phone went off and Margaret shook him to wake him up and answer it. She reached across him and turned on the table lamp, picked up his phone and handed it to him. He looked at the display and saw the call was coming from the Dakota County Sheriff which set off an alarm bell in his head and snapped him awake.

Marc's feet thumped onto the floor as he quickly sat up on the edge of the bed and answered the call.

"Yeah, Marc Kadella." He listened for over a full minute without saying another word. Finally, he replied with, "Shit. Okay, I'll be there as soon as I can and thanks."

"What?" an anxious Margaret asked as Marc looked at the clock reading 2:30 A.M.

"It's Brittany," Marc sighed. "She tried to commit suicide."

"Oh, God no! Is she all right? What happened?"

"Her parents went to midnight Mass. When they got home, Barbara went in to say goodnight and they found her. She was barely alive. She took a bunch of sleeping pills and others. The deputy who called just now didn't know what. I'm guessing Citalopram.

"Anyway, there were still protesters out front and a couple of deputies. Floyd got them, and they took her to Fairview in Burnsville. The deputy that called said they're not sure but believe she's going to make it."

Brittany would be held in the hospital for observation for a week. On the night before she was to be discharged, two young nurses working the graveyard shift strolled casually toward the bank of elevators. It was time for their break and they were headed down to the cafeteria for a cup of really bad machine brewed coffee and a chance to sit and relax for a few minutes.

When they got to the elevators, a young, fairly good-looking doctor came through the stairwell door wearing a white doctor's smock and a stethoscope looped around his neck. He was apparently new since neither could remember seeing him before, but on this shift, doctors came and went frequently. The sight of a new one was hardly unusual. The young women smiled, said hello, which he acknowledged with a bright smile just as their elevator arrived.

The doctor, keeping his head angled downward to avoid any security cameras stopped at Brittany's room. The chair next to the door that should have held a sheriff's deputy was empty. Probably in the men's room, the doctor surmised. No matter. If the cop came back, he was ready with the name of a real doctor to use if necessary.

He stood next to the bed holding Brittany's wrist as if he were checking her pulse while she slept under the influence of a sedative. He quickly read over the notes on her chart and was relieved to see that she was doing fine and expected to make a quick, full recovery. Satisfied, the disguised Bob Olson slipped out of her room and walked down the hall to the stairwell door. Within minutes he was in his car and on his way home.

FORTY-THREE

"Is your client strong enough and psychologically stable enough to assist in her defense?" Judge Connors asked Marc.

The four of them, the judge and the three lawyers were in the judge's chambers doing last minute motions and scheduling. It was Thursday morning and jury selection was still scheduled for the coming Monday.

"Yes, judge," Marc said. "She seems to be doing better as we get closer to the trial. She's anxious to get it going."

"How about you?" Connors said looking at the prosecution. "You've had your psychiatrist examine her and are you satisfied she can assist in her defense?"

"Yes, your Honor," Hart answered the judge. "He has not actually examined her but he has been through her charts and is confident she is able to assist in her defense."

"Okay. Moving forward," he said. "We're going to start jury selection, Monday morning, 9:00 A.M. at the Olmstead County Courthouse in Rochester. It's all arranged. Have you been there before?"

"No," Marc and Vanderbeck said.

"Yes. I did a trial there last year," Hart replied. "It's really quite nice. The courthouse is on the Zumbro River in downtown, a couple of blocks from the Mayo Clinic."

Connors handed both the prosecution and defense a copy of a document seven pages in length. "Here's a list of one hundred prospective jurors. Names, ages, addresses, etc." Connors said. "We're going to get twelve jurors and four alternates. As you know, because this is a first-degree-murder case, we will call each prospective juror into the courtroom, one at a time. I will question each first, then Mr. Kadella, then either of you," he said to the prosecution. "You two decide which of you will do the questioning. One of you, not both.

"If a juror is selected, he or she will be sequestered immediately from any other potential jurors until we have all twelve and the four alternates. All of these people have been told this will be a three to four-week trial and they will be sequestered the entire time. They have not been told where the trial will take place. We didn't want to give them a heads up and have them figure out it was the Riley case and have that leak to the media.

"The defense will get fifteen peremptory challenges and the prosecution nine as set out in the rules of criminal procedure. Jury selection will be done by Friday, the thirtieth and we will give opening statements first thing Monday morning, February second."

Before continuing, Connors looked over all three lawyers with a serious expression. "This trial will not, I repeat, not take longer than four weeks."

Vanderbeck started to speak but was abruptly cut off by Connors holding a hand up, palm out. "I don't want to hear it, Mr. Vanderbeck. Four weeks. I am not going to keep the jurors locked up away from their families and their lives longer than that. After the first two weeks, we can evaluate how fast things are moving. If it looks like we need to speed it up, we'll start staying late and work weekends. So, I suggest you plan your cases accordingly and get things moving.

"Witness lists. You've exchanged a final witness list?"

"Yes, your Honor," they all replied.

"Good. The jury list; I know there's not much time for you to go over them. If it will help at all to give you or your staff more time, we'll call them in the order listed on the sheet you have." Connors held his list up and said, "They are listed randomly and not in alphabetical order. Agnes Moore, first on the list will be the first one called. Got it? Good. Anything else?" he asked then paused for a response.

"Okay then," the judge continued when no one asked anything. "Monday morning. There's a nice Holiday Inn right across the river from the courthouse. There's a skyway to walk through between the motel and courthouse and I took the liberty to reserve two rooms for each of you plus a conference room for your use. Obviously, you can stay wherever you like. The Holiday Inn is pretty convenient. One last thing. I know the news about where we are doing this will leak out to the media today. But these lists of prospective jurors, there are only three copies and if it gets leaked to the media I will have somebody's ass for it. And I will find out. Just so you know; there is a minor change in each of yours different from each other's and mine. Only I know what those are and if your copy gets leaked," he sternly looked directly at Vanderbeck, "I will find out whose copy it was." This last part was a lie but Connors figured it would keep the jurors' names safe from being made public and having the media hound them.

"I'll see everybody Monday morning."

Later that same day, during her four o'clock show, Melinda Pace reported quite accurately, when, where and how the jury selection was to take place. She even reported the fact that the jurors would be selected in Rochester, then moved to Hastings and be sequestered during the three to four-week trial. Much to her disappointment, the juror list had not been leaked to her. Certainly, good fortune for those on the list.

"Did you get your list?" Barry Cline asked Marc. Barry was standing at Sandy's desk, one of the office staff. He had been talking to her about some papers she was working on for him when Marc came through the door into the office suite.

"Yeah, I did," Marc acknowledged. "Want to help me go over it?"

"Sure, give me a few minutes."

Marc made a copy and gave it to their paralegal, Jeff Modell. Jeff was in that age group that grew up with the internet. If there was anything out there about any of the people on the list, he would find it. Sandy, a few years older than Jeff, was also adept at mining the internet and she would lend a hand.

Before Barry was done talking to Sandy, Madeline came through the door which caused Barry to stop breathing. She walked past the staff area, said hello to everyone as she did and went directly into Marc's office.

Carolyn had been watching Barry's reaction to Maddy and when she closed Marc's door she said to him, "Breathe dummy."

"Huh? Oh, yeah," he replied to which Carolyn and Sandy both laughed.

"Men, you're all alike," Sandy said.

"Right. And women are so different," Barry said. "I'll remind you of that the next time Butch Koll stops by and the both of you start drooling."

"That's different," Carolyn said. "But never mind how."

That afternoon, Marc, Maddy and Barry went over the list looking for obvious pluses and minuses of the names. The list included some cursory information about each of the people. Things such as name, address, age, occupation, marital status, spouse's name and occupation. Like any jury trial, selection was much more art than science. A jury selection consulting industry had developed that was more sophisticated in its guesswork and claimed to be accurate. They tended to be quite expensive and very few criminal defendants could afford to hire one. The prosecution with the virtually unlimited resources of the state would certainly have a team of consultants. Were they worth the expense? Some lawyers swore by them, some scoffed at them.

By the end of the day, the three of them, Marc, Maddy and Barry had placed all one hundred names into one of three categories: 1) definite yes; 2) definite no; 3) maybe. The definite yes were young, single men and women without children. All three of them agreed these would be most likely to sympathize with or, be more open-minded to Brittany. The problem was there were only a dozen names in that category and the prosecution would likely try to get them removed. The other end of the spectrum was the definite no list. There were over thirty names on that list, mostly men and women with young children. Of the remaining fifty to sixty, all had some question marks, but the final jury would likely come from those people.

"What are you going to do about the publicity?" Maddy asked Marc.

"I've been thinking about it and I think the best thing to do is go after it directly. Don't try to be cute about it. Ask each juror up front if they've seen or heard about it on TV or in the media."

"What if they say no?" Barry asked.

"Then they're probably lying," Marc said. "Unless they're on our list of 'yes' jurors, I might use a peremptory challenge. We'll see. If they admit bias, the judge should drop them. I'll at least indoctrinate them to the idea that the TV and news reports may not know what they're talking about; that what they see on TV are leaks, not evidence. Get them to promise to ignore it and keep an open mind."

"What about things like abortions, miscarriages, and political groups that may indicate a bias?" Madeline asked.

"We argued about that and the judge had it all put in the juror questionnaire that they all answered. Supposedly, those things were covered that way. Connors didn't want us to get too personal, especially with the women. If they had a miscarriage or abortion or lost a child, they were dropped as potential jurors."

Marc tells Maddy he is not going to challenge any jurors for pretrial publicity unless their bias is blatant. He tells her it is pointless since whether they admit it or not, they have all heard about the case.

"Can you get the cameras kept out of the courtroom?" Barry asked.

"Sure. The prosecution went nuts, the media went nuts, but the judge ruled against me. Um, Maddy," he said to his investigator. "Since the subject came up, would you mind sitting at the defense table, you know, a little dolled up wearing a low-cut, backless cocktail dress?"

Barry choked back his laughter as Madeline narrowed her eyes at him and said, "You do know I carry a gun don't you?"

"Oh yeah, sorry I forgot," Marc sheepishly said. "So, how about a bikini?" he added as he ducked when she threw a yellow legal pad at him. Even she had to laugh at that juvenile remark.

"That's enough for today," Marc said. "We'll see what Jeff and Sandy come up with off the internet and work on it more this weekend."

As they were leaving Marc told Jeff and Sandy they could knock off for the night.

"I'm okay," Jeff said. "I'm going to stay for a while and keep looking. I, ah, you know, like Brittany and I want to help her."

Sandy wiggled her eyebrows and winked at Marc. Jeff saw it and started to protest but Sandy cut him off and said, "I'll stay for a while and help him. Our lives are so boring anyway this might be fun."

Marc took a twenty-dollar bill from his pocket, gave it to Jeff and said, "Order in pizza. I'll see you tomorrow."

FORTY-FOUR

By noon on the day after Melinda Pace broadcast the news that jury selection would take place in Rochester, the media had descended like a horde of locusts. Rochester, Minnesota is one of the best known, most widely publicized and acclaimed small cities on the planet. The Mayo family started their world-renowned medical facility as a family practice by the patriarch, William Worrall Mayo in 1863. In the 1880s he was joined by his two sons, Dr. William James Mayo and Dr. Charles Horace Mayo. From that modest beginning in what was a sleepy little farming community straddling the Zumbro River in southeast Minnesota, one of the two or three most respected medical facilities on Earth has grown. Kings, Presidents and despots do not go to Cuba for their socialist "free" healthcare. They go to Minnesota with one notable and humorous exception. The socialist dictator of Venezuela, Hugo Chavez went to Fidel's worker's paradise and by the time they were done with him, he was likely wishing he had gone to Rochester. Unfortunately, the kind and decent citizens of this very pleasant city were about to get hit by a media storm.

The last weekend in January, which is what this was, is typically as bad as the weather becomes. This year was to be no exception. On Friday morning the air temperatures ranged from minus eight on the southern border with Iowa to a really bone-chilling minus thirty-five in International Falls on the Canadian border. Coupled with a brisk fifteen to twenty miles an hour westerly wind made it a dangerous day to be outdoors.

Every television station, newspaper and several large radio stations were setting up shop. CNN had a crew on hand and all of the major networks, including the ones on cable, made sure there was an affiliate crew from the Twin Cities ready to report in. Among them, standing in line to check in at the downtown Holiday Inn, was the intrepid Ms. Gabriella Shriqui. She looked outside, across the river at the back of the government center and an involuntary shiver swept over her when a gust of wind blew between the buildings along the frozen over Zumbro River.

When Gabriella got to her room, she dejectedly dropped her single suitcase on the bed and opened the drapes. She stood at the window watching the traffic go by four stories below on Broadway Ave. There were very few pedestrians out and those that were scurried along the sidewalks, bundled up in large coats, heavy boots and fur-lined gloves, their breath making long streams of steam. The traffic on the street at midday was light which made her wonder why it was moving so slowly. The street itself looked as frozen as ice, which it was, colored white and very hard.

Gabriella shivered again, folded her arms across her chest, rubbed her hands on her biceps as if to warm herself and said out loud, "It even looks freeze-your-ass-off cold out there."

Her phone went off and she retrieved it from her coat pocket, looked at the caller ID and said, "Hey, Hunter. Tell me again why I need to spend this weekend in a Rochester Holiday Inn when nothing happens until Monday morning?"

"Because the competition is there. Why, Rochester is a lovely city. Where else would you rather be?"

"At home wrapped in a blanket."

"It's fourteen below here," Oswood said.

"Well, we're kicking your ass. It's a balmy eleven below here. Again, why am I here?"

"Because the network wants us there and they're paying for it. The reason I called, to see if you can get a couple of 'man on the street' interviews…"

"Man on the street! Are you nuts? I'm not going out there," she protested.

"Yes, you are," Oswood laughed.

"How about I try the skyway first?"

"No, we want the cold weather background."

"You're serious?" she said. "I thought you were just jerking my chain."

"No, I'm not. Take the van and you and Kyle get out there and get some interviews. Send them back live. Get four or five and we'll edit them."

"What do you want me to ask them? How do you like not being able to feel your toes, fingers and face?"

Oswood laughed heartily and finally said, "Don't be such a wuss. Get out there. You'll live. Just get a few quotes about the usual blather: how do you feel about the trial coming there? That kind of thing."

"What are you talking about? The trial is not coming here."

"What are you talking about? We monitor the news, and everyone is reporting that the case is going to be tried in Rochester."

Gabriella, clearly confused, said, "I understood that only jury selection was going to be done here then they would be moved back to Hastings."

"Huh. Well, I don't know but everyone is reporting the trial was going to be there."

"Are you saying I'm going to be living in this Holiday Inn for the next month or so if the trial is here?"

"Probably. Why, is that a problem? We'll cross that bridge when we come to it. In the meantime, go get some interviews."

214

"Okay. So, I have to go out there. All right. Talk to you later."

At the same time, Gabriella was conversing with her boss, Marc, Maddy, Connie Mickelson and the entire office were chuckling while watching a reporter on one of the local channels. The man was reporting, obviously from a skyway, about the "breaking news" that the Brittany Riley trial was to be conducted in Rochester.

The report led the midday news and between the reporter prattling on and the inane questions the busty blonde anchor asked, the segment took up almost eight minutes of air time. When they went to a commercial, Carolyn switched to another channel and caught the tail end of them reporting the same thing. For the next twenty minutes, they checked all of the networks and the cable news channels. All of them were making the same mistake. CNN even had two trial lawyers discussing the significance of it and had an interview with a lawyer who practiced in Rochester.

"That's enough," Marc said to Carolyn with a big grin.

Carolyn pressed the power button on the remote and Connie said, "That was fun. We're going to have to do some more of that. Leak bad information to these idiots just for the amusement. Leave the phones, girls. I'll take everybody across the street and buy lunch."

When they got back from lunch, Maddy took off and Marc huddled in the conference room with Jeff Modell and Sandy. The two of them were about halfway done with their internet search of the jury list. Marc wanted to hear what they had found, so far. On the whole, it wasn't much. Unlike TV and the movies, most people lead fairly drab, repetitive, even boring lives. Marriage, mortgages, jobs and kids happen which precludes a lot of glamour and intrigue. This list of names was no exception. Plus, the juror questionnaire that each had filled out had eliminated a lot of potential problems and biases.

Around two, by prearrangement, Connie, Barry and Chis Grafton came into the conference room after Jeff and Sandy left. Marc knew what was coming. They needed to discuss business. The four lawyers were all independent of each other. What they had was an office sharing arrangement. But they were all friends as well as colleagues and anything that affects one likely affected all of them. The Brittany Riley case was currently affecting all of them. Plus, they had these meetings about once a month just to help each other out if needed.

"Okay," Connie began after each had taken a seat at the conference room table. "How's everyone doing?"

"I'm okay," Barry said. "December was bad but January, compared to a year ago is actually a little better."

215

"Chris?" Connie asked.

"I'm down almost twenty percent. But I'm not sure what's causing it." Chris Grafton was a corporate lawyer that handled small business accounts. "It could be the economy and the weather. My clients are telling me their businesses are also down so…"

"It causes a ripple effect on others. Are you okay?" Connie asked.

"Yeah, I am. If I need a short-term loan, I'll let you know."

"Marc?"

"Right now, I'm fine. I need to talk to the Rileys. The defense fund isn't going to last much longer. We've got a lot of expenses coming up. I'll see them this weekend. There's untapped revenue in a home equity loan they can get. Barbara already told me that."

"So, it sounds like we're not in too bad of shape. We need to get that Riley trial done," she said looking at Marc. "You know I love you guys, and if you need any help, let me know."

Connie was the beneficiary of several successful marriages and subsequent divorces. On top of that, she had a very successful law practice and had inherited from her parents a sizeable estate including the building they were seated in. She had helped all of them out on several occasions, cash flow being what it is and was always willing to lend a hand. Despite what most people believe, the practice of law is a tough, competitive way to make a living and very few lawyers get rich.

Gabriella and her cameraman, Kyle Bronson, an affable, balding overweight, forty-something married father of three were wrapping up her final interview. So far, they had only met one man, a sixty-year-old self-confessed court watcher, who knew everything about the Riley case coming to Rochester. Gabriella, despite the cold, was able to talk to the man for almost fifteen minutes before he had to leave.

Gabriella was dressed in warm boots, insulated underwear and a heavy fur-lined very chic black parka. Even with all of that, she was almost stiff from the cold. To wrap it up, Gabriella, runny nose and all looked into the camera and said, "I must say, these have to be the nicest people I've ever met. The people in the Cities, as pleasant as they normally are, would not stand outside in this weather to talk to anyone, let alone a reporter.

"And one last thing Hunter, just so you know, someday, no matter how long it takes, I'm going to cut your balls off for making me stand out here and freeze my ass off to do this."

Everyone at the station who saw and heard the last remark wanted desperately to put it on the air, especially Melinda. Hunter Oswood, who laughed as loud as anyone, edited it out himself just to make sure no one could sneak it past him. He did manage to keep a copy for himself to be used at Gabriella's next performance review.

FORTY-FIVE

Marc looked around the windowless, oak-paneled courtroom where he would be spending most of the week. As usual, despite all of the courtroom experience he had and the jury trials he had done, he was barely able to sleep the night before. Wide awake by 5:00 A.M., he got up, shaved, showered and went downstairs for breakfast to get ready for the day.

He arrived early, barely minutes past 7:00 A.M. The moment he stepped off the elevator, he was immediately confronted by a mass of media members waiting for the door of Courtroom Seven to open. The waiting area on the sixth floor of the Olmstead County Government Center's court division was not especially large. It was mostly used for witnesses waiting to be called and wasn't suited for a mob like this. Marc had all he could do to muscle his way through while saying "no comment" all the way to the single entryway door.

Marc showed the two burly male sheriff's deputies his I.D. and while they checked for his name on their list, he noticed Gabriella Shriqui standing in front of a window that overlooked the frozen Zumbro. He said both "hello" and "no comment" to her at the same time. She smiled back as the guard opened the door for Marc.

Once inside the bar, he laid claim to the table he wanted, the one on the right-hand side of the courtroom. Marc set his briefcase and overcoat on top of the table which would put him closest to the witness stand.

Unlike most courts, the pathway to the bar was not in the middle of the gallery. It was on the left-hand side, along the wall. When he entered, he walked up to the gate which was on that same left side of the courtroom as was the jury box. Even though he had used the skyway to walk over the river from the Holiday Inn to the courthouse, he still wore a heavy winter coat. He wanted to use it as an additional prop to secure the table he wanted. A minute later, before Marc had seated himself, another deputy, a woman, came in from the back hallway.

They greeted each other with a pleasant "good morning" and Marc said, "Maybe you ought to let them in to get them out of the hall."

"The judge's clerk is preparing a drawing, a lottery to allow some of them in. If we let them all in we wouldn't have room for anyone else," the woman said as she took up station in front of the bench.

"Make the media sit in the back two rows," Marc said which made the woman chuckle.

There are five hard, uncomfortable wooden benches in this courtroom's gallery. There is a space along both walls, with the bench seats in between them, to allow people to come and go without crawling over everyone in that row. Each bench is long enough to accommodate about fifteen normal sized people fairly comfortably. Except, after maybe two hours, a normal person's butt and lower back will become pretty sore, which Marc believed is why the benches are intentionally made uncomfortable; so people wouldn't loiter. There are courtroom junkies, people that use trials as entertainment, who are experienced enough to carry a small pillow with them if they can sneak it past security.

The first row was reserved for Brittany's family and staff for the lawyers. Marc told Barbara and Floyd they did not have to attend but Barbara insisted. By eight o'clock the two of them along with Barbara's sister, Charlotte Daniels, were seated behind Marc and Brittany. Taking up most of the row, behind the other table, were nine members of the prosecution, staff and jury consultants. At the table to Marc's left, closest to the empty jury box, were Lowell Vanderbeck and Danica Hart.

Marc, Vanderbeck and Hart had conferred with Judge Connors in chambers to make sure everyone understood the rules. The judge reminded them that this was a first-degree murder trial and the prospective jurors must be questioned one at a time. The judge would first ask a series of routine questions, most of which had been included in the pre-selection questionnaire dealing with the overt bias and hardship of being sequestered for a long trial. Marc, for the defense, would be allowed to ask questions first and then the prosecution. This would continue until there were twelve jurors and four alternates. Connors had made it clear that he was not going to let this go beyond Friday.

"I'm so nervous," Brittany whispered to Marc. "I'm glad I'm sitting down. Who are all those people?" she asked indicating with a nod toward the prosecution crew seated behind them. A couple of them, an older man and a younger woman, were leaning over the rail conversing with Vanderbeck and Hart.

"That's the prosecution team," Marc told her. "I'm so good they need a whole team," he smiled.

Brittany smiled and laughed at his little joke and then said, "I hope so."

The two of them did not notice several reporters scribbling notes about this exchange. Later that day, Channel 7 in Minneapolis would report that Brittany was laughing and joking as if her murder trial was just another joke not to be taken seriously. It was yet another report that went national on the news and viral through the internet.

"The two talking to the lawyers are probably jury consultants, people who think they are experts at picking juries."

"Are they?" Brittany said.

"Are they what?"

"Experts and why don't we have any?" Brittany said.

"Who knows?" Marc replied. "No one really knows how to pick a jury. They think they're experts and know more than the rest of us. Maybe they do. I'm supposed to have one coming. I thought he'd be here by now," Marc said.

He heard the exterior door open and swiveled in his chair to look. "Speak of the devil," Marc said when he saw his officemate, Barry Cline come in. Barry was also an experienced criminal defense lawyer and wanted to help with Brittany's' case. Marc had submitted a *Notice of Representation* to the court and the prosecution about Barry to allow this. Barry had cleared most of his calendar for the week and Marc was glad to have his input and assistance. Barry was delighted to get the free publicity as well.

He apologized for being late due to underestimating the drive time. He took a seat next to Brittany and the three of them chatted quietly while waiting for the judge.

A minute after Barry's arrival, the judge's clerk, Marion Kellogg and Connors' personal court reporter, Bill Franzen came out and set up their positions. Kellogg was seated to the judge's right and Franzen to his left, between the judge and the witness stand. Barely a minute after they appeared, Connors came into the courtroom and the trial of the State of Minnesota vs. Brittany Ann Riley was officially underway.

Connors spent roughly ten minutes giving the crowd in the gallery a brief description of how jury selection would proceed. He was under no obligation to give the description of the procedure but decided to do so which would also serve to inform the public through the media.

When the judge was almost finished, the outer doors opened and the attorney general herself came marching in, followed by two young staff members. Peterson walked up to the gate and said, "I apologize for the interruption, your Honor. I've decided this case is so important that I need to give it my personal attention." She turned slightly toward the gallery and the camera in the corner televising the proceedings and continued by saying, "I will be personally sitting in to see to it the people of Minnesota are provided with justice."

Despite the fact that he was bristling with indignation, especially at the posturing politician's last remark, Connors said, "Welcome, Madam Attorney General. If you would be so kind as to take a seat, I'd like to continue," he finished with more than a touch of sarcasm.

220

Peterson handed her coat to one of the flunkies who trailed behind her. The two of them, not finding a place to sit, went out to wait in the hall. The attorney general went through the gate and took a seat at the prosecution table.

Marc sat quietly, his left elbow on the table top, his chin in his left palm, observing this little farce and trying not to smile. Barry Cline turned his chair to face the wall so the reporters would not see him stifling a laugh.

Agnes Moore, the first name on the jury panel list, was led into the courtroom by the female deputy Marc had spoken to earlier. Agnes was a short woman, barely five feet and a little on the plump side. She was wearing her best navy-blue jacket, skirt, white blouse and sensible black shoes. Noticeably nervous, she raised her left hand then switched to her right with an embarrassed giggle, was sworn in and took the witness stand.

Agnes was a forty-four-year-old mother of three teenagers. She was married to the same man, Frank, for nineteen years. Agnes had worked in one of the Mayo Clinic cafeterias as a shift supervisor. Frank had owned a car repair business for the past twelve years. An excellent mechanic, he had earned a reputation for honesty and quality workmanship. Almost ninety percent of his business was from repeat customers. Frank and Agnes Moore were about as Midwest America as could be found.

The search of Agnes' background had not uncovered a single flaw. Marc had originally placed her on his "No" list. A church-going, albeit Lutheran, middle-class woman with a solid family was not likely to be very sympathetic to a case involving infanticide. Then Jeff Modell turned up a piece of news that raised some eyebrows.

When Agnes was nineteen, Jeff was able to uncover several visits to a Planned Parenthood Clinic. He also unearthed a bill for three hundred seventy-five dollars paid by Agnes' mother. Agnes had an abortion. The question was; would this make her more or less sympathetic? Marc had moved her name from his "no" list to the "maybes".

Judge Connors started out by lightly asking her a few simple questions to get her to talk and calm down. When he got into more substantive areas, the judge was basically asking the same questions that were on the questionnaire she and all of those selected for the jury pool had filled out. A copy of each questionnaire had been provided to both the defense and prosecution. The judge also took it upon himself to elicit answers to how much influence the media coverage had on her. Was she willing to admit to a preconceived bias? If so, could she set that aside?

221

When Connors finished, he handed the questioning over to Marc.

Marc began by introducing himself, Barry and Brittany then transitioned into his questioning. He had decided to meet the publicity issue head-on. He spent almost ten minutes on the subject with her. Not really asking questions to find out if she had heard of the case but to get her to promise to set that aside and listen to the evidence. Agnes, with an almost imperceptible touch of hesitation, promised that she would do that.

Marc took almost ten more minutes asking her questions about the concepts of innocent until proven guilty, proof beyond a reasonable doubt and the prosecution's burden of proof. Like almost every American, Agnes owned a television set, so the terminology was familiar to her. What Marc was mainly trying to do was to indoctrinate her into what her obligations would be and to elicit a promise that she would be fair, impartial and leave any biases she may have at the courtroom door. It was pointless to try to find twelve people who had not heard about this case. Oddly enough, there would be at least two or three who genuinely had not and two or three more willing to lie about it.

After what appeared to be a mini-conference with Peterson and Vanderbeck, Danica Hart began her turn questioning of Agnes. Most of the main issues had been thoroughly gone over by Judge Connors and Kadella already. Even so, Danica went over many of the same issues, except media bias. This hardly surprised Marc and Barry. Obviously, the prosecution was fine with each juror having watched and read as much about the case as possible. Agnes had already promised to set aside any potential bias. Hart's main job was to also indoctrinate the witness that it was the state who was looking out for "The People" and it was their job to obtain justice.

Then, just before Hart finished, like a too curious child who has been told not to touch a hot object but can't resist it anyway, Hart gave Agnes one more chance.

"You're sure you have not formed an opinion about guilt or innocence?" Hart asked.

Agnes sat quietly, her head slanted downward, kneading her hands together, then said, "Well, to be honest, I'm just not sure. I mean, I'll try, your Honor," she said looking at Connors, "But I just don't know how anyone could do that to her daughter."

As soon as the words came out, Marc was on his feet. Before he could say anything, Connors held up a hand to stop him and said, "Thank you for your time, Mrs. Moore. You're excused."

As the deputy was leading her out of the courtroom, Connors checked the time and said, "We'll take a fifteen-minute break now. I'll see counsel in chambers."

"We took almost an hour questioning the first one," Connors began as he removed his robe and took his chair while the lawyers found seats. "We have to move it along or we'll be here until spring. If I have to, I'll put a time limit on it. For now, let's try to just speed it up a bit and cut out the repetition. Suggestions? Objections?"

"Yes," Attorney General Peterson said, "He should have had to use one of his peremptory challenges on that juror."

"Anything else?" Connors asked ignoring her. "Okay. Mr. Kadella hang on a minute. Madam Attorney General, I'd like a word with you please."

Connors waited until everyone else had left then said to Marc, "I asked you to stay so I wouldn't be accused of any ex parte communications." He then turned to Peterson and as politely as possible said, "Madam Attorney General, with all due respect, you are entitled to assist in the trial of this case. However, if you ever make a grandstand entrance and disrupt my court like that again, you personally will write a ten-thousand-dollar check to the court and I won't hesitate to admonish you publicly. Now if you'll excuse me, I need to use the restroom."

Peterson, whose eyes had widened to the size of saucers, clamped her lips together and stormed out. As Marc was leaving, he looked back at Connors, smiled and gave him a thumbs up.

Barely two minutes later, the AG was holding a press conference in the very crowded hallway. She explained that something had come up and she had to get back to St. Paul right away. Peterson assured them her personal interest in the case would not wane. She had no doubt Brittany was guilty and would be brought to justice.

FORTY-SIX

Marc, with Brittany walking next to him, trudged through the skyway over the Zumbro River, heading back to the Holiday Inn. He was a little crabby, tired and very hungry. It was almost seven o'clock and he had nothing to eat since the noon lunch break. For lunch, even though the temperature had only climbed to a positive two degrees, they all needed some fresh air. Marc, Barry and the Rileys had gone to a Subway sandwich shop about a block from the courthouse. After being indoors in the overheated building, the cold, fresh air and sunshine felt refreshing.

It was now the end of the second day of jury selection and so far only four jurors had been picked; two men and two women. They were all white which, given the make up of southeastern Minnesota, was no surprise. With a white defendant, the racial composition of the jury shouldn't be a factor. After adjourning for the day, Judge Connors had called the lawyers into chambers and let his displeasure be known, again, at how slowly things were going. He was especially annoyed with Vanderbeck. The prosecutor kept going over the same ground with each of the veniremen that the judge and Marc had already covered, and his style was slow and deliberate. Vanderbeck was taking twice as long as Marc to cover the same ground.

Marc was feeling pretty good about the four jurors selected. Three of them, one of the men and both women were on his list of "maybes". There was nothing about any of them to raise alarm bells or he would have used a peremptory challenge to excuse them.

One of the women was a single, twenty-six-year-old nurse at Mayo who was given paid leave by the clinic to serve. The other woman was a thirty-two-year-old, divorced single mother of two. She assured the court that she and her ex got along fine and he would watch the kids while she was gone. She was one of six assistant principals at Rochester John Marshall High School and time away would not be a problem.

The first man selected was a sixty-two-year-old retired dentist. Marc liked him because he believed that most people with that much higher education would be more likely to think rationally and not let their emotions make decisions for them.

The fourth one was on Marc's "Yes" list and Marc was pleasantly surprised that he made the cut. A twenty-two-year-old single college student taking a break from school. He was a nice-looking young man who might be sympathetic to a girl that looks as good as Brittany does. Also, when he claimed he had not heard about the case, he seemed quite believable. Knowing males that age are far more interested in video

224

games, beer and girls than the news, it didn't seem to be much of a stretch to believe he had not heard of the case.

Vanderbeck had completed his questioning of the young man and then he and Hart huddled with their jury consultants. Marc could see a quiet yet heated exchange between Vanderbeck and the lead consultant who was vehemently shaking his head "no". While Marc continued to watch, fully expecting the prosecution to use one of their nine peremptory challenges to bump him, Vanderbeck turned to Connors and accepted the young man. When he did this, Danica Hart looked right at Marc and rolled her eyes.

The good news when the session adjourned was that Barbara and Floyd were going home. Putting up with the two of them, especially Barbara's meddling all day for two days was stretching Marc's patience. At one point he even had to have a stern talk with Barbara to stop the kibitzing and second-guessing.

The bad news was Barry had to leave. One of his clients had an employee who was jammed up and needed a lawyer. Barry's client ran a legitimate car dealership and at least a half dozen illegitimate chop shops throughout the Upper Midwest. The owner was well insulated and even though the cops knew who he was, they couldn't get to him. But the nature of his illegitimate business was such that Barry had a steady stream of clients from a man who paid the attorney fees for them with cashier's checks. It was a little problematic ethically, but with each of them, Barry made sure the man paying the bills signed a statement acknowledging who the client was.

Marc and Brittany reached the hotel elevators and Marc asked her if she wanted to get some dinner. She begged off saying she was tired and would get something from room service, which was fine with Marc. He would rather eat alone and work some more on the jury pool list.

Wednesday morning Connors began promptly at 9:00 A.M. The next prospective juror brought in was a thirty-four-year-old male doctor in the urology department at Mayo. A very good-looking married man with two preschool children whose wife was staying home until the kids started school. Time off from the clinic would not be a problem.

Marc quickly went through his indoctrination questions and informed the court the doctor was acceptable. He was originally on Marc's list of "Maybes" as a 6 on a scale of 1 to 10. Last night at dinner, Marc had moved him from a 6 to an 8.

Vanderbeck spent barely five minutes questioning the man then also informed Connors he was acceptable.

The doctor was led away to be taken home to pack for the duration of the trial. While this was happening, one of the deputies came to the

225

bar and over to Marc. He bent down to whisper in his ear. The deputy was an older man riding out his time until retirement. Marc had gotten to know him enough to say hello and chat. "There's a woman outside who says she works for you and wants to get in."

"What's her name?" Marc asked thinking it might be Sandy with more information on jurors.

"Shoot. I didn't get it or I forgot."

"What does she look like?" Marc asked.

"Well, I should probably sit down before my knees buckle. On the other hand, I can die happy now having been close enough to see and smell such a woman."

Marc laughed and said, "Have Madeline come in, please."

While the deputy went to get Maddy, the next venireman was sworn and seated. Connors began his routine of asking the now boring, standard questions. A moment later he noticed an obvious stirring and buzz go through the gallery and looked up to see Maddy walk toward the gate.

"I am really sorry, your Honor," she said with obvious sincerity.

"It's quite all right, Ms. Rivers," Connors said with a smile. "Please come in and have a seat," he gestured with his left hand toward Marc's table.

She quickly took the chair Barry had used. She dropped her purse next to the table, turned to give a grinning Brittany, who was very happy to see her, a hug. Marc leaned over behind Brittany and whispered to Madeline, "Always need to make a grand entrance."

Maddy dropped her left hand below the table behind Brittany, smiled at Marc and extended her middle finger at him which almost made him laugh.

Over the next hour, they dismissed two more possible jurors. One Marc dismissed was a thirty-year-old woman, married mother of three who was on Marc's "no" list. Sandy had discovered she was a Republican member of a pro-life group. Marc brought that out during questioning, but she denied it would influence her decision. Vanderbeck argued vehemently to keep her and Connors ruled she would not be dismissed for cause just because of her political opinions. Marc used one of his precious fifteen peremptory challenges on her.

The next one up was another twenty-something single man. He was acceptable to Marc and Judge Connors so Vanderbeck used a peremptory on him.

The judge took a short break after which the pace continued at a quicker rate. By noon, they had gone through three more and selected one more bringing the total number of jurors to six.

A half hour before the lunch break, Madeline left to secure a table for them back at the Holiday Inn restaurant. When she got there the place was already full but there was a young man at the hostess stand. Maddy had little trouble convincing him to get her a table which he promptly did.

"I am so glad you're here," Brittany said for at least the tenth time.

"Marc can be a pretty boring date," Maddy answered.

"You should've seen the doctor that was picked before you got here. What a honey!" Brittany said.

"Really? Tell me," she urged Brittany.

"Married with two kids," Marc drolly interjected.

"Forget it," Maddy said emphatically. "No more married doctors," she continued referring to a bad romance in which she had once been involved.

"What's going on with the search for the elusive Bob Olson?" Marc asked.

Maddy sighed but before she could answer the waitress appeared and took their order. When she left, Marc asked, "Anything?"

"No, not really. Sorry," she said looking at Brittany. "I'm down to a couple of girls that worked at Macy's last summer." She pulled a steno pad from her purse and flipped through it until she found the page she wanted. "...a Leslie Dungey; twenty-four years old, student at the U, living in Richfield with a boyfriend. I found him. He said they broke up in August, she moved out and he hasn't seen or talked to her since. He heard she moved east with the guy she had been seeing behind his back. He wasn't sure where and didn't care to know."

"Is he angry, bitter?" Marc asked.

"No, and with good reason. His new girlfriend was there when I met with him. Apparently, he had found solace in the arms of another as they say.

"The other one, the other missing girl, is a Julie Makie. Twenty-one..."

"I remember Julie," Brittany said. "She worked in the jewelry department right next to where I worked. We became friends, sort of. I mean, you know, we'd take lunch together sometimes. Things like that. She was really nice. She had to quit to go home. Her dad got sick and she wanted to go home and help her mom."

Brittany pressed the index and middle finger of each hand to her temples, closed her eyes and thought for a moment. "She wasn't from Minnesota," Brittany said, her fingers still pressed against her head. "She was from out west. Oh!" she snapped her head up. "I remember! Oregon. She's from Oregon."

"Can you remember where?" Maddy asked.

"Let me think. I remember it was a man's name..."

"Eugene?" Marc and Maddy asked together.

"Yes, that's it. Eugene, Oregon."

"Good. I'll see what I can do to find her," Maddy said.

Their lunches arrived and the three of them made light, small talk while they ate. They steered clear of the trial since none of them wanted to talk about it anyway. Instead, they conversed mostly about what Minnesotans normally talk about this time of year; the weather.

The afternoon session started with the notable absence of Lowell Vanderbeck. Marc and Danica Hart met with Judge Connors before court resumed. Danica lied and said something came up in their office that required Vanderbeck's immediate attention. Hart would finish up the jury selection for the prosecution and promised to speed it up.

Hart proved to be true to her word. Much less inclined to posture and pontificate, more efficient and with less interest in the jury consultants, she helped move the selection process briskly along. By 11:00 A.M. Friday, they had their jury. Twelve with four alternates. The first twelve consisted of seven men, including the lone African-American and five women. Of those, two were on Marc's "Yes" list, two from his "No" list and the rest were from the "Maybe" list. The "Maybes" were spread out on Marc's one to ten scale evenly; four from one through five and four from six through ten. The four alternates were one from the "Yes" list, two "Maybes" and one "No".

Looking over the final list, Marc thought they were not a good jury for either side but not bad either. Marc needed just one to get a hung jury.

The Rileys' had returned to court this morning for the final selections. Marc spent a few minutes chatting with them while the gallery emptied after court adjourned. While they chatted, Marc noticed a quiet yet obviously heated exchange between Hart and the lead jury consultant. The consultants left and the Rileys, including Brittany, went out right behind them. Marc's former client, Butch Koll and his bouncer friend, Andy Whitman were waiting in the hall to escort the Rileys through the crowd.

Marc and Hart had become, if not friends, at least friendly adversaries. She came over to his table and hoisted herself up to sit on the tabletop.

"Ever use a consultant team?" she asked.

"No," Marc replied looking up at her from his chair. "My clients can never afford them."

"Between you and me, I don't think they add shit to the process. They're expensive and pompous as hell. They're know-it-alls who've never tried a case. Vanderbeck likes them but I think they're a waste of money. I'm with you; take the first twelve through the door. Just question them enough to make sure there's brain activity then get on with it."

Marc laughed and said, "I wish I had the balls to try it sometime."

Hart chuckled and said, "Me too." She hopped down from the table and said, "See you Monday morning."

Melinda Pace, as she had done all week, was live at four o'clock, then the show was rerun at six-thirty. She had Andrea Briscomb on air discussing the jury selection process and giving her "expert" opinion about it. Of course, Melinda's show wasn't the only one doing this. It was a good week for former prosecutors, retired judges and defense lawyers to get face time on TV. The national news outlets, especially the cable networks, were doing the same thing. The consensus opinion from them was decidedly running against Marc. Briscomb was especially critical of him even going so far as to say he may have already lost Brittany's case.

FORTY-SEVEN

It was mid-afternoon when Marc trudged up the back staircase to his second-floor office. His leather satchel briefcase, one of two he would be using for this trial, hung heavily at his side. The building, as usual, was a little too warm and he removed his winter overcoat before beginning his journey up the stairs. Between a week of not eating right, not sleeping well and overall lack of meaningful exercise, by the time he reached the top, he had to pause to catch his breath. Vowing to himself, again, once this trial was over, he would lose the ten to fifteen pounds he needed to lose and get back in shape.

He greeted everyone, then Marc and Barry Cline spent two hours going over the jury list. Barry agreed that it could be better, could be worse and was probably all right. About as good as he could have hoped for, all things considered.

Next, he got together with the office paralegal, Jeff Modell. They went over their witness list making sure Marc had interview notes on each one, so he knew what their testimony would be. They also made sure that each of them had been issued a subpoena to make sure they would testify. Even cooperative witnesses can get cold feet and it was prudent to drop a subpoena on each of them no matter how friendly they seemed.

Jeff left, and Marc closed his door to work on his opening statement. The opening statement is the lawyer's opportunity to verbally walk the jury through their case and tell the jury what evidence they will see and what each witness will say. As anyone who owns a television in America should know, the defense is under no obligation to prove anything. It's the prosecution that has the burden of proof. One of Marc's primary responsibilities during the prosecution's opening statement is to keep track of what the prosecution claims they will present to the jury versus what they actually deliver. There are specific elements to any crime and the prosecution must present evidence of each one of those elements or they lose. Additionally, this is another chance for Marc to hammer home the concepts of the burden of proof, of innocent until proven guilty and guilt beyond a reasonable doubt. It would also be his chance to look at them as both a group and as individuals and remind them of the promise they made during jury selection. Marc had elicited a promise under oath from each and every one of them that they would ignore what they had heard from the media and decide the case based strictly on the evidence presented.

The first thing he did was to go over what he believed the prosecution would say in their opening. He reviewed all of the evidence and laid it out in a logical sequence the way he would present it to the jury. Marc then went over their witness list and made sure his trial notebook had either copies of their statements or typed notes of what their testimony would be. For most of them, he had both. Also, for each witness, he had detailed notes, even specific questions, written out as to what he wanted to get from each of them on cross-examination.

Around seven o'clock, tired, hungry and done with his opening preparation, the office phone rang. He mentally debated whether or not to answer it then finally, after five rings, succumbed.

"I knew you'd still be there," he heard Madeline say.

"I'm about done. Just making sure I'm ready for Monday morning. I'd like to take the weekend off to get some rest. What's up?"

"I finally tracked down Julie Makie's parents," Maddy said.

"That's nice. Who's Julie Makie?" Marc asked.

"The girl that worked at Macy's with Brittany, or, at least, she worked by her. Remember?"

"Oh, sure, yeah. I remember now. Did you talk to her?"

"No, I talked to her mother. She's a very nice lady. Julie's not home. She's in China."

"China! What the hell is she doing in China?"

"She's on some kind of Christian missionary thing."

"Seriously? Why can't these people leave everybody alone?"

"Don't be so cynical," Maddy chided him. "They do a lot of good things. Besides, Wendy said Julie isn't all that religious. She just went with a friend for the experience of going to China."

"Who's Wendy? I'm getting confused."

"Wendy's her mother. Anyway, I explained why I needed to talk to Julie. Wendy said she's been following the case and admitted Julie told her she knew Brittany, but Wendy was a little skeptical. I told her it was true and…"

"Is there a point to this?"

"You need to go home and go to bed you crabass. Better yet, go to Margaret's. Did you sleep at all this week? Let me finish. Wendy was going to call the church and see if she could get a message to Julie. Wendy says they are supposed to be back in the next week or two, she wasn't exactly sure. Wendy will have Julie call me."

"Okay. That still doesn't mean she can help us."

"I realize that! Don't get cranky with me, buster."

"You're right, I'm sorry," Marc laughed. "I need to get out of here."

"Are you still going out to the Rileys' tomorrow and see them, Brittany and their neighbors?"

"Yeah, about ten o'clock. Why?"

"Want some company?" she asked.

"God bless you. Of course," Marc replied.

"I'll come to your place at about 9:30. You can drive. See you then."

Marc used two fingers to separate the curtains covering the bay window in the Rileys' living room. He was watching the protesters across the street as they milled about with their various signs. It was a clear, crisp, sunny winter day and since it was a Saturday morning, the street was almost blocked by the turnout.

At the end of the block, to Marc's right, several enterprising young men had set up a coffee and doughnut stand. There were two lines with at least fifteen people in each constantly waiting to be served. Two of the young men did the serving while others ran a shuttle service supplying the coffee and pastries. The deputies had tried to make them move but the crowd reaction caused the cops to back down. Apparently, they weren't causing any trouble, so they let them be and the deputies were given coffee and doughnuts gratis from the guys.

Marc turned back to the interior of the house. Maddy, Barbara and Brittany were seated at the dining room table and Floyd was downstairs.

"I'm going to run next door and talk to the Wilsons. When I get back, we'll go," he said to Madeline.

He went out the back and trudged through the almost knee-deep snow in the backyards. Marty Wilson was expecting him and let him in through the patio door after he brushed himself off. Inside he was greeted by Marty's wife, Elaine, their two friendly Golden Labs, Zeus and Ike and Marc noticed the pleasant aroma of a wood burning fireplace.

The Wilson's were a retired couple who had lived next door to the Rileys since the Rileys moved in. Marty was seventy-four, quite bald but liked to brag except in front of Elaine, that he still weighed what he did in high school. Elaine was white-haired, a little bit on the plump side after raising four kids and the polar opposite of Barbara Riley who neither of them particularly cared for.

"I have a little task for you two if you don't mind," Marc began. Both of them, sitting opposite the fireplace from Marc and sweetly holding hands, assured them they would help any way they could. They had watched Brittany grow up since the day she was brought home from the hospital. Brittany told Marc the Wilson home was a warmer, more comfortable place for her than her real home. Elaine could get teary-eyed just thinking about what Brittany was going through. Neither of them believed for an instant that Brittany could do such a thing and their hearts ached terribly over what had happened to Becky. Obviously, they would do anything to help her.

Marc took about three minutes explaining what he needed. It was a simple task but one that could be crucial to Brittany's defense. It may even be decisive, he told them.

"Remember, do it separately and then when you're done, check with each other's results. If they don't match, do it again. I need you to be careful and accurate. Okay?"

They both confirmed that they understood him and would do it that very day. Elaine, the more computer literate one of the two, would email him their results later that afternoon.

FORTY-EIGHT

Marc spent the weekend before the trial with his love, Margaret Tennant. The stress of a long vacation together was gone, and they were back together having slipped right into their comfort zone with each other.

The two days were about as relaxing as Marc could make them. Never leaving his head was the realization that serious business was going to start first thing Monday morning. The stress was always there even when he wasn't thinking about it. Just below the surface constantly tugging at him, was the question of if he was as prepared as he could be or as he should be. The two of them talked about it. Margaret was a trial judge and knew exactly what he was going through having been there as a lawyer herself, although not with the stakes Marc played with. A first-degree murder case was at the top of the critical meter. A young woman's life was literally in his hands. At the same time, despite the angst he constantly felt, he felt pretty good about their chances. A strong circumstantial case can be more difficult to find reasonable doubt than an eyewitness case. Except the more Marc prepared for the trial, the more he came to believe this was not a strong circumstantial case.

The warmth, comfort and security he felt in bed, naked with Margaret helped him sleep like a baby. By Monday morning, he was rested, refreshed and ready to go.

Marc arrived at the courthouse in Hastings before 7:30 A.M. believing he would be early enough to find good parking. He drove around through the front lot without finding a space and found out why. In front of the main doors, spilling beyond the sidewalks and blocking the circular drive in front of the building, was a crowd of well over two hundred people. On top of that, the sheriff had blocked off at least a quarter of the lot, closest to the building, for media vehicles.

Marc parked his car in the back lot and walked quickly toward the building. Keeping his head down as much as he could to avoid being recognized, he hurried past at least six TV reporters. Each of them, along with their camera operators, were conducting interviews of the crowd.

Standing at the back of the mob, hoping not to be recognized, he casually asked an older man, "Why isn't anyone moving?"

"They're not letting anyone in until eight o'clock, leastwise, that's the rumor going around," the man told him. He stared at Marc with a quizzical expression and said, "You look familiar. Are you a lawyer or something?"

At that moment, Marc spotted a deputy he recognized standing inside the exit door. "No, I'm nobody," he answered the man then hurried off toward the exit doorway. The crowd on this side of the building was fairly thin and he almost made it. A few feet before he got to the door, he heard a familiar voice and footsteps hurrying up behind him.

"Marc! Mr. Kadella," Gabriella Shriqui was almost shouting.

If it was anyone else he would have ignored her. Marc genuinely liked Gabriella. He had been interviewed by her many times for this case and a couple of others and always found her to be polite, respectful and professional.

"Hey, Gabriella," he said as he turned to her. Before she could ask him a question, he said, "You look lovely this fine brisk winter morning."

"Oh, stuff that," she whispered after covering her microphone. "I'm freezing my ass off out here. Would you mind...?"

"What's that scent you're wearing? It smells great," Marc said.

"Never mind that," Gabriella said trying not to laugh. "I have a few questions..."

"And you still have those temptation eyes..."

"Stop trying to deflect this by flirting with me," she laughed.

"Gabriella," Marc said turning serious. "You people always do this. Try to get people to say something they shouldn't. Do you want a quote?"

"Yes, sure," she answered.

"Here it is. Ready?" he said looking at her cameraman. "My client maintains her innocence. Other than that, I have no comment."

During all of this Marc had been slowly backing up toward the door. By the time he got there, everyone in the vicinity was watching. Someone in the crowd recognized him and shouts of "It's her lawyer!" were starting up. Fortunately, the deputy at the door recognized him and opened the door to let him in.

Having arrived as early as he did, Marc went into the courtroom and staked his claim to the table he wanted. The deputy guarding the courtroom door had let him in. Marc placed his briefcase and overcoat on the table closest to the jury box. He wanted Brittany to be as close to the jurors as possible. He wanted them to see her every day. He wanted them to look at her, watch her and humanize her as much as possible and to get them wondering: "How could this demure, pretty, wholesome girl-next-door possibly do what the prosecution says she did?" At least, that was his theory.

The courtroom they would all be almost living in for the next month was the largest one in the building. From the back, looking toward the front of the room and the judge's bench, there were three separate sets of benches in the gallery. Each bench could accommodate between seven and eight people and the seats were cushioned. Two aisles separated them for people to walk up and down.

On the left of the courtroom next to Marc's table was the jury box with twelve reasonably comfortable, padded chairs. There were four more comfortable chairs in front of the jury box for the alternates. In the front of the room, from left to right, were the witness stand judge's bench and to the left of the judge's seat, the court clerk's desk. It was a modern well-lit, fairly comfortable courtroom done in an oak motif.

After Marc arrived, a deputy roped off the front two rows directly behind the defense table. These would be reserved for the family and others involved on Brittany's behalf. At 8:30, the Rileys were escorted into the courtroom. Butch and Andy were with them along with two sheriff's deputies. Much to Sheriff Cale's displeasure, Judge Connors had ordered the sheriff to provide protection for Brittany coming and going from court.

A few minutes later, the prosecution team arrived again including the attorney general herself, Anne Peterson. Along with Vanderbeck and Hart, there were four additional lawyers, two who would be there throughout the trial to help the trial lawyers. The other two were simply aides of Peterson. There were seven lawyers on behalf of the people of Minnesota, three at the table and four in chairs in front of the bar, all lined up against one, young, pretty, widowed mother. Marc smiled at the absurdity of it and hoped it would look as ludicrous as bullying and overbearing to the jury as it was to him.

By now, the courtroom was beginning to fill up. The members of the media who had been selected to sit in were filling the second, third and fourth rows along the right-hand side of the room. Behind and above them, with a clear, unobstructed view, was the single camera that would beam the proceedings live to an insatiable, voyeuristic public who seemingly could not get enough of courtroom reality television.

The lawyers were asked to meet with Connors in chambers a little before nine. Marc, Vanderbeck, Hart and Attorney General Peterson went back to see him. Connors wanted to know if there were any last-minute issues to discuss which there were not. He made it clear that opening statements were to be done before lunch and testimony would begin that afternoon.

While the trial was beginning, Melinda Pace and her producer Robbie Nelson were meeting with Hunter Oswood and Madison Eyler, the station's general manager. They went over scheduling and details for Melinda's show. It had been decided that starting today in her normal four o'clock afternoon time slot, they would rerun the previous day's show. At 6:30, Melinda would go live with a report and commentary of that day's court proceedings. The station had never tried this before but there had never been a trial with this level of ratings appeal. The station had set up copying equipment and had a pair of full-time techs to view and copy the entire day's feed from the live courtroom camera. In addition, they agreed to preempt any programming being aired to run live feeds over the air. As the meeting was breaking up, Oswood bluntly told Robbie, in Melinda's presence to keep a lid on her drinking.

FORTY-NINE

As Marc had guessed, Danica Hart gave the prosecution's opening statement. Opening statements are supposed to be an opportunity to tell the jury what the case is about and to verbally walk them through the evidence that is to be presented to the jury to make the case. It is not meant to be a time to argue the case to convince the jury they should find in your favor.

Marc's job during Hart's opening was to take extensive notes of what she told the jury. If she told them they would hear testimony or receive exhibits then failed to deliver on any of these things, Marc would be sure to let the jury know this during his closing argument.

He also liked to watch the jurors as much as he could. He wanted to see if they would give any nonverbal indicators of what they were thinking. As they were led into the courtroom and seated, the four alternates taking chairs in front of the jury box, Marc undoubtedly noticed something. Every one of them took a long look at all of the lawyers on the prosecution team. The looks on the faces of several of them were plainly not positive. In fact, he saw two of the women and one older man look back and forth between the small herd on the prosecution's side and Marc with just pretty, modest Brittany sitting beside him.

Danica Hart spent over two hours explaining their case. Hart presented herself well, had a nice, easy manner and a voice that, unknown to Marc, had years of singing lessons behind it. In Marc's opinion, she made one serious mistake. When he wasn't taking notes, Marc was closely watching the jurors. Again, he was trying to gauge their nonverbal response to her.

At first, all sixteen, including the four alternates, were sitting upright paying very close attention. At least half of them started out taking notes themselves. The mistake Marc believed she made was giving them too much detail. Hart, by memory, explained what every witness was going to tell them and what every piece of evidence was that they would see.

Gradually, she began to lose them. She didn't lose them all at once and not entirely, but an objective observer could see it. It started with the note takers. One by one they gradually stopped writing or at least slowed. Marc also noticed two or three others openly yawn or stifle one. Unfortunately for Hart, and this was easy to do, she was concentrating so much on what she was saying and where she wanted to take them that she failed to notice where her audience was. To top it off, Hart's big finale, the part where she really wanted to hit a home run was, to Marc, pretty much a total flop. She went over the ten-day period when Becky first turned up missing until Barbara notified the authorities. Instead of highlighting this time frame as a whole, Hart informed the jury of Brittany's behavior day-by-day. She went over in detail everything the cops had learned about Brittany's behavior. By the time she finished detailing every bit of each day including such mundane details as what time she got up, what time she went to work and what time she got home, the jury was gone. In fact, at least half of them were fidgeting uncomfortably in their chairs obviously in need of a restroom break.

When she finished Marc looked over at the prosecution table and all of them were beaming with pride. The jurors, all of them, were looking at the judge like little kids hoping dad would stop the car and take a break. Fortunately for Hart, opening statements are probably the least important part of the trial. If you screw it up, presenting your case will give you an opportunity to correct it.

Following a short break, Connors looked up at the clock and saw it was now after 11:00. He turned to Marc and asked, "Are you going to give an opening statement now, Mr. Kadella?

The defense has the choice of making its opening statement after the prosecution or waiting until the prosecution is finished presenting its case. Marc had been undecided about what he wanted to do until this very moment.

Marc stood up to address the judge and said, "I'll do so now, your Honor."

He stood in the well of the court a respectful distance from the jury and began by introducing himself and his client.

"Ladies and gentlemen, my name is Marc Kadella and I represent the accused, Brittany Riley. I use the word 'accused' to describe her because that is who and what she is. She is accused and nothing more."

Marc spoke for about an hour. Without notes of any kind, while slowly pacing around the courtroom he spelled out for the jury the prosecution's case in terms of what they did not have and could not present to them. No witnesses, no fingerprints, no forensics tying Brittany Riley to the death of her daughter. He avoided going into any detail the evidence the defense would present for its case. At this point in the trial, it was possible he might not have to put on a case at all. Highly unlikely but he did not want to promise them something then not deliver it.

Marc concluded by reminding them of their oath. Their promise to keep an open mind and wait until all of the evidence was in before making a decision. He talked about the presumption of innocence and the burden of proof and while he did these things, he moved slowly before them and made sure he made eye contact with each of them. Trials are theatre and like any good story, the defense especially wants the jury to become emotionally invested in defense counsel and the defendant. It's very difficult to make the jury like your client. But if you can do it, you're probably half-way to reasonable doubt. While Marc was making eye contact with them, he actually made several of them nod their heads and smile at him.

"If you do that, ladies and gentlemen, if you abide by your oath, wait for all of the evidence and follow the law, you will find this young woman not guilty and send her home."

When he finished, Judge Connors said, "We'll break for lunch now. The prosecution will call its first witness at one o'clock."

Every television news report in America broadcasted over the lunch hour gave an update of the trial. Included was footage of Danica Hart talking to the jury. Each station cherry picked a piece of film to highlight Brittany's dilemma. Every one of the news reports had a highlight clip of Hart making a damaging statement about the evidence to be presented followed by a commentary supporting the strength of the prosecution's case. All of the reports had an "expert" talking head, a defense lawyer, a former prosecutor or a retired judge to give their highly regarded two cents worth. On the whole, those opinions were running about ninety to ten in favor of the prosecution. According to the media, Brittany Riley was in grave trouble.

As Marc had anticipated, because it is chronologically and logically what he would have done, young Jackson Carson, the boy who found Becky Rileys' remains, was the first witness called.

Most ten-year-old kids would have trouble just walking up to the witness stand. They would typically be so nervous, and their legs would be so weak they could barely move. Especially in a courtroom as packed with people as this one was.

Jackson Carson swaggered, and that was the word to describe his walk and attitude, swaggered up the right-hand aisle, through the gate and directly to the witness stand. He stood in the box and looked out over the crowd as unconcerned as if he had done this a hundred times. The clerk swore him in and he sat down.

Connors took a couple of minutes to chat with him, off the record just to make sure he was comfortable and ready. Having been thoroughly prepared by Danica Hart, Jackson was fine and knew enough to call Connors, your Honor. Satisfied, Connors offered the witness to Hart.

In Minnesota state courts, lawyers must conduct their questioning of witnesses while seated at their table. Many state and federal courts will allow the lawyers to stand at a podium about ten or twelve feet, maybe more, away from the witness box. This is to prevent lawyers from physically intimidating a witness. If the lawyer has an exhibit or a

240

document to give to the witness, the lawyer must ask the court for permission to do so. Even then, he or she is not allowed to hover over the witness. That behavior is a TV and movie thing and is not acceptable conduct.

"May I call you Jackie?" Hart asked trying to be as friendly as possible.

"No, I told you before, I hate that name," Jackson answered with obvious annoyance which elicited restrained laughter through the courtroom. "Jack or Jackson."

"I'm sorry. You're right, I forgot and apologize," A slightly red-faced, chastened Hart replied. Marc Kadella, suppressing a smile, made a mental note to ask Hart what it's like to get slapped down in open court by a ten-year-old.

"Jackson," she said, starting over, "do you remember what happened on October third of last year?"

"I don't think I'll ever forget it," Jackson said as he leaned forward a few inches to speak directly into the microphone.

Hart, having conducted hundreds of direct examinations over the course of her career, expertly walked Jackson through the events of that day. When questioning a witness that you have called to help your case, the lawyer's role is to ask short, open-ended questions. The idea is to let the witness tell the jury what he or she saw or did that is pertinent to your case. Let the witness tell his story.

Since this was the first witness of the trial, Hart decided to let the jury hear all of it. Let Jackson tell them everything he did from the time he woke up until the sheriff's office was done questioning him and they went home. Obviously, none of this had anything to do with Brittany Rileys' guilt or innocence. It was necessary, however, since an element of the crime is to establish that the jury could reasonably infer the crime took place in Dakota County. Or, at least enough of the crime took place there to support the question of jurisdiction.

Hart then spent a little time going over the fact that Jackson had no idea how the body got there. That he did not see anyone carrying anything into the river and leaving it. "How have you been since this happened?" Hart asked.

"Okay," Jackson quietly answered, uncomfortable being asked personal questions about his well-being.

"Are you sleeping okay?"

"Most of the time," he answered.

"Are you seeing a counselor?"

"Your Honor," Marc politely said as he rose from his chair. This line of questioning was clearly objectionable. It was entirely designed to draw on the jurors' emotions. "Look what this has done to this bright, delightful, young boy. Someone needs to pay for it." Except, these questions have nothing to do with guilt or innocence.

"That's enough, Ms. Hart," Connors told her.

"Yes, your Honor," Hart said. "I have no further questions."

Marc took a moment to mentally debate whether or not to ask him anything. He finally decided on a couple of quick questions.

"Hello, Jackson," Marc lightly began. "My name is Marc Kadella and I am the lawyer for Brittany Riley. I have just a couple of questions for you.

"Have you ever seen Brittany before?" he asked indicating the young woman to his left.

"I've seen her on TV a lot."

"Sure. But before the day you were hunting with your dad, had you ever seen her?"

"No, sir. I haven't," Jackson answered.

Jackson was excused and calmly strolled out of the courtroom.

Jackson's father, Eric, was called next. The prosecution had originally listed every member of the hunting party on their witness list. Connors had pressured them into cutting the number down to just two, Eric and his friend Chris Givens. The other three had nothing more to offer so Connors wanted them dropped to move the trial along.

Vanderbeck took the testimony of the two hunters. Unlike young Jackson, these two had little to offer except confirming what Jackson found and where he found it and then calling the sheriff. What they did after that wasn't much.

Marc asked very few questions of either of them on cross-examination. Questions designed to have the men verify that they had not seen anyone dump the body, had never seen Brittany before except on TV and had nothing to offer regarding guilt or innocence.

By the time Chris Givens was done, it was almost 2:30 and the jury was looking uninterested. When Marc finished, and Givens was excused, Connors called for a break.

Next up was the man who led the forensics team that conducted the search of the area where the body was found. The jury had to endure the showing of the film of the search in its entirety. When it was finished Vanderbeck took almost another hour going over the removal of the body and the pictures taken of the scene at the water's edge, including showing a color photo of Becky's remains still in the water.

Marc had warned Brittany about this and did his best to prepare her for the picture of her daughter as she was when found in the river. Brittany did her best to look as neutral as possible but was unable to keep her eyes on the TV screen where the picture was displayed. Marc watched the jury and to his dismay, almost every one of them at some point glanced at Brittany to see her reaction. Fortunately, she held her composure fairly well except for a few tears that leaked out and trickled down her cheeks.

When the show was over, Vanderbeck passed the witness to Marc. The only question he had was to elicit an admission that the crime scene crew uncovered no physical evidence that could be tied to Brittany Riley or anyone else.

Marc finished his short cross-exam, the witness was excused, and Connors called the lawyers up to the bench.

"Do you have a quick witness to put on?" he asked Vanderbeck.

"Not really your Honor," Hart replied. "We're going to get into investigators now."

"Okay. We'll call it a day, but this took too long today. The jury got bored. Everybody needs to step it up. If I need to we'll start early and stay late. That could include the weekend." He continued sternly looking at all of them. "We'll start tomorrow promptly at nine. Have your witnesses ready to go."

On her live 6:30 show, Melinda Pace had two guests. A man named Steve Farben and Andrea Briscomb. Farben was a former federal prosecutor who was now a partner in a well-known personal injury firm. In his late fifties, the mostly bald lawyer had taken his government pension and moved to private practice to make some serious money before retirement. Farben had agreed to be an on-air talking head for the publicity to his firm. Commercial exposure like this could not be purchased.

Melinda's other guest was the criminal defense lawyer she had been using, Andrea Briscomb. Briscomb was suppressing her annoyance at sharing the spotlight with anyone especially Farben. She had conducted a couple of trials against him while he was with the U.S. Attorney's office and considered him a snake. Borderline ethical with a win at all costs, the truth be damned attitude. Thanks to Robbie Nelson's research, Melinda knew all about the animosity between them and was perfectly willing to poke them both to bring it out on-air.

Farben's take on the day's proceedings was decidedly favorable toward the prosecution. He went over everything ignoring the bad parts and emphasizing only the good on behalf of the state's case.

Briscomb, put on the defensive, stuck to the obvious that it was the first day of testimony and nothing of significance came out. Farben stuck her with a mild put down that defense lawyers always downplayed evidence against their client, ignoring the fact that he was doing the very same thing. The show wrapped up with Briscomb taking a pretty good shot at Hart by telling the audience that a ten-year-old boy had put the lawyer in her place. When Melinda was finishing up with a final remark, the two lawyers sat quietly with forced smiles and annoyed expressions.

The station had set up an audience of twenty people to watch the show and provide feedback. If this group was a fair indication, the public was going to eat this up with a spoon. Melinda and the station management could not have been happier.

FIFTY

When court adjourned for the day, it was already after 5:00 P.M. Marc, Brittany and the Rileys waited another half hour for the crowd to thin out. It was safe enough for Butch, Andy and the deputies to sneak Brittany out the back. By early February, the days were lengthening enough to the point where it was no longer totally dark when Marc hurried through the windswept parking lot to his car.

The air temperature for most of the day held steady in the single digits. Beginning around four o'clock a warm front was moving in and the temp was already up to twenty degrees and still rising. The wind was picking up from the west. When Marc reached his car, before opening the door, he raised his head, tilted it upward slightly, faced into the wind and drew in a deep breath through his nose. He could feel and smell the moisture in the air and guessed six to eight more inches of snow on the ground by morning. It was one of those winters where it was either cold or snowing. The cold of the past several days was lifting and the snow was on its way. The weather geeks were predicting temps in the mid-thirties by morning and snow off and on for the next several days.

Marc stopped at a fast food chain restaurant and by the time he arrived back at his office it was almost seven. Despite the sign at the entrance to the building's parking lot proclaiming it to be private parking, there were two media vans in it waiting for him.

Because of the hour, there were only a couple of tenant's cars still there. Marc parked as close to the door as he could but by the time he opened his car door, they were on him. He decided the best thing to do was be a little cooperative. There were two cameras and two reporters; one from a local station, one from CNN. Both immediately asked the same question.

"How did it go in court today?"

"Fine," Marc answered. "No surprises. It was the first day. We have a long way to go."

"Is it true you offered to accept a plea to second-degree..." one of them began asking.

Marc wearily shook his head and said, "I've answered that question at least a dozen times. No, it is not true. In fact,..."

"Our sources insist it is true," the reporter for CNN said.

"And who exactly are these sources?"

"We can't tell you that," the woman replied.

"So, they just remain sources and you report it as if it was Moses on Mount Sinai. Goodnight," Marc said as he began walking toward the door. "I have to prepare for tomorrow."

Marc stood in his living room wearing a T-shirt and sweatpants, sipping his first cup of coffee, staring out the bay window. There looked to be, he estimated, about four inches of new snow already down and more falling. He had fallen into bed just before midnight and fortunately, fell asleep immediately. His internal clock went off five minutes before his alarm was set to go off and he got up right away. Marc checked the time, decided on one more cup of caffeine and then he better get moving early.

Despite arriving before 8:00 A.M. Marc was still unable to find a spot in the lot closer to the building. Fortunately, the county plow had already cleaned both lots, so he didn't have to wade through four or five inches of fresh wet snow. When he was halfway to the building, he saw the prosecution team, including A.G. Peterson, pile out of two black Suburbans. They had parked in the two spots closest to the building with "Reserved" signs on them.

Marc stopped for a moment to stare at the prosecution herd heading through the crowd toward the building. "Now that really sucks. They get reserved parking and I …" he said out loud to no one. He shook his head, shifted his briefcase from his left hand to his right and quickened his pace to get out of the snow. He finished going through security and his phone went off. Marc saw it was coming from Barbara Riley and he took a moment to decide if he wanted to answer. When the sixth ring finished, he put it to his ear and said hello.

"The deputies served me and Floyd with subpoenas this morning," an angry Barbara said without preamble.

"Not a surprise," Marc said. "We talked about this, remember?"

"I know but…"

"It's no big deal. They're going to want to sequester you from the courtroom until you testify. Is there a date and time on it when they want you to appear?" he asked.

"No, there isn't."

"Stay home for now. I'll find out what's going on and call you back. Have the guys bring Brittany in, but you and Floyd might as well wait."

Marc had anticipated this. All three of the Rileys were on both the prosecution's and the defense's witness lists. Barbara was obviously the one they were after. He believed the next few witnesses were going to be the investigative deputies and they would need Barbara to corroborate their belief that Brittany was a pathological liar.

Marc set his briefcase on the defense table and hung his overcoat on the portable coat rack along the wall. He turned from the coat rack and just about ran into Danica Hart.

"Sorry," she smiled. "We need to talk about Barbara Riley. We served her this morning."

"I heard," Marc said. "When do you want her?"

"That's for us to decide," Vanderbeck said. He had been standing behind Hart looking annoyed.

"Lowell, please," Hart said. "Not every little thing needs to be adversarial." Hart turned back to Marc and said, "Is there any reason they won't be available with a couple hours' notice? We'll send a sheriff for them."

"No, not really," Marc said. "It's up to you, of course. But Floyd's a waste of time. Barbara's running the show in that house."

"We're not sure exactly when we'll get to them. Probably not before Thursday," Hart said. At that moment A.G. Peterson joined them, looked at Marc and said a pleasant good morning and extended her hand to him.

"Good morning," Marc replied. "I'm sorry but I'm not sure what to call you. Madam Attorney General or just…"

"Anne will be fine." She smiled surprising Marc with her informality.

"Okay, Anne." He looked at Hart and said, "I told them to stay home. Why don't we tell the judge what's going on and then I'll call them."

Shannon Keenan, one of the four investigators was called to the stand promptly at nine o'clock. As she was being sworn in, a man and a woman entered and sat down on the bench with Butch Koll and Andy Whitmore. Tony Carvelli silently shook hands with both men. Vivian Donahue handed her cashmere topcoat to Tony who gave it to Andy to place on the empty seat next to him.

Vanderbeck did the direct examination of Detective Keenan. He started out by having her talk about her credentials, to have Keenan tell the jury about her education, years on the job and her experience as an investigator and then to establish her in the minds of the jury as a professional to be taken seriously.

Keenan was being used to explain to the jury what steps the sheriff's office took to find the child and how seriously the sheriff and all of the personnel involved treated a missing child case. Not just the sheriff but every local and state police department and agency would assist to leave no stone unturned.

Shannon Keenan made an excellent witness. She had testified in court many times and was quite poised, comfortable and well prepared. Coaching a witness and preparing a witness are two very different things. Coaching a witness means putting words in her mouth, telling her what to say. Obviously, this is not allowed. Preparing a witness is going over their testimony to make it smooth and credible and helping the witness through any potential nervousness or problems, but letting the witness tell the jury what they know about the case. Keenan was very well prepared. Except in Marc's opinion, Vanderbeck made a mistake that is difficult to avoid.

During the morning break, Marc introduced Vivian and Tony to his client. Brittany had seen them at her bail hearing and knew who she was but did not have the chance to meet her. They shook hands and a tear trickled down Brittany's cheek. Seeing this Vivian held out her arms and gave the younger woman an affectionate hug.

After that Vivian went through the gate into the courtroom well and was warmly greeted by Anne Peterson. They chatted for a minute then Vivian bluntly asked her, "Anne, why are you here? I must tell you, as friendly as possible, with all of the lawyers on your side, it looks a little ridiculous, like you're ganging up on this young girl."

"I was wondering about that myself, Vivian. Do you think so?"

"Yes, and it doesn't make you look good. Stay or go, it's up to you but…"

"I think I'll go. Thanks. No one else would tell me that. Why are you here? I heard you paid her bail."

"I believe she's innocent. Or, at least deserves her day in court. Besides, you know the media and me. I love to tweak them and give them something to gossip about. Great to see you again," Vivian said to a woman she secretly loathed. *But* she thought with smug satisfaction, *I did get her to leave.*

Court resumed after the break with a very noticeable absence of Attorney General Peterson and her two toadies. Marc silently caught Danica Hart's attention, tilted his head to look at Peterson's empty chair then back to Hart who was concealing a large smile from Lowell Vanderbeck.

Keenan was on the stand not counting breaks and lunch, a total of over four hours. Using her notes, which is permissible to refresh her memory, she told the jury, in detail, everything that Keenan and her partner, Kristin Williams, did. Every minute they spent driving around with Brittany. Every apartment complex they visited and whatever they did at each one to locate the missing Bob Olson. Each and every person they talked to in an effort to bolster their suspicion that Bob Olson did not exist, and Brittany was not being honest.

Possibly the most damaging thing she testified to, was the lock on the outside of Becky's bedroom. A picture of it was put up on the TV screen and Keenan explained to the jury exactly what it was. She tried to give her opinion about why it was there, but Marc objected, and Connors sustained him. That likely didn't matter since it was obvious the latch

248

was there to keep Becky locked in her room. While Keenan testified about the latch, Marc stole glances at the jury and several of them, mostly the women, had a look of distaste if not disgust about it.

Vanderbeck, for the most part, did an excellent job of asking her open-ended questions to allow Keenan to testify. The one thing he did too much of, the mistake Marc believed he made, was to interrupt her and ask her a question and to highlight a point he wanted to make by repeating her testimony.

"After you finished at this apartment complex and found no evidence of the mysteriously vanished Bob Olson, what did you do next?" was a question or a variation of it that he used so many times it became predictable. By the time they finished most of the jury seemed lost except every one of them got the message that Vanderbeck wanted them to get. Bob Olson did not exist, and Brittany Riley led the cops on a wild goose chase looking for him. It was also clear that this intelligent, educated, experienced detective believed Brittany was lying. Without saying it, that message came across loud and clear.

Keenan tried to testify what Brittany's friends had told them. She was looking for a way to bring out the lies Brittany told during the time Becky was missing and before Barbara called the police. This was clearly hearsay and since Brittany's friends were on both witness lists, they could testify themselves.

Marc objected as soon as Keenan started down that path. Judge Connors, an experienced judge and trial lawyer himself knew exactly what the prosecution was trying to do. He quickly sustained Marc's objection and gave Vanderbeck a mild admonishment for the effort, warning him not to try it.

Score one for the defense, Marc thought. He hoped the jury would see this as the state trying to pull something underhanded.

Judge Connors called for a short break when Keenan finished her direct and before Marc could-cross examine her.

On cross-examination, Marc decided to not waste a lot of time. One by one he went over the list of people she had personally interviewed and asked the exact same line of questions.

"Isn't it true you asked Annabelle Oslund her opinion of Brittany as a mother?" was an example of Marc's question.

"Yes," Keenan always replied.

"And it's also true that Ms. Oslund had nothing but praise for Ms. Riley as a parent?"

"Yes."

"That Becky was always well cared for. Always clean, well fed, clean clothes and was a very happy little girl, correct?"

"Yes."

"And she also told you, because you specifically asked everyone who knew her that Brittany was a loving, caring mother, didn't she?"

Marc got Keenan to admit they asked everyone about Brittany as a mother. She also had to admit they were unable to find anyone, not a single person, who knew Brittany and Becky, who had anything bad to say about her as a parent.

He then shifted his inquiry to the search of Brittany's apartment which Keenan had overseen. Marc had a list of every item removed by the deputies and went over every item on it. What he got was Keenan to admit they found nothing in the search of Brittany's apartment, her cell phone, computer or anything else taken from her apartment to indicate Brittany had anything to do with her daughter's disappearance.

FIFTY-ONE

Shannon Keenan's partner, Kristen Williams, was called to the stand next. Hart would conduct her exam and she started off basically the same way Vanderbeck had with Keenan. Hart walked the witness through her experience, education and any pertinent awards and commendations. Williams then testified about riding around with Brittany visiting various apartments in Burnsville, restaurants and other places Brittany claimed they had been together. She also used her notes but did not go into the detail that Keenan had. Hart used this testimony mostly to bolster what Keenan had told the jury and to point out that two veteran detectives believed Brittany was lying about the missing Bob Olson.

"After about two weeks of this, we were all very suspicious of her story. It was decided that Shannon and I would start to investigate Brittany Riley. You have to remember, every law enforcement officer and department in Minnesota was looking for her daughter. Plus, the Rileys were conducting searches throughout Dakota County with thousands of volunteers trying to find her. At that point, we pretty much assumed she was dead, and we had a homicide to investigate and without even a hint that Bob Olson existed, Brittany was the obvious suspect."

"What did you do at that point?"

"We began by interviewing her closest friends first," Williams told the jury. Hart used the same questioning technique with Williams that Vanderbeck had used with Keenan. Whenever Williams paused, which, of course, had been carefully prearranged and rehearsed, Hart would repeat a significant point Williams had just made and put it back to her in the form of a question.

For the next two hours, the two of them went through the entire list of people the female detectives had interviewed. They started with Brittany's three best girlfriends, then ex-boyfriends, relatives and acquaintances. With each one, Williams would inform the jury of what their relationship was to Brittany. She would then tell the jury enough of their interview to make it clear what they had to say but not quite enough to draw a hearsay objection.

Testifying as to what you claim somebody else told you is the very definition of hearsay and is normally not allowed. Marc could have objected, but what Williams was telling the jury wasn't harmful to his case. Plus, too many objections can alienate a jury and make them believe you're trying to keep something from them and every one of the people she interviewed and talked about was on the prosecution's witness list and were going to testify anyway. And if they didn't, they were all under subpoena by Marc and he would bring them in. Marc let it go for a while then, after the sixth or seventh time they did it, he had enough.

"Objection, your Honor," he said as he arose from his chair. "Your Honor, these little statements the witness keeps making claiming someone they interviewed said such and such are clearly hearsay. I've let it go hoping they'd stop. If they want to have the jury hear what someone said, they can have that person testify themselves."

By making a lengthy objection, Marc was explaining to the jury what was going on. The judge certainly did not need Marc to explain it to him. But it would help the jury understand and maybe lead them to believe the prosecution was trying to pull something over on them.

"I agree," Connors said. "Sustained. No more of it, Ms. Hart."

"Sorry, your Honor," a slightly chastened Danica Hart said as Marc sat down.

"Did you interview any co-workers of the defendant?"

"No, I did not. Stu Doyle, one of our other investigators working the case did. I believe he did so while trying to locate…"

"Objection," Marc said as he stood up again. "Detective Doyle should be able to testify as to what he did."

"Sustained," Connors said while making a note in his trial notebook. "Move along Ms. Hart," he continued without bothering to look up.

Williams then began to testify about her internet search of Brittany and her friends' social media sites. Before he had a chance to stand Connors turned his head away from the witness to look at Marc.

"Objection, your Honor," Marc said as he again stood up. "What they're about to show the jury is highly prejudicial and offers no probative value." What this particular objection means is that the testimony about to be given is being offered to inflame the juror's emotions and offers nothing in the way of proving the defendant committed the crime charged. What Hart and Williams were about to present were the results of Williams' internet search. They had been the focus of a significant and at times, heated argument in chambers several weeks ago. Connors had already ruled he would allow it. Marc, as Connors expected, was renewing his objection to get it on the trial record and let the jury know the material they were to be shown proved nothing.

Connors looked at Hart, who had also stood up, waiting for her response.

"It goes to motive, your Honor and is central to our theory of the case," she said.

"Overruled," Connors said. He then gestured the lawyers to come up to the bench.

"How long is this going to be?" he asked Hart.

252

"At least an hour and a half," she replied.

Connors looked at the clock again and the fidgeting, semi-bored jurors and said, "I'm going to call it a day. The weather being what it is it's going to be a slow ride home. We'll pick it up here in the morning."

Melinda and Robbie were meeting in Melinda's office with defense attorney Andrea Briscomb. It was almost 6:00 P.M. and they had to wrap up their pre-production meeting. Of the day's testimony, they would show for the defense the thirty seconds worth of film when Kadella objected to what would be shown in court the next day. The three of them were reviewing it so Briscomb would have an explanation ready to tell the audience what was going on. Melinda and Robbie had already been over this with Briscomb's counterpart, Steven Farben. It would be easier if the two of them didn't despise each other so much that they could be in the same room at the same time to do it.

Farben would have two segments of film to explain. One was slightly more than a minute long and the other almost two minutes. Both were segments of testimony from one of the women investigators that any fool could see made Brittany look like a liar.

They nailed down Briscomb's response to the film she was to explain and then took a few minutes to go over a few "spontaneous" questions. When they finished, satisfied that their guest was prepared, Robbie packed up everything to go to the booth to oversee the show.

"Just between us," Melinda said, "you're right about Farben. He is an arrogant ass."

Robby heard Melinda say this to Briscomb and was able to get out of the room without laughing. Melinda had said the exact same words to Farben referring to Briscomb less than half an hour ago.

"You should've tried a case against him," Briscomb almost sneered. "This is pleasant compared to that."

"I just want you to know how much I appreciate your input and professionalism. It balances Farben and makes the show look fairer."

The show itself went smoothly except for one small, not quite heated exchange between the two lawyers. Briscomb was supposedly taking the defense side. Even so, she was forced to admit Brittany was obviously lying, especially during the ten days when her daughter was missing, and she did not report it.

The show wrapped up with all three of them agreeing it would be difficult for her to get out from under her lies. And both lawyers agreed her attorney looked completely over his head.

The phones at the station did not stop ringing until almost an hour after the show aired. Over ninety-five percent of the callers agreeing with

Melinda and her guests and thanking her for putting on an objective, balanced commentary about the trial.

Later that night, relaxing on the couch in the living room of his sparse, one-bedroom apartment, Bob Olson watched Melinda's show for the third time. He had his stockinged feet on his cheap wooden coffee table enjoying the show and the results. After the third viewing, he decided he wanted to risk attending the trial; at least for one day. Maybe one day next week if he could get some time off from work.

The next day almost every paper in the country ran a story about the previous day's testimony. It was also prominent on all of the morning TV talk shows and cable news throughout the day. Of course, they all used the word "alleged" a lot, but it was evident they believed Brittany was going to be caught in her web of lies.

Marc had been seated at his desk for over three hours going over his trial book. His door stood open and the office was dark, silent and empty. He was just about done reviewing and editing his cross-exam of Detective Williams to be done first thing tomorrow. Earlier, while going over his and Madeline's interview notes of the next batch of witnesses, he had taken a call from Margaret Tennant.

Margaret called to check up on him to see how he was doing. Being a trial judge and before that a trial lawyer herself, she understood the burden and stress he was under. Concerned about him, she called just to let him know she was thinking about him.

Tired after another long day, Marc gathered up what he needed for court in the morning.

"How's your trial going?" a voice came from his doorway breaking the silence.

Marc jumped two inches off his chair and almost fell over backward when he bounced down. His breathing stopped, and he placed a hand over his chest in a futile effort to slow down his heart.

"Jesus Christ, Connie! You just took ten years off my life," Marc shouted. "Make some noise when you come in!"

Connie Mickelson, his good friend, colleague and landlord was standing in his doorway. She had one hand over her mouth to hold back a laugh and an embarrassed look in her eyes.

"I'm sorry," she said laughing a little bit.

"It's not funny," he calmly replied as his breathing and heart returned to normal.

"Depends on where you're standing," Connie said as she sat in one of his client chairs. "I drove by and saw the light on. Figured you were here. How's it going?"

"So far, okay," he shrugged.

"Are you eating and getting some sleep?" his friend asked.

"Doing my best, Mom," he smiled.

"Kiss my ass, smartass. You know what I mean." Connie could out cuss most sailors.

"Yeah, I do. Vivian Donahue and Tony showed up today. She pretty much chased Anne Peterson away. It was pretty funny."

"You don't seem too stressed yet."

"It's there," Marc conceded. "She's innocent and if I screw this up she's going to prison for the rest of her life. Life without possibility of parole. It's hard to sleep well."

"We've been over your case. It's solid. You're going to win. Okay?"

"We'll see. I hope you're right."

"Get out of here. Go see Margaret. Get laid. Get a good night's sleep."

"I'll see Margaret this weekend. I hate driving all the way to Hastings from her place in the morning. Too much traffic," he answered as they both stood to leave.

"Anything you need, anything any of us can do to help…"

"I know, thanks, Connie."

FIFTY-TWO

The next morning, the snowstorm had moved into Wisconsin, the streets were clear, the sun was out, and the weather geeks were forecasting several days of pleasant weather. Marc began his trek from the already almost full far parking lot. He looked at the building and saw the mob. As he got closer he could see Sheriff Cale and at least a dozen deputies trying to herd them away from the doors.

To Marc's left was the jail, euphemistically called the adult detention center. To his right were the county government offices and between them was the courthouse. All three sections were connected to form one large building. In front of the court section is a circular drive that people can use as a drop-off and pick-up area. In front of the jail and county offices are sidewalks. The problem Cale was having was that there simply is not enough area or a convenient place for this crowd of protesters to go. Especially with the snow piled up.

The protestors wanted to be admitted into the building but that was not going to happen. Cale finally decided to cordon off a section of the sidewalk by the jail. There would not be enough room for all of them on the sidewalk itself which meant a large number would have to leave or stand in almost knee-deep snow.

Cale stood watching his deputies line up and slowly began moving the crowd away from the front of the building. Marc tried to make his way past alongside them to get to the door where another deputy stood inside watching and waiting for him. When he was about halfway there, someone in the crowd recognized him and began yelling, "There he is! That's her lawyer! Get him!" The mass of moving people, later estimated at almost five hundred, stopped, went completely silent for two to three seconds then all hell broke loose.

When he heard the man yell, Marc stopped and turned his head to the crowd. Just as he did, at least fifty of them broke through the thin cordon of deputies and charged after him screaming and yelling obscenities knocking four or five of the deputies to the ground. Marc stood frozen in disbelief for two seconds then his survival instincts took over and he sprinted toward the door.

The deputy standing inside the door waiting for him immediately opened it and stepped out to help. Just as Marc was about to reach the safety of the doorway, a young man, faster than the others, caught him and grabbed his left sleeve and stopped him. Instinctively Marc spun around, brought his hard leather briefcase up and smashed it into the face of his attacker. The young man's nose exploded, his hands went to his face and he staggered back into the crowd.

The deputy reached for Marc to pull him in but was a fraction of a second too late. A woman, in her mid-forties, swung her purse, the size of a small suitcase and drilled Marc across the side of his head. Marc staggered back, and the deputy grabbed him by the front of his overcoat and almost tossed him through the door to safety.

By now, there was absolute chaos on the steps in front of the building. Another twenty-five to thirty protestors decided to join in and at least twenty more deputies rushed from the jail and the court building to quell the mini-riot.

The entire uprising lasted less than fifteen minutes. At the sight of the deputies charging from the buildings, most of the idiots began to scatter. By the time it was completely over, there were a dozen arrests and another fifteen people needed minor medical care for small cuts, bruises and abrasions, including three deputies, one of whom was going to have a serious black eye the next day.

Of those arrested, the woman who had drilled Marc with her purse was included. The deputy who had rescued Marc went after her himself and made sure the handcuffs were nice and tight.

Much to their delight, the camera crews, including CNN, were already filming when the melee broke out. The entire disturbance would be on the internet within minutes. To say it went viral would be a gross understatement. Within a week, three hundred million viewers worldwide would see it. Even the President would get in on it, apologizing to the world, once again, for America's shortcomings.

Marc, seated in a mostly empty courtroom, had just swallowed two Aleve provided by the judge's clerk when Connors came through the door. The judge was wearing slacks, a white shirt and tie and without his robe, walked over to Marc.

"You okay?" he asked sincerely.

"Yeah, I'm fine," Marc replied.

"We can postpone if you need to see a doctor."

"No, let's keep going. I'm embarrassed as much as anything."

"Why?"

"A woman hit me with her purse," he answered looking a bit embarrassed. "Although just between you and me, I did drill one of them pretty good with my briefcase."

"Did you really?" the judge smiled. "Well, keep it quiet. I'll talk to Cale and get you parking in back. We should have done it right away."

"Thanks, judge."

Kristin Williams was reminded she was still under oath when she took the stand at nine o'clock. A large, flat screen TV on a portable stand had been wheeled in and positioned on the opposite side of the room facing the jury. Williams was going to testify about what she had found on the internet social media sites and the prosecution was going to put it up on a TV screen for the jury to see.

Marc knew this was coming and believed that Connors allowing it to be admitted as evidence could very easily be reversible error. That was the reason he had objected, again, to allowing it. If he did not put an objection on the record, in the event of an appeal, the appellate court could not even consider it.

Marc knew that Brittany was about to take a beating. What Williams was about to testify to might be the worst testimony about her for the entire trial. He had been over this with her and made it very clear she was not to show any emotional response. She was to keep a neutral expression and act as if everything coming out was exactly what they expected. Brittany promised to do it no matter what.

Williams started out by informing the jury about the decision to begin investigating Brittany. The longer they searched for the elusive Bob Olson the less credible Brittany's story became. Even though Shannon Keenan had already testified to these things, it wasn't worth the bother to object.

Williams, with Hart tossing her easy questions, told the jury what she found on the internet. She first went to obvious sites beginning with Facebook. At this point, one of the younger lawyers with the state used a laptop to put Brittany's Facebook page on the TV screen.

What Williams found, and what was put up on the TV, was entry after entry of Brittany writing about the difficulties of being a young single mother. She wrote about how much having a young child weighed her down and disrupted her life. That sometimes when her friends were out partying and having fun, she was stuck at home with a kid. Every one of these ended with Brittany admitting that Becky was the joy of her life and the sun rises and sets with her. That last part was quickly and conveniently glossed over.

Williams then moved on to a couple of dating sites that Brittany was signed up on, Match.com and Zoosk and went over her entry for each, one at a time, with the profile on the TV screen. While the laptop operator used a highlight marker on the screen, Williams went over each item. She pointed out inconsistencies, exaggerations and outright lies Brittany had used. And on the profiles of both sites, in answer to the question: Do you have any children? Brittany had answered "no".

After the morning break, Hart started in on the most damning testimony. Williams had gone over the Facebook pages of Brittany's best friends. What she found was the usual kind of drivel that young people, especially young women, liked to share. Mostly gossipy nonsense if not outright lies about themselves, their friends and especially boyfriends. And of course, their social lives.

For some reason, they seemed to enjoy bragging about how drunk they could get and how many guys they hooked up with. Brittany had assured Marc that it was mostly exaggeration, but it was up on the screen for the world to see. The worst of it was the pictures. The prosecution, after much discussion with the judge, was allowed to put into evidence and show on the TV eight pictures from each site of Brittany's three best friends. Most of them were silly, even mildly humorous selfies, taken at parties and bars. The problem was all of them had Brittany in the picture showing her having a grand old time and obviously drinking too much. A few of them were shots of her sitting on the laps of different young men making out in public with them.

The worst of them were the ones saved until the end. The pictures taken at the bars during the time Becky was missing. The last one, the one that was left up on the screen and the jury would have in their memory, was the one of Brittany standing on the bar, braless in her soaking wet T-shirt, proudly holding her trophy for winning the contest. Brittany would later tell Marc it took more self-control than she believed she had not to crawl under the table and hide.

As bad as it was, Marc knew it could have been worse. If it had been him using that picture, he would have timed it so it was the last thing the jury saw on Friday, so they would have the image in their minds all weekend. He just hoped some of the men on the jury would not be as appalled as the women.

FIFTY-THREE

The courtroom audience was filing back into their seats following lunch. Marc was giving a quick read to his notes to cross-examine Kristin Williams. He felt a tug on his left coat sleeve and lifted his head to look at Brittany. She turned her head toward the gallery, specifically the row directly behind them. Marc looked and saw Tony Carvelli and Vivian Donahue seated next to Butch and Andy.

Over the lunch hour, Marc had spoken by phone with Barbara Riley. She informed him that the refinance of their house was done, and that money would be available soon. Also, someone had donated one hundred thousand dollars, anonymously, to Brittany's online defense fund. The news had significantly boosted Marc's spirits with the knowledge the case probably would not bankrupt him.

Marc stood up, stepped to the bar between the well of the court and the gallery to speak to his friends. He shook hands with Tony and Vivian then leaned over to whisper to Vivian.

"Do we have you to thank for the anonymous donation to Brittany's defense fund?"

With a faux-innocent look on her face, Vivian looked directly at Marc and said, "I'm sure I don't know what you mean."

Marc, with a skeptical expression, said, "Uh, huh. Okay."

Vivian motioned for him to lean closer, so she could whisper in his ear. "But if you need more, let Anthony know."

Marc took her hand lightly kissed the back of it and patted it with his other hand and said, "Thanks."

He then turned to Butch and Andy and said, "I've told you guys you don't have to sit here all day."

"And we've told you, we're going to protect her and you," Andy replied.

Vivian motioned to Brittany to come to her and Marc stepped aside while they hugged. He looked up as the last of the crowd trickled in and saw Maddy Rivers walk up the aisle toward him.

She sat down next to Tony who put his arm around her shoulders and kissed her on the cheek. "Hello, beautiful," her friend and sometime mentor said.

Maddy leaned forward to greet Vivian and Brittany. She looked at Butch and Andy who were both sneaking peeks at her and said, "Hey, guys."

Marc was about to speak to her when he heard the bailiff say, "All rise." Judge Connors entered. Marc looked at Maddy and quietly said, "Gotta go," as everyone stood.

Kristin Williams was recalled to the stand once again reminded she was still under oath and stepped into the witness box. Judge Connors, while looking past Marc at Maddy, told Marc he could question the witness.

The cross-examination is supposed to be limited to the evidence and testimony brought out during the direct exam of the witness. Usually, especially in a capital case, the defense will be given some latitude to go beyond that restriction.

Marc started off by going over the same things he had crossed Shannon Keenan about except in much less detail, mostly to establish that they tried to find people to denigrate Brittany as a mother. He knew they had found a few people to testify that Brittany had made remarks about the difficulty of raising a child by herself. Those would be dealt with when they testified.

He moved into her slide show of things Williams had discovered on the internet. She had found an old Myspace posting of Brittany and friends partying and underage drinking. There were more than two dozen pictures of the girls posing with drinks, with boys and sexually suggestive pictures of Brittany with multiple guys. Nothing explicit but certainly enough to give the jury the impression she was quite the party girl.

Each of the photos was clearly dated and Marc replayed them all and went over the dates on each one. All of them were taken when Brittany was in her late teens. At least two years before Becky was born, which Marc was able to get Williams to admit. He also made her admit this fact was completely ignored during her earlier testimony.

Marc then hit a button on his laptop and the picture on the TV screen changed to Brittany's Facebook home page.

"You recognize the image on the screen don't you, Detective Williams?"

"Of course."

"It's Brittany Riley's Facebook home page, correct?"

During the direct exam, Hart made a point of always referring to Brittany as either the defendant or the accused. Not once did she use Brittany's name. This was, of course, a subliminal message to the jury to dehumanize her in their eyes. Does this work? No one really knows. To counter that, Marc made sure he always referred to her by name for the exact opposite reason, to make her look as human as possible. Does this work? Again, no one really knows.

"When you were sworn in, you swore to tell the truth, the whole truth and nothing but the truth, do you remember that?"

"Objection!" Hart said rising from her chair. "Where's he going with this?"

"Overruled but there better be some relevance here," Connors said looking sternly at Marc. "Answer the question."

"Yes, I remember that."

"During your direct exam, you and Ms. Hart went over a lot of postings Brittany Riley had on her Facebook site, isn't that correct?"

"Yes, we did."

"And the ones you showed the jury were ones in which Ms. Riley complained about the difficulties of being a young, single mother correct?"

"Yes, that's right."

"You didn't show the jury this one, did you?" Marc asked as he pushed the button on his laptop to change the image on the TV. In place of Brittany's Facebook home page, a posting she had written appeared. It read "I was off from work today and got to spend the whole day with my baby. She is beautiful! She is perfect! When she looks at me with those beautiful little eyes, I almost cry with joy. I will love her until the day I die." It was dated less than two months before Becky disappeared.

After reading it, the entire jury panel turned to look at Brittany. She stared at the screen and maintained her composure except for a single tear that trickled down her cheek.

"Um, no I didn't," Williams quietly answered.

"How about this one?" Marc asked as he tapped the laptop key and put another of Brittany's postings on the TV screen. "Did you show this one to the jury?"

The image changed to another of Brittany's written postings very similar to the first one. It was dated two days after the first one Marc had shown the jury.

"No," Williams quietly answered.

"How about this one?" And he repeated the procedure and put up another written posting just like the previous two. Marc elicited the same response from Williams and kept doing it ten more times before Hart finally objected.

"Your Honor," Hart said. "He's being repetitious and…"

Marc would not admit it, but he was grateful Hart had finally objected. When Hart and Williams did the same thing during the direct exam, Marc let them go because the jury became bored with it. Fortunately, Hart objected before they became bored with him. In fact, he only had a few more he wanted to use anyway.

"How many more of these questions are you planning on asking?" Connors asked Marc.

"Your Honor, they went through quite a lengthy list. I should be allowed the same thing," Marc replied after standing.

"He has a point, Ms. Hart," Connors said.

Marc had prepared for this and was ready to respond and hopefully win some points with the jury.

"However, your Honor," Marc said, "in the interest of moving this along, I'll use just one more example."

"Are you satisfied?" Connors asked Hart.

"Yes, your Honor," she said and sat down.

Marc stared at the screen on his laptop pretending to search for the one he wanted. After a minute or so, he tapped a key again and the new Facebook entry appeared on the TV screen.

"I haven't been this happy since Greg died. I think I'm in love and Bob is great with Becky. I think he'd make a great dad for her and I'm really hoping this works out. Becky likes him, and this could really be the one. I hope so!" It was dated two days before Becky disappeared.

"You ignored this one, too, didn't you?"

"Objection! Argumentative," Hart said.

"Sustained," Connors ruled. "The jury will disregard that last question."

Marc knew the question was inappropriate, but he asked it anyway. The judge could order the jury to ignore it but would they? The next question, he believed was probably more objectionable.

Marc pointed a finger at the TV screen and asked, "In your professional opinion, Detective Williams, would you say someone would write that two days before…"

"Objection! Speculative," Hart practically yelled as she jumped out of her chair. "And he needs to be sanctioned!"

"Overruled," Connors said.

"Your Honor," Hart persisted. "She's not a psychiatrist…"

"I'll rephrase," Marc said, delighted to get the chance to say it again by rephrasing it.

"Very well. The objection is sustained, the defendant will rephrase the question," Connors ruled.

"Detective Williams," Marc began, "in your experience, in your years as an investigator with law enforcement, have you ever seen such a case where the accused would write something similar concerning the victim two days before the crime was committed?" A question which was worse for the prosecution than the one Marc initially asked.

"No, um, I have not," Williams quietly answered.

"Detective Williams, I only went back a couple of months for the postings by Brittany Riley that I showed to the jury today. Would it surprise you to know, that going back to when Becky was born, there are over two hundred such postings on Ms. Rileys' Facebook account?"

"No, ah, I guess not."

"And yet, you showed none of these to the jury did you?"

Williams hesitated and looked at Hart to see if she would object. Not getting one, she simply said, "No."

"Would you like to change your answer about claiming you told the whole truth to the jury?"

"Objection," Hart said much more quietly this time.

"Sustained," Connors said. He looked at the clock and said, "Fifteen-minute break."

Marc clicked a couple more keys and Brittany's home page from the dating site Zoosk.com appeared.

"Detective Williams, on the TV screen is the home page from Zoosk.com of Brittany Riley, do you recognize it?"

"Yes, of course," Williams replied, noticeably more guarded.

"In fact, during your direct exam you went over this posting in great detail did you not?"

"Yes, I suppose you could say that."

"Pointing out things that were surely exaggerated and let's be totally candid, some things that were not true Ms. Riley put on her profile?"

"Yes," Williams answered. "She lied about not having a child."

"Yes, she did. No point denying it," Marc agreed.

He clicked his laptop a couple more times and her profile from Match.com appeared on the screen.

"This is Brittany's profile from Match.com, do you recognize this?"

"Yes."

"You went over this one line by line during your direct exam also, pointing out pretty much the same exaggerations and the same lie, didn't you?"

"Yes."

"Would you say that everyone who fills out a profile such as these is being completely honest?"

"Objection," Hart stood and said. "This witness is not an expert in this particular area."

"Mr. Kadella?" Connors asked looking for a rebuttal from Marc.

"I'm not asking her as an expert, your Honor, just her opinion as an adult woman."

"Overruled," Connors said. "The witness may answer."

"I couldn't say. I really have no idea what people put on these things. If I had to guess, I believe people would be honest."

Marc hit a key on his laptop and a new Match.com profile appeared. An audible gasp came from the jury box and the jurors involuntarily leaned forward when the image appeared. Marc said nothing for ten seconds while the jury stared. The jurors turned back toward the witness who was fidgeting in her seat, her cheeks a light pink. Staring back on the TV screen was a flattering photo of Detective Kristin Williams.

"Objection!" Hart stood. "The witness is not on trial…"

"Her credibility is at issue, your Honor," Marc calmly said.

"Overruled."

"Is that your picture and your Match.com profile, Detective Williams?"

"Yes, it is."

"Did you graduate magna cum laude from Wisconsin, Eau Claire?"

"No," Williams quietly answered.

Marc started going over her profile line-by-line questioning everything she had put on it. Most of the entries were accurate but there were several more that she had to admit were a little inflated.

Following the fifth such admission by her, she said, "Okay, you're right. People aren't one hundred percent honest when they fill out these things. But I didn't lie about not having children. I cannot believe anyone would."

"Does the name Lisa Monroe sound familiar to you, Detective?"

"No, it doesn't," Williams answered.

"How about Cheryl Dean? Does that ring a bell?" Marc asked.

"No," Williams answered looking puzzled.

"Robyn Grogan?"

"Objection your Honor, relevance. Where's he going with this?" Hart said.

"Excellent question," Connors said. "Mr. Kadella, where are you going?"

"If the court will indulge me for just a couple more minutes, your Honor, I'll get there," Marc answered.

"All right. Objection overruled, for now."

"Robyn Grogan," Marc repeated.

"No, I don't believe I know the name."

"How about Chloe Stewart, Alexis Regan or Jamie Westlund?"

"No, none of them," Williams said.

"Every one of these young women is between the ages of twenty and twenty-three. Each of them is single and has one or two young children and every one of them lied about it on Match.com. And if need be, I will bring them into this court and they will testify to it."

"Is there a question for the witness?" Hart asked trying to disrupt Marc.

"Does it really surprise you," Marc began ignoring Hart, "that a young, single girl, looking for companionship would lie about having a child while trying to meet someone and then tell him later?" It was a question Williams could answer either way, yes or no. But the real answer was obvious, and Marc knew the jury would get it.

"No, I guess not," Williams quietly answered.

Marc hit a couple more keys, scrolled down on what he was looking at then hit two more keys to put up a new image. On the screen was one of the photos of Brittany partying with friends.

"During your direct exam, you testified quite a bit about Brittany's behavior. At one point even using the word irresponsible, do you remember that?"

"Yes," Williams apprehensively answered.

"How old was Brittany Riley at the time this picture was taken?"

"Um, I'm not sure. I don't recall her date of birth."

Marc told her what it was and said, "She was seventeen."

Marc hit a key on the laptop and another picture of Brittany appeared that the prosecution had used. It was another party picture of Brittany sitting on a guy's lap with a beer in her hand.

"According to the date stamped on this photo, how old was she when it was taken?"

"She would have been, um, eighteen."

"And this one?" Marc asked after changing the image on the TV.

"Yeah, um eighteen again," Williams quietly answered.

With that answer, Marc hit a key and the TV screen went blank.

"Detective Williams, how old were you when you were suspended from Memorial High School in Eau Claire for smoking marijuana with several other students in the boy's locker room?"

"Objection," Hart said.

"Overruled," Connors answered.

"Detective?" Marc said.

"Seventeen."

"And the first time you were arrested for underage drinking while in college at UW-Eau Claire?"

"Eighteen."

"And the second time?"

"Nineteen," Williams said shifting around in her chair.

"And you were only twenty when you were arrested for trespassing…"

"That was a legitimate student protest," Williams blurted out.

"Really? And what were you protesting at the age of twenty?" Marc asked.

Williams sat silently for ten seconds then said, "I can't remember."

"Must have been really important."

"Objection," Hart said.

"Withdrawn, your Honor. I apologize," Marc said. He looked at Williams who was trying to burn holes in him with her eyes. "Isn't it fair to say that these events that you did when you were a kid should be classified as youthful indiscretions?"

"Yes, it would be," Williams conceded.

"And isn't it reasonable to say that virtually everyone did things in their youth that when they get older, they wish they had not done?"

"Yes," Williams agreed. "Even you, I'll bet."

"Oh," Marc said holding up a hand "Mea culpa, mea culpa. Especially me. I don't even want to think about it," he added to much laughter in the court. Marc looked over at the prosecution table and asked, "What about Mr. Vanderbeck? On second thought, probably not. Withdrawn." Marc quickly said as Vanderbeck started to stand. "I have nothing further for this witness."

"We'll adjourn for the day," Connors said after the laughter died down.

FIFTY-FOUR

The jury filed out as the room was emptying of spectators. Marc was packing up when Brittany asked him, "How did you find out those things about her?"

Marc smiled at her, swiveled his chair around to face the gallery, pointed at Madeline and said, "You can thank her. She has a way of getting people to tell her things they shouldn't, especially men."

Vivian Donahue stood up and walked through the gate to Marc's table. Vivian took his hand and firmly shook it. "Watching you this afternoon was worth the price of admission. You did great and I can't believe how fast the time went by."

"That's kind of you Vivian but we have a long way to go," he said as they released each other's hands.

By this time, Tony and Maddy had joined Marc and Brittany and by now the courtroom was empty except for them.

"I was thinking," Vivian continued. "If you think it would help I'd be willing to act as a character witness for her."

"Bad idea," Tony said.

"He's right," Marc interjected. "I appreciate the offer…"

"Me too," Brittany chimed in.

"But first of all, you don't know her well enough. And if you get on that witness stand and testify about someone's character, that leaves your character wide open. They'll go after anything you've ever done and your family."

Marc leaned close to her and whispered in her ear, "Including the dearly departed Leo Balkus."

"That's only a rumor," she said with a twinkle in her eye.

"It would still come out," Marc answered her. "I appreciate the offer, Vivian. Really. But I'm not sure it would help. I wouldn't want to put you through it." He then said to Tony, "Give her driver a call and have him pull around to the back. You guys," he indicated to Butch and Andy, "escort the ladies out to avoid the press."

"So, I'm not one of the ladies that need to be escorted out?" Maddy said giving him an evil look.

"You walked right into that one," Tony said.

"Actually, I was hoping you'd escort me out," Marc said. "We'll go out front then I'll sneak back to my car, okay?"

Marc, with Madeline next to him, held an impromptu press conference in the second-floor hallway. He politely answered a few questions, mostly reminding them the trial was far from over. When the press was satisfied, they melted away and Marc went back into the courtroom to sneak out the back to where his car was parked.

Maddy went down the stairs to the first floor. She was striding toward the front door when Gabriella Shriqui, without a camera operator, approached her.

"Hi, um, you're Madeline Rivers aren't you?"

Maddy recognized her and cautiously replied, "Yes."

"Hi, I'm Gabriella Shriqui," she said and extended her hand to Maddy. They shook hands and Gabriella said, "I see you with Marc, Mr. Kadella, a lot so I found out who you are and what you do and decided I wanted to meet you."

"I'm not sure I want to talk to the media right…"

"I'm sorry," Gabriella interrupted. "No camera, no microphone, nothing at all, totally off the record. But…"

"Yes," Maddy flashed her best, most dazzling smile. "Here comes the 'but'".

"You're right," Gabriella laughed. "But I would love to interview you. There aren't too many gorgeous women private investigators and from what I've heard, you'd make a great interview."

"I don't know," Maddy said with noticeable skepticism.

"You don't trust us and…"

"With the way, the media is covering this case and how you people have treated Brittany, can you blame me?"

"No, I don't," Gabriella admitted. "It hasn't been our finest hour. And between you and me, I'm a little ashamed to be a part of it. Tell you what," Gabriella continued. "Talk to Marc. Ask him about me and see what he thinks. Here's my card. If you change your mind, give me a call. I promise I'll play it straight. Plus, I'd be okay with you getting some good publicity out of it."

"That wouldn't hurt my business," Madeline admitted. "I'll talk to Marc and see what he says," Maddy replied, starting to lower her guard a bit.

"If nothing else, I'm glad I got to meet you," Gabriella said extending her hand to Maddy again.

"Me too," Maddy smiled. "I've seen you around too and Marc usually has nice things to say about you."

Marc made the connection from Highway 61 onto 494 westbound and decided he needed a night off. He was about as prepared for the upcoming witnesses as he was going to be and another evening in the office probably would not add much.

He considered calling Margaret and spending the night with her but decided against it. With morning rush hour, the drive from her house to the court in Hastings would take an extra hour. The idea of a quiet evening at home sounded very appealing.

"That's interesting," he said out loud to himself. "I must be getting old. There was a time when I would have crawled out of bed at 3:00 A.M. and gone out into a blizzard to get laid. Now, I'm looking forward to a quiet evening at home in front of the television. It's kind of sad, pathetic even."

Marc stopped at a grocery store a couple of blocks from his apartment. Needing a decent meal, he splurged and bought a nice New York sirloin, shocked at the price. He also got a potato to bake and a bag of salad. It was a good, quick and easy single man's meal. On his way out, he grabbed a copy of that morning's Star Tribune and headed home.

While waiting for the baker in the oven, he hated microwaved food, he kicked back on the couch to read the paper. Marc turned the television on to check out the national news broadcasts. All of them had a one or two-minute segment on the mini-riot by the protestors. Only one, CNN, showed the film of him getting hit by the angry woman. The anchor for each took a moment to make pious proclamations scolding the people involved. Of course, each of them went on to wonder how anyone could be driven to such behavior and where could it possibly come from. He sipped at a beer and read the paper's take on the previous day's testimony. On the whole, the article was reasonably accurate. He found three or four things he would disagree with, but not as bad as usual.

At 6:15 the local news broadcast went to a commercial break and after two minutes, just before the weather report, Melinda Pace appeared on the screen to do a promotional spot for her 6:30 show. Marc made a mental note to watch it, went back to the sports section of the paper and two minutes later his cell phone rang.

He spent the next several minutes talking to Maddy about the proposed interview with Gabriella. Marc assured her it would be okay, that Gabriella would be straight, and the publicity would do her business some good.

"I have to go," Marc said. "Melinda Pace is coming on and I want to watch it."

"Really? You're going to watch that bitch after the way she has treated you and Brittany?"

"I get a call from her almost every day to come on her show."

"You're not going to are you?"

"Probably not until after the trial. We'll see. Here she comes. Gotta go." And he ended the call.

"Good evening and welcome to the *Court Reporter*. I'm Melinda Pace and my lone guest this evening is former Federal Prosecutor, Steven Farben. Good evening, Steve.

"Interesting day in the Brittany Riley trial, wouldn't you say, Steve?"

"I agree, Melinda," Farben said, "and not a good day for Brittany Riley. She's quite the little party girl."

At that moment, on the screen behind the set's anchor desk where the two of them were seated, a photo of Brittany appeared. It was an enlarged photo of her standing on the bar displaying the trophy for winning the wet T-shirt contest. Brittany had a huge smile and was triumphantly holding the trophy above her head. In the interest of TV modesty, but in actuality to add to the titillation, the word CENSORED in red capital letters was superimposed across her breasts.

Melinda looked into the camera with an earnest, sober, stern expression and solemnly said, "It almost breaks my heart, but I must point out the date stamped on this photo. Ladies and gentlemen, this was taken five days after her beautiful little girl, Becky, went missing and five days before it was reported to the police. And let me remind you, Brittany never did call the authorities. It was Brittany's mother, Barbara Riley who called them. God only knows how long Brittany would have gone on partying.

"This is what came out in court today. And there was plenty more of this behavior by Brittany that time does not allow us to show you." All the while the photo of Brittany standing on the bar in her soaking wet T-shirt remained on the screen directly behind Melinda.

When she finished, the camera moved in for a close-up of Melinda's face centering on her eyes. As it did so, Robbie Nelson signaled Melinda and just as the camera focused on her watery, tear-filled eyes, Melinda lightly sobbed. "I'm sorry. I need to take a short break."

They went to a commercial, Melinda smiled and asked Robbie, "How was that?"

Steven Farben laughed, and Robbie sarcastically said, "Delightfully cynical, Melinda, one of your best."

"Oh, screw you," Melinda laughed. "It's just showbiz. Don't take it so seriously."

"I'm sorry, folks. Sometimes these things can be a little hard to deal with," Melinda said into the camera with a sad smile. Robbie standing beside the same camera rolled his eyes and shook his head. They were back from the commercial break and Brittany's picture had been replaced by one of Becky. The images could not have been more starkly contrasting.

During the next several minutes, the two of them discussed Kristin Williams' testimony. Carefully chosen clips of her actual testimony would be played and then Farber would give his opinion. Of course, as a former prosecutor, his take was always detrimental to Brittany. What they did not tell the audience was that the film clips and testimony they were shown was from detective Williams direct examination by Danica Hart.

"To be fair and balanced, as we always strive to be, I thought Brittany's lawyer did a good job when he cross-examined Williams," Melinda said. "He scored a couple of good points for her defense."

"Oh, not really," Farben said staring into the camera with an obvious condescending attitude. "I mean I guess he did okay for someone with the level of experience he has. But," at this point the wet T-shirt photo of Brittany went up behind them again, "he's going to have a tough time overcoming the image of the uncensored version of this photo."

"Before we go to break, there is a short clip you need to see," Melinda said turning to look directly at the camera.

For the next one minute and twenty seconds, the audience watched a silent film of Brittany Riley seated at the defense table laughing. She was obviously whispering back and forth with Marc Kadella making light of something. It was made to appear as if Brittany was having a grand old time and the whole thing was quite amusing. What wasn't shown or explained was that this exchange took place during a break. The judge, jury and most of the gallery were not in the courtroom. And there was no sound to let the audience know exactly what it was about.

When the film of Brittany was finished, the camera was on a wide shot to show both Melinda and Farben at the anchor desk. They were solemnly looking at each other. Melinda lightly shook her head and asked, "What is wrong with her? Does she not know how serious this is?"

"Yeah, well," Farben said raising his hands, palms up from the desktop and shrugging his shoulders. "I don't know." He folded his hands on the desk and continued, "I'm not a psychiatrist, but you'd think her lawyer would make sure she knew how to behave in court, especially on trial for murder."

"Well, it's just amazing," Melinda said then looked at the camera. "We'll be right back."

They wrapped up the show after the break by showing ninety seconds of the mini-riot centered around Marc Kadella. Three times they played the images of Marc being grabbed by the first man to get to him then Marc, swinging his briefcase and drilling the fool in the face and then the irate woman nailing Marc on the side of the head with her purse. This was followed by an edited version of the sheriff's deputies hauling people away in handcuffs toward the jail. The camera stayed with one woman in particular who was being walked over to the jail. Gabriella Shriqui was walking with her and asking the woman over and over, "Why did you hit Brittany's lawyer with your purse?" The short, somewhat plump middle-aged woman whose hands were cuffed behind her back, was trying to shield her face from the camera. She refused to answer and eventually made it inside the jail.

"It's shameful and I don't understand what could possibly drive some people to act like this," Melinda said.

When Robbie heard Melinda say this, he smiled and thought, *apparently the word irony is not in Melinda's vocabulary.*

"You'd think people would understand that everyone deserves to be represented by a lawyer," Farben agreed. "I guarantee you that the woman who hit him with her purse has a lawyer by now."

"I'm just glad no one was seriously injured," Melinda said.

Farben had left and Melinda and Robbie were in her office by themselves. Robbie said, "I've been thinking, Melinda. What if Brittany is really innocent? You have practically declared her guilty and your audience agrees. What if she isn't? Shouldn't we try to be a little more even-handed?"

Melinda stared at him for a moment then said, "Innocent? Look, it's not our job to determine whether or not she's guilty or innocent. Robert, dear, let me remind you, if you want to stay in this business you better accept the fact it is about two things: ratings and money. This is show business, not a morality play. My pay and bonuses and yours are tied to ratings. Right now, we are kicking ass. The trial will work itself out. People don't want even-handed, touchy-feely bullshit. Hard opinions draw the audience. I know it's cynical, but we are giving them what they want."

"Yeah, you're right, it is cynical," Robbie agreed.

Marc pushed the power button on his television remote. He sat staring at the blank screen for ten or twelve seconds then finished his beer. He thought about what he had just watched, laughed a little bit and stood up to have his supper. He also needed to call Margaret to make plans for the weekend. He missed her and wanted to discuss the case with her and get some advice and input from her.

FIFTY-FIVE

A cold front had moved in from Canada during the night dropping the air temperature to a brisk minus ten. Before Marc drove into the private parking lot behind the courthouse, he stopped his car next to a sheriff's deputy. There were two of them standing guard at the lot's entrance making sure no unauthorized cars parked back there.

Marc rolled down his window and the deputy said, "Morning, Mr. Kadella."

"Morning, Carl. It's a little cool today," Marc answered. "Here take this," he said as he handed the man a cardboard cup holder with two large hot coffees he had picked up for them at the Starbucks across the highway.

"Oh man! Thanks, Mr. Kadella," Carl said as he took the offering from Marc.

"There's cream and sugar if you want it. I wasn't sure. Oh, and please stop calling me Mr. Kadella. Marc is just fine. Enjoy."

Marc parked his car and walked toward the building. It had snowed a little just before the cold came through and the snow was so frozen it crunched under his feet.

Brittany Riley removed her winter coat and hung it on the coat rack next to the defense table. She cupped her hands together and blew warm breath into them to warm them up.

Having seen Brittany come in, Marc turned around to say hello to Butch and Andy. The two men handed their coats to Brittany and she hung them up on the same coat rack.

"Good morning," Marc said to his client.

"Hi," Brittany said as she took her chair, "My mom got a call this morning from them," she said indicating the prosecutors who were just arriving. "They want her here after lunch."

"Okay, that's fine," Marc said.

Marc turned toward Danica Hart and said good morning to her and she smiled and replied in kind. A deputy came through the gate, leaned over to whisper to Marc. "Um, some of the guys were wondering if Maddy Rivers was gonna be here today? The deputy asked.

"What's that ring on your finger for?" Marc laughed.

"I may be married but I'm not blind," the man said as he walked away.

The morning session was taken up with young men who had recently dated Brittany. The state had found four of them. There had been a significant amount of arguing over allowing them to testify at all. None

274

of them had any personal knowledge of the crime and could offer nothing in the way of guilt or innocence. Marc had argued vehemently and unsuccessfully that their testimony was being offered for the sole purpose of making Brittany look like a promiscuous party girl. The prosecution argued their testimony was offered to bolster their claim of motive that Brittany was a young mother saddled with a child she didn't want and eventually murdered her.

Vanderbeck would conduct the direct exam of each of these young men. Marc found this mildly amusing since the arrogant Lowell Vanderbeck was supposed to be first chair for the prosecution. Normally minor witnesses such as these would be handled by the second chair lawyer, Danica Hart.

First up was a young man named Nick Hanley. Nick was a twenty-four-year-old attractive kid who had met Brittany at a party. He testified that they had dated for a couple of weeks. During the entire time, not once did Brittany tell him she had a child. He found out when she was digging through her wallet looking for something, he couldn't remember what, while he watched. She opened it up and he saw a picture of a young blonde girl who looked a lot like Brittany. Nick said he asked her about the kid and she very reluctantly admitted she had a daughter. A few days later, not ready to become a father, Nick broke it off with her.

Marc's cross-examination was very soft and only lasted about ten minutes. He got the witness to admit Brittany was a very pleasant, likeable young woman. Nick was noticeably uncomfortable and at one point even looked at Brittany and apologized to her.

He eagerly admitted he had no knowledge of the crime and could offer no testimony as to guilt or innocence.

"In your opinion, having gotten to know her, would you believe she could commit the crime she is charged with?"

This was a question that seemingly violated the cardinal rule of witness examination. Never ask a question unless you know the answer. Except, both Marc and Maddy had talked to all of this morning's witnesses and he did know the answer.

"Objection!" Vanderbeck thundered. "This witness is hardly qualified as a medical professional."

By this point, Marc was standing ready to address the court.

"Mr. Kadella," Connors said.

"Your Honor, the state is offering this testimony as proof of motive. As such, the witness can give his opinion as to whether or not he believes she would do such a thing. Plus, I am not claiming he is a trained psychologist. He's an ex-boyfriend who got to know her."

"I'll allow it. Objection overruled. The witness will answer."

"No! That's nuts. The girl I knew wouldn't do such a thing," Nick said as Marc and Vanderbeck sat back down.

Marc passed the witness back to Vanderbeck for redirect. He stuttered around for a few minutes trying to undo the damage. He drew several objections from Marc for going over testimony he had elicited during the direct exam. All of the objections were sustained and Vanderbeck finally gave up.

The next two young men called by the state, Steve Driscoll and Tim Stevens, went pretty much the same way as Nick Hanley did. Vanderbeck would walk them through their background to establish their credibility. He would then take them through their brief relations with Brittany. It was all routine and by the end of the morning was becoming a bit boring, until Vanderbeck got to the last one, David Hunt.

Marc knew what was coming and had prepared Brittany for it to make sure she did not respond.

Hunt had met her in a bar with several other girls. They became quite friendly, especially after Brittany had a few drinks. One of Brittany's friends mentioned her daughter and when Hunt asked her about Becky, she reluctantly admitted she was a single mom.

The damaging part was Hunt telling the jury Brittany went on to say that sometimes she wished she didn't have a kid. That sometimes being a single mom really sucked, her words he testified, and that she would be better off without the burden.

About the best, Marc could do to soften this was to get Hunt to admit a couple of things. First that Hunt had physically and noticeably backed off and cooled toward her when he found out about Becky. And that Brittany had too much to drink.

"The state calls Barbara Riley," Hart announced after Connors indicated he was ready to begin the afternoon session.

Barbara strolled up the aisle on the left-hand side of the gallery. Every head in the place turned to watch her and Marc almost laughed at the spectacle. *The Queen making her entrance* was the thought that went through his head because Barbara looked fabulous.

She spent an hour at the hair salon that morning and was dressed to kill. She looked at least ten years younger than her forty-eight years. Her makeup was perfect, and she wore just enough jewelry to look elegant and charming. It was the exact look Marc wanted her to have; the Queen Bee of the Riley household.

Hart herself had interviewed Barbara preparing their case. Barbara foolishly had not been represented during the interview. Marc did not represent Barbara and he advised her to get a lawyer to go with her, but she had almost arrogantly dismissed the notion.

Marc had received a copy of the report and on paper, it didn't look too damaging except he knew where they were headed. Hart had carefully probed her relationship with Brittany back to the cradle.

For almost three hours, Hart walked her through the pertinent parts of Brittany's life. What she got out of Barbara, at least so it seemed, was that Brittany was a habitual, if not pathological liar. Especially toward her mother after she got into high school. Marc knew none of this was particularly problematic. He had Brittany's psychiatrist willing to testify that this mother-daughter relationship among teenage girls was quite normal. The damaging part was the lies Brittany told her during the ten days Becky was missing and Brittany failed to tell her or report it to the police.

Marc had decided to go right after her during his cross exam. He didn't like the woman anyway and saw no reason to coddle her. He had to be careful not to be too aggressive to avoid alienating the jury. The last thing he wanted was to make this vain, narcissistic woman look sympathetic to the jury.

"Mrs. Riley," he began, "isn't it true that both you and your husband were in the delivery room when Becky was born?"

"Yes, that's true," Barbara answered.

"Along with the baby's father, Greg Mead, is that correct?"

"Yes, Greg was there."

"Isn't it true when the nurse had the baby cleaned up and went to hand her to the mother, Brittany, you stepped in and took the child from the nurse?"

"Yes, I did," Barbara answered looking puzzled wondering why he would be asking this.

"It was your decision to name the baby Becky Ann, wasn't it?"

"Well, I ah, I guess, um yes, I guess I chose that name. I suggested it to Brittany. But it was ultimately her decision."

"Did she suggest any other names?"

"Not that I recall," Brittany lied.

"How about Emily?"

"Yes, that's right. I forgot. A dreadful name."

"Did Brittany argue with you about you naming her baby Becky Ann?"

"No, she was fine with that name."

"It was your decision to have Becky baptized when and where, wasn't it?"

"Objection," Hart stood and said. What's the relevance?"

"Mr. Kadella?" Connors asked.

Marc stood and said, "Your Honor, they probed every aspect of the witness's relationship with her daughter, I'm merely going down that same path to explain that relationship."

"Overruled," Connors said.

"The child needed to be baptized."

"Is that a yes?" Marc asked still keeping his inflection as neutral as possible.

"Yes," Barbara conceded.

"Your son-in-law, Greg Mead, died in a car accident a few months after Becky was born, didn't he?"

"Yes, that's right," Barbara answered visibly relaxing.

"It was your decision for Brittany to change her name and Becky's name from Mead to Riley wasn't it?"

"I ah, don't remember."

"Isn't it true you hired the lawyer to help with the name change?"

"Yes, I did."

"And you paid the lawyer to help get their names legally changed, didn't you?"

"Yes."

"Isn't it true that you decided which personal injury lawyer to hire to handle Brittany's wrongful death claim for her husband's accident?"

"I don't see what…"

"Please just answer the question, Mrs. Riley," Marc politely said.

"All right, yes. I suppose I did."

"It was your decision to have Brittany bring Becky to your house each day for babysitting while Brittany worked, wasn't it?"

"We offered. She was our granddaughter."

"You kept a separate dresser in Brittany's old bedroom filled with clothes for Becky didn't you?"

"Yes. The child needed clothes."

"And even though Brittany always brought Becky to your house bathed and wearing clean clothes, you decided every day to bathe her and change her clothing didn't you?"

By now everyone in the courtroom was beginning to feel a little uncomfortable, a little creepy. Marc continued on for another twenty minutes with this line of questioning. Each question beginning the exact same way.

"It was your decision to…"

Finally, out of frustration, Barbara blurted out, "You're trying to make it look like I thought I was Becky's mother."

At that exact point, Marc thought *gotcha*, looked up at Connors and said, "I have no further questions, your Honor."

278

Hart tried her best to rehabilitate Barbara as a prosecution witness but too little, too late.

Judge Connors adjourned for the day after that.

That evening, Melinda Pace's show ignored the cross exam of Barbara Riley completely. Instead, again showing carefully edited soundbites, Melinda and her guests, both lawyers were back, concentrated on the testimony of the ex-boyfriends and Barbara's direct exam. The gist of it was that Brittany was unable to tell the truth, secretly wanted Becky dead and was a sleep around tramp. Andrea Briscomb, to her credit, tried to bring the discussion around to Barbara's control problem but Andrea didn't have much luck.

The networks and newspapers all followed the same line. Sex and lies in a notorious trial would sell more than a domineering mother or mother-daughter relationship problems.

FIFTY-SIX

The next morning Marc was seated at the defense table concentrating on his case notes for Friday's testimony. The previous evening, he had talked to his lady friend, Margaret Tennant, for an hour about his case and the trial. By 8:30 he was snoring in his recliner and by 9:00 he was in bed sound asleep to get the first solid night's sleep he had in weeks.

The clanging hangers on the coat rack made him aware that Brittany had arrived. She hung up her coat and her escorts' coats then dropped into the seat next to him.

"How were things at home last night?" Marc asked referring to Barbara.

"Fine," Brittany said.

"Good morning Marc," he heard Barbara say from the bench behind them.

Marc turned to look at her and saw her genuinely smiling at him while folding her coat to hold it in her lap.

"Here, let me have that," Marc offered and took her coat and Floyd's to hang them on the coat rack.

"Um, about yesterday…."

"Don't worry about it," Barbara answered him. "You did your job. Really, I understand."

"Good, thanks. Morning, guys," he said to Butch and Andy who were sitting impassively.

Madeline Rivers had deliberately waited in her car until almost nine o'clock before heading to the courthouse. The air temperature was a balmy five below zero this morning. This accounted for the sparse crowd of protesters in front of the building when she arrived. Minnesotans can find winter activities even in sub-zero weather but standing outside doing nothing isn't normally one of them. This was much to her delight, if not at all surprising, the meticulously attired Ms. Rivers hurried up the steps and passed quickly through security.

When she reached the top of the stairs, the hall in front of the courtroom was empty except for a solitary figure seated on one of the benches. Maddy recognized him right away. When he saw her, he stood up and walked toward her.

"Hello," the man said flashing a perfect grin and extending his right hand. "You're Maddy Rivers. I've heard good things about you. I'm Stu Doyle, an investigator with the Sheriff's Department."

"Yeah, I recognize the name," Maddy replied as they shook hands. "Nice to meet you," she politely said.

"Not at all, the pleasure's mine," Doyle said as Maddy extracted her hand. "Listen, I'd really like to get to know you better. Maybe meet for coffee or a drink sometime."

"I'm in a hurry," Maddy said. "I'll think about it but I gotta go. I have to talk to my boss," she said as she brushed past him and went into the courtroom.

While she walked up the left-hand aisle to the bench behind Marc, the door to the chambers area opened and the judge entered. Maddy smiled politely at Floyd and Barbara Riley, removed her winter coat and sat down next to Floyd when Connors told them all to be seated.

Marc turned and looked at Madeline and she gestured for him to come to her. He silently rolled his chair back to the rail and Maddy whispered to him that Stu Doyle was in the hall waiting to be called. Marc nodded to her acknowledging the news then rolled back to the table.

Connors solemnly looked over the crowd then told the state's lawyers to call their next witness. In less than a minute, Stu Doyle was sworn and seated.

Marc had guessed correctly that Doyle and his partner, Paul Anderson, would be called on Friday. The lawyers had met with Connors this morning for a few minutes and Hart had assured him they were on schedule. Connors admitted he did not want to take testimony over the weekend. His grandson was in a hockey tournament in Duluth and he had planned on going.

Vanderbeck would conduct the direct exam of Doyle. He started out as he normally did by having Doyle tell the jury his résumé. Doyle had been in law enforcement for over fifteen years. He had testified in trials too many times to remember and made an excellent witness. Aside from being a very attractive man, with little effort, he came across as a calm, intelligent professional who knew his business. He already told the jury about his list of commendations, awards and law enforcement courses. Marc could see where a jury could take to the man. Vanderbeck again made the same mistake he seemed prone to make. It took him, including a longer than usual morning break, until after 11:00 to finish Doyle's direct testimony. Vanderbeck went into too much detail, at least in Marc's opinion, for what little Doyle had to offer. Vanderbeck took Doyle through every step he personally took, day-by-day, in his efforts to find the missing Bob Olson. By the time he was finished, even Marc was having trouble staying awake.

Before Marc could begin his cross, Connors called the lawyers to the bench. He looked at Marc and asked. "How much do you have? The reason I'm asking, I've got a motion on another case I'm going to hear

281

in chambers over lunch. In fact, I've been told the lawyers are already here. If you're going to go much longer, I'll break now."

"We would not object to breaking now," Vanderbeck chimed in.

"No, judge, I don't have much," Marc replied. "But I'd prefer to get it done now." He wanted the jury to go to lunch knowing Doyle did not really have much to offer.

"Okay. We'll do it now."

Everyone took their seats and Connors gave Marc permission to proceed.

"Detective Doyle," Marc began, "I have just a couple of questions for you, but they concern only your personal involvement in the investigation. By that, I mean what you personally did and not what you may have seen or heard from one of your colleagues. Okay?"

"Sure," Doyle said.

"You did not personally come across any evidence of any kind that would tie Brittany Riley to this crime did you?"

Doyle looked past Marc at the back of the courtroom, thought about it for a moment then finally said, "No, I did not."

"Your part of the investigation was almost exclusively the search for Bob Olson, was it not?"

"Yes."

"Isn't it true that Brittany Riley was very cooperative with you in that search?"

"Yes, she was."

"And she was very insistent that Bob Olson was a real person who had abducted Becky Riley wasn't she?"

"Yes, she was," Doyle agreed.

"Isn't it also true that other than the fact you were unable to identify him, unable to find him, you personally never found any reason to doubt Ms. Rileys' sincerity, did you?"

"Um, no, I did not. But it was…"

"I'm sorry detective, you've answered the question honestly and completely," Marc said, cutting him off.

"One last question," Marc said. "Isn't it possible that Bob Olson was in disguise when dating Brittany Riley and using a fake I.D. which is why you did not find him?"

"Yes, it's possible," Doyle admitted.

Doyle was excused and as he was walking out, he actually smiled and winked at Madeline. Unfortunately for him, Gabriella Shriqui saw him do it, rolled her eyes and made a mental note to warn Maddy.

Judge Connors finished his other hearing early and the afternoon session started on time.

Vanderbeck called investigator Paul Anderson as his next witness. A moment later Anderson came in through the hallway doors followed closely by Tony Carvelli escorting Vivian Donahue. Anderson walked up the aisle on the right as Tony and Vivian went up the left. Anderson was sworn in and seated while Tony and Vivian sat down next to Maddy Rivers.

Vanderbeck again used simple questions to Anderson about his background and experience in law enforcement. Again, the object being to enhance the witness's credibility in the eyes of the jury. Anderson had testified many times and was quite comfortable with it. His demeanor and clear, calm way of telling his story played well with any jury. A professional they could believe.

Anderson and Vanderbeck made a smooth transition from Anderson's personal credentials into the Riley case. He basically followed the same script that he had with his partner, Stu Doyle, relating to the jury his initial involvement. They had spent most of their time in the search for Bob Olson. Anderson testified he began having doubts about Brittany's version of events before the others. He claimed his early suspicions were the result of interviewing some of Brittany's friends. It seemed a little odd, a little too convenient, that none of them, including her family members, had ever met the missing Bob Olson.

Anderson told the jury what they were doing as far as investigating goes, which after a while wasn't much. By then they had exhausted all leads and were not getting anywhere. It was about then it was decided to arrest her for child neglect. Anderson tried to say she was certainly guilty of that. This drew an objection from Marc and a stern admonishment from the judge.

He testified about the news of the body being found and Vanderbeck transitioned the testimony to the search of the Rileys' home. Anderson explained that he obtained a search warrant and led the team to the Rileys' and the subsequent search.

Vanderbeck asked Connors for permission to approach the witness. It was granted, and he walked up to Anderson and handed him a document. Vanderbeck stepped a few feet away but did not sit down.

"I have given you a document marked for identification as state's Exhibit 7. Do you recognize this document?" Vanderbeck asked.

"Yes, I do," Anderson replied.

"What is it?"

"It's a life insurance policy I found in a desk drawer in the den of the home of Floyd and Barbara Riley while we conducted our search."

Vanderbeck then had Anderson explain all of the details Vanderbeck believed were pertinent. Anderson first told them the date it was purchased which was barely three months before Becky disappeared. He then told them the amount of the death benefit, half a million dollars on the life of Becky Riley and of course, the beneficiary who was Brittney Riley.

Vanderbeck took the policy, verbally offered it into evidence and receiving no objection from Marc, had the clerk mark it as entered. He then slowly walked over to the jury box and handed it to the forewoman. While the jurors passed the document around to each other, Vanderbeck returned to his chair.

Along the wall next to the defense table was a cart with a blanket over it. Vanderbeck nodded to one of his flunkies who stood and wheeled the cart in front of the witness. The young man removed the blanket and exposed the six cinder blocks and the rope removed from the Rileys' garage. They had been marked as state's Exhibits 8 through 14.

Vanderbeck had Anderson identify the cinder blocks and rope by the evidence tags he had placed on each item as the ones from the Rileys. They were entered into evidence and the cart was placed next to the table with the cinder block and rope found on Becky Riley in the river. Obviously, they were the same. Anderson tried to testify that they were an exact match to the rope and cinder block used to drown Becky Riley.

"Objection," Marc said as he stood. "This witness did not…"

Connors help up a hand to stop him and said to Anderson, "Did you personally conduct tests on the rope and cinder blocks found in the garage?"

"No, your Honor," Anderson admitted.

"Cause of death your Honor," Marc said. "He claims she drowned."

Connors again directly addressed the witness and asked, "Did you personally determine the cause of death to be drowning?"

"No, your Honor, I did not," Anderson had to admit.

"The jury will disregard those references," Connors ordered the jury to basically pretend they did not hear something they just heard. "Move on Mr. Vanderbeck."

Having accomplished what he needed from Anderson, the life insurance policy as motive and the discovery of the rope and cinder blocks, Vanderbeck ended his examination of Anderson.

By now it was after 3:30 and Connors needed a break.

When court resumed, Connors turned the witness over to Marc for cross-exam.

Marc asked for permission to approach the witness and it was granted. He walked up to the witness and handed him a document.

For the record, he said, "I've handed you a document entitled Fidelity Investment Account, is that correct, Detective Anderson?"

"Yes, I believe so."

"I've highlighted the part that reads account owner. Will you read the name to the jury?"

"Brittany Riley."

"I've highlighted the date of this account statement, the period it covers. It is for July of last year, is it not?"

"Yes, it is."

"That would be the same month Becky Riley disappeared, was it not?"

"Yes, it was."

"In the lower right-hand corner on the first page, I've highlighted something. Would you tell the jury what this is, please?"

"It is the total amount in the account."

"What is that total?"

"One hundred twenty-seven thousand six hundred thirty-eight dollars and seven cents."

"In the upper right-hand corner is the statement date. What is that date, detective?"

"August third."

"So, on August third of last year, a few days after Becky disappeared, Brittany Riley had one hundred twenty-seven thousand dollars in an investment account. Is that correct?"

"Objection, your Honor," Vanderbeck foolishly said. "Where is the relevance?"

"Overruled," Connors quickly said. "The witness will answer."

"It appears so, yes."

"Your office, the sheriff's office subpoenaed these records, didn't you?"

"Objection," Vanderbeck tried again.

"He's the lead investigator, your Honor. He knows."

"Overruled", Connors said.

"Um, yes, I believe we did."

"You believe you did, or you know so?" Marc asked still standing only a few feet from Anderson.

"Yes, we did."

"And you received two years worth of account statements from Fidelity of the investment account of Brittany Riley including the one in your hand didn't you?"

"Yes, we did," Anderson admitted setting the document on the railing in front of him and leaning away from it as if it might bite him.

"Did you tell the jury that Brittany Riley had one hundred twenty-seven thousand dollars in this account when Becky was abducted?"

"No, we saw no need…"

"I didn't ask if you saw a need. I asked if you told the jury this. Did you?"

"No, I did not."

Marc walked back to his table and picked up another document, went back to Anderson and handed it to him.

"Detective Anderson, I have handed you another document. It is another account statement from the same Fidelity account, isn't it?"

"It appears so," Anderson said.

Marc picked up the one Anderson had set down, handed it back to him and said, "Please detective, compare the account numbers on both documents to be sure."

Anderson did so then said, "Yes, they're from the same account."

Marc retrieved the first one then stepped back and said, "Please read the highlighted date range of the statement you are holding, the month it covers."

Anderson read it to the jury.

"This is the same month that the life insurance policy was taken out on Becky Riley, correct?"

"Yes, it is."

"On page three, under the heading withdrawals, I have highlighted a date and an amount. Please read that to the jury."

Anderson read them.

Marc walked over to the jury box and retrieved the life insurance policy Vanderbeck had given the jury to examine that was now on the rail in front of the jurors. He then walked to his table and picked up another document, walked back to the witness and handed both to Anderson.

"The date the insurance policy was signed is the exact same date as the day of the withdrawal from Brittany's account that you just read to the jury, is it not?"

"Yes, it is."

"The other document I just handed you is an account summary of the life insurance policy; state's Exhibit 7 is it not? Please check and compare the policy number on both."

Anderson did that and admitted they were the same.

"On the life insurance policy investment account summary, I have highlighted a deposit and the date of the deposit. Read those to the jury."

Anderson read them to the jury.

"They are the exact same date and amount as the withdrawal from Brittany Rileys' savings, aren't they?"

"Yes, they are."

Marc went back to his table and sat down. He looked at Anderson and said, "Detective, when you found the life insurance policy, state's

Exhibit 7, after you read it over, saw whose life it was on and who the beneficiary was, you immediately thought; *Ah, ha! Got it! Motive! Here it is!* Didn't you?"

"Yes, I guess so," Anderson answered almost flippantly.

"You guess so?"

"Well, motive would be up to the lawyers to determine…"

"I'm not asking them, detective. I'm asking you as a veteran investigator, did you not believe you had found motive when you saw the insurance policy?"

"Sure, I did," Anderson admitted.

"You didn't tell the jury that the same day the insurance policy was executed, Brittany Riley transferred thirty thousand dollars from her personal savings into the investment account of the insurance policy for her daughter, did you?"

Anderson visibly squirmed in his seat, then said, "No, I didn't."

Marc narrowed his eyes, pursed his lips and glowered at Anderson for a full ten seconds. "You swore to tell the whole truth did you not?" he practically shouted.

"Objection!" Vanderbeck yelled as he jumped to his feet.

Marc slapped his hand on the table as he stood and yelled, "I object to the amount of information these people are trying to keep from this jury!"

"That's it!" Connors said as he hammered his gavel. "Timeout. I'll see the lawyers in chambers, now!"

As Connors was leaving the bench Marc leaned down and whispered in Brittany's ear, "I'm about to get my ass chewed but it was worth it."

He turned around and saw the disappointed mother look on Madeline's face and the smirk on Carvelli's and winked at them both.

Marc joined everyone in the judge's chambers in time to hear Vanderbeck demanding that Marc be sanctioned if not disbarred.

"Calm down," Connors told Vanderbeck. "Maybe you should bring these things out on direct instead of letting him do it."

"As for you," he said turning to Marc. "I'm not even sure if what you did was wrong, but no more histrionics. Any more of it and I will have a large piece of your ass in the form of a check. Do I make myself clear?"

"Yes, your Honor," Marc said without meaning it.

"It's after four, your cross-exam is done, and I don't care if you don't like it. We're going to call it a day and give everyone a break. I've had enough."

"Your Honor, I demand …" Vanderbeck started to say.

"Demand?" Connors said.

287

"Request, your Honor, an opportunity to redirect before we adjourn for the weekend," Vanderbeck said while Hart looked at him with a horrified expression on her face.

"Really? You want to go back out there and go over everything he just did to your case again?" Connors asked.

"No, your Honor," Hart interjected taking the opportunity to stop Vanderbeck from likely making things worse. Vanderbeck started to speak to her but she held up a hand and cut him off. "Lowell, we can't unring the bell they just heard. Leave it alone."

A furious Vanderbeck turned and stomped off and the rest of them followed him back into the courtroom.

While waiting for the gallery to empty, Brittany asked Marc what happened in chambers. Maddy had joined them at the table and listened while Marc answered her.

"No big deal. Connors told me to knock it off. But I got exactly what I wanted. I have no doubt they were counting on me to do a much longer cross of Stu Doyle this morning so that their direct exam of Anderson would be the last thing done today. They wanted the jury to have that insurance policy to be the last thing they heard to think about over this weekend. Instead, the last thing they heard was my claim that the prosecution is trying to hide things from them. Let the jury think that over until Monday morning."

FIFTY-SEVEN

Marc was planted on the couch in front of Margaret Tennant's sixty-inch flat screen. They were flipping through the channels checking the 5:30 network and cable newscasts. Each of them had their own "legal expert" giving a one to two-minute summary of the day's testimony of the Riley trial. Almost all of them showed film of Paul Anderson testifying about the life insurance policy. This would be followed by a serious, somber opinion by their "legal expert" on how devastating the day's testimony was for Brittany.

"You know, you're getting your ass kicked, according to the news reports," Margaret said.

"Think so?"

"Yes, I read both the Minneapolis and St. Paul papers every day and it doesn't look good for you."

"Should I be worried and when is dinner, I'm hungry?"

"No, you should not be worried. I saw your cross of the cop this afternoon, what's-his-name?"

"Anderson."

"And I thought you drilled him. We'll eat in a few minutes." She poked a finger into his ribs and in mock seriousness said, "You'd better not be too tired tonight."

"I'll do my best, ma'am."

They finished their meal and Marc helped clean up afterward. It was almost 6:30 and Marc wanted to catch Melinda Pace's show.

"Why do you torture yourself by watching this woman?" Margaret asked.

Marc thought it over for a moment then said, "Curiosity? I'm not sure. It's like watching a car accident and taking some perverse delight in the scene. You know you shouldn't, but you just can't look away."

Marc hit the power button on the remote and a close-up of Melinda came up on the screen. The show was starting, and she was introducing herself and her two guests, the lawyers Steve Farben and Andrea Briscomb.

Melinda was seated in the middle of the anchor desk with Farben to her right and Briscomb to her left. She turned first to the former prosecutor Farben and said, "Interesting day at the Riley trial today, wouldn't you say?"

"Definitely and another day of bad news for the defense," Farben said into the camera.

For the next three minutes, they showed Stu Doyle testifying about all of the steps the sheriff's office had taken in their effort to locate Bob Olson.

"He's kind of cute," Margaret commented trying to tweak Marc a bit.

"From what I hear, he thinks so too. He hit on Maddy today. She told Gabriella Shriqui, the reporter with Channel 8. Gabriella told her he is a married womanizer. Maddy says she might teach him a lesson."

"Oooo! If she does, tell her I want to hear about it."

Marc looked at her, shook his head and said, "I'll never cross a woman again. You people are vicious."

The camera came back with a wide shot of all three people on the set. Melinda was cued by the director in the booth and she asked Farben, "What do you think?"

"I think Brittany Riley's lies are catching up with her. Obviously, the police did everything they could to find this mystery boyfriend. They left no stone unturned and found nothing to back up her story," Farben replied.

Melinda turned to Briscomb and asked, "As a defense lawyer, how do you think Brittany's lawyer, Marc Kadella, handled this witness."

"Well, Melinda, I'm reluctant to denigrate a colleague but Kadella seems to be a bit over his head," Briscomb said acting as if it bothered her to say it.

"Let's look at a bit of his cross-exam," Melinda said into the camera.

The edited version of Marc's exam of Doyle made it look as if he was grasping at minor points. It ran for just under two minutes. While it was being shown, Margaret asked Marc, "Do you know her?"

"Who, Briscomb?"

"Yeah."

"No, not really. I met her at a couple of seminars. Enough to say hello. Why, do you know her?"

"I went to law school with her. She was a conniving, back-stabbing bitch then and it looks like she hasn't changed. I haven't had her in my courtroom yet."

The screen was again filled with the three people at the anchor desk.

"It was a pretty weak cross-exam," Briscomb said.

"For sure," Farben, agreed. "Most of his examinations have been. He's not getting much out of the prosecution's witnesses to help his client. I've heard he's a respectable trial lawyer, but so far, we're not seeing it."

Margaret, seething while watching this said, "If he ever shows up in my courtroom, I'm going to cut his nuts off."

"See what I mean about vicious women?" Marc said.

"Who does this asshole think he is?"

290

"Relax. This whole thing is a staged set-up. She's totally playing for ratings."

At that moment, Melinda's show went to a commercial break.

Marc watched the three minutes of commercials while Margaret opened a fresh bottle of wine. When she came back and sat down, Marc pointed at the screen and said, "Her ratings must be really good. This is a local show and the advertisers are all national brand names. Interesting."

The second half of the show was devoted to the testimony of Paul Anderson. While Marc and Margaret watched, the next ten minutes were filled with a carefully edited version of the prosecution introducing the life insurance policy and the items taken from the Rileys' garage. Both lawyers and Melinda agreed the life insurance policy may be the "smoking gun" that would nail down a conviction of Brittany Riley

The only part of Marc's cross-examination of the detective they showed was the moment Vanderbeck objected. They then showed Marc slapping his hand down on the table standing and yelling, "I object!" but edited out what else Marc said about keeping things from the jury. Then the judge calling a recess.

"Clearly, Kadella lost his grip there," Melinda said.

"Absolutely," Briscomb agreed. "And it won't do his client any good."

"It was a brilliant moment for the state. Now the jury's last image of the week, the one they'll each have all weekend is the life insurance policy and Brittany's out-of-control lawyer. Devastating day for Britany Riley," Farben chimed in.

"Wow," Marc softly said as he changed the channel. "I thought my cross went pretty well."

Margaret was sitting up on her knees staring in disbelief at what she had just seen. "I watched most of your cross myself with a couple of other judges. We all agreed you did great. What the hell are they talking about?"

"So, you saw it, right?"

"Yes, we all agreed you hammered him. And that business about the state keeping things from the jury was brilliant, if somewhat unethical. The last thing the jury heard was you telling them the prosecution was keeping things from them."

"Brilliant! Really? Wow, I'm not sure anyone has ever called me brilliant before," he said laughing as she punched him on the shoulder.

Marc's phone was buzzing but it didn't wake him. Margaret slapped him on his bare butt and whispered in his ear to wake up and answer it.

"Hello," he groggily said while noting from the bedside clock it was after midnight.

"I'm sorry, did I wake you?" he heard Maddy Rivers ask.

"No, it's okay. I was just sleeping anyway."

"Oh, God. Did I wake Margaret?"

"Yep."

"Apologize for me please."

"Okay, what's up?"

"I thought you'd want to know. She's back."

"That's great. I'll talk to you tomorrow," Marc said still half asleep.

"What? Wait. Don't you want to know who?"

"I suppose."

"Julie Makie."

"And who is she?"

"She's the girl that worked at Macy's with Brittany. She was in China. Remember?"

"Oh, yeah. Now I remember," he said, fully awake now.

"You ready for this? She returned my call this evening, about an hour ago. She's in Oregon so..."

"Madeline, get to the point please," Marc politely interrupted.

"Okay. Anyway, I emailed six sketch artist drawings of men to her, including the one of Bob Olson. She identified Olson immediately."

"She recognized him?"

"You got it. Says she remembers him hanging around Macy's. She even talked to him. She said she thought he was kind of hot, but he was obviously checking out Brittany."

"Now what?" Marc said while putting on his shorts and undershirt.

I told her we'd call her tomorrow. I filled her in on the trial and she said she'd be happy to testify but she has no money to get here..."

"No problem. We'll take care of it."

"I told her that. But she can't come back until next week. Her dad's going into the hospital for more treatment. Cancer."

"I remember. Next week will be fine. I'll call you tomorrow. We'll call her from my office. Nice job, sweetheart. I owe you one."

"Did you remember to add her name to your witness list?"

Marc paused for a second thinking, then said, "Yes I did. I remember it now. I remember thinking it over and decided to put her on the list."

"All right! Talk to you tomorrow."

FIFTY-EIGHT

Marc and Madeline arrived at Marc's office simultaneously, Maddy driving into the lot right behind him. It was just before 10:00 A.M. and the air temperature was warmed to a plus twenty. The sun was shining brilliantly, there wasn't a hint of a breeze and it was predicted to be a very pleasant winter day. It was the sort of day the natives broke their cabin fever and got out to enjoy. Of course, because it was so nice out, the semi-professional protestors were slowly parading around the front and side of the building.

When Marc drove past them he noticed a CNN van and camera crew conducting interviews on the sidewalk. A couple of the protestors saw him and pointed him out to the reporter as Marc pulled into the lot behind the building. Maddy parked next to him and the two of them walked toward the back door and saw the camera crew already waiting for them.

Marc was dressed in jeans, sneakers, a light sweater and a modest winter jacket. No hat, no gloves, no scarf. Maddy was similarly dressed except she was wearing four-inch heeled, suede half boots with a light blue silk scarf stylishly draped around her neck. Seeing the reporter waiting for them at the building's back door, Marc almost started laughing.

When they got close enough to be heard, before the reporter could ask a question, Marc said, "Don't tell me, let me guess. You must be Nanook of New Jersey."

The man was dressed as if he was starting out on the Iditarod dog sled race. He was wearing a fur-lined Elmer Fudd hat with the ear flaps down, a heavy wool scarf, insulated and hooded winter coat, large fur-lined mittens and insulated, heavy boots that came up to mid-calf.

"How did you know I'm from New Jersey?" the man asked.

Ignoring the question, Marc said to Maddy, "Notice the dull, drab, pathetic look of the East Coast candy-ass whiner."

Maddy laughed then said, "Very similar to its close cousin, the West Coast candy-ass whiner."

"Ha, ha, ha. Very funny. At least we're not crazy enough to live here in this frozen wilderness," the reporter said.

"He's got us there," Maddy said to Marc.

"Excellent point for which we have no explanation. Are you filming all of this?" Marc asked the cameraman who nodded his head to indicate he was.

"After taking that shot at you I suppose we could give you a couple of minutes," Marc said.

293

While the protestors stood a respectful distance away and watched, Marc politely answered a few questions. Most of them were innocuous nonsense. The few that were pertinent were mostly answered with a no comment or an extremely vague answer. The whole thing took less than ten minutes. The reporter's main interest was getting Marc to give an opinion about the trial. Of course, all he would say is that it is still too early to tell.

"Do you realize that conventional wisdom has it that you're way behind and seem to be over your head?"

"Conventional wisdom," Marc laughed. "That's an interesting phrase to describe the media in this country. I'm not sure I'd use the word wisdom when describing how they cover trials. But they're certainly entitled to their opinion. Look, I really have to go."

While the interview was taking place, every time the reporter was speaking while he asked a question the cameraman would aim the camera at Madeline. After the third time, she scratched her nose with the middle finger of her left hand. The man got the message and stopped doing it.

While Marc and Maddy walked up the back stairs to his office, Maddy asked him, "Do you think he'll play it straight?"

"Who knows and who cares?"

"I can see it now, 'Brittany Riley's lawyer thinks the media are all idiots'."

Marc stopped on the next to last step, looked at her and said, "How could that hurt me?"

Marc's desk phone was set on speaker so both of them could listen and converse. Maddy made the call and after the fourth ring Marc asked, "You're sure it's not too early out there?"

"No, she said…" Maddy stopped when the voice of a young woman said hello.

"Hi, Julie, this is Maddy Rivers."

"Morning, Maddy."

"I'm with Brittany's lawyer, Marc Kadella in his office."

"Okay."

"Hello, Julie. This is Marc. How are you this morning?"

"I'm fine, Mr. Kadella."

"Please, call me Marc."

The three of them went over the conversation Maddy and Julie had the previous evening. Julie reaffirmed that she recognized the man in the drawing having seen him a couple of times in mid-July at Macy's. When Marc gently pressed her about the time when this happened, she was certain because it was shortly before she quit working there. It was at this time she found out her father had cancer and she went home to be there for him and to help her mother.

Julie was not only willing to testify for Brittany but quite eager. She said she was absolutely certain Brittany could not have done something so horrible. Marc assured her he would take care of all of her travel arrangements and expenses and he made sure she had his office and cell numbers before ending the call.

"Julie, one last thing, I don't want you talking to anyone about this. If it leaks to the press, they will be all over you and your family. Just keep it to yourself for now."

Julie agreed, and they ended the call.

"What do you think?" Marc asked Maddy.

"She didn't vary a bit from what she told me last night."

"She sounds credible."

"They'll go after her," Maddy said referring to the prosecution.

"I know. I'll have Jeff do a thorough background search on her including Facebook and all of that other internet nonsense."

"It's amazing what some of these kids put out there for the world to see."

"No kidding. I'll smooth her out once she gets here. As long as she sticks to the truth, she'll be fine. When are you doing your interview with Gabriella?"

"We're going to meet for lunch and go over it and then go to the station and do it. I'm really nervous about it. What should I wear?"

"A thong bikini," Marc immediately answered.

That made her laugh and say, "And show off my Carl Fornich scars?" This was a reference to the first case the two of them had together. Carl was a serial killer Maddy had fought and thrown to his death through a window in her apartment.

"How are they?" Marc politely asked.

"Not bad but no bikini on TV."

"Wear something professional and don't get too carried away fixing your hair or putting on makeup," Marc seriously told her. "You'll do fine just being yourself. Let me give you some advice. Don't anticipate questions. Let her finish asking you the question and take all of the time you need to answer it. This is more of a puff piece anyway, a human-interest thing. Gabriella isn't out to play 'gotcha' with this."

"I made it clear, no questions about the trial. You think she'll try to set me up for some? Get me to say something about Brittany?"

Marc thought about the question for a brief moment then said, "No, I don't. She strikes me as pretty straight. In all of the times I've talked to her she's been very professional. Relax. Have some fun with it. It's okay to joke around and laugh a bit. Be yourself. Just don't shoot anyone. Besides, it can't hurt your business."

"Don't shoot anyone! Won't that take most of the fun out of it? What are you up to today?" she asked.

"I'm going to spend some time here getting ready for next week. Then, I'm going out to the Rileys' this afternoon."

"Have fun with that. Are they still being mobbed with protestors?"

"Not as bad, but it's Saturday and the weather's nice so, we'll see. One other thing. Keep this business about Julie Makie to yourself. Talk to no one including Brittany and the Rileys. I need to figure out exactly how I want to handle her testimony."

"Sure, no problem."

Maddy met Gabriella precisely at noon, just as they agreed. Maddy was barely out of her car when Gabriella drove up, waved at Maddy and put her car in the slot next to Maddy's. They had agreed to meet at a trendy and pricey French bistro named *Oceane* in an upscale mall located in an upscale neighborhood of an upscale suburb west of Minneapolis. Maddy had been there a couple of times on dates. Gabriella was here for the first time.

The lunchtime crowd had filled the dining area and left eight or nine people waiting to be seated. The two beautiful women, led by Maddy, spoke to the young man in charge of seating and within a minute they had a table.

They ordered lunch on Gabriella's expense account and spent the next hour getting to know each other. Gabriella started off by asking Maddy about herself, her background and how she got into the private investigator business. Gabriella took notes to prepare for the interview. They exhausted that topic after a while and Gabriella put the notebook she was writing on back in her purse.

"I have a confession to make," Gabriella said, a little nervously.

"Oh?" Maddy said, giving Gabriella a suspicious look, her natural investigator's alarm going off in her head.

"No, no," Gabriella protested waving a hand at her. "It's um, well, I'm not sure how to say this." She paused, looking nervously at Maddy and then continued by saying, "First of all, I'm not gay." This comment caused Maddy to almost choke on the soda she was sipping. "Alright, alright, here it is," Gabriella said as if to start over. "I'm not from around here and I don't have any girlfriends. You know, someone to get together with and just be friends with. I see you with Marc and I did a little digging to find out who you are. We're about the same age and I just thought you might be someone I'd like to get to know."

"I'm flattered," Maddy said.

"Really? I can't believe how nervous this made me. How do men do this? Ask girls out."

"Yes, really. Believe it or not, I'm in the same boat you are. All of my friends are lawyers or cops. Besides, Marc has good things to say about you."

"Does he really?"

"Yeah, he does. Says you're good and professional. No games, no agenda, no bullshit."

"That's nice to hear. He'd be a good one, I think. A little too old. If he was maybe ten years younger and no kids…" Gabriella let the thought drift off.

"I've had the same thought." Maddy smiled. "Besides, he's involved, and I think it's pretty serious. A judge."

"Too bad. Why is it so hard to meet a decent, normal guy?" Gabriella asked.

"Marc has a theory," Maddy said. "He calls it: The Curse of the Beautiful Woman. He claims decent, normal guys are too intimidated to approach beautiful women, which you certainly are. That just leaves the assholes who never met a mirror they didn't fall in love with. Insecure little boys."

"That actually makes sense. That does seem to be the type I attract. The assholes who would love to spend their time in front of a mirror," Gabriella said. She checked the time on her watch and continued, "We should go. They'll be waiting."

As the two women walked to their respective cars, Madeline hooked Gabriella's right arm with her left and said, "Louis, I think this is the beginning of a beautiful friendship."

Both of them laughed and Gabriella said, "That's one of my all-time favorite movies."

"Is it really? See, we already have something in common," Maddy said.

"Casablanca and being hit on by assholes," Gabriella said which elicited another hearty laugh.

FIFTY-NINE

"Did you come in through the front or the back?" Marc heard the deputy ask him.

It was Monday morning and Marc was at the defense table setting up for the day's testimony. He looked at the man, an older deputy whose name escaped him, and said, "Through the back, why?"

"You should go down to the lobby and take a look at what's going on outside. Go ahead. I'll watch your stuff."

Marc gave the man a puzzled look, shrugged and started toward the hallway door. He made his way through the crowd on the second floor, went down the stairs and a minute later was looking at what the deputy meant. To his left, as he looked through a window by the entryway, was a small crowd. They were milling about on the sidewalk in front of the county offices, loosely watched over by three deputies. What he looked at were thirty-five to forty people, a number of whom carried signs with slogans painted on them. He read the slogans such as "Free Brittany Now!", "Brittany Is Innocent", "Brittany Is Being Framed".

While Marc stood silently watching them, one of the sheriff's deputies, the sergeant in charge of the door security team, silently slid up next to him. The two of them watched the crowd and the deputy said, "Seems you've created some fans."

"Interesting," Marc said. "The other side still seems to be a bit more popular."

To their right, crowded along the sidewalks stretching from the jail a couple hundred yards to the back parking lot were the anti-Brittany demonstrators. Even on a chilly morning, there were at least three hundred of them.

"Don't any of these people have jobs?" Marc asked turning back to the pro-Brittany crowd.

"Guess not," the deputy said. "Just so you know; the office pool odds have dropped quite a bit. It's now down to three to two in favor of a conviction. The word is you're doing pretty well."

"What were the odds originally?"

"Five to one."

"If I had known, I would have taken some of that." Marc pulled some bills from his pocket, peeled one of them off and handed it to the sergeant. "Here, put me down for twenty and if the odds go back up, let me know. I'm gonna win this thing."

"You got it," the man said as he took Marc's money.

Marc took one more look at the pro-Brittany side and noticed one of them, a man, staring back at him. While Marc watched, the man smiled and gave Marc a thumbs up sign, a gesture Marc returned.

298

The man who gave Marc the thumbs up signal watched as Marc retreated from the window and walked away. He continued to stare for a moment then looked at his watch, stepped off the sidewalk and headed toward the parking lot. Bob Olson, in a new disguise, decided it was time to go to work.

The day's testimony was taken up entirely by the staff from the medical examiner's office. Hart was the one who took the testimony of all of these individuals for the state. Following routine evidentiary procedure, Hart was going to call everyone involved in the chain of custody of the body. The purpose is to establish that the cause of death and time of death are as accurate as possible and that the autopsy is performed without any taint. The actual cause of death was unknown, and the time of death was at best, a guess based not on a clock but a calendar.

First up were the two responders who recovered and transported the remains. Marcia Clark, one of the two medical examiner responders called to the scene was first up. Hart quickly went over the day's events that brought her and her partner, Jerry Hoy to recover Becky's remains.

Hart got her to the river bank and the main purpose of her testimony. As Clark described what they did, Hart had photos up on the television screen giving graphic, visual details of the area where the body was found and more importantly, several close-ups of Becky in the water. An especially pitiful one was left up on the screen while Clark explained how difficult it had been to recover the body and keep what was left of it, the skeletal remains, intact.

The final photo was one of the tiny little body, covered up, lying on the gurney. The contrast between the size of the gurney and the remains of the little girl actually caused three or four of the jurors to gasp and sob.

The showing of the photos was designed for one purpose. It was designed to tug at the hearts of the jurors. "Look at this tiny little baby and what was done to her. Somebody needs to pay!"

The content of this testimony and the photo display had been the subject of a heated argument several weeks ago. Marc, of course, had argued vehemently that these photos should not be allowed at all. Neither of the medical examiner's team had taken them. The person who shot the pictures had already testified and the photos admitted. Showing them again to the jury would have no additional probative value. Connors came down in the middle, allowing a few of them but not all. The most damaging one, the one the state would have loved to be shown, was the picture of a live, beautiful blonde-haired, blue-eyed, Becky Riley holding her favorite teddy bear and smiling adorably at the camera. Of course, while Clark testified and just before the first photo went up on the screen, Marc renewed his objection for the jury to have it on the official record.

The rest of the morning session, after the break, was taken up by Clark's partner Jerry Hoy. His testimony was an exact duplication of Clark's and Hart was allowed to go through the same routine with the same highly prejudicial photos. While this was taking place, Marc spent a lot of time observing the jury. It was clear the shock effect, the emotional value of the photos was dissipated. By the time Hoy was finished, Marc noticed a number of yawns and even stifled yawns from the jury. Apparently, they were getting used to seeing this type of evidence.

Marc's cross-examination of both witnesses was short and to the point. He simply made them both admit they found no evidence connecting Becky's death to anyone, especially Brittany Riley. And could add nothing as far as cause of death or time of death or even where the death occurred.

For her part, while this testimony and photo display was taking place, Brittany had all she could do to keep control of herself. Marc had known what was coming and of course warned her ahead of time about it. Not once could she bring herself to look at the TV screen. She sat as impassively as she possibly could, her hands folded tightly together on the table, doing her best to keep herself together. Marc had expressly gone over this with her. The less emotion she showed, the less it could be misconstrued, except, no matter what she did, someone would take it wrong.

"Please state your name and occupation," Hart asked the mostly bald, elderly man seated on the witness stand.

"Sebastian Carnes. I am the Dakota County Medical examiner," the man replied. Carnes was in his late forties but looked like he was in his mid-sixties. He was, in appearance, exactly what you would think of as a pathologist. He sported a short, mostly grey beard, a bow-tie and reading glasses perched on his forehead with the rapidly receding hairline.

Danica Hart, being more efficient and less inclined to play for the court's TV camera than her colleague, moved the doctor through his credentials much more expeditiously but not less thoroughly than Vanderbeck would have. Even so, being the professional witness and inveterate showman that Carnes was, he was not going to be rushed. Someone should have warned Hart that when the good doctor testified at a trial, any trial, he savored the spotlight and made the most of his time on stage.

Despite Hart's attempt to move him along, the doctor took up the entire afternoon. He gave the jury a lengthy dissertation of his curriculum vitae, which included details of several highly publicized trials. Obviously, he wanted the jury to know they had a true expert, maybe even a minor celebrity before them.

Throughout most of the man's testimony, Marc paid scant attention to what he was saying. Almost all of it was a corroboration of the autopsy report which Marc had been over until he practically had it memorized. Watching the juror's eyes glaze over and a couple of them even nod off, he thought about a stunt he had always wanted to try. Marc wondered just how much trouble he would get into if he folded his arms on the tabletop and put his head down. Then to really set it off, make soft snoring noises. The image amused him, and he almost started laughing.

By the time Carnes finished going over every detail of everything he had done, it was after 4:30.

"In your opinion, doctor, was this child's death an accident?" Hart asked.

"Obviously not. It was clearly a homicide."

"In your opinion, doctor, if you have one, what was the cause of death?"

This was a question that made Marc's antennae go off.

"This child was deliberately drowned," he said.

"Thank you, doctor," Hart said, hoping against hope she had just slipped a fastball past Marc, or, at least, because of the preparation she had done with Carnes, it would get the doctor through what was coming. "I have no further questions."

Marc barely waited for the judge to give him permission to begin his questioning.

"I noticed, doctor, that she just asked you for your opinion about the cause of death and not your medical opinion. Isn't that unusual?"

"Not necessarily, no."

"Oh, really? So, if I ask you your opinion about, for example, the composition of these cinder blocks on the table in front of you, could you give me an opinion?"

"Well, um, no…"

"Because you're a doctor, not a bricklayer, correct?"

"Yes, of course."

"So, I'll ask it. In your medical opinion, what is the cause of death of Becky Ann Riley, doctor?" Marc politely asked knowing what he would say.

"In my medical opinion, I stand by my previous statement that she was deliberately drowned," Carnes answered feeling quite smug about himself.

"Really? And explain to the court and this jury exactly what medical evidence you have uncovered to reach that conclusion, please, doctor."

"Well, clearly everything associated with the body is consistent with…"

"Ah, there it is, the phrase I knew was coming…" Marc cut him off.

"Objection!" Hart was on her feet. "He needs to let the witness finish his answer."

"Sustained. The witness will be allowed to finish his answer," Connors ruled.

"Consistent with what, doctor?" Marc asked anyway.

"Consistent with drowning," Carnes said slumping down in the chair a bit.

Marc clasped his hands together, placed them on the table in front of him, leaned forward across the table and glared at the M.E. for a full ten seconds.

"Is the term 'consistent with' the same as a 'medical certainty', doctor?" Marc very quietly asked.

"I'm sorry, I didn't hear you," Carnes said.

"Isn't it true, doctor," Marc said more loudly without changing his position, staring at Carnes, "that 'consistent with' and 'medical certainty' are not the same thing?"

"Well, no but…"

"In fact, doctor, isn't it true that you, as an expert, should be telling this jury how this child died to a medical certainty, yes or no?"

"Yes," he quietly answered.

"Doctor, isn't it time for you to admit to this jury that you have no idea how Becky actually died?"

"Look," Carnes began trying to reacquire control. "Obviously everything points to…"

"Points to? Now you want to go with 'points to'?"

"Objection, argumentative," Hart said.

"Overruled," Connors said surprising even Marc.

"You started off with 'consistent with' and now you want to switch to 'points to' a drowning. Shouldn't you be testifying only to a medical certainty, doctor?"

"Yes," Carnes meekly agreed.

"Then, doctor, time for you to be honest with this jury. Isn't it true, doctor, you have no idea, not to a medical certainty, how this child died, do you doctor?"

302

"No, I don't," Carnes finally conceded. Marc stood up, looked at Connors and said, "Your Honor, I move that this witness's entire testimony be stricken from the record as being totally unreliable."

Danica Hart, knowing her case would disappear if Connors granted Marc's request, practically jumped out of her chair. If the medical examiner's testimony was struck from the official record, there would be no expert medical testimony of a murder. There would be no way to know legally if this was an accident or a homicide. If that happened, the defense would move for the case to be dismissed and Brittany Riley goes home today for good.

"Denied," Connors ruled before a relieved Hart had a chance to speak. "The jury can infer what it wants from his testimony and give it whatever weight they desire. Continue, Mr. Kadella."

"I have no further questions, your Honor," Marc said having gotten the admission he wanted, no cause of death.

Melinda opened her show with several minutes of film and discussion about how and where the body had been found and removed. The three of them, Melinda and the two lawyers, conversed quietly, almost reverently, while the screen behind them flashed the photos taken of Becky Riley's remains lying among the cattails.

The pictures had been a subject of a very heated debate between Melinda and her producer, Robbie Nelson. Robbie tried to make her believe that showing the audience the photos of Becky in the water was taking the show to a new low. Melinda, never one to take her eyes off the ball of TV ratings, fell back on the old cliché, "the people have the right to know." That, combined with the fact that it was her show, ended the argument.

The real purpose of this macabre slideshow was to allow Melinda another opportunity to slash and burn Brittany.

"It disgusts me, that she could sit there and not even bother to look at what she did to her baby," Melinda said looking at Steve Farben. With that comment, the picture on the screen behind them switched from Becky's skeleton in the river to the shot of Becky holding her teddy bear, smiling at the camera.

"It's likely," Andrea Briscomb interjected, "that her lawyer prepared her for this and told her not to look. He told her to keep her composure and not give anyone anything to misconstrue."

A brief exchange took place among the three of them about this, but Melinda had the last word just before the commercial break. "She didn't look because she knows what she did."

The second half of the show was taken up by a discussion of the medical examiner's testimony. Farben was the one that explained to the audience that it was necessary for the doctor to go over all of the details of the autopsy. To be sure that the defense could not trip him up by making him admit he missed something.

"True enough," Briscomb agreed, "but at the end of it, he still had to admit he had no cause of death. Kadella scored some points with that."

"Not really," Farben countered almost disdainfully. "She was tied to a cinderblock and thrown in the Mississippi. The jury will figure it out."

The print media and national networks ran the same basic theme the next day. It was almost as if they were taking their cue from Melinda's show. In a way they were. She was becoming a significant source for their stories, so they could start with the lame disclaimer, "It has been reported that..." Of course, this is totally unprofessional and unreliable, but it did provide cover for them. They could point to someone else and truthfully say whatever they reported had been reported elsewhere first.

Thirty minutes after the show, Cordelia Davis, an associate producer for Melinda, knocked on Melinda's door. Without waiting for a reply, she entered carrying several pages of note paper.

"What's the Twitter world saying?" Melinda asked.

"You're a god," Cordelia answered. "Here's one," she continued as she read a note from one of the pages. "God bless you, Melinda. Thank the Lord we have people like you to report the truth. Hashtag Brittany rot in hell.

"That's one of the calmer ones. Most of them are positive. I brought a sampling for you to read," Cordelia handed her the pages of notes. "I'm going to take off. See you tomorrow."

SIXTY

"The state calls Nolan Leffler," Danica Hart announced.

It was Thursday morning and the prosecution was in the home stretch of its case. The previous two days had been taken up by witnesses that did not add much, if anything at all, to the issue of guilt or innocence. The first four of them had been argued about strenuously but eventually allowed.

The cops had rounded up four people who they talked to while conducting the search for Bob Olson. Three of them were people who managed apartment complexes where the cops had stopped. The fourth was a woman married to a man named Bob Olson who lived in one of the buildings. Each of them testified that Brittany seemed uninterested, aloof and unconcerned. Being lay people and not professional psychologists, their opinions should not have been allowed at all. Marc believed that for Connors to allow this testimony might be reversible error except the judge gave very explicit instructions to the jury about the fact that these were not professional opinions and should not be given that level of weight.

Marc's cross-examination was short and to the point. He made each of them admit they did not know Brittany Riley, had no idea what she was really thinking and what they told the jury was mostly a guess. Each of the four left the witness stand quite annoyed with Brittany's lawyer for ruining their moment in the spotlight, on TV and likely their dreams of a book deal.

The more damaging testimony inadvertently came from Brittany's three best friends. It was Vanderbeck who conducted their exams and with each one he went through the "Brittany as a party girl" slide show again. Since each friend had been there with her and had even taken most of the photos, this was clearly fair game. It was obvious that the three young women were uncomfortable and did not want to testify against their friend. Marc and Maddy had both extensively interviewed all three and assured them to tell the truth, answer honestly and things would work out.

When he finished with each of them, Vanderbeck made sure the picture of Brittany and the wet T-shirt trophy was left on the screen. Marc would walk over to the TV and shut it off before beginning his cross exam. The third and final time he did so, he said, "I think we've all seen this one enough." He looked at Vanderbeck and added, "Although it does seem to be the one Mr. Vanderbeck likes the most." This comment elicited a roar of laughter from the gallery, the jury and even the judge who had to gavel for order while a red-faced Vanderbeck stared holes through Marc.

Marc's cross of Brittany's friends was limited to a few well-prepared questions. Each of the girls very willingly admitted that during the time Brittany said she was dating Bob Olson, her friends believed he was real. Mostly this was so because Brittany was too busy with him to socialize with them. Whenever any of the girls had a steady boyfriend, it wasn't unusual to spend more time with the boyfriend and not much with each other.

"I have just one more question," Marc would conclude with each of them. "Did the police, sheriff's deputies or prosecutors ask you about Brittany as a mother? Ask you what kind of a mother she was?"

Each of her friends answered the same basic way. "Yes, all of them did many times. In fact, they wouldn't leave it alone. I kept telling them Brittany was a great mother. Becky was always clean and fed. She had nice clothes and was the happiest little girl you could find. But that was never good enough. It was never what they wanted to hear. They kept at it asking, 'are you sure'? What was she like at home? Didn't she say she wished she didn't have the child? Stuff like that. They wouldn't leave it alone. No matter what I said they obviously wanted me to say Brittany was a bad mom."

"Was she a bad mom?" Marc would ask.

"No, she loved that little girl with all her heart. Becky was the world to her."

Nolan Leffler was sworn in and took the stand. He told the jury his name, occupation and current place of employment. Leffler was a forensics expert with the Bureau of Criminal Apprehension for the state of Minnesota.

Hart took a better part of an hour slowly and carefully allowing the witness to spell out his education, training and qualifications. Leffler was going to testify that the hair found in Brittany's trunk was Becky's and the cinder block and rope to which Becky was tied, matched what was taken from the Rileys' garage during the search.

Leffler was a pro at testifying and was very good at explaining his testing methods in understandable language that did not come across as condescending. With the use of photos put up on the TV screen, Hart and Leffler almost casually explained the testing methods of the hair found in the trunk of Brittany's car and the comparison to the hair that remained on the skull of Becky Riley.

The two of them did the same thing with the cinder block pulled from the river. The forensics expert thoroughly explained the testing methods used and the positive match with the cinder blocks found in the Rileys' garage. Leffler was also able to positively match the cinder block with particles found in Brittany's trunk. What could have been a very boring scientific demonstration was actually quite interesting. When they finished with his direct exam, every member of the jury was completely captivated. And they all got the message. Leffler believed Becky Riley and the cinder block to which she was tethered, had been in Brittany's trunk.

"Isn't it true, Mr. Leffler," Marc began his cross-examination after the break, "your tests cannot determine when the hair was left in the car's trunk?"

"That's true, but..."

"Nonresponsive, your Honor," Marc said.

"Just answer the question," Connors admonished Leffler.

"Yes or no, please," Marc told him.

"Yes, that's true."

"There were cinder block particles spread throughout the trunk, wasn't there?"

"I'm not sure what you mean," Leffler replied.

"If you put a forty-pound cinder block in the trunk of your car, it wouldn't slide around while the car was moving, would it?"

"Well, no, I suppose not," Leffler agreed.

"It would sit in the spot where it was placed?"

"Yes, it would be too heavy to slide around."

"And isn't it true that you would expect to find residue particles of that cinder block in the spot where it was placed?"

"Yes," the witness agreed.

"Isn't it also true that there were particles spread throughout the trunk of the car?"

"Yes, there were."

Marc was tempted to ask him to explain why, but he avoided temptation. Not knowing what the man could come up with, he decided to move on and later Marc would bring his own witness to explain it.

"Mr. Leffler, would you explain to the jury, the concept of fiber transference?"

"When two articles consisting of fibers rub against each other, fibers from each will be transferred to the other article," Leffler said looking at the jury.

"For example," Marc continued, "if a blanket rubs up against carpeting, you would expect to find fibers from the blanket on the carpet and carpet fibers on the blanket?"

"Yes, exactly so."

Marc asked Connors for permission to approach the witness and it was granted. He took an exhibit off of the exhibit table and handed it to Leffler. It was a multicolored cloth object in a clear plastic bag.

"Mr. Leffler, I handed you state's Exhibit number 1. Do you recognize it?"

"Yes."

"And what is it?"

"It's what was left of a blanket found in the river with the remains of the victim."

"Did you run tests on this item?"

"Yes, I did."

"What is the blanket made from?"

"It is fifty percent cotton and fifty percent orlon."

"Isn't it true that if you were to rub this blanket against carpeting, you would find fiber transference?"

"Yes," Leffler answered softly, realizing where Marc was going.

"Yet, isn't it true you found no fiber particles of this blanket in the trunk of Brittany Riley's car, did you?"

"No, um, I did not."

"Did you test Exhibit 1 for any carpet fibers from the trunk of the car?"

"Yes, I did," Leffler admitted.

"You didn't find any carpet fibers on the blanket, did you?"

"No, I did not."

"You did not tell the jury this during your examination by Ms. Hart, did you?"

"She didn't ask," Leffler said believing this would exonerate him."

"No, she didn't, did she?" Marc said then quickly added, "Withdrawn, your Honor."

Marc went through the exact same routine with the remnant of Becky's pink pajamas and the rope found tied to her ankle. The results were the same. No fibers from any of these objects were found in the trunk and no carpet fibers from the trunk were found on the pajamas or rope.

Marc also went through the same routine of having Leffler admit this was also not told to the jury during the direct exam.

"Mr. Leffler," Hart began her re-direct exam, "isn't it possible that there might not be no fiber transference at all?"

"Yes, that is possible," Leffler agreed.

"Would it also be possible that after being in the river for two months, the river would wash away fiber transference from the items the defense attorney asked you about?"

"Not just possible but quite likely," Leffler said.

"Nothing further, your Honor," Hart concluded.

"Mr. Leffler," Marc said on re-cross, "isn't it true that the odds of there being no fiber transference in the trunk of Ms. Riley's car if the victim was in that car are virtually zero?" He was taking a chance with this question. He didn't know how the witness would answer it so he was counting on the jury's common sense to figure out the real answer would be no.

"I don't know…" Leffler began.

"Yes or no, Mr. Leffler," Marc interrupted him sounding impatient.

The witness sat silently for a moment thinking about his answer then finally said, "Yes, I suppose that is true."

Connors called for the lunch break and while they waited for the crowd to dissipate, Maddy asked Marc, "How could they have missed that?"

"Because the Attorney General's office doesn't handle enough of these cases. I guarantee you, if LeAnn Miller was trying it, she would not have missed it and she would have dealt with it," Marc said referring to the Dakota County Attorney.

When they returned from lunch, Barbara and Floyd Riley were not in attendance. Marc had guessed, correctly as it turned out, that the next witness would be the psychiatrist the state had hired. A lot of his testimony was going to be about the relationship between Brittany and Barbara, so Marc discouraged her from attending.

Judge Connors' clerk came out and informed the lawyers that the judge was on a conference call. He was trying to resolve a dispute between two lawyers taking a deposition for a case assigned to him. Connors sent his apology and let them know he would be out as soon as he was done.

When court finally resumed, Vanderbeck called the state's next witness, Lawrence Randall. Randall was a sixty-four-year-old psychiatrist. He received his M.D. from the University of Chicago and was a practicing psychiatrist for several years before realizing he didn't really like listening to other people's problems all day. He obtained a position with the University of Kentucky, College of Medicine where he taught and wrote for twenty years. In his early fifties, he discovered the pleasure and profit of being a professional witness. Having put in twenty years and earning a full taxpayer-funded pension, he quit his day job and hired himself out to trial lawyers.

The reason for going over an expert witness's qualifications is to make the jury believe his opinion carries more weight. Following forty minutes of testimony about his education, experience, awards and publications, Vanderbeck was finally getting to the point. The doctor's role was to explain why a seemingly normal mother would murder her daughter. Randall spent an hour explaining the various reasons why someone could commit this act. He offered numerous examples, most of which were related to postpartum depression.

"That's normally found in newborn or very young babies' deaths isn't it doctor?" Vanderbeck asked. This is a leading question, but Marc did not bother to object.

"That's true," Randall answered.

"Have you had the opportunity to examine Brittany Riley?"

"No, but I have done a thorough analysis of her medical and personal history and in my medical, professional opinion, she is suffering from PTSD, post-traumatic stress disorder as a result of the death of her husband. She is harboring deep-seated anger and resentment at him and life in general for leaving her alone to raise a child."

"In your medical opinion, could this cause someone to kill their child?"

"Yes, in fact, there are a number of cases of this that have occurred."

"Would the person who did this, the mother, know that what she is doing is wrong."

"Of course. Hiding the body would be a clear indication of that."

"Would this also explain someone not reporting her daughter missing for ten days?"

This, again, was a leading question that Marc could object to but Vanderbeck could easily rephrase it and get the answer they had rehearsed anyway. He didn't object because there is no need to make the jury believe he does not want them to hear the answer.

"Certainly, at least in part. It's likely that she wanted some time to celebrate her new-found freedom. And she was also in a state of denial that anything was wrong; that nothing out of the ordinary had occurred."

"Just a couple more questions, doctor. In your professional opinion is this common?"

"I wouldn't say it is common, but it does happen."

"What about a mother-daughter conflict, doctor? If the child's mother was afraid of a domineering grandmother, the child's mother's mother, could this be the reason for hiding the fact of the child's disappearance?"

"I suppose it could contribute to it, but as I said, the PTSD is the far more likely cause."

"Thank you, doctor. I have nothing further."

"I'm sorry, doctor, I forgot," Marc began, "how much time did you spend personally interviewing Brittany Riley?"

"It really isn't necessary…"

"Nonresponsive, your Honor," Marc said without taking his eyes off of the witness to send him an unmistakable message as to who was in charge of the questioning.

"Answer the question," Connors told him.

"None but..."

"Yes, I know, you reviewed her history," Marc said with mild sarcasm.

"Did you interview her parents?"

"No, again..."

"Did you interview anyone that knows her? Neighbors, friends, physicians, anyone at all?"

"Objection," Vanderbeck said trying to disrupt Marc.

"Overruled, sit down," Connors told him. "Answer the question, doctor."

"No, I did not."

Marc continued to lean on the table top, his hands folded together while he stared directly at the state's expert witness.

"Because it's not necessary, correct?"

"Yes," he steadfastly agreed.

"Because you made a thorough review of her history, isn't that true?"

"Yes, I did."

"Who provided you with that history?"

"Well, the, uh, prosecution. Mr. Vanderbeck, I believe."

"Did he leave anything out?"

"Objection!" Vanderbeck yelled as he jumped to his feet. "How dare he suggest..."

"Overruled," Connors sternly said. "Sit down, Mr. Vanderbeck."

"Um, ah, I'm not sure. How would I know?"

"Exactly, doctor. How would you know?"

"Your Honor!" Vanderbeck yelled as he again jumped out of his seat.

"Move along, Mr. Kadella, you've made your point."

"You were a professor in the medical school at Kentucky until you retired at the age of fifty-two, is that correct?" Marc asked looking at a note in his trial book.

"Yes, that's correct. I was fifty-two."

"Have you been in private practice since then seeing patients?"

"No, I have not treated patients."

Marc again leaned forward on the table, his hands clasped together on the tabletop, staring directly at Randall and asked, "You've been a professional witness since then, haven't you?"

"I wouldn't put it that way..."

"Stop it, doctor! Tell this jury the truth. You've been a professional witness for twelve years, haven't you?"

While Marc was drilling Randall between the eyes with this question, Vanderbeck started to get up to object. Before he had a chance to say a word, Judge Connors gave him a firm look and held up his hand to stop him.

"Yes, I suppose," Randall quietly admitted.

"You're now sixty-four is that correct?"

"Yes."

"In the past twelve years, since your retirement, how many criminal trials have you testified in?"

"Oh, I don't know. I don't keep a running count," he said chuckling at what he thought was a little joke.

"How about forty-six, doctor? Would that number sound about right? Roughly three to four per year."

"Yes, that is probably accurate," he agreed.

"And of those forty-six, how many times did you testify for the prosecution and how many times for the defendant?"

"Objection, relevance," Vanderbeck stood up and said. When he did this, his co-counsel Danica Hart cringed, and Marc silently thought, "Thank you."

"Goes to credibility, your Honor," Marc said without standing or moving his head to look at the judge.

"Obviously," Connors said. "Overruled."

"I'm not sure," Randall replied.

"Would forty-three sound right?"

"I, ah," Randall said as he squirmed a bit, "yes," he conceded.

"And for last ten years you have not testified in a criminal trial for the defense even one time, isn't that true?"

"If you say so, yes, it's probably accurate."

"How much did the prosecution pay you to testify today?"

"I am compensated for my time, I do not sell my testimony," Randall indignantly answered.

"I'll rephrase. How much did the taxpayers of the state of Minnesota pay you to compensate you for your time?" Marc took a second to look at Danica Hart who stared straight ahead not daring to return Marc's look.

"Seventy-five thousand dollars," Randall answered.

"Plus expenses which included first-class airfare and a suite at the airport Hilton in Bloomington, isn't that correct, doctor?" Marc asked.

"Yes," the doctor agreed almost too smugly.

Marc silently stared at the witness for several seconds to let that news sink in with the jury. Since they were staying in a Budget Inn, the admission about the suite at a Hilton would be especially annoying.

"I have nothing further..." Marc began. "I'm sorry, your Honor. On second thought, I do have a couple more questions." Marc did this deliberately to make sure he had the jury's attention.

"Proceed," Connors said.

"Brittany Riley is currently under the care of a psychiatrist, isn't she?"

"Yes, I believe so."

"Dr. Lorraine Butler?"

"Yes."

"As part of your review of Brittany Riley's history, were you given the session notes from Dr. Butler?"

"Yes, I was."

"And in those session notes was there a single reference to post-traumatic stress disorder."

"A difference of opinion between two professionals."

"Is that a no, doctor?"

"Yes, that is correct."

"To be clear, there were no references in Dr. Butler's session notes to PTSD were there?"

"No," Randall finally admitted.

"How many hour-long sessions did Dr. Butler have with Ms. Riley?"

"I'm not sure."

"Well, doctor, considering the amount of session notes you were provided, would you believe twelve hours is an accurate number?"

"Yes, that seems accurate."

"So, Dr. Butler spent twelve hours with Ms. Riley in her office conducting individual therapy with her and you spent a grand total of none. Is that true?"

"Objection," Vanderbeck stood and said while Danica Hart silently wished he would stop making it look like he was trying to keep things from the jury.

"Overruled. Answer the question, doctor."

"Yes, that's true but..."

"Nonresponsive," Marc said.

"Is your answer, yes, doctor?" Connors asked.

"Yes, your Honor," Randall admitted.

"Leave it at that. Do you have anything else, Mr. Kadella?"

"One more question, your Honor."

"Go ahead."

"Isn't it true that your belief that PTSD caused Brittany Riley to murder her daughter is totally based on the premise that she, in fact, committed this act?"

"Yes, that's correct."

"I have no further questions."

Before Vanderbeck could begin to attempt to rehabilitate their expert testimony, Hart leaned over and whispered in Vanderbeck's ear. There followed a brief, quiet but heated exchange between them.

"Redirect, Mr. Vanderbeck?" Connors asked.

Reluctantly, Vanderbeck stood and said, "No questions, your Honor."

SIXTY-ONE

The three lawyers left the judge's chambers and made their way into the courtroom. The prosecution had one more part of their case to present and there had been another discussion about it before court began this Friday morning. They made a short videotape of the scene at the river's edge where the body was found. The relevance of the tape had been argued before trial and Judge Connors was going to allow it. Marc had made enough of an objection to it for the record in case of an appeal. Having seen it beforehand he was not overly concerned about it but he didn't want the prosecution to know that. He wanted to keep up the appearance that he was dead set against allowing the tape to be shown.

During the conference in chambers, Marc admitted he would be presenting a defense. The judge looked at his calendar and decided they were going to take testimony on Saturday this week. He wanted to get the case to the jury as soon as possible so they could get back to their lives. Keeping a jury sequestered is hard on them although half of them were probably thinking about book deals.

As the trial had moved along, invariably it had slowed down and the middle part was a bit boring. Over the past several days the crowd had thinned, and the gallery had been barely half full. As Marc walked through the courtroom to the defense table, he looked over the audience and was a little surprised to see the benches were once again packed. Evidently, the prosecution had leaked the news that something significant was going to happen today. A sly, knowing smile appeared on Marc's face as he took his seat next to his client.

Judge Connors took the bench, gave everyone permission to be seated and told the prosecution to begin.

Hart stood up and called the name Linda Johnson to the stand. A professionally dressed, slender woman of medium height and short dark hair entered the courtroom. She made her way up to the witness stand was sworn and seated.

Hart had Johnson explain her occupation, experience, education and other qualifications to the jury. She was a photographer with the Minnesota Bureau of Criminal Apprehension. She was qualified as both a photographer of still camera photos and a videographer.

Hart asked for and received permission to approach the witness. She picked up an evidence bag with an object in it, walked up to Johnson and handed it to her.

"Agent Johnson, I have handed you an object marked state's Exhibit 17, do you recognize it?"

"Yes, it's a DVD of a video I made."

"The state offers state's exhibit seventeen into evidence, your Honor."

"Mr. Kadella?" Connors asked.

"Renew my objection as to relevance and prejudicial with no probative value."

"Noted. Overruled. You may continue, Ms. Hart."

"Agent Johnson, explain to the jury the contents of the DVD. What is on it."

Linda Johnson, a veteran witness knew enough to look at the jury while she talked to them. She explained to them that the prosecution had brought her in to film a demonstration at the site where the remains of Becky Riley were found. Johnson gave them a fairly detailed description of what was on the tape, when it was filmed and how long it was. When she finished, having satisfied the evidentiary requirements to validate the video's authenticity, Hart passed the witness to Marc.

"Agent Johnson, the date you filmed the video contained in state's Exhibit 17 was Tuesday, October 8, is that correct?"

"Yes, that's correct." The woman replied,

"That was four days after the remains of the victim were found, is that also correct?"

"Yes, I believe it was."

Marc looked at the bench and saw a deputy whisper in the judge's ear. "I have no further questions, your Honor'" Marc said.

The deputy stepped away and Connors motioned the lawyers to come forward. When they reached the bench, Connors said. "I got a phone call I need to take. We'll take an early break now."

On the way back to his table, Marc saw Maddy Rivers walking up the aisle toward him. She stood at the rail and when Marc got to her, she said, "She'll be here this afternoon at 1:00."

"Perfect, thanks," Marc answered as Connors ordered the break and quickly headed back to his chambers.

When court resumed Hart called her next witness, Sunday Porter. A young woman a few years older than Brittany was shown into the court. Her resemblance to Brittany Riley was startling and a slight buzz went through the gallery.

She was sworn and took the stand. Hart went through the standard, routine procedure of getting name, address, and occupation on the record. She was a part-time actress hired by the prosecution to take part in a film production. Porter admitted when she found out what it was about and what it was for, she felt a little odd about it. But needing the money, she had agreed to do it.

At that point, Hart removed the disk from the evidence bag and placed it in the DVD player wired to the television. While the BCA agent, Linda Johnson filmed and handled the technical part, Porter performed and narrated what they were doing. The entire movie lasted a little more than thirty minutes. The relevant part, the reason for doing it, was the filming of Porter in the water.

Wearing knee-high rubber boots, the young woman carried a cinder block with a piece of rope attached to it and tied to the ankle of a doll. These items, through this witness, were all marked and entered into evidence. What the film supposedly proved was that a woman the size of Brittany Riley could carry these objects by herself. Porter waded into the water and dropped the cinder block and doll in the exact same spot where Becky was found, the pole that the CSU people had placed in the river marking the spot was still there.

When the film was finished, Hart stood and asked, "At this time your Honor, the state requests that the defendant stand next to the witness for a comparison of their size."

"Mr. Kadella?" Connors said.

"No objections, your Honor," Marc replied. He then whispered to Brittany to go up to the witness stand and stand next to Porter but be very careful not to say a word.

Porter stepped down into the well and the two young women stood side-by-side. They could have been sisters and Hart had them stand there so the jury could get a good look.

"Your Honor, I would like the record to reflect that the witness and the defendant are the same height and size."

"So noted. You may return to your seat, Ms. Riley," Connors politely said.

"I have no more questions," Hart said.

"Mr. Kadella?"

"I have no questions, but I reserve the right to recall her."

"Very well," Connors said. He looked at Porter and said, "Keep yourself available. You can go for now."

"The prosecution rests, your Honor," Hart informed him.

Marc stood up and made the obligatory request that the case be dismissed for failure of the prosecution to present sufficient evidence to support the charges. Connors quickly denied it. Marc then assured him he would be ready to begin his case at 1:00 and Connors broke for lunch.

SIXTY-TWO

Arriving back at the courtroom following the lunch break, Marc was pleased to find Jeff Modell, his office paralegal, seated at the table. As Marc and Brittany passed through the gate Marc asked Jeff, "All set?"

Without answering his boss, Jeff smiled at Brittany and offered to take her coat. As he did this, Marc reached toward Jeff with his overcoat thinking Jeff would take it too. Instead, Jeff turned his back to him just as the coat slipped out of Marc's hand to fall crumpled on the floor.

Jeff hung up Brittany's coat and turned back to the table, ignored Marc and his overcoat and quickly sat down next to Brittany.

"Don't worry, I'll get it," Marc said to Jeff as he bent down to pick up his coat.

"Okay," Jeff said without taking his eyes off of Brittany or his right hand from the back of her chair. "How are you doing?" Jeff asked Brittany.

"Okay," she smiled at the obviously smitten young man.

"You've got some fans out there," Jeff said referring to the pro-Brittany marchers in front of the building. During the week their numbers had grown to over one-hundred. Sheriff Cale was a very displeased man because he had to waste eight to ten deputies to keep the two sides separate. The yelling back and forth was causing concern about the possibility of a clash between them.

"It's nice to know not everyone thinks I'm a monster," she replied.

"Hey! Yoo-hoo," Marc quietly said waving a hand to get Jeff's attention. When he finally took his eyes off of Brittany and looked at Marc, Marc asked, "Are you ready?"

"Oh, yeah. Sure. All set and in the order you gave me."

"Pay attention."

Marc turned around and saw Maddy watching Jeff with a big smile on her face. At that moment, Tony Carvelli and Vivian Donahue reached the front row to sit with the defense supporters. Marc wheeled his chair back to the rail to say hello and chat with them.

"How ya' doing, counselor?" Tony asked.

"Okay," Marc shrugged. "Hello, welcome back," he said when he spotted Brittany's aunt, Charlotte Daniels, sitting with the Rileys.

A minute or so later, the judge came out, took the bench and when everyone returned to their seats, told Marc to call his first witness.

Marc stood and said, "Your Honor, the defense calls Lennon McCartney." The sound of this name, being what it was, caused an immediate buzz through the gallery. A moment later, a woman carrying a leather folder and wearing the dark green pants and tan shirt uniform of an agent of the Minnesota Department of Natural Resources came through the door. She was a fairly tall, fit, and attractive woman with medium length brown hair worn in a ponytail. After being sworn in, she took the stand gave her name including spelling both names, her address and occupation.

Judge Connors, who had indicated to the court reporter to go off the record, asked her, smiling, "Lennon McCartney? Really? Mom a big Beatles fan?"

"Mom and Dad. Dad already had the last name and Mom came up with the first name. Most of the time I like it. It's certainly different and gets people's attention."

Connors told the court reporter to go back on the record and informed Marc he could begin.

Marc had her begin with her education and work record. She told the jury her history with the DNR what her job description was and the geographic zone in which she worked and patrolled.

"Is the area along the river where the remains of Becky Riley were found in your patrol area?"

"Yes, it is."

"Do you routinely patrol this area?"

"Yes, at least once a week. It's an open fishing and hunting spot along the river so I keep an eye out for illegal hunting and fishing there and several other places along the river. I also keep track of the river level, how high or low the river is to monitor flooding."

"Did you patrol this area during the months of August and September of last year?"

"For most of it. I took a couple of weeks of vacation in mid-September."

"Tell the jury what your normal routine would be at this spot on the river."

She explained that she would check any hunters or people fishing for licenses and the amount of game or fish taken. Most of the time, during the week, there would not be anyone there for her to check. Those were the times she would walk the shoreline measuring the height of the river.

"I have to ask, Agent McCartney," Marc began. "If you routinely walk the shoreline measuring the water level how is it you failed to find the body of Becky Riley?" This question had been thoroughly prepared so the witness would not be blindsided by the prosecution with it.

"As you probably recall, we had a lot of snow the previous winter and rain in the spring and early summer. The river's water level was unusually high and the foliage growth, especially the cattails along the river bank, was quite thick. Where the body was found, it would have been farther out in the river than it was when it was found. I'm not even sure you would have seen it even if you had been looking for it which, of course, I wasn't."

Marc asked for and received permission to approach the witness. He picked up a stack of photos and handed McCartney the first one.

"Agent McCartney, I'm showing you a photo marked for identification as defense Exhibit A. Do you recognize it?"

"Yes," she answered. At that moment, Jeff clicked a key on his laptop and the same photo appeared on the TV screen.

"Is Exhibit A the same as the photo on the television screen in the courtroom?"

"Yes, it is."

"Describe for the jury what this picture is."

"Objection," Vanderbeck said. "Foundation."

"Sustained."

"Who took this picture?" Marc asked.

"I did," McCartney replied.

Marc looked at Connors who, being satisfied, told him to proceed. "What is it?"

"It's a photo of the spot where the body was found. You can see the pole the police placed in the water to mark the spot. It was taken, on October 31, Halloween. The date is in the lower right-hand corner."

For the next half hour, Marc stood next to the witness box handing Agent McCartney a series of photos of that area of the river. He went through the same routine with her marking and identifying them and comparing each to the picture Jeff put up on the TV. They were a series of pictures she had taken as the water level of the river rose and then receded beginning in the spring until early autumn. Each one had a measuring device, usually a metal rod stuck in the ground, to show the rising and falling levels.

"I'm showing you defense Exhibit K. Do you recognize it?"

"Yes, it was taken on August eighth. You can see the date." At that point, she opened her leather folder and checked it. "I took that photo on August eighth and then I came back on the twelfth and according to my notes, the river had already receded almost a foot."

During her testimony, there was absolute silence in the courtroom. It was evident to everyone where Marc was going, with the possible exception of Lowell Vanderbeck.

"Your Honor," Vanderbeck stood and said before Hart could stop him. "I fail to see the relevance?"

Connors looked at Marc who said, "We're getting there, your Honor."

"Overruled."

Marc handed her another photo, went through the routine record building questions and asked her to identify it while Jeff put it on the TV screen.

"It's the photo taken on August twelfth."

"Is that the same pole marking the same spot as Exhibit K?" Marc asked as he walked over to the TV.

"Yes, it is."

"Agent McCartney, what is this brown, dirty area on the photo marked Exhibit L a foot or so to the left of your measuring pole?"

"That is the top of a depression where the water had eroded the river bank."

Marc looked at Jeff who put another photo up alongside Exhibit L showing the full eroded area, one of the photos she had already identified and had been entered into evidence.

"Is this the same area after the water level went down, the same eroded area as Exhibit L?"

"Yes, it is. I took that picture on October first after returning from vacation.

A third photo of the same spot went up on the screen alongside the first two.

"Do you recognize this photo?"

"Well, yes. It's a picture of the scene where the body was found."

"Did you take this picture?"

"No, I did not."

"Can you read this, please?" Marc asked pointing to a marker on the photo.

"State's Exhibit 6."

"And do you recognize this?" Marc asked pointing to the object in the photo.

"Yes, it is the pole the police placed in the water to mark the spot where the little girl was found."

Marc walked back to the witness stand and handed her another photo. They went through the identification routine and Marc stood back and let her explain to the jury what it was.

McCartney and Marc's criminalist, Jason Briggs, had tied a rope to a post at the high-water mark along the shore. It was set into the ground at the top of the eroded area. They then tied the rope to the pole in the watermarking the spot where Becky was found. In the photo taken by Briggs with McCartney's camera, was Agent McCartney, standing in the river next to the pole to demonstrate how high the water was on August eighth, about the time Becky was put in the river. The water level would have been up to McCartney's chest.

"Agent McCartney, I would now like you to come off of the witness stand."

When she did, Marc had her pick up the cinder block found in the river with Becky tied to it. The brick weighed almost forty pounds and when she got it, she just held it with her right hand down at her side and faced the jury.

"Agent McCartney, place your left hand on yourself where the water level was on August eighth."

She placed her left hand just below her breasts which made it obvious the cinder block would have been completely underwater.

"In your opinion, could you have carried that cinder block that far into the river and dropped it off?"

"Objection, your Honor. Calls for speculation."

"Overruled, you may answer."

"I don't think so. Carrying something this heavy underwater would be very difficult."

"How about if you were also carrying a thirty-pound child in the other hand?"

"Objection…'

"Sustained. You've made your point."

Marc took the cinder block and made an exaggerated effort to put it back.

"Your Honor," he said turning to the judge while McCartney remained standing. "I would like to have Ms. Riley stand next to the witness for a comparison."

"Objection," Vanderbeck said.

"Overruled. Go ahead."

Brittany walked up to them and the two women stood side-by-side facing the jury. McCartney was at least three inches taller and twenty to thirty pounds heavier. The image and message were quite clear. It was highly unlikely someone Brittany's size could have carried that cinder block and Becky that far into the river.

Vanderbeck conducted the cross-exam for the prosecution which began after the break. The state's attorney did about as good a job as anyone could have, actually impressing Marc. He had McCartney on the stand for almost two hours trying to find a way to crack her story. Having been grilled the same way by Marc's officemate, Barry Cline, McCartney was calm and almost casual in dealing with it. Of course, she also had truth on her side. You don't have to keep track of lies when you don't tell any.

322

The best Vanderbeck could do was get her to admit it was possible to heft the cinder block up onto a shoulder and carry it into the water that way. It was at least something he could argue in closing.

Marc was kicked back on his couch in his apartment when The *Court Reporter* came on that evening at 6:30. He watched with amusement as Melinda Pace and the former fed prosecutor, Steve Farben, argued with defense attorney Andrea Briscomb. Briscomb was arguing that Marc had kicked a large hole in the state's case with the afternoon's testimony. Melinda and Farben still believed a conviction was coming because Kadella didn't come close to proving she didn't do it.

"He doesn't have to prove she didn't do it," Briscomb countered.

"A baby is dead. There's plenty of circumstantial evidence pointing at the mother. In a case like this, the jury is going to want someone to pay for that," Farben argued.

"Yes, I admit that's probably a good point," Briscomb conceded.

Melinda, as usual, got in the last word. "Besides, who's to say she didn't have help? Someone could have been helping her. It certainly makes sense."

Once again, the phone lines at the station lit up congratulating Melinda for not being fooled. Tricky defense lawyers should not be able to get away with confusing the jury with sideshow nonsense. This was still ninety percent the public's sentiment.

SIXTY-THREE

"Your Honor, the defense calls Dr. Jason Briggs," Marc said, calling his next witness. Despite the fact that Judge Connors had not announced that testimony would be taken this Saturday, word had leaked out and the gallery was full again. Marc's witness was led in, sworn and took the stand.

Briggs was almost a professional witness. He had testified in over a hundred trials and was fully prepared by Marc for this one. Like all experts, they started his testimony by building a record of his qualifications. Then the two of them spent a few minutes explaining to the jury what a criminalist did. Essentially, he was a forensic scientist. He was a crime scene and evidence investigator.

Marc received permission to approach the witness and brought a stack of photos with him. These were the same photos of the scene at the river he had gone over with the DNR Agent McCartney the day before. For the trial record and before they could be admitted into evidence, Marc had to have the ones Briggs had taken authenticated by him and verify that he had taken them. Jeff Modell was in attendance again and as Marc went over each picture, Jeff took the opportunity to put them up on the television screen again. Marc took his time to give the jury another good look and Briggs testified that he was the one who took each picture.

They then moved on to the cinder blocks and rope. Briggs admitted the cinder block found in the water attached to Becky Riley's skeleton was an exact match in composition to the ones taken from the Rileys' garage. He also admitted the rope attached to Becky's ankle matched the rope from the garage.

"There is a problem with the rope attached to the victim's ankle," Briggs said.

"Explain that to the jury, please."

"The cut marks don't match." At that point, Jeff put a magnified photo of the river rope up on the screen. "The cut marks on the ends of the rope taken from the river do not match the cut from the one found in the garage. The cuts on both ends of the rope from the river match each other which could only happen if it was cut using the same instrument, a knife or scissors of some kind. I compared the cut marks on the river rope with every knife and scissors at the Rileys' and found none that made that exact cut. But I did find a knife at the Rileys' home that definitely left the cut mark on the end of the rope taken from the Rileys' garage."

Marc held up a knife, received permission to approach the witness and gave it to Briggs. A couple of quick questions and he identified it as the knife he tested that matched the garage rope.

"Is it possible the river rope could have been cut from the garage rope with a different knife or scissors than the one you found?"

"Of course," Briggs answered. "It seems a little odd..."

"Objection, speculation," Hart said.

"He's been qualified as an expert, your Honor," Marc said.

"Yeah, but he's straying a little far off here. I'm going to sustain."

Having scored about all he could with the rope, Marc moved on to the trunk of Brittany's car. Briggs main point was to let the jury know because of how much cinder block residue there was in the trunk and that it was spread throughout, there had to be several blocks in there and not just one. He had to admit that there could have been several in the trunk sometime before and then a single one later.

The most damaging testimony by the defense expert was regarding Becky's blanket, pajamas and the river rope. There was absolutely no residue of any of these items in Brittany's trunk. Briggs was absolutely adamant that there would be. Maybe not all three but at least one of them.

"Why didn't you have an autopsy performed, Dr. Briggs?"

"Autopsies aren't cheap. They will run at least five thousand dollars. Given the condition of the remains and the fact the state's medical examiner was unable to determine a cause of death, it seemed unlikely that a second autopsy would be very helpful."

They took the morning break and then Hart conducted the state's cross exam of Briggs. Hart was very thorough and did an excellent job of going over, in great detail, every possible negative admission to be made of Briggs testimony. The problem she had was that there was really nothing new to bring out. No surprises for the jury. Everything she went over had already been testified to during his direct exam. When she finished, Marc didn't bother to re-direct.

Marc's next three witnesses, in order, were Brittany's aunt and uncle, Charlotte and John Daniels and her brother Timothy Riley. None of them had anything to offer regarding the question of guilt or innocence. None had anything to say about any evidence or exhibits. What they did offer was more testimony about the police and prosecutor's investigation.

Each of them had been brought into the sheriff's department at least twice for an interview. They all testified that, as with everyone the sheriff's department interviewed, it was obvious what they were seeking. They were determined to find people who knew Brittany to testify that she was a bad mother.

Both of the Daniels testified that the police were almost obsessed by it. No matter how many times they told the detectives that they had never seen anything to indicate Brittany was a bad parent, the police would not let it alone. John Daniels even testified he became so tired of it that, on one occasion, he finally just got up and left.

With the Daniels, Hart made a little bit of a score by getting them to admit they did not see Brittany very often to underscore that their knowledge of Brittany as a parent was somewhat limited. It sounded a little weak, even to Hart.

Tim Riley went over the same basic theme during his direct exam also. Tim should have been more credible since he personally saw his sister and niece several times a week, except Tim had a more difficult time with Vanderbeck's cross exam. Even though Marc had anticipated it and brought it out on direct, Tim still spent a long half hour being humiliated with his drug abuse history. Marc objected several times and Connors finally called a halt to it. But again, the state was unable to elicit any damaging testimony about Brittany as a mother.

The remainder of the day was taken up by Floyd and Barbara Riley. They too had been hounded by the investigator's attempts to have them make claims that Brittany was a bad mother. Both of them had been interviewed multiple times allegedly for various things but the discussion always came back to Brittany's parenting.

Marc also had Floyd testify about the cinder blocks and rope. He could not recall where the rope came from or why he had it. Like almost every garage in America, there are any number of things in them that the owner could not recall where they came from or how they ended up in the garage.

Floyd did remember the cinder blocks. He specifically remembered buying them at a local large box hardware-type store, Menard's. He was even able to remember the approximate date when they were purchased and testified he had to make two separate purchases of them. He also specifically remembered buying several extra ones in case they were needed. When Marc asked him why he didn't return them, he merely shrugged and told the jury it wasn't worth the bother. They weren't very expensive, and he kept them in case he might need them for repairs to the wall he built around the patio.

The most significant and helpful part of Barbara's testimony was her admission that the life insurance policy taken out on Becky was Barbara's idea. The premiums, including the investment portion, were barely eighty dollars a month. It could be used for college or whatever Becky wanted. If she wanted to keep it, the premium would never increase, and she would have a couple of million dollars to retire on at age sixty-five. It was an excellent investment. While explaining to the jury that the insurance policy was for her granddaughter's future, Barbara had to stop three or four times to maintain her composure and not break down.

It was Hart's job to cross-examine them. Since the cross is supposed to be limited to what was brought out during the direct exam, and the fact that Barbara had testified for the state already, there wasn't much that would be helpful to the prosecution.

SIXTY-FOUR

When Marc arrived for court on Monday morning, the prosecution team was already there. Seeing a prosecutor in court this early made Marc's mental alarm bell go off. Something was up and it wasn't likely a good thing. Before Marc could place his briefcase on the table, Vanderbeck was next to him.

"We need to see the judge," Vanderbeck said.

"What about?"

Vanderbeck looked quickly at Hart who flipped a hand at Vanderbeck and said, "Tell him. He has every right to know."

"We're going to ask the judge to allow us to reopen our case. He's waiting for us," Vanderbeck curtly said as he walked off toward the door to the back hallway.

Marc and Danica Hart walked together trailing Vanderbeck. Marc asked her, "What's this about?"

A clearly frustrated Hart said, "It's not my idea. Talk to him."

All three lawyers stood in front of Judge Connors desk while Vanderbeck began. "Your Honor, the state requests that we be allowed to reopen our case in chief."

Before Marc could object, Connors held up a hand to him and politely said, "Let's hear him out first, Marc."

"Judge, it is obvious she must have had an accomplice, someone to help her dispose of the body. We believe we should be entitled to a recess and an opportunity to reopen our case to pursue this theory. It was the defense that rushed this case to trial. We believe if we had been given adequate time to investigate we would have found him or her."

"You didn't find Bob Olson, but you believe you would have found this mysterious accomplice?" Marc asked.

"There is no Bob Olson. That's a lie and you know it," Vanderbeck hotly said while Hart's eyes narrowed. Marc's brow furrowed, and he took on a clearly angered expression. With this response from Marc, Vanderbeck took a step back realizing he had gone too far.

Marc, thoroughly fed up with the arrogant Assistant Attorney General, took a step toward Vanderbeck and snarled, "You're accusing me of suborning perjury? You might want to be a little careful here, buster."

"I didn't mean that…" Vanderbeck stammered looking at Connors for help.

"All right you two. Lowell, he has a point. Be careful who you accuse of something that serious."

"I apologize. I didn't mean that."

"Do you have any evidence, anything at all, pointing to a specific person who may have been involved?" Connors asked.

"Not at this time, but…"

"Then there will be no mention, not a word about it in front of that jury. Am I understood?"

"Your Honor," Vanderbeck began. "She had to have had help. That is the only rational explanation…"

"You had your chance. You had the same opportunity to investigate that he did. Allowing you to reopen now would be reversible error and I won't do it. End of discussion."

As the three lawyers were leaving the judge's chambers, Vanderbeck in the lead, Marc gently took Hart's arm and whispered, "What the hell was that all about? He had to know it would be denied."

"I don't know," Hart replied. "He told me about it this morning, too. I told him it was bullshit, but he didn't care."

"Why do I get the feeling I don't trust him?"

"No comment," Hart said.

"The defense calls Cory Graham," Marc said.

A young man, in his mid-twenties, took the stand wearing a short sleeve white shirt buttoned to the throat and khaki slacks. The only thing missing to complete the picture was a plastic pen holder in his shirt pocket.

He croaked out his name and occupation, a techie in the IT department at Menards.

"You seem a little nervous," Marc said. "Have you ever testified in a trial before?"

"Um, no sir. I ah, have not," he replied.

"Relax," Marc said. "Take a deep breath. You'll be fine. We just need a little information from you okay?"

"Yes," he said feeling a little better.

"Menards was served with a subpoena requesting some records you have, is that correct?" This is a leading question but before Vanderbeck could stand to object, Hart grabbed his arm to stop him.

"Yes. I was told by my boss to find any receipts we had for purchases of cinder blocks by a customer, Floyd Riley."

"Did you find any?"

"Yes, two."

Marc received permission to approach and carried two clear plastic evidence bags, each with a single slip of paper in them, to the witness. He went through the routine of having him identify them and testify to their contents. One was a receipt for the purchase of one hundred sixty cinder blocks and the second one was dated three weeks later for an additional twenty-six for a total of one hundred and eighty-six. He then testified he did a search of every purchase made on the Rileys' credit card and found no other purchases for cinder blocks.

Hart, speaking for the state, had no questions. A greatly relieved Cory Graham fled as quickly as he could.

Marc called the Rileys' neighbor, Marty Wilson. He took the stand gave his name, address and occupation; retired, and explained he and his wife lived next door to the Rileys. Marc took some time hearing him explain his relationship with the Rileys, especially Brittany. Since their own four children were all grown and gone, they had become close to both the Riley children, especially Brittany.

He testified about being interviewed by the investigators and that they were mostly interested in Brittany as a mother. Like everyone else called to testify, Wilson had nothing but positive things to say about Brittany and her relationship with Becky.

"In your heart of hearts, Mr. Wilson, having known Brittany Riley since she was a small child," Marc placed his left hand on Brittany's right arm, "do you believe she could have done this?"

"Objection," Hart said standing. "This witness is hardly qualified to give such an opinion."

"He's known her almost her entire life…" Marc began.

"Overruled. The witness can answer, and the jury can give it whatever weight they want. You may answer, sir."

"Not in a million years could I believe that."

"Have you ever helped Floyd Riley with any projects around his house?"

"Sure, in fact, I helped him put up his cinder block wall around his patio."

"If you know, why were there two separate purchases of the cinder blocks?"

"We screwed up our calculations, so we had to make a second purchase."

"How were the cinder blocks delivered, do you know?"

"Sure. Menards delivered the first big batch, I forget how many. Then, to save the cost of delivery, we picked up the second batch."

"Was Brittany's car used?"

"Yes, we put several of the bricks in her trunk. We also used my pickup and Floyd's van.

"Mr. Wilson, a few weeks ago, I asked you and your wife Elaine to perform a task for me. Did you do that?"

"Yes, we both did, separately just as you asked."

"Explain to the jury what that was."

"Well, it was simple enough. I went over to the Rileys' and counted all of the blocks we used to put up their patio wall. I counted them twice just to be sure."

"How many were there?"

"Both times I counted exactly one hundred and eighty."

Marc approached him and handed him the plastic bags with the Menards receipts. He had Wilson again verify the number purchased and compared it with the number used to build the wall.

"How many cinder blocks were left over?"

"Must have been six. I remember there were a few. I helped Floyd put them in the garage."

"To be clear," Marc said, "there were one hundred and eighty cinder blocks used to build the wall and six left over?"

"That would be correct." Wilson agreed.

Elaine Wilson testified next and basically parroted what her husband had said. She was also allowed to give her opinion about Brittany's ability to kill Becky over Hart's objection. She had counted the cinder blocks twice herself and came up with the same number as her husband.

On cross- exam, Hart tried to get both of them to admit they loved Brittany Riley as a daughter to which they both agreed. Then she tried to get them to admit they would say anything to protect her. Again, they both agreed they likely would.

Marc had prepared them for this and on re-direct, he had them testify that even though they would help her, they were telling the truth.

When the court broke for lunch, Hart stepped over to Marc and said, "We're going to go count those bricks on that wall."

Marc smiled and said, "I knew you would. That's why I counted them myself. One eighty it is."

"Shit," a disappointed Hart muttered.

The entire afternoon session was taken up by Brittany's treating psychiatrist, Dr. Lorraine McDowell. They went through the usual routine of placing her credentials on the record and before the jury then moved into the substance of her testimony. The doctor spent a good deal of time rebutting the state's expert regarding PTSD.

"She's not suffering from post-traumatic stress disorder," McDowell stated. "She is suffering from depression due to the death of her child. Also, the media, both locally and nationally have basically labeled her a monster for committing infanticide."

"In your opinion, how is she holding up?" Marc asked.

"Pretty well, all things considered. Between the depression and the fear, stress and anxiety she's dealing with, she's doing well. I see these same symptoms in cancer patients, to give you some idea of what it's like."

"Objection, your Honor. Relevance," Vanderbeck said.

"Overruled but move it along Mr. Kadella."

"During the course of your treatment of Brittany Riley, did the two of you discuss the ten-day period when Becky was missing and her failure to report it?"

"Yes, we did, at length."

"And doctor, did you form a professional opinion about why she failed to report her daughter's abduction?"

"Yes, I did."

"Explain to the jury what your opinion is."

"To be blunt, she's terrified of her mother, Barbara."

With little prompting from Marc, McDowell spent almost an hour going over the history of the Riley family. McDowell gave the jury a full and complete picture of the dysfunctional Rileys and Barbara's treatment of Brittany since childhood. Brittany was simply afraid to disappoint her mother. Having known ahead of time what was coming, Marc had warned Barbara not to be in court, to which she had reluctantly agreed.

Marc then walked her through the events of those ten days. It was McDowell's opinion that Brittany was simply lying to keep Becky's abduction from Barbara and was in fact, trying to find her daughter and get her back. The socializing with her friends was all part of her attempt to convince her family, her friends and even herself that everything was fine and Becky would be home and no one would be the wiser.

Vanderbeck handled the cross exam and he was going to try to diminish her and prop up his own psychiatric expert, especially regarding PTSD. Marc had anticipated this and had set up Vanderbeck knowing his arrogance would get in his way.

"So, you don't believe the defendant snapped because of PTSD, doctor?"

"I don't believe she killed her daughter at all."

"You don't believe she was suffering from PTSD, isn't that true?"

"Yes, that's correct."

"Have you taught any courses or written any papers on PTSD, doctor?"

"No, I have not."

"You're not an expert on PTSD, are you, doctor?"

"Well," she started out slowly, "I have treated almost two hundred patients with PTSD…"

"Nonresponsive," an almost panicky Vanderbeck said to Judge Connors.

"You opened the door. You may as well finish your answer, doctor."

"As I was saying. I work with the VA hospital in Minneapolis and have treated almost two hundred PTSD patients, some going back to the Viet Nam war. I may not have written any papers, but I do have a bit of experience with PTSD patients."

Vanderbeck did his best to stumble through the rest of his cross-exam but the damage had been done. He kept at her for another hour without scoring much to discredit her or help his case. He ended it shortly after five o'clock and Connors adjourned.

The show Melinda Pace aired at 6:30 had only Steve Farben, the ex-prosecutor as a guest. Barely thirty seconds into it, Melinda made the claim that the prosecution had found an accomplice of Brittany and the judge was refusing to allow them to reopen their case. Her entire show was devoted to this new "evidence" and the judge's refusal to allow it into testimony.

In between film clips of the scene at the river where the body was found and Melinda's outrage, Farben solemnly explained the judge's decision. Judge Connors had discretion once the prosecution rested to refuse them permission to reopen their case. But in Farben's opinion, with evidence as significant as this, justice demanded it be allowed in.

The next day, television and newspapers across the country were reporting the accomplice story. Of course, the usual disclaimers were used: "It has been reported that…" and "We could not independently confirm but…" How many readers or viewers paid attention to the disclaimers was anyone's guess.

The next day Judge Connors took a large bite out of the ass of Lowell Vanderbeck. Vanderbeck, for his part, looking as innocent as a newborn, denied any knowledge of how this story got started. Marc merely sat back and smiled.

SIXTY-FIVE

Marc awoke with a start, feeling as if he had been sleeping for just a few minutes. He rolled his head to his left to look at his alarm clock. The digital read showed the time to be not quite 4:30 A.M. Seeing the time, he realized there was a good reason he felt as if he had barely slept because he had barely slept. Marc had tossed and turned, dozed off and on and finally fell asleep between 1:30 and 2:00 A.M.

He rolled to his right, his back to the clock and tried to go back to sleep. Marc lay there for another fifteen minutes before giving up and tossing the blankets aside. He shut off the alarm on the clock, picked up a pair of sweatpants off of the bedroom floor and headed toward the bathroom.

A half hour later he was standing at the living room window watching the snow come down. The weather geeks had called for another three to four inches by morning. Because it was so late in the winter, no one was going to get too excited about three inches of snow. That much would barely affect rush hour traffic.

Standing in the dark, the only light coming from the small kitchen, he was sipping his coffee when his phone went off. A jolt of fear gripped him and he immediately thought about his son and daughter, worried that something happened. Marc snatched the phone from the coffee table, looked at the caller I.D. breathed a sigh of relief and answered it.

"Good God, Connie," Marc said without preamble. "Are you trying to give me a heart attack? Do you know what time it is?"

"Good morning, Marc," Connie Mickelson said ignoring his admonishment. "Don't bullshit me. I knew you'd be up. So, is today the day you put your client on the stand?"

"Why do you want to know? What are you trying to do, win the office pool?"

"No, smartass. I know you. You've been trying to decide for weeks. I've been following the trial and I figured you must be down to her. So, knucklehead, I thought I'd call and give you some support. But if you don't want…"

"You're right. I'm sorry," Marc quietly apologized. "I'm a bit stressed. And I actually decided a couple weeks ago she has to testify. The jury needs to hear from her, I think. They need to hear her say she didn't do this."

"And today's the day and you've been second guessing yourself all night."

"Yeah, I have. It's just, well. I'm not sure if it's worth the risk. I think I have this thing bagged…"

"Really? According to our self-proclaimed media professionals, you're getting your ass kicked."

"That's what I hear. Fortunately, Melinda Pace isn't on the jury," Marc laughed.

"Marc go with your first instinct. Is Brittany ready for it?"

"Yes, I think so."

"Then she'll probably do just fine."

"Yeah, you're right. Hey, thanks, Mom. I'll call you later and let you know how it went."

Marc swiveled around in his chair to face the gallery just to look them over. The usual support group was there on behalf of Brittany plus a few more. In the front row were Brittany's two new best friends, the large Butch Koll and his even bigger friend Andy Whitmore. With them were all three Rileys, including her brother, Tim. The second row contained Maddy Rivers, Tony Carvelli, Vivian Donahue and Brittany's aunt and uncle, Charlotte and John Daniels. Marc stood up and walked to the rail. Starting with the bodyguards, he went down the line, shook hands with each of them and took a minute to thank each of them individually for being there.

Obviously, Connie Mickelson wasn't the only one who had guessed what was coming today. Before retaking his seat, he noticed Gabriella Shriqui directly across the aisle from Madeline. She looked up at Marc, smiled and wiggled her fingers at him. He returned the smile, sat back down and swiveled back to the table next to Brittany.

"How are you doing?" he asked as he took her right hand in his left.

"I'm pretty nervous."

"You'll be fine. Once I get you to start talking, you'll be fine. And it's okay to be nervous. Who wouldn't be? Just remember, when Hart cross-examines you, she's going to want you to get angry and lash out at her. Don't do it."

"I know. I understand. Are you sure she will question me?"

"Yeah, they'd be damn fools to let a man come after you. If it is Vanderbeck, same thing applies. Take your time and do your best to stay calm. I'll do what I can to help you. Don't worry. You did great when Barry cross-examined you and he's better at it than either of them."

Judge Connors took the bench and when everyone sat back down, told Marc he could begin. Marc called Brittany Riley to the stand a slight buzz went through the crowd and Brittany was sworn and seated.

Marc started her out by having her tell her life's story to the jury. She had done this in sessions with Dr. McDowell and they had used those session notes to prepare her testimony. This allowed Marc to move her along and prevent the prosecution from using those notes to impeach her. The doctor's notes had been given to the prosecution as well and if she testified about something that was significantly different, Marc believed Hart would drill her with the inconsistency.

A half hour into the direct exam, Vanderbeck stood and objected as to the relevance. Marc was a little surprised it was Vanderbeck who objected since it is normal that the lawyer who will conduct the questioning should be the one to handle objections.

"May we approach, your Honor?" Vanderbeck asked before Connors ruled on his objection.

The three lawyers stood at the bench and Vanderbeck said, "This is all very interesting your Honor but totally irrelevant."

Before Marc could say anything Connors said, "No, the jury wants to hear from her. I'm going to allow it."

"Objection overruled," the judge said while the lawyers went back to their tables.

Marc and Brittany continued and by the time 10:30 rolled around, the entire courtroom was convinced the Rileys were one messed up family. Having been fully warned ahead of time what was coming, the three of them, Barbara, Floyd and Tim, sat stoically in the front row keeping their thoughts to themselves. With a tiny exception, a single tear trickled from each of Barbara's eyes when the jury looked at her after Connors called for a break.

After the morning break, for the last forty-five minutes of the direct exam, Brittany told the jury about her brief marriage, her young husband's death and her life with Becky. This was the first time since the trial started that the jury saw her brighten, enlivened and appearing happy. She went into almost trivial detail describing the day-to-day routine of loving and caring for her daughter.

"I have sat in that chair," Brittany said, unfolding her hands from her lap and pointing at the defense table, "for weeks listening to people accuse me of a terrible crime. I go to my parents' house at night and I try not to pay attention, but I can't help see how much people hate me…"

"Your Honor," Vanderbeck softly said as he rose from his chair."

"I'm going to allow it. Please sit down."

"As hard as that is to handle," she continued, "It's nothing next to hearing my baby described as 'remains' and 'the body' and listen to people explain how she was found." Brittany stopped here, took a deep breath and a drink from a glass of water she had.

"I, ah, I, I, just want to crawl in a hole sometimes," she sobbed, and the tears started to flow. "I just want it to be a bad dream. To wake up and, ah," she sobbed again. "To, ah, have my baby back…" She stopped and put her left hand turned into a fist, to her mouth and looked away from the jury. Marc stood up and showed a handkerchief to the judge who motioned for him to come forward. Marc handed her his handkerchief which she immediately used to wipe her eyes and blow her nose.

Marc returned to his chair and quietly sat waiting for her to indicate she was all right. While waiting, he took the opportunity to sneak a look at the jury. If he could have, he would have whooped for joy. Including the men, there wasn't a dry eye to be found.

Brittany took several more sips of water and a couple of deep breaths before looking at the judge and saying, "Sorry." He smiled at her and indicated to Marc to continue.

"Brittany," he began without the formality of calling her Ms. Riley, "I only have one more question. Did you kill your daughter, Becky and throw her body in the Mississippi River?"

Brittany took another deep breath, turned to look at the jury and softly, almost in a whisper, said, "No."

Judge Connors adjourned for lunch and Brittany sat down next to Marc. As the jury filed out almost every one of them turned to give her a quick, sympathetic look. Marc noticed this and if he could, he would have ended the trial that exact minute. Instead, he put his arm around Brittany's shoulders, gave her a little hug and said, "You did just fine."

"I wish it was over," she quietly said.

"It will be soon."

Maddy sat down in the chair on the other side of Brittany and held her hand "I'm proud of you. That took a lot of courage."

"We're all set?" Marc asked Maddy.

"Yes, for the tenth time."

"Sorry. I'm just, you know, that way."

"It's okay," Madeline said. "Yes, we're set."

337

SIXTY-SIX

"You may proceed," Connors said looking at the prosecution table.

"Thank you, your Honor," Vanderbeck replied.

Upon hearing Vanderbeck's voice responding to the judge, Marc's eyebrows went up and he stole a quick glance at Danica Hart. Hart slyly returned Marc's curious look. She had both hands flat on the table and raised just her thumbs as if to say, "What can I tell you? It's not my idea."

Marc pressed his lips in a tight smile, looked at Brittany who was staring at him and winked at her. Having a man go after Brittany when there was a woman who could do it and do it better in Marc's opinion, was a serious mistake.

Vanderbeck started out softly, probably a concession to Hart and her influence. He went over the day Becky first came up missing and what Brittany claimed she did, getting her to simply repeat her story of how she searched for Bob Olson and her daughter.

"You spent the entire day driving around trying to find them, is that your testimony?"

"Yes."

"And you saw no one, talked to no one, told no one what happened, is that correct?"

"Yes."

"You didn't call the police, your parents, your friends, no one, is that true?"

"Yes," she agreed.

"And after spending the entire day in this exhausting, fruitless search for your daughter, you went out partying with your friends that very night didn't you?" At that moment one of the photos of Brittany and her friends at a bar appeared on the television screen.

"Yes, but…" she tried to explain.

"And that evening," Vanderbeck said cutting her off, "you did not tell any of these three best friends your daughter was missing did you?"

"No," she quietly answered.

Using this same technique Vanderbeck took her through the entire period before Becky's disappearance was reported to the police. Every day was recalled in great detail and he again forced her to admit she did not tell anyone. In fact, he made her admit over and over that she spent the entire ten-day period lying to her friends, co-workers and family.

Vanderbeck spent almost twenty minutes on just the night of the wet T-shirt contest. Of course, the picture of her holding the trophy was up on the TV during this line of questioning. To break up his rhythm, Marc finally objected and to his surprise, Connors sustained him and told Vanderbeck to move along and remove the photo from the TV screen.

During most of this, Marc kept a close eye on the jury to gauge their response. At times, this stoic bunch of Minnesotans was very difficult to read. All of them watched and listened mostly stone-faced. Fortunately, Marc's officemate, Barry Cline, had put Brittany through a mock cross-exam far worse than what Vanderbeck was doing or what he could get away with. Brittany was handling it fairly well, although at times she was noticeably embarrassed.

Just before he got to the day when Barbara notified the police, Vanderbeck abruptly switched gears.

"Isn't it true, Ms. Riley, on the Saturday when over three thousand volunteers went to Lebanon Hills, a park in Eagan, to search for your daughter, you were not there? Yes or no."

"No, I wasn't."

"Because you knew she wasn't there because you and your accomplice threw her body…"

"Your Honor!" Marc jumped from his seat.

"You're risking a mistrial, Mr. Vanderbeck," the judge sternly admonished him.

"I believe I have the right to probe into her use of an accomplice," Vanderbeck defiantly said.

At that moment the light went on in Marc's head and before a visibly angry Connors could reply, Marc almost yelled out, "Your Honor, please. May we approach?"

By now there was a noticeable buzz flowing through the gallery; almost everyone wondering where this business of an accomplice came from. If they were wondering, the jurors must be as well.

Connors motioned the lawyers to come forward and as they did he banged his gavel twice and snarled for quiet.

"Your Honor," Marc whispered. "He's doing it intentionally. He's trying to provoke you into ordering a mistrial."

"I resent…" Vanderbeck started to protest.

"Be quiet," Connors said glaring at the prosecutor. The judge leaned back in his chair, narrowed his eyes to angry slits and said. "We'll recess for fifteen minutes. Take the jury out and I want the lawyers in chambers."

No one in the gallery, the jury or watching on TV knew exactly what had happened. But it was apparent the judge was extremely displeased.

By the time they got back to the judge's chambers, Connors had taken several deep breaths and was much calmer. Marc didn't wait for the judge to begin.

"Judge, he's getting his ass handed to him and he's…"

"I resent that…"

"...trying to provoke a mistrial. He wants another bite at the apple. And more time to investigate and..."

"That is preposterous," Vanderbeck tried to protest.

Connors was standing casually behind his large, over-stuffed, leather chair. He was leaning on the back of it listening to this exchange. Vanderbeck and Marc were both standing in front of his desk glaring at each other while Hart sat on a couch across the room.

"The problem you have is," Connors said addressing Vanderbeck, "I believe him." Before Vanderbeck could protest again, the judge held up his left-hand palm out, to cut him off.

Connors pointed his index finger at him and said, "I specifically warned you about this. You admitted you have no evidence of an accomplice. You're at best, fishing and I'm not going to allow it. There will be no mistrial. Not at this point. But before you leave today, you will get your personal checkbook out and write a check to the court for five hundred dollars. The next time you try this you will add a zero on that."

"The jury needs to be told..." Marc started to say.

"I'll take care of it," Connors assured him. "You can go now."

Marc and Danica Hart followed a steaming Vanderbeck into the courtroom. A few minutes later, court resumed.

Connors addressed the jury and firmly explained to them that they were to absolutely disregard any reference to an accomplice. He went over it very thoroughly to make sure they understood that there was no evidence of an accomplice and the prosecution had no business bringing the subject up. When he finished he gave Vanderbeck permission to continue.

Vanderbeck spent the next hour going over every detail about the mysterious and vanished boyfriend, Bob Olson. He made excellent use of the fact that she dated him for weeks, claimed they had a sexual relationship yet not a single friend, family member or even casual acquaintance had ever met him, seen them together or even spoke to him. No friends, no family, no co-workers knew anything about him. And Brittany never met any of his friends, family or co-workers.

"You want this jury to believe that this went on for over two weeks then, poof, he disappeared and took your daughter with him?"

"Yes, because it's true," she meekly replied.

By this point, Vanderbeck was risking an objection for badgering her but Marc decided to let it go. Observing the jury, he believed they were giving off a definite vibe that Vanderbeck was going a little too far.

"Isn't it true," Vanderbeck quietly said, "no one ever saw this alleged boyfriend, Bob Olson, because he doesn't exist..."

"No," Brittany said emphatically.

"And that, along with all of the other lies you told, this was just another one?"

"No, that's not true."

"And isn't it true that you murdered your daughter then threw her in the river like so much garbage just to get your single girl, party lifestyle back?"

"No! That's not true," she yelled back at him.

"I have nothing further, your Honor."

"Re-direct?" Connors asked Marc.

"No, your Honor," Marc replied.

"The witness is excused," Connors told Brittany. While Brittany hurried back to the defense table, Maddy Rivers got up and started walking toward the exit. "Call your next witness, Mr. Kadella."

"The defense calls Julie Makie, your Honor."

"Objection, your Honor," a puzzled Vanderbeck stood and said.

"She's on my witness list, your Honor."

"Overruled."

Maddy came back in holding the elbow of a young woman. Makie was a sandy-haired pretty girl in a simple, unadorned way. Dressed in slacks, a sweater and plain flat shoes, she came across as everyone's daughter or cousin you'd like to have. She passed through the gate, looked at Brittany and gave her a little smile. For her part, Brittany looked totally shocked to see her.

She was sworn, seated and gave her name and address. Marc, having thoroughly prepared her, had her explain who she was, where she worked and where she had been since the previous summer. Julie admitted to the jury that Marc had flown her back to Minnesota several days ago and put her up in a nice hotel by the airport.

At this point, Vanderbeck requested a meeting in chambers, which was granted. The jury took a quick break while the lawyers went backstage again.

"Your Honor, we were not notified about this witness," Vanderbeck meekly complained.

"She was a co-worker of Brittany's. She's on our witness list. If your investigators didn't find her to interview, that's not my problem. You had notice by way of the witness list. I don't have to drive witnesses to the sheriff's office for you," Marc replied.

"We knew of her, your Honor. We could not find her. She vanished."

"I found her. Or, more precisely my investigator found her. Again, not my problem."

"We're being ambushed, your Honor," Vanderbeck tried to protest.

"That does appear to be the case and he's done a nice job of it," Connors replied. "What is she going to testify about?"

"The mysterious Bob Olson."

"She saw him?"

"Yes, your Honor."

"This ought to be good," Connors said.

"Your Honor, we need some time to prepare…"

"No, you had months to find her. You just admitted you knew about her. Although," he turned to Marc, "I am a little uncomfortable with you keeping her hidden in a hotel."

"Judge, you said it. They had months to find her. We did. She volunteered to testify but couldn't afford to fly back. So we flew her back, put her in a hotel for a few days. She's our witness. We did nothing wrong."

"I agree," Connors said with a shrug. "Let's go."

Julie made a great witness. She was calm, smart, articulate and quite sure of herself. With just a few questions from Marc, she took the jury through her story.

Just before she got to the bombshell of identifying Bob Olson, Marc placed a large poster board with the six drawings Maddy had emailed her. At that point, Marc motioned for Hart and Vanderbeck to join him at the bench.

"Do you want me to put Ms. Rivers on the stand to confirm this? She's here and we can do it."

"We'll stipulate, your Honor," Hart conceded. When she got back to her table Hart made a statement for the record stipulating that these were the drawings emailed to Makie.

Marc had Julie tell the jury that when she received them she recognized one immediately. It was the drawing of Bob Olson.

"You're sure you saw him before?"

"Yes."

"When and where?"

By the time she finished Connors was pounding his gavel for quiet. Several members of the media had scrambled out of the courtroom, barely waiting to hit the door before using their phones.

Hart conducted the cross-exam, but it was ineffective. Having had no chance to interview her or prepare an examination, the best Hart could do was try to make her appear less credible. Hart's best effort was to take shots at her for not coming forward sooner. To make it look like Julie and Brittany had become best friends and had concocted this entire story about seeing Bob Olson in a last-second effort to fool the jury. It came across as weak and desperate. Julie testified they were hardly best friends and admitted she knew Brittany had been arrested but heard nothing about Bob Olson. Because of that, she had no idea she might have information and could be a witness. It wasn't long before Hart gave it up.

Marc rested his case. Connors asked the prosecution if they were calling any rebuttal witnesses and when informed they were not, ordered both sides to give closing arguments the next day. Marc again made the obligatory formal request for dismissal which Connors quickly denied.

The jury filed out, the gallery started to empty, and Julie Makie greeted Brittany with a hug.

"Why didn't you tell me you found her? I wouldn't have been so stressed out."

"I didn't want your testimony to be tainted. I wanted Vanderbeck to pound you about Olson and then spring our little surprise. I just hope it worked."

Melinda Pace received her cue from the director that the cameras were running. She stared straight at the camera and said, "Stop the presses, ladies and gentlemen. Notify Hollywood that we have the winner for the next Academy Award for best actress on a witness stand. In all my years as a lawyer, reporter and journalist covering trials, I have never seen a performance to match what Brittany Riley put on today."

The camera went to a wide shot to show all three people, Melinda, Farben and Briscomb on the set. Another twenty-two minutes of carefully edited highlights and commentary. At the end of it, Melinda scoffed at Brittany's performance and the "alleged" sighting of Bob Olson by a last-second witness she referred to as Brittany's best friend. Farben disagreeing a bit with Melinda conceded it was a good day for the defense but believed she would still be found guilty. Andrea Briscomb flat out told both of them they were wrong. She predicted that the jury, after several days of deliberations, would acquit her. Briscomb then went on to remind the audience that a not guilty is a long way from innocent.

343

SIXTY-SEVEN

To Marc's surprise, Danica Hart arose from her chair when Judge Connors told the prosecution to begin their closing argument. This is the final spotlight moment of a trial; the last chance to sway a jury to decide the case your way. Marc would have bet just about anything that Vanderbeck would be the one to give it. Hart, arguing to the jury was of greater concern. He believed she would be more professional, dispassionate and convincing than Vanderbeck.

The closing statement or, more normally and accurately called the closing argument is the lawyers' chance to argue their case to the jury. It is one last chance to pull their evidence, witnesses and exhibits together to convince the jury to see things their way.

While listening to Hart, Marc quickly realized she was simply going to mostly ignore the defense case. Apparently, she decided their best bet was to walk the jury through the prosecution's case.

She started out by giving the jury a brief explanation of what a circumstantial evidence case is. Essentially, it is one in which there are no eyewitnesses to the event. The evidence is laid out for the jury and the conclusion is clear.

Hart skillfully used the television screen to go over every piece of evidence, each witness's testimony and all of the exhibits. During the presentation, she hammered two main themes: "Who stood to gain and use your common sense?" Hart was also careful not to overdo either of them. She interspersed both the question of "who stood to gain" and "use your common sense" not too much and not too few times throughout her argument.

The one piece of the defense case she could not ignore was the testimony of Julie Makie. If the state was to get a conviction, they had to show, beyond a reasonable doubt that the story of the missing boyfriend was a fantasy. Hart gave it her best shot and made Marc squirm a little and wondered if she wasn't pulling it off.

Using a voice inflection bordering on obvious sarcasm, she tried punching holes in Makie's credibility as the conveniently reclusive best friend, co-worker who came riding in at the last minute. What a significant coincidence it was that out of the hundreds of people who were questioned, Julie Makie was the only one to have seen the mysterious and vanished Bob Olson. Hart again made the point to the jury to use their common sense and disregard Makie's testimony as an obvious last-ditch effort to help a friend.

Hart concluded her presentation of the evidence by going over the most damning part of the story. Again, using the television to put up the photos they had all seen many times, she relived Brittany's behavior during the ten days before Becky was reported missing. Of course, the very last photo to be displayed was the wet T-shirt contest winner.

When this went up on the screen, Hart, who had been standing a respectful distance in front of the jury, took two steps toward Brittany. She silently stared at her for several seconds, looked at the image on the TV then turned back to the jury.

Marc slipped his left hand under the table where Brittany had her hands clasped together. She grabbed his fingers so tightly he almost let out a yell. While Hart continued, the two of them sat silently, Brittany trembling and praying she would finish soon.

Hart looked at the jury, slightly shook her head, pointed at the television and said, "This is what she was up to while her daughter decomposed in the mud, the weeds and the filth of the Mississippi River."

Marc, his fingers still being crushed under the table by Brittany, looked over the jury and noticed more than a few sniffles and tears. He considered objecting since there was no evidence that Becky had been put in the river at that time. He decided against it. Why draw even more attention to it when Hart was moving on?

While keeping the wet T-shirt photo on the screen, Hart began to slowly pace in front of the jury.

"Let's talk about reasonable doubt for a moment," she began. "Reasonable doubt does not mean beyond all doubt. Use your common sense, use your common sense, use your common sense," she repeated while slowly making eye contact with every juror. "Motive, ladies and gentlemen. Who stood to gain? Who was going to be relieved of the burden of raising a child by herself? Brittany Riley. Who was going to be able to go back to her party girl lifestyle? Brittany Riley. Who was going to be paid five hundred thousand dollars from an insurance policy?" Hart paused, shrugged her shoulders, looked over the jury and said, "Brittany Riley. And all of the evidence points right at her and no one else. Use your common sense and find Brittany Riley guilty on all counts."

Hart had spoken for two and a half hours without notes and it seemed to take less than half that time. Before she started, Marc felt very confident about his case; maybe a little too confident. Hart's presentation had slapped him back to the reality that this case could still be lost.

Connors was back on the bench precisely at one o'clock. It was his intention to get the closing arguments over and get the case to the jury today.

Marc started out, as Hart had done, by thanking the jury for their time, service and sacrifice.

In less than half the time that Hart took, Marc went over the state's case and the holes he had punched in it. The explanation of the ten days when Brittany failed to report her daughter missing backed up by her psychiatrist. The efforts Brittany made to find Becky. Marc used the pictures of the DNR agent to show them the extreme improbability bordering on impossibility that Brittany could have carried that cinder block and a thirty-pound child into the deep water of the river. All the while he did this, he was using a large whiteboard that had been wheeled into the courtroom. It was placed less than ten feet in front of the jury. With each piece of the state's evidence he talked about, he wrote a letter on the whiteboard, beginning with the letter A. But they were scattered and spread out. Not listed in a straight line. When he finished with the last one, he placed the marker he was using on the tray of the framework. He stepped close to the jury box and looked them all over.

"Here's what they're trying to do," he almost whispered. "They're trying to get you to do their job for them. They're trying to get you to connect the dots for them." Marc stepped back and pointed at the scattered letters on the whiteboard symbolizing the state's evidence.

"The prosecution has thrown their evidence up on the wall and with a sly wink and a nod, they are trying to get you to draw the line from Point A to their conclusion to find guilt." Marc stepped back to the whiteboard and using the marker, drew a crooked and convoluted line through all of the letters he had written on the board. Marc finished drawing his line, looked at the jury and stunned that he had not drawn an objection, continued. "That's not your job. That's their job. They are supposed to connect the dots for you, not you for them."

He flipped the whiteboard over to show the other side to the jury. On this side, he had previously written the same number of letters only they were in a straight line across the board.

"This is what they are supposed to do for you. Start here, at Point A," he said using the marker to point at the letter A. "And draw a straight line from A to B to C to D until they get to guilty beyond a reasonable doubt." He rapped the board with the knuckles of his left hand and said, "This is what it is supposed to look like, and it is not your job to make it so, it's theirs. It's not your job to connect the dots for them. It is their job to connect the dots for you. The reason they aren't able to do that is because Brittany Riley is not guilty.

"Julie Makie," Marc said as he walked back toward the jury. "Ms. Hart did an admirable job of trying to show that Ms. Makie lacked credibility. Why? Julie Makie had no reason to lie. She was an acquaintance of Brittany's, a co-worker. She wasn't a close friend, let alone a best friend, who might be convinced to lie. They worked in departments at Macy's that were close to each other, they had lunch

346

together a few times. That's it. They didn't socialize together. Didn't go out together, they were casual acquaintances from work. Then, just before this happened, Julie had to go home to be with her family. Her dad had cancer and she went to help her mother. After her dad became better, she went to China and was out of touch from this highly publicized trial. What possible reason did she have to come back here and lie? The truth is she has no reason to lie and she didn't.

"The prosecution did everything they could to portray Bob Olson as a figment of Brittany Riley's imagination; a massive lie that she concocted to place blame on someone else. They scoffed at the notion that he was real. Then along comes Julie Makie and under oath, without ever having spoken to Brittany Riley about this, identifies the drawing Brittany helped make as someone she saw while working at Macy's. Someone she saw checking out Brittany in the Men's Department near where Julie worked. The state has come up with nothing to refute her testimony. Bob Olson is a real person.

"The defense has no obligation to find the real culprit. This isn't TV and I'm not Perry Mason. It's up to the police to solve this crime and not the defense. But we did it. We did find him or at least identify him sufficiently to create reasonable doubt.

"The Holy Grail of the state's case, the most important piece of evidence they needed to bolster their claim that Brittany wanted to free herself from motherhood was to find someone, anyone, to testify that she was a bad mother. Using the power of the government, they sent their investigators to every corner of this state and talked to everyone and anyone who knew Brittany, searching desperately for someone to tell them this; to tell them Brittany Riley was a bad mother who wanted to get out from under the burden of raising a child on her own. In fact, they did it over and over and even went beyond harassing some of them to badger them into saying this. And ladies and gentlemen, they found no one. Not a single person who really knew her who had anything to say except that she was a loving, caring young mother for whom the sun rose and set with her daughter.

"Finally, Ms. Hart skillfully used the themes of who would gain by Becky's death and to 'use your common sense'. I agree with her. Use your common sense. If you are going to believe the state, what you have to believe is that Barbara Riley insisted Brittany take out an insurance policy for Becky to use as an investment and savings account. Brittany then took thirty thousand dollars from the proceeds of her husband's death, her own money, and deposited it into that policy on the same day the policy was obtained. Then barely two months later, this young woman, who everyone said was a loving, caring mother woke up one day and decided to murder her daughter. The beautiful little girl who was the light of her life. And they, the prosecution, want you to use your common sense to believe this." At this point, Marc paused and stood in front of the jury and silently looked each of them in the eye.

"Use your common sense, ladies and gentlemen. There is reasonable doubt all throughout this case. Find Brittany Riley not guilty and let her go home and try to pick up the pieces of her life."

SIXTY-EIGHT

Marc looked at the clock on the dashboard which read 7:12 A.M. He stopped at the stop sign where County 42 meets Minnesota 55. Before making the right-hand turn onto 55 to head toward Hastings, he patiently waited for a large semi with a line of several cars to go by.

Marc spent last evening and this morning thinking over the trial and what he would have, could have or should have done differently. It's always easier to say "don't second guess yourself" than to actually not second guess yourself. This morning, while he drove the last few miles to the courthouse, he satisfied himself that he had done as good a job as anyone reasonably could and with that thought, let it go.

The day before, after Marc's closing argument, the lawyers met with Connors one more time to discuss jury instructions. Marc and Danica Hart were satisfied with what the judge had decided upon. Vanderbeck took this one last chance to weaken the instruction on reasonable doubt. Connors was not to be swayed and brushed Vanderbeck aside.

Judge Connors gave the jury their instructions and by five o'clock sent them off to deliberate. The jury was led out and the only people who left the courtroom were the judge and court personnel. Virtually no one else, at first, even moved. They all hung around and after a little while, the crowd began wandering in and out of the courtroom, until 8:00 when Connor's clerk announced the jury was done for the night.

On his way home, Marc stopped at his office to pick up case files and correspondence from his desk, things he could work on the next morning at the courthouse. He awoke at 6:00 A.M. and was out the door by 6:30. There was no reason for him to go to the courthouse this early. The jury probably wouldn't start before 8:00 and Connors' clerk would call if they came in with a verdict. Something in the back of his mind told him it was going to be this morning and he could not stop himself from getting there as early as possible.

As he drove up to the private parking in the back of the building, a deputy held up a hand to stop him. Marc buzzed his window down and the woman, who Marc recognized but could not remember her name, greeted him.

"Good morning, Mr. Kadella. I'm sorry but I can't let you park back here anymore. Sherriff Cale's orders. He says the trial is over and you'll have to park out front."

"Really? Does he know he may have a riot on his hands when the jury comes in?"

She leaned a little closer into Marc's open window and said, "Believe me, all of the deputies know. We've been trying to get him to

349

bring in some help from the state, but…" she shrugged her shoulders and raised her eyebrows. "Sorry."

Marc approached the deputy guarding the courtroom door. Before he could say anything she opened it and held it for him. "Thanks, Carla," he said to her. Carla Mason had been one of six deputies in the courtroom during the entire trial. Marc had made a special effort to learn their names. He always figured it can't hurt to be friendly with people who carry guns.

He placed his coat and briefcase in one of the client conference rooms then went back to see if Connors or his clerk were in. His clerk was at her desk and he knocked on her open door.

"Morning, Marion," he said when she looked up and saw him.

"You're here early," she replied.

"Couldn't sleep. Is the judge in yet?"

"Yeah, he's around somewhere. The jury's already at it."

"Oh, really?" Marc asked a bit surprised. "I'll be around in one of the conference rooms by the exit doors."

"Okay. Let me know if you go anywhere, please."

"Sure, no problem."

Marc retreated to the small room and started to work through the pile he had brought along. Judge Connors stopped by to say hello and starting shortly after 8:00, Marc began taking phone calls. On the drive in this morning, he had stopped at a Starbucks for a large coffee and bought a copy of both the Minneapolis and St. Paul papers. Since the phone was going to continue to interrupt him anyway, he set aside his work. His mind wasn't on it and he was more curious about what the papers had to say.

In between phone calls, the arrival of Brittany and her support group, he managed to read the paper's accounts of yesterday's events. To his surprise, both papers had very good things to say about him and his closing. The gist of it was that what had appeared to be a for sure conviction was no longer as certain.

Just before 9:00 he heard a light rap on the door and looked up to see the tempting dark eyes of Gabriella Shriqui when she poked her head through the door.

"Good morning, Gabriella."

"Mind if I join you? If you're busy…" she said when she saw the files on the table.

"Nah, come on in. I was going to try to do this," he said waving a hand at the letters and documents on the table, "but I'm not getting anywhere with it anyway."

Gabriella sat down across the table from him and Marc said, "We are off the record? No microphones or hidden cameras?"

"No, none of that," she laughed. "Yes, we're off the record. Seriously," she continued, "how are you doing and how's Brittany holding up?"

"I'm okay. I just spoke to Brittany. They're down in the cafeteria. She didn't sleep a wink last night. None of them did. They're all pretty stressed."

"I can't even imagine. I wanted to tell you how sorry I am about how we, the media, treated her. I'm not going to give you any bullshit about the public's right to know or any other crap like that. Innocent or guilty, she did not deserve to be treated the way she was."

"Thanks, Gabriella. I don't mean to make you feel worse, but she is innocent."

"I believe that, now. And from what I'm hearing from my cynical brethren, it's running about sixty-forty in your favor."

"What are you doing here already?"

"Got a call from a source, told me the jury started up again at 7:00. So, here I am in case..."

"How do you get calls like that? I don't get calls like that."

"We, ah, have a cash expense account for such matters."

The two of them chatted for the better part of an hour. Every few minutes they were interrupted by a phone call to Marc. Madeline called, and Marc gave the phone to Gabriella. Marc finished glancing through the papers, mostly the sports sections, while the two women gabbed for twenty minutes.

At 10:00 there was a knock on the door and the judge's clerk opened it, looked at the two of them and said, "They're in. The judge wants the verdict read at 11:00."

"Thanks, Marion." Marc looked at Gabriella as the door closed and said, "Get out. I gotta make some calls."

"What do you think?" Gabriella asked as she stood to leave.

"I don't know," Marc shrugged. "Really, I can't guess these things."

Gabriella reached across the table and took Marc's right hand in both of hers, looked him in the eyes and said, "Good luck. I really mean that. I hope you win."

Marc nervously smiled at her and said, "Thanks, kid. Now go. I have calls to make."

When eleven o'clock rolled around, every local TV station, all of the networks, both broadcast and cable, were preempting their programming and carrying the courtroom feed live. They all had their

351

"expert" commentators either live in-studio or on the phone line ready to give their view of why the jury was either right or wrong. Later, the numbers would show that more people nationwide watched the verdict being read than voted in the last presidential election.

There is an old belief among defense lawyers that if the jurors look at your client when they come into the courtroom with the verdict, it's good news. Marc tended to believe it but he had not told Brittany this. She had enough on her plate as it was.

At 11:10 Connors took the bench and after everyone sat down, the judge spent a few minutes lecturing the crowd on court decorum. While he did this, Marc glanced over at Danica Hart. Their eyes met briefly and each smiled and nodded at the other.

The jurors were led in and Marc's heart jumped a bit when he saw each and every one of them look directly at Brittany. At least half of them even smiled. The verdict form was handed to the judge who read it and sent it back to the jury foreman. Connors looked down at Marc and Brittany and politely told her to stand which they both did.

The foreman, the retired dentist named Allan Cheever, rose and looked at the judge. Connors nodded slightly giving him permission to speak. By this point, no one in the courtroom was breathing.

"We the jury, in the matter of the State of Minnesota versus Brittany Ann Riley, unanimously find the defendant not guilty of all charges."

The instant she heard the man say "not guilty" Brittany burst into tears, brought her hands to her face and started to collapse. When her knees started to buckle Marc grabbed her under the arms and gently lowered her to her chair. The courtroom erupted, and it took Connors three full minutes of gavel pounding to get the place quiet again.

An hour later, Marc stood at the entrance to the courthouse looking out toward the parking areas. To his left, by the administration building, were almost two hundred marchers carrying signs supportive of Brittany. To his right, along the sidewalk in front of the jail, was more than twice that number in the anti-Brittany crowd. In between them were more than fifty sheriff's deputies from Dakota and several other surrounding counties. Apparently, Sheriff Cale had seen the light and called in the cavalry. So far they had kept the crowd separated and peaceful.

Butch Koll said to Marc, "We'll walk her out over by the friendlier crowd on the left over by those TV vans. The deputies think she'll be okay. They've been gauging the mood out there and they believe it's pretty quiet. That's my truck in the reserved spot up front. We'll get her there."

Marc and Butch turned away from the window and walked back to Brittany. Along with Butch and Andy, Maddy was there wearing a handgun holstered to her belt. Interesting that none of the deputies said a word to her about it. There were also four deputies, including a woman and three large men. The woman, the one Marc knew as Carla, was helping Brittany put on a bulletproof vest.

"Melinda wants film of her leaving the building all the way up to her getting in the car," Robbie Nelson reminded Gabriella and her cameraman, Kyle Bronson for the third or fourth time.

"I don't work for Melinda," an irritated Gabriella said in retort.

Robbie gave her his best wounded puppy look and said, "Gabriella, give me a break. You know what she's like. If I don't get this film for her I'll never hear the end of it."

"Here, hold this," Kyle told Robbie as he handed him the camera. Kyle opened the passenger door and used the back of the seat to climb up on the roof. Robbie handed Kyle the camera. Kyle stood up on the roof, looked through the camera's lens and declared himself to be all set.

"I'm going to try to squeeze through the crowd and see if I can get a quote," Gabriella told Robbie.

"Good luck with that," Robbie replied as he watched her try to muscle her way through the crowd in front of the van.

Gabriella, carrying her recording equipment by a strap on her shoulder, managed to squeeze through the crowd. She recognized Butch Koll's truck and believed they would pass close to her. Unknown to her, not that Gabriella or Brittany would have recognized him from the drawings of him Bob Olson stood less than twenty feet from Gabriella. He was toward the back of the crowd, up on his toes, trying to get a glimpse of Brittany as she was escorted to the parking lot.

The small crowd of security surrounding the diminutive blonde Brittany went out through the door. When they saw them heading their way with Brittany in the middle, the pro-Brittany crowd began to cheer and applaud. Those lined up on the jail side of the complex kept a respectful distance and with a few exceptions, were silently, sullenly watching.

Despite the deputies aligned along the route, the pro-marchers surged forward as if to greet a hero. Suddenly, less than fifty feet from Butch's truck, a young woman squeezed through the crowd to the front when Brittany was about to pass by her. In her hand was a .38 caliber handgun that belonged to her father. Brittany, less than fifteen feet from her assailant, looked directly at the girl as the first shot exploded from the barrel.

The first three shots hit Brittany squarely in the chest. Fortunately, the vest absorbed all three with little more damage than severe bruising. A man in the crowd standing next to the girl grabbed her right wrist and jerked it upward. This caused the fifth shot to sail over the building and land harmlessly in a snow-covered field a half mile away. Unfortunately, he was less than a second too late.

The fourth shot was the bullet that did the damage. Because the first three shots knocked her backwards into Butch, the fourth one missed the vest, blew through the left side of her neck and took a one-inch section of her carotid artery with it. It then punched through Butch Koll's coat, took out a good part of two ribs, went through his left lung and lodged in his back.

Bedlam exploded.

In an instant the shooter was on the ground, her hands cuffed behind her. Both sections of the crowd broke into hysteria and stampeded toward the parking lot. Almost three dozen of them would end up in the hospital that day, most for relatively minor scrapes and bruises but several with serious broken bones or concussions.

While Carla, the deputy, tried valiantly to stop the blood from spurting out of her neck, Marc found himself holding Brittany's head in his lap. Madeline and another deputy were helping Butch and Andy was sprinting toward Butch's suburban.

Brittany's blood was everywhere. Carla had it on her face, her hair and the front of her uniform blouse was soaked in it. In less than a minute, every bit of color drained from Brittany's face and even if a surgeon had been there, she still would not have been saved.

While the tears streamed down Marc's bloody face, he looked down at her as she moved her lips trying to speak. He leaned down, blood still erupting from the wound and put his left ear on her lips.

"Thank you, Marc," she whispered.

Brittany Riley lived for another minute or so. Marc stared down into her eyes, oblivious to the chaos swirling around them. She didn't speak again, and he could think of nothing to say as the light in her eyes flickered out.

SIXTY-NINE

April

Spring came early to Minnesota and the rest of the upper Midwest. By mid-March, daytime temperatures were pushing into the 60's. The snow was gone, the ice was coming off of the lakes and most of the golf courses were open before April 1st.

The trial of Brittany Riley was already receding to a painful, even embarrassing, memory. The Minneapolis newspaper combined with a local TV station commissioned a statewide poll a few days after her death. Somewhat disturbingly, 63% of those polled believed she got what she deserved.

The young woman who shot and killed Brittany became the focus of attention for a week or so. Her name was Katelyn Parker, a twenty-four-year-old single woman who had lost a baby due to a miscarriage. After losing her baby three years ago, she became a hard-core, anti-abortion, right-to-life advocate. The authorities conducted a search of her apartment and found hundreds of newspaper clippings concerning the disappearance of Becky Riley and all of the subsequent events, especially the trial. One of the detectives thought to check what she had stored in her DVR library. It was completely full of shows of *The Court Reporter* starring Melinda Pace.

Of course, every television news outlet in America found a reason to broadcast the shooting, over and over. The anchor who solemnly introduced the film always issued a standard warning about upcoming disturbing images. This was allegedly done to give parents a chance to remove children from the room. Some cynics might say it is really a notification to be sure to watch because something gruesome was about to be shown, so sit tight.

A week after the death of Brittany Riley, the Rileys held a double funeral for Brittany and Becky. They were buried next to Brittany's husband and Becky's father, Greg Mead. Becky was finally laid to rest between her parents.

Marc attended with Margaret Tennant and sat behind the Rileys with Maddy, Tony Carvelli, Vivian Donahue, Andy Whitmore, Gabriella Shriqui and Robbie Nelson. Gabriella had called Marc to ask if he thought it would be okay for her to attend, not as a reporter but as just another mourner. She brought Robbie along just for a little companionship. The only one not in attendance was the still hospitalized Butch Koll.

The sheriff's office cordoned off a section of the cemetery for the media. They were out in full force filming the burial for "the public's right to know". It would be the lead story throughout the day from coast to coast, a sad and tragic ending to the story, or so they would opine.

After the shooting, Butch and Brittany had been rushed to a hospital in Hastings in an ambulance that one of the sheriff's deputies presciently had standing by. Brittany was officially pronounced DOA, but the presence of the ambulance probably saved Butch's life. He spent two days in intensive care then was taken by helicopter to Regions Hospital in St. Paul. Regions is far more suited to handle gunshot wounds. The surgeons were able to repair the damage and in a few months, Butch would be almost good as new. Marc, Maddy, Andy and a busload of friends visited him daily which started driving him a little crazy after a week or so.

Marc, with Margaret Tennant on his arm, was walking slowly away from the gravesite when a woman approached them. It was Brittany's psychiatrist, Lorraine McDowell. They talked for a few minutes then the doctor gave Marc her card and he promised to call and make an appointment. Three days later he had his first session with her to help him cope with what he had been through.

Marc was in his office, leaning on the sill of the open window behind his desk. A beautiful April day was forecast; sunny with temps in the low seventies. He smiled while he watched two girls in their mid-teens walking down the sidewalk across the street. They were both dressed in skin-tight jeans that accentuated their cute little butts. He then realized they were both younger than his daughter and feeling a little embarrassed, looked around the room to see if anyone had noticed.

Marc softly laughed to himself then quietly said, "Getting back to normal."

At about the same time that Marc was enjoying the view from his office window, Gabriella entered her boss's office. Hunter Oswood pointed to a chair in front of his desk and after she sat down said, "So, kid, what's up?"

This was a meeting Gabriella had requested and she wasn't quite sure how to begin. After a moment, she looked at Hunter and said, "What are we doing? What is this bullshit we do all about?"

Oswood leaned back in his leather executive chair, placed his hands behind his head and said, "Ah. Having the 'what is this all about' dilemma, are you?"

"I suppose, yeah," Gabriella agreed.

"Don't feel too bad. Most reporters if they have a conscience and a soul which, I'll grant you most lose, go through this." Oswood came forward, leaned on his desk with his hands lightly clasped together on the desktop.

"Believe it or not, Gabriella, we do give people the news. Not all of it is what we used to call hard news, but it is still news. Stories that need to be reported, for the most part, are reported.

"Keep something in mind. Whether we like it or not, this TV station is, as are all media outlets, a business. We are in business to make money and that includes the news division. I don't know about you, but I like getting paid. We don't do this as a charity."

Gabriella started to protest but Oswood held up a hand to stop her.

"Sure, there's a public service aspect to it, but if we don't make money, like any business, sooner or later we close the doors. Look at what's happening to newspapers in this country. They're dying thanks to the internet and other things.

"Look, the various media outlets in this country, combined, spend millions of dollars on studies, polls and focus groups to find out what the public wants. So we feed it to them. If you ask individuals, 98% of them will claim they don't like it and don't pay attention to it. But our ratings and research tell us this is a lie. Some people, and an awful lot of them, are watching and paying attention to us.

"Let me give you an example. Last week, I think Wednesday, we ran a two and a half minute on-air segment, including film, of a cop rescuing a cat from a tree in West St. Paul. Two and a half minutes of news airtime! That's the kind of shit people say they want. That night, we got over four hundred calls and several thousand tweets or twitters or whatever you call them on that segment. Our research told us over 90% was a positive response to the story. Personally, it would have been a far better story and certainly more newsworthy and a lot more interesting if the cop had pulled his gun and shot the damn cat out of the tree."

They both chuckled at the thought then Oswood said, "That would have been worth two minutes of film."

"Am I going to become as cynical as you?" Gabriella asked.

"I hope not, but likely. Look, Gabriella, you're good at what you do. You have a good future in this business. And the camera certainly likes you. Here's something for you to think about. You might want to start learning more about what goes on behind the camera and in the business offices. It can't hurt your career."

"So, you really believe we do give them the news? Or, at least, the news they want?"

"Yeah, I do. The real news stories do get broadcast. Or, at least what we believe is news. That argument is for another time."

Gabriella thanked him for taking the time to meet with her. She turned the handle on his door to open it, looked back at Oswood and said, "The fault, dear Brutus, is not in our stars, but in ourselves."

"Willie was a smart guy," Oswood answered her.

That evening, Gabriella was alone in her apartment enjoying a quiet evening. Dressed in comfortable dark blue sweats and white cotton socks, she sat cross-legged on her couch. The TV was on showing a vapid sitcom she paid no attention to and she sipped a glass of Zinfandel while reading the paper.

Gabriella was scanning the small headlines in the Nation section when a story caught her eye. She put her wine glass on the coffee table and read the story twice. Something clicked in the back of her mind causing her to get up, go into her small kitchen and check the calendar on the wall. She did a quick mental calculation then retrieved the laptop from the bag she left by the door.

Gabriella, her reporter's curiosity having been piqued, carried her laptop back to the couch and resumed her position. She turned off the TV, set the paper aside and spent the next hour doing research on her computer. She opened a file into which she would make notes and copy her findings, then finally stopped to refill her glass.

When she got back to the couch, she shut down her laptop and stared at the blank TV screen sipping the wine for several minutes.

"Jesus Christ," she whispered to herself. "Could it be possible? Am I drunk? I need to talk to somebody," she said as she reached for her phone.

Gabriella punched the dialer and listened while it rang. During the third ring, she heard a familiar voice greet her by saying "Hey Gabriella, what's up?"

Gabriella paused for a brief moment then said, "I think I may have found something, and I need to talk to you about it. Can we meet for lunch tomorrow?"

"What's wrong? You sound a little upset. Everything okay?"

"No, no. I'm okay. Can we meet? I'll tell you all about it then."

"Sure."

The two friends agreed to a noon lunch date at a place they had been to before.

"Are you sure you're okay? I can come over now."

"No, really, I'm fine. Thanks, Maddy. But it is important so, I'll see you tomorrow?"

"Of course, I'll be there."

SEVENTY

Maddy and Gabriella met at a popular Perkins on the west side of Minneapolis. As usual, whenever these two walked through a restaurant together even the other women turned their heads and watched as they were led to a booth in the back.

They both ordered a light lunch of salads and when the waitress left, Gabriella got down to business. For the better part of an hour, she explained to Maddy what she surmised and why. She showed Maddy everything she had researched including dates and times. Maddy asked many questions, most of which Gabriella had an answer to and several she had not thought of herself. Between the two of them, one a professional investigator the other a professional reporter, both with very inquisitive minds, the two women analyzed everything Gabriella had found.

When they finished, there was a pause in the discussion and Maddy leaned back on the bench seat, heavily sighed and said, "God I hope you're wrong."

"So do I!"

Maddy leaned forward again, looked across the table at her friend and said, "It's not enough to even get the cops interested. We need some real evidence."

"I know," Gabriella quietly replied. "What do you think? You think I'm crazy or..."

"No, not at all," Maddy said. "What I think is that I owe it to Brittany Riley to check this out, to do a little road work, investigate this and follow up the trail you've uncovered. Or, at least, see if it's a trail and not just a string of coincidences."

"Thank you, I think. Tell me if this is a good idea. We find a sketch artist, like the ones the cops use. Have him draw his picture then..."

"...add the details from the sketch of Bob Olson to see if they match up," Maddy said finishing the statement. "That's a great idea. Let me call Tony, I'm sure he'll know the guy with MPD."

Two hours later the two women, along with Tony Carvelli and an MPD detective friend of his, Owen Jefferson, were sitting next to a man at a computer. They were sitting in a tech room at the police department in the bowels of the Old City Hall in downtown Minneapolis. Gabriella described the suspect strictly from her memory and not from a photo and the sketch artist came up with two drawings for them. One was of Bob Olson which was identical to the one Brittany Riley had described. The other was a drawing of the man Gabriella had begun to suspect. Gabriella also had a copy of Brittany's original sketch and they laid all three of them on a table, side by side for comparison.

"They're a match," Carvelli said. "No doubt about it."

"Yeah," Owen Jefferson agreed, "but they could also be a match for a hundred other guys that age. It's not enough."

"Gus," Maddy said to the artist, "Can you do some more? Do another five or six of him with various disguises?"

"Sure," Gus said turning back to his desktop.

For the next hour, working with suggestions from his gallery, Gus came up with six more drawings of Bob Olson in various disguises. When he finished, he gave the two women a copy of each. They thanked him and the four of them went out the Fourth Street exit.

"Now what?" Jefferson asked them.

"We're going to do a little investigating out of state. We've got some things to check on," Maddy replied.

"Be careful you two," Carvelli said sounding like a father to two daughters.

"Hey, who are you talking to? I'm the soul of discretion," Maddy smiled.

"Oh, yeah, that's right. Well, in your case, try not to put anyone in the hospital," Carvelli said.

"Listen," Jefferson interjected while handing each of the women his business card. "Stay in touch. If you find anything let me know."

While they walked to their cars, Gabriella said to Maddy, "You know, I can't pay you up front. I'll pay you as best..."

Maddy stopped, looked at her friend and said, "You'll pay me nothing. I'm doing this because it needs to be done and it's up to you and me to do it. Besides I told you, I owe it to Brittany."

"Thank you," Gabriella quietly replied.

"We need to keep in touch. Talk a couple of times a day, okay?"

They reached their cars, parked next to each other in a ramp, gave each other a hug, wished each other good luck and went their separate ways. As part of their lunchtime discussion, the two women had decided on a specific course of action. Maddy knew people where she was headed, and Gabriella had a couple of contacts with local TV stations where she needed to go.

Eight days later, while Madeline was still out of town, Gabriella met with Detective Jefferson at his office. She had been in constant contact with Maddy and with what the two of them had discovered, Gabriella was hoping it would be enough to get an investigation going and possibly a search warrant.

360

Jefferson and Gabriella were meeting in a small conference room at the downtown police headquarters. Gabriella went over the details of her trip and her investigation into the disappearance and death of a six-year-old girl in Missouri.

"The death is almost the exact same thing as Becky Riley's death. The girl was snatched off the street a block from her home. Her body was found in a lake in the Missouri Botanical Garden. She had been tied to a cinder block with clothesline, carried into the lake then tossed in. The mother was alibied by three people. No one was charged.

"I took the pictures, the drawings we had done, around to local bars, restaurants and stores. An owner of a convenience store identified this one," she continued sliding one of the drawings across the table to the cop. It was one with a baseball cap and mustache for a disguise.

"How could he be sure?" the skeptical cop asked.

"He was very sure. He said he had never seen the guy before then all of a sudden he was stopping almost every day. He also remembered that after the news of the kidnapping, he never saw him again."

"You say Ms. Rivers has more?"

"Yes," Gabriella told him. She then spent a few minutes giving him a brief rundown of what Maddy had found.

Jefferson thought it over for a minute then said, "It's a little circumstantial. The thing about guys like this though, when they get busted they usually can't shut up. They confess everything. Like they're relieved to finally get caught and stopped.

"Tell you what. Rivers will be back tomorrow night? Let's get together day after tomorrow and we'll go over everything. The glitch might be that this isn't really our case. This is Dakota County. If she's back, the two of you come in ten o'clock Friday morning."

"What do you think, Owen?" Gabriella asked.

Jefferson thought about it for a few seconds then said, "I'm about seventy percent convinced. But we may have enough to bring him in and maybe enough for a search warrant. We'll see."

The next night, late Thursday, Gabriella was in her cubicle on the otherwise empty third floor of the station's building. She had been a last-minute replacement on the anchor desk for the ten o'clock late news and was packing up getting ready to go home when the phone went off. She looked at the screen, answered it and said, "I was hoping you'd call, any more news? Where are you? Are you back in town?"

"Yeah, I'm back. I'm in my car heading toward your place. That man I told you about, the school psychologist," Maddy said. "He emailed me our guy's file, lock, stock and barrel."

"Your source will be in a lot of trouble if this gets out," Gabriella said.

"He didn't think so. Especially, if what I told him turns out to be true. I glanced through everything and our boy definitely had issues."

"What kind of issues?" Gabriella asked.

"I'll tell you when I get there. It's not good."

"All right, I'm leaving now and I'll see you…"

"Hello, Gabriella," a voice behind her said.

Gabriella jumped about four inches off of her chair and put her left hand over her heart. Still holding the phone by her mouth, she said, "Robbie, geez you startled me."

Robbie was standing at the entrance to her cubicle wearing a look she had never seen before. The normally smiling and affable younger man who had a huge crush on her was looking down on Gabriella with a humorless expression on his face and almost dead look in his eyes. "What's up?" Gabriella asked as casually as she could. Without ending the call with Maddy, she discreetly set her phone on her desktop.

"I came by a while ago looking for you," he said with no inflection in his voice. "You weren't here. Tell me, how was St. Louis?"

A stab of fear ran through her, but she remained outwardly calm. "What are you talking about? I wasn't in St. Louis. I went to Michigan," she lied.

Robbie removed a glossy, folded paper from his back pocket and tossed it on her desk. It was a four-color brochure from the Missouri Botanical Gardens.

"How did you like the Botanical Gardens? Beautiful isn't it?"

Knowing she was in serious trouble and praying Maddy was listening and was now heading to the station and not Gabriella's apartment, Gabriella decided to go on offense. "Who the hell do you think you are going through my desk?"

Ignoring her feigned indignation, Robbie continued by calmly saying, "It's a great place to dump the body of some whiney, spoiled brat, don't you think? It took them a lot longer to find that one than any of the others." When he said this, he was looking at her with a nasty smirk, almost sinister. He cocked his head back, looked up at the ceiling and started to laugh when Gabriella made her move.

Seeing her chance, possibly the only one she would get, Gabriella launched herself at him head first. Like a battering ram, the top of her head hit him right in the solar plexus driving him back, off his feet and down, banging his head on the cubicle wall across from Gabriella's. The blow stunned and staggered her, but she didn't go down. While he was lying on the floor trying to regain his breath, Gabriella stepped into him and kicked him in the groin as hard as she could. The pain went up into his chest like a wave of fire. He curled up, placed his hands on his crotch and instinctively rolled on the floor two or three times to get away from her.

Still, a little stunned herself, Gabriella knew her only real hope was escape. She grabbed her phone and looked around to make a break for it just as Robbie was starting to recover. He was still on the floor groaning and in obvious pain, but he was also very effectively blocking her only escape route. Realizing she didn't have a chance to get past him, she looked to her left and ran to the door leading up to the roof.

Gabriella burst through the door onto the roof and was almost knocked down by the wind. As she looked around for a place to hide, an enormous boom of thunder roared overhead, and a brilliant flash of lightning lit up the sky and the rooftop allowing her to see the air conditioning unit.

The weather forecast had predicted a large thunderstorm for that night which was rolling in from the western suburbs. Gabriella sprinted across the roof, fighting the wind, and praying Maddy had heard the conversation with Robbie.

She ducked behind the four-foot high covering of the A/C unit and brought the phone to her ear. "Maddy, are you still there?" she whispered.

"Yes! What happened? Are you all right? Where are you?"

The thunder continued to rumble, the lightning crashed, and the wind whipped around the roof. It had not started raining yet but it was only a few minutes off.

"I can barely hear. Can you hear me?" Gabriella whispered.

"Yes, I can. Where are you? What's going on? I'm on my way to the station. I'll be there in three or four minutes."

"I'm on the roof hiding. He knows, Maddy! He knows! He'll be up here to get me soon. Southeast corner. Third floor. Door to the roof. Please hurry."

"Southeast corner, third floor. I'm coming."

At that moment through the sound of the storm, Gabriella heard the door for the roof crash open. She squatted behind the A/C unit and tried to listen for him. She tried to hear the sound of his shoes scraping across the pebble-strewn rooftop.

Two, maybe three minutes went by. She occasionally heard the sound of him walking around. She thought she heard it in front of the air conditioner. She hunched down a little more, then duck-walked backward to the edge of the A/C covering. Gabriella, barely breathing for fear of making a sound, silently listened hoping he was moving away. Suddenly a hand grabbed her by the back of her hair and jerked her head back.

"Hello, Gabriella," he said looking down into her eyes and placed the blade of a knife against her throat. "Come with me, you stuck up bitch," he snarled while dragging her by the hair across the roof. When they reached the three-foot brick wall at the edge, he flung her down causing her to hit her head on the wall. Stunned, she got to her knees as he knelt down in front of her. He grabbed the hair on top of her head with his left hand while pointing the knife at her face with his right.

"I could've loved you. I could've made you happy. I would've done anything for you," he said as tears trickled from his eyes.

"We still can. You don't have to do this, Robbie," Gabriella pleaded.

"It's too late, it's too late," he cried. "You couldn't leave it alone. You had to keep digging..."

"No, Robbie, please. It's not too late. You need help, we can..."

"I don't need any goddamn help! It's too late!" he screamed above the howling wind as the rain began to come down.

Still holding her by the hair, he stood up and started to pull her up with him. Another flash of lightning lit up the sky after which a strong, firm, serious voice said, "Put the knife down and let her go."

They both looked toward the sound of the voice and a wave of relief washed over Gabriella as Robbie let go of her hair and allowed her to slump down on her butt. Standing twelve feet from them in a shooter's stance holding her Ladysmith .357 revolver was a very grim looking Madeline Rivers.

Another bolt of lightning flashed which caused Maddy to flinch, blink her eyes several times and shake her head in confusion. The image she was looking at suddenly changed and she yelled, "Drop the goddamn knife, Carl. I swear I'll shoot again."

"Go to hell, bitch! You're both gonna die!" Robbie yelled back.

"I mean it, Carl. I mean it. Drop the knife now, Carl, or I swear I'll shoot."

Enraged, he again grabbed Gabriella by her hair, Robbie looked down at Gabriella, raised the knife above his head and before he could strike heard Maddy yell, "Don't, Carl, I..." Then she began pulling the trigger and didn't stop until the gun was empty.

The first bullet struck him in the right shoulder and spun him around to face her. The next five all hit him in the chest and literally blew him backwards over the ledge, off the roof and down into the parking lot.

Madeline calmly walked over to the ledge and looked down at Robbie's lifeless body, the blood beginning to pool on the asphalt. She stared down at him for ten seconds or so and the image fluctuated back and forth in her mind from seeing Robbie to seeing another man lying lifeless in the rain on the roof of a car. She blinked several times at the image and it finally stayed as Robbie lying in the parking lot in a pool of blood, his lifeless body twisted and broken, the knife still in his hand.

At that moment the skies opened, and the rain started. The two women looked at each other; the tears flowed through the smiles as they held each other in the rain. Gabriella stepped back and asked, "Who the hell is Carl?"

"What? What are you talking about?" Maddy asked.

"Who's Carl? You kept calling Robbie, Carl, telling him to put the knife down. Who's Carl?"

"Are you sure?"

"Yes."

Maddy shook her head and said, "I can't talk about it now. I'll tell you later."

"Let's get inside," Gabriella suggested.

The two of them, huddled together holding each other, started toward the door, then suddenly Maddy said, "Oh shit," and started to run. When they got down the stairs to the third floor as they ran past Gabriella's cubicle, Gabriella asked, "Why are we running?"

Maddy stopped, turned and said, "Look, call 911. Call the cops. Then call Marc. I gotta get downstairs. I left the security guard handcuffed and gagged. I'm gonna have some serious explaining to do."

SEVENTY-ONE

Marc drove his SUV into the station's parking lot and was immediately stopped by a uniformed police officer.

He handed the officer his attorney license card and explained why he was there. The officer politely told him to wait where he was while the officer went to find a superior.

While he waited he noticed that the rain had stopped. He looked to his left and saw Robbie lying on the asphalt illuminated by the lights of a dozen police cars and other emergency vehicles. The area around the body was already cordoned off with yellow crime scene tape. Two CSU people, a man and a woman, were taking photos and an assistant M.E. Marc recognized, was examining the body.

A tall, good-looking black man looked into his window and handed Marc's attorney I.D. back to him and said, "I'm Detective Owen Jefferson, Mr. Kadella, I've been expecting you. Park your car over there," he continued as he pointed to a spot away from the crime scene, "Then I'll take you in to talk to your clients."

Marc and the detective were almost to the entrance of the building when Marc asked, "Are they under arrest?"

Jefferson stopped, thought for a moment then said, "Nothing's been decided. We're still investigating, and I haven't heard their story. When I got here, they told me they had called you so, I sat them down in the lobby and stationed an officer with them just to keep everything orderly.

"I should tell you this, too. A couple of weeks ago, the two of them came to me with their suspicions about this guy," he said nodding toward the body. "In fact, I talked to Ms. Shriqui day before yesterday and the two of them were supposed to meet with me tomorrow in my office."

"What suspicions? What are you talking about?" Marc asked looking puzzled.

"You don't know?"

"No. Know what?"

Jefferson held up a hand and said, "Look, I'll let them tell you, then we'll talk. Okay?"

A minute later Marc led the two women into a glass-enclosed conference room on the main floor a short distance from the lobby. They all took chairs. Marc looked at the two of them and said, "Okay, what's going on?"

"You start," Maddy said to Gabriella.

"About three weeks ago, I was reading the paper when I saw a little article about the body of a young girl being found in a park in St. Louis. She was found in a pond in that park. She had been missing for over a year. They even gave the date she disappeared.

"Then I remembered hearing about another little girl being abducted just after Christmas in Rockford, Illinois. So, I checked my calendar and realized Robbie Nelson, Melinda Pace's producer, had been in St. Louis at the same time the girl there went missing and in Rockford last Christmas."

"A little thin," Marc said.

"Very thin, but a little too much of a coincidence, too. I've known Robbie for a while, in fact, he had a big crush on me and pretty much told me his life's story.

"After checking my calendar, I spent an hour or so on the computer checking for abductions of girls in places where Robbie has lived during the times he was there. I found at least seven more possibilities."

"Jesus Christ," Marc whispered.

"The next day I got together with Maddy and told her what I found."

"I called Tony and he put us in touch with Detective Jefferson and a department sketch artist," Maddy said.

"I had the sketch artist draw a picture of Robbie, and then we had him add features of the sketch of Bob Olson that Brittany had done," Gabriella said.

"It matched," Marc quietly said.

"Dead on," Maddy agreed.

"We had him do some other drawings of Robbie adding different disguises…"

"Because we had talked to Detective Jefferson who told us what we had wasn't enough for either a search warrant or an arrest warrant," Maddy interjected, "we agreed to do some more digging. I went to Illinois and Gabriella went to St. Louis."

"I found a store owner who identified one of the disguised drawings of Robbie as someone he remembered. He also swears after the abduction in St. Louis, it was all over the news, that he never saw the guy again," Gabriella said.

"And," Maddy said picking up the story, "when I went to Illinois I found out a lot about him, especially in Rockford. People who knew him and knew the family all figured there was something wrong. His father took off when he was very young, seven or eight. He had a younger sister, Lucie. I talked to an aunt, his mother's sister, who said the mother blatantly favored the daughter. She said she believed his mother took it out on Robbie for the father leaving.

"I also got a copy of a file on him from a school psychologist and he believes the mother even sexually abused him."

"We figured we at least had enough to have him brought in for questioning and get a search warrant," Gabriella said.

367

Gabriella paused, looked at Maddy and continued, "Then, tonight, he overheard me talking to Maddy and he had discovered I went to St. Louis. He found a brochure I brought back from the same place where the girl's remains were found."

The two of them then told Marc the story of what happened that evening on the roof. Maddy even told him about the flashbacks she had to the night she was attacked in her apartment by a former client of Marc's.

When they finished, Marc told them to keep all of this to themselves for now. He would set up an interview with Jefferson but until then, avoid the media who were already lined up outside to find out what happened.

They left the conference room and Marc found Jefferson. The first thing he said was, "Did you find the knife?"

"Oh, yeah, he still had it in his hand," Jefferson replied.

"We got a self-defense here and it looks like our DOA is a serial killer of little girls. From what they told me, they had enough for at least a probable cause arrest and search warrant," Marc told him.

"So, they found more?"

"Yeah, I'll bring them in for a statement tomorrow at 10:00 A.M. Will that work for you?"

"Yeah, see you then."

The next day the police obtained a search warrant for Robbie's apartment. What they found would make Madeline Rivers and Gabriella Shriqui national heroes.

In a spare bedroom, they discovered Robbie's trophy collection. He had saved an item or two from every one of his victims, a toy, a piece of clothing, a stuffed animal, something to commemorate his gruesome sickness.

They also discovered a number of wigs, hats, glasses, a make-up kit and false noses for several disguises. Apparently, he had been perfecting his craft for many years.

Maddy and Gabriella gave complete statements to the police, at least most of it. The investigation was headed by Owen Jefferson who agreed there were some things that need not be included.

Maddy, off the record, told him about the personal psych file she had obtained on Robbie. In order to protect her source and keep him out of any potential trouble, Jefferson agreed with her that since no prosecution was going to happen, it wasn't really necessary.

At the end of the interview, Jefferson said to her, "Here take this." He handed her a small stuffed Teddy Bear. Around its neck was a tiny gold chain with the name *Becky* engraved on a small gold plaque. "I thought you might want to give this back to the family."

Melinda Pace's show, like most of the media the day after the shooting, was devoted to her deceased producer. The gist of it was: You just never know what is in somebody's heart. Of course, her ratings were through the roof and she uttered not a peep showing any remorse, contrition, guilt or apology about what she had done to Brittany Riley and her family. There wasn't any forthcoming from anyone else as well. Like Melinda was prone to say, "It's just showbiz and we're only giving them what they want."

Also Available on Amazon

Certain Justice

A Marc Kadella Legal Mystery No. 4

Thirteen Years Ago

The two men sat silently staring through the windshield of the dark blue Chevy sedan. The passenger, whom the driver called Big, had his window open an inch while he smoked. Big was flicking the ashes out of the wet window and staining the outside of it with gray, wet, cigarette ash. It was a cold, wet, windy, miserable night, especially for mid-September. While Big stared silently into the night the driver, whom Big referred to as Little, fidgeted anxiously in his seat and occasionally coughed lightly due to his partner's smoking.

Big crushed out his cigarette in the car's ashtray, careful not to toss it out the window and possibly leave DNA evidence for the cops. When he did this, Little broke the silence by saying, "Roll your damn window down and let some air in."

Without turning his head, Big replied, "Roll yours down. It's raining out there."

A gust of wind came across Lake of the Isles shaking the oak tree they were under on Parker Street. The sudden burst of wind shook the big tree causing a small torrent of rainwater to splatter down on the car. A second, less powerful wind burst broke off a tiny, leafy branch from the tree that landed on the windshield directly in front of Little. The sudden appearance of the oak leaves and the noise it made caused Little to jump in his seat, bring his hand to his heart and say, "Jesus Christ!" Big, who rarely smiled and almost never laughed, cracked a brief grin at his partner's discomfort.

"Time?" Big asked.

Little checked the digital read on his watch and said, "At least five more minutes."

Big's real name was Howie Traynor. At twenty-seven he was already a career criminal and no stranger to jail cells. He was a first-rate burglar because his nerves were almost non-existent so that nothing seemed to faze him.

At a very early age, his parents began to notice that Howie was a little off. He seemed to be a little too quiet and unhappy. When he started school, his teachers didn't tell his parents he didn't play well with the other kids. He didn't play with them at all. He showed no interest in making friends, rarely participated in kids' activities and basically kept to himself. By the time he entered high school he had become a bit of a bully who scared just about everyone, including his teachers and was someone to avoid.

During his junior year, his parents took him to a psychologist who somewhat reluctantly told them that Howie appeared to be a pure sociopath. A person without empathy or any real feelings for or a connection with other people. A Minnesota Multiphasic Personality Inventory was administered, and Howie's results revealed a 49 profile. He was quite intelligent but had a marked disregard for social norms, mores and standards. He was essentially someone with little or no conscience or regard for anyone else.

The oddity was that people exhibiting these traits normally come from economically depressed, fractured environments. Howie was the anomaly. John Traynor, his father, was a dentist with a very successful practice. His mother, Monica was a surgical nurse. Between them, they made an excellent living and provided well for Howie, his brother Martin who was three years older and a sister Alison, two years younger. The family had an upper-middle-class home life in an upscale neighborhood of a Minneapolis suburb. The family was caring, loving, nurturing and almost exactly what any child should have. His brother and sister showed none of the antisocial traits of Howie and both had become normal, self-supporting, law-abiding adults. Howie was simply not wired right.

His criminal life began while still in high school. There was nothing too serious at first. Joyriding in stolen cars with a couple of other boys with behavioral issues; shoplifting items he didn't really need and one arrest for burglarizing a house.

Howie's behavior in school steadily worsened as the years went by. None of it was very serious just antisocial to the point that everyone in the building breathed a sigh of relief when he dropped out two months before graduation. He gave no explanation why. One day he simply walked into the principal's office and announced he was leaving. No one, not even his parents, bothered to try to talk him out of it.

From that day until tonight, his family having given up on him years ago, left Howie unburdened with human ties or any responsibilities

371

and he bounced around from one loser job to another. His adult life was spent in and out of trouble, jail and the workhouse without a care in the world. Howie was a criminal. He knew he was a criminal and simply accepted it as a fact.

Howie made most of his money from home invasion burglaries. With his total lack of conscience, he justified it by simply believing it was what he was meant to do and that was that. The only legitimate job he had that he liked was as a nightclub bouncer.

Howie was big only in comparison to the man in the front seat next to him. Howie was a touch over six feet and one hundred eighty rock solid pounds. While not at work, Howie could be found at a boxing school in North Minneapolis training and working out.

When he first started working as a bouncer, his actual size rarely intimidated the average drunken idiot, until the drunken idiot crossed the line with Howie. One night, a well-known and very large Viking football player tried to show off to his entourage. Howie politely asked the man and his friends to settle down, but the football player thought he would have some fun with the smaller Howie. One punch from Howie and the fool's eyes rolled back in his head, his knees buckled and the table they were seated at shattered when he fell on it. No one messed with Howie after that story got around.

Howie's partner was a man named Jimmy Oliver. Eight years older than Howie. He was Little to Howie being Big because he was barely five foot six and rail thin. Howie hooked up with him because Jimmy was a first-rate safe cracker and knew all of the best places in the Cities to fence stolen property. Jimmy kept it well hidden, but he was scared to death of Howie who reeked of menace. Jimmy had witnessed Howie scaring cops with little more than a nasty look.

It was Jimmy who had scoped out the job they were on tonight. Jimmy had taken a job using a false identification and forged documents with a home cleaning service. This would be the second job he had come up with while cleaning homes with this company and he figured the cops would find the connection after one more. The third one would be it then he would have to move on.

The house they were going to hit was a sixteen-room beauty overlooking Lake of the Isles surrounded by a six-foot high, spike-topped, wrought iron fence. Jimmy had been inside with a weekly cleaning crew three times. The third time the home's owner, a seventy-eight-year-old widow, was arguing with her daughter about selling the place. The daughter was adamant that it wasn't safe for her mother to live there alone and the place was simply too much for her. The daughter also let it slip that they would be out of town and the place would be empty for several days, including the night Big and Little now found themselves sitting patiently across the street.

The two men were parked in between two other cars on a side street in this very upscale Minneapolis neighborhood. They were less than one hundred feet from the corner where Parker Street met Lake of the Isles Boulevard. Despite the lateness of the hour, almost 11:00 P.M., the darkness and the storm, they could clearly see by the ambient light reflecting off of the lake barely a hundred yards across the grass in front of them. Lake of the Isles is one of the chain of lakes that gave the City of Minneapolis, and the Los Angeles Lakers, its nickname; The City of Lakes. Surrounded by beautiful, expensive homes, many dating back to the turn of the nineteenth century, the area would be a crown jewel in just about any city in the world.

"Time," Big said again a few minutes later.

"Any minute now," Little replied.

They watched as a man in tights marked with reflective tape, despite the weather, jog past the corner on the path surrounding the lake. When Big saw the jogger he muttered, "asshole" just as the lights from a car on Lake of the Isles Boulevard illuminated the man and a moment later a police patrol car passed by the corner.

"Right on time," Little said. "Every eighteen to twenty-four minutes." Little had done a thorough recon of the house and neighborhood and had spent several nights timing the cops patrolling around the lakes.

"Let's go," Big said as he opened his car door. Having removed the single bulb from the interior light, the car remained in darkness as the two men got out. Hunched over against the wind and light rain, they quickly ran across Parker Street to the back door of the house.

Next to an alley that ran behind the building was a small, unattached one car garage facing Parker Street. It was constructed of the same brick material as the house from over eighty years ago and looked tiny, almost ridiculous, next to the seven thousand square foot home. Above the door was an old-style exterior light to illuminate the small, barely ten-foot driveway. Little had previously loosened the bulb of the light above the garage door and the area in front of the garage was quite dark. Between the missing garage light, the weather and the all black clothing the men wore, the two of them were practically invisible.

The corner of the house met the corner of the garage at this point and there was an entryway door into the house. The lock on the door looked as if it had last been replaced in the '50s. It took Big less than a minute, even in the dark, to pick the lock and the two of them were in.

They both carried a flashlight with the lens taped over leaving a hole for the light to come through about the size of a pencil's eraser. Once inside, they turned the flashlights on and Little went up the single flight of stairs and into the kitchen. With Big casually following him, Little went through the kitchen and into a hallway closet. Inside the closet, while Big shined his flashlight on it, Little removed the cover to the alarm box and quickly attached a bypass hook up to the alarm before the alarm company could be notified of their intrusion.

Little turned around and said, "Okay. We're good to go."

"You're sure there's no one here?" Big asked for at least the fifth time that evening.

"They're out of town," Little replied. "Six minutes. No more."

"I know the drill, asshole," Big snarled causing Little to flinch. "You go do the safe. I'll check upstairs."

Little hurried toward the far end of the first floor where the study was. Having already discovered and photographed the safe, he was extremely confident he would have it open in under two minutes.

While Little went toward the study, Big started up the carpeted, open stairway to the upstairs bedrooms. Little had told him the bulk of the items worth taking, the solid silver utensils, candlesticks and other items, many of which were expensive antiques, were on the main floor. While working with the cleaning crew, Little was able to scout the upstairs and told Big to take no more than one minute to go through the master bedroom only. There wasn't anything in the other rooms worth the time and effort.

Big almost carelessly opened the door to the master bedroom which caused the door to bang slightly against an antique armoire standing behind it. The noise it made, while not very loud, made a significant impact on the silence of the room.

Big ignored the noise and while standing in the doorway, began to play the flashlight around the room. In the middle of the bedroom, directly in front of the door was a king size, four poster bed, complete with a canopy above it. He slowly moved the light over the bed then heard the obviously frightened and shaky voice of an old woman say, "Who are you and what do you want?"

Big didn't hesitate an instant. He didn't think about what to do or take a moment to consider it. He simply reacted. In barely a second he leapt over the bed's baseboard, flew across the length of the large bed and came down directly on top of her. He heard the air rush out of her lungs as he clamped his left hand down on her mouth and with his right hand he grabbed a pillow, roughly pushed it down to cover her face and used both of his powerful hands to hold the pillow in place.

The elderly woman tried her best to fight back. She kicked her legs and thrashed about back and forth and with her hands she tried to claw at his arm. The poor woman never had a chance. Less than thirty seconds after it started her back arched, her eyelids fluttered, and her body went completely lax.

Big held the pillow over her face for another minute to be sure she was dead. He got off the still body, found his flashlight and surveyed what he had done. Then he did something even he could not have explained. Big pulled the blankets down, took the woman's hands and gently folded them together and placed them on her stomach. He then covered her up to her chin with the blankets, put the pillow he used to kill her back where it was and fluffed the pillow under her head. Despite the sudden and violent attack, she looked quite peaceful and serene. Apparently satisfied he returned to his task.

Big opened the door to the study and found his partner seated at a desk with the contents of the safe spread out on its surface.

"Hey," Little began when he saw his partner. "We did okay. Looks to be about seven or eight grand in cash and if the jewelry is real and it looks like it, gotta be another hundred here easy. Everything okay upstairs?"

"Yeah, everything's fine," Big lied. "Why?"

"What do you have there?" Little asked indicating the black cloth sack Big carried.

"Silver," he answered.

Little looked at his watch and said, "Times up, we need to go."

"I know you told the other officer what happened, Carlotta, but I need you to tell me," Detective Tony Carvelli patiently said to the obviously distraught Latina woman.

Carvelli and his young partner, Antwone Spenser, a recently promoted detective with the Minneapolis Police Department, were seated in matching, obviously expensive cloth covered wing-backed chairs. The two men were facing two women, both of whom appeared to be the same approximate age. The women were seated together on a sofa and the four of them were in the main living room of the house on Parker and Lake of the Isles.

Carlotta took a deep breath, squeezed the hand of the woman next to her and said, with barely a trace of an accent, "I got here at eight just like every day. As soon as I came into this room, I noticed some things missing. I looked around for a few minutes and could tell that a lot of the silver things were gone. Then I realized Mrs. Benson wasn't downstairs.

She's almost always here when I get here," she explained. "So, I hurried upstairs and went into her bedroom. She was still in bed and not moving."

Carlotta stopped and wiped a couple of tears away, looked at the woman seated next to her and said, "I guess I knew right away she was dead. Her eyes were closed, she wasn't moving, and her face was really pale." She sniffled and said to the other woman, "I'm so sorry, Miss Janet."

"It's all right, Carlotta," the woman said rubbing the back and shoulders of the upset housekeeper.

Carlotta turned back to the two detectives and continued, "I checked to see if she was breathing, which she wasn't, then I came downstairs and called Miss Janet from the kitchen."

"I called 911 then drove here as quickly as I could. There was a police car already here when I arrived," Janet Benson Milliken, the victim's daughter said. "I came inside and before they could stop me, hurried upstairs to Mom's bedroom.

"I came back down, and we talked to your officer, the tall black man. And we both told him what happened. He had us sit down here and told us not to move around or touch anything. More police and other people started arriving and we've just been waiting. Do you think my mother was murdered by burglars?"

"It's too soon to tell," Carvelli softly replied.

"It's all my fault," the daughter said fighting back a sob. "We were supposed to be at my cousin's cabin, but something came up at my job and I decided to stay for a couple more days."

"Wait, wait, wait," Carvelli soothingly said looking into the daughter's eyes. "This is not your fault. If this was done by the guy who did the burglary, he's the one to blame. Don't do that to yourself. Don't start second-guessing things. It won't bring your mother back and it isn't true. We'll get this guy and put him away."

"Sarge," Carvelli heard a voice say coming from the living room's entryway. It was the same officer the two women had first talked to. "Sergeant Waschke just pulled up," the man said referring to the arrival of a homicide detective.

"Thanks, Jefferson," Carvelli replied looking up at the man. He turned back to his partner and asked, "Did you get everything?"

"Yeah, I did, Sarge," the much younger man answered.

Carvelli looked at the women and said, "We should clear out of here and let the crime scene people do their job. You'll get me a list of the missing items?" he asked the victim's daughter.

"Yes, as soon as I can. The insurance company will have an inventory of everything. I made sure of that. There are also photos."

376

"That's smart. Good job," Carvelli said.

Leaving Jefferson at the door, the four of them went out through the front door. Carvelli nodded his head at the beefy man coming through the front gate. They all waited at the bottom of the steps as the man approached.

Carvelli and Waschke shook hands and Carvelli introduced the homicide detective to the two women.

"I'm sorry for your loss," Waschke sincerely told Janet. "I should go take a look," he said to Carvelli.

Carvelli indicated to his partner to stay with the women while he and Waschke started up the front steps to go inside. Jefferson was at the door with a clipboard making a record of everyone who entered the crime scene. He took down Waschke's name and badge number. As the two men were walking up the stairs, Waschke said to Carvelli, "Keep an eye on him. He's sharp as a razor and he'll make a damn fine detective and soon."

"Where's Collins?" Carvelli asked referring to Waschke's current partner.

"He's got his old lady knocked up again and they had some doctor's appointment this morning."

"Another kid?" Carvelli asked. "What's that, five or six?"

"Yeah, something like that. I'm not even sure he can keep track."

"Maybe you ought to have a little talk with him about how to avoid it."

"I've tried. He won't listen," Waschke growled as he walked into the bedroom.

He greeted the two people from the medical examiner's office who moved away from the body to allow Waschke to look over the elderly woman.

Waschke looked over the woman's face for a moment then asked the tech standing next to him, "What's this on her cheek?"

The tech leaned over next to Waschke and with a pen, pointed at a very lightly discolored area along the right jawline. "That right here?"

"Yeah."

"It could be bruising. Look at this." He picked up a pillow lying next to the woman and pointed to a very light stain on it.

"What is it?"

"Can't say for sure," the tech said. "But it could be a bit of lipstick. Even if a woman washes it off before bed she wouldn't get all of it. We'll know more when the CSU guys run some tests. Could be trace saliva on it too."

"He held a pillow over her face," Waschke said as he straightened up.

"Maybe, we'll know more in a day or two."

"Put a rush on it, will you Paul? I got a call from the chief this morning who got a call from the mayor about this. I guess this is a pretty prominent family."

"Sure, Jake. Gonna be a lot of political heat on you for this one. Sucks to be you."

"Thanks for the reminder," Waschke sarcastically answered.

The two detectives had just stepped through the doorway leading to the front yard when a small Cadillac limousine pulled up and double parked in front of the house. They stopped and watched as a very attractive woman in her early fifties exited the back seat of the car. When she did this, the victim's daughter walked quickly to the gate in the wrought iron fence. The two women gave each other an affectionate, consoling hug then walked up the sidewalk toward the house.

"Who is she?" Carvelli asked.

"I do believe that is Vivian Donahue, top dog of the Corwin family. You know them?" Waschke answered his friend.

"I know of them. Since this looks like a homicide and I'm in burglary, I'll let you deal with her," Carvelli said. He then turned and went back into the house.

Waschke walked up to the women as the older one was consoling the housekeeper. Waschke gave a slight jerk of his head at Carvelli's partner to indicate he could leave which the young detective did as quickly as seemed polite. Janet introduced him to Vivian Donahue and explained that her mother was Vivian's aunt. Janet had called her earlier after calling 911. Waschke immediately realized this explained the call from the mayor to the chief of police and the subsequent call to him.

"May I see my aunt?" Vivian politely asked.

"I believe they're about ready to move her," Waschke replied. "Plus, it's a crime scene and the fewer people that go in there right now, the better."

"There's nothing much to see," Janet said to her cousin. "Mom looked like she was peacefully asleep."

"You're sure there was a burglary?" Vivian asked Jake.

"Yes, absolutely," Janet answered before Jake could respond.

"Is her death a homicide? She had a bad heart..." Vivian began to say.

"As long as she took her meds she was fine. I made sure each week her pillbox was filled for each day. I checked the one for yesterday and she had taken her pills," Janet interjected.

"We don't know," Waschke said to Vivian.

"She'll have to have an autopsy?"

378

"I'm afraid so," Waschke shrugged.

"Oh, God, how ghastly," Vivian said. "But I suppose we have to know." She handed Waschke a personal card with her name and private number on it. "Please keep me informed as much as you can, Sergeant. I don't mean to interfere but…"

"I understand," Jake replied. "I'll do what I can," he continued while thinking, *if you can't use the kind of clout she has what's the point of having it?* Jake handed one of his cards to each of the three women and told them if they thought of anything to call him.

Vivian Donohue slipped her left arm through Waschke's right arm and led him several steps away from the daughter and housekeeper.

"I won't hold you to it but tell me what you think," she quietly said when she let go of his arm and looked up at him. Waschke was a large, veteran cop who knew how to intimidate people with just a look. Rarely did he ever experience the uneasiness he felt because of the look this woman was giving him.

"It's probably a burglary gone bad. Likely he found her and smothered her with a pillow."

"Will you catch him?"

Jake took a deep breath, scratched his chin and thought about his answer. "I'll be honest, the odds are not good. If we can recover some of the stolen property…"

"Which isn't likely," Vivian said.

"Usually not," he agreed. "We have our best people on it. We'll do our best. I promise you that."

Marc Kadella wearily sat on a padded bench in the hallway outside courtroom 1523 in the Hennepin County Government Center. The pain in his lower back was finally gone. The stress of doing his first homicide trial had tightened up his lower back muscles for the duration of the trial. Four days and no relief. The case had been given to the jury only two hours ago and the pain was already gone.

Marc leaned back against the hallway wall and vacantly stared across the empty space at the government side of the big building. He found himself taking simple pleasure watching through the windows as the county employees worked at their desks or busily scurried about. It felt good to have his mind in neutral; not thinking about the trial or what he should be doing to prepare for it. It was over. He had given it his best shot and there was nothing more he could do.

Marc thought about his client, Howie Traynor. He was accused of first and second-degree murder in the death of an elderly woman during the commission of a burglary. Going into the trial, Marc believed he could beat the first-degree charge but probably not the second-degree.

His client was likely looking at three serious felony convictions, including assault on a police officer. If convicted of everything but the first-degree murder charge, he was looking at thirty years, minimum.

It had been eight months since the crime was committed. Fall and winter had come and gone and a lot had happened during that time. The murder of a member of a well-known, respected, politically prominent family had generated a lot of publicity and media attention. Being a novice at dealing with the press, Marc could only hope he didn't come across as too much of an inexperienced fool. For a solid hour after the case went to the jury, Marc, and the lead prosecutor, Rhea Watson, had both given multiple impromptu interviews here in the hallway. While replaying it in his mind, Marc appreciated the quiet and solitude even more.

Marc began to go over the trial in his head. He knew it was a bad idea to do this. It would lead to second-guessing himself and thinking of new things he should have done. But he couldn't help himself.

The first thing he mentally replayed was his cross-examination of the medical examiner who had conducted the autopsy. During the man's direct exam, he testified that there were microscopic cotton fibers found in the victim's mouth and nose. These fibers, he testified, were an exact match with the pillow found next to the body. A lab tech had previously testified that there were traces of lipstick that matched the lipstick worn by the deceased. Also, DNA analysis showed saliva from the same spot on the pillow as the lipstick. This allowed the ME to testify that, in his medical opinion, someone held that pillow over the face of the victim and was the proximate cause of the heart attack that killed her.

Replaying the cross exam, Marc was satisfied he had done as good a job as anyone could trying to find reasonable doubt about the cause of death. He was able to get the doctor to admit the lipstick and saliva on the pillow could have happened simply by the deceased rolling on her side or putting her mouth on it while she slept. And this could have caused the small cotton particles to enter her nose and mouth.

The problem he had was the bruising on the jawline. There was simply no reasonable explanation for how that could have happened except by someone holding the pillow over her fragile face. Between that and the DNA evidence from the hair and skin found under the victim's fingernails, a 99% match, Howie's goose was cooked. Howie Traynor was going down for the murder of Lucille Benson, second-degree felony murder. Marc believed he was not going to get first-degree premeditated murder. Howie did not go up those stairs intending to kill anyone. According to the state's star witness, Jimmy Oliver, they believed no one was home, so how could anyone have gone into that bedroom planning to kill someone who wasn't supposed to be there? Clearly, the prosecution had overcharged.

Marc thought it over for another fifteen or twenty minutes then satisfied himself that he had done a good job. Not only that but being honest with himself, he wasn't the least bit upset that Howie was going to prison for a long time. The simple truth was even if Howie did not admit it, he was guilty as hell. And like just about everyone else who came in contact with him, Howie Traynor scared the hell out of Marc.

"Replaying the case? Second guessing yourself?" Marc heard the voice of his counterpart, Rhea Watson say to him. He had been so lost in thought he didn't notice her walk up next to him.

Marc looked up at her, smiled and said, "Hey, Rhea."

"Mind if I join you?" she asked.

"No, not at all. Have a seat," Marc replied as he picked up the briefcase he had set on the seat next to him and put it on the floor.

"Yeah, I was thinking it over," Marc agreed as the lawyer sat down, crossed her legs and pulled her skirt down to her knees.

"Don't," she said. "You did a good job. Old Mickey would have been proud of you. He may have been a bit of a drunk and notorious womanizer, but he was a damn fine trial lawyer. I bet you learned a lot from him."

"Yeah, I did," he agreed. "Learned a lot the hard way the past few days."

"That's probably the best way. You beat us on the first-degree charge. I think we got you on everything else. I'll make you a new offer. He pleads to second-degree, we recommend thirty years. Peterson will go along with it," she said referring to the judge. "Otherwise, we're going to ask for an upward departure on the homicide and consecutive sentencing on everything else. He'll get forty for sure. This guy scares everybody, including the judge."

The thirty-year offer was ten years more than the original offer they had made six months ago.

"I'll go across the street and tell him but don't hold your breath," Marc said as he stood and retrieved his briefcase.

"Tell him it's good for another hour only. I'll be upstairs for a couple more hours. If he says okay, call me and we'll see Peterson yet today."

"You think the jury will be back today?" Marc asked as the two of them walked toward the elevators.

"Doubtful. They have way too much to go through with all of the charges on your guy."

"Please don't call him my guy," Marc protested as he pushed both the up and down buttons at the elevator bank. "I'll call you one way or the other after I talk to him," Marc said as he stepped onto the elevator that arrived to take him downstairs.

"Will the defendant please rise," Judge Ross Peterson intoned.

Marc arose from his chair immediately, but his client stood up as if this was little more than an annoyance.

The jury had come back with a verdict before noon on the day after the trial concluded. It was now two hours later after allowing for lunch and to get all of the parties, including the media, together. In the back row, a serious looking man in a charcoal suit and stylish tie sat patiently waiting for the verdict to be read. He was the current head of the security for Vivian Corwin Donahue. He was to call her as soon as he had the news. Vivian was not a woman who liked to be kept waiting.

The jury foreman, a man named Elliot Sanders, held up the paper with the verdicts written out. He cleared his throat and read the charges and the verdict for each.

Marc had guessed correctly. The first one the foreman read was the murder one charge and the finding of not guilty. Every other charge, the felony murder second degree; assault on a police officer; resisting arrest; multiple breaking and entering and burglary charges were all guilty verdicts.

While each was being read, Marc was thinking that with the not guilty of first-degree murder, Traynor could not be sentenced to life without parole. Later that day, he would find himself wondering if that was a good or bad thing.

When the foreman finished, Peterson ordered a presentence investigation report and set the date for sentencing thirty days out. He thanked and dismissed the jury and adjourned.

Before Traynor could be led away, he turned to Marc and sarcastically snarled, "Nice job, rookie. I won't forget it."

On the day of his sentencing, Marc and his client stood silently and patiently while Judge Peterson went over the list of reasons he was sentencing Howie to forty years in prison. This was a significant upward departure than what the sentencing guidelines called for and the judge was obligated to make a record of his reasons for it. In the event of an appeal, which Marc was extremely grateful he would not have to handle, the appeals court would have to know why the longer than normal sentence was given.

The judge finished, looked at Howie and asked, "Do you have anything to say?"

Howie opened his mouth as if to say something causing Marc to cringe at the thought of what might come out, then Traynor simply said, about as politely as he was capable of, "No, I guess not, your Honor."

Marc got off the elevator on the second floor of the building. He had his cell phone in hand and before he had walked twenty feet, he could hear the phone he dialed already ringing.

"Hey, Cara, it's Marc," he said.

"What did he get?"

"Forty years total. It's all yours now," Marc told the lawyer with the Minnesota State Public Defenders office. They would be handling Howie's appeal and Marc was delighted to wash his hands of it. "And good luck."

"Thanks," she responded a touch sarcastically. "I'll have someone get started on it. Do you want us to keep you informed?"

"Not really," Marc replied. He had arrived at the elevators in the corner of the building to go down into the underground parking area. He pushed the button and said, "I've seen all of Howie Traynor I care to."

Made in the USA
Middletown, DE
05 July 2021

43619640R00214